UNDOING HIS INNOCENT ENEMY

HEIDI RICE

IN BED WITH HER BILLIONAIRE BODYGUARD

PIPPA ROSCOE

MILLS & BOON

First published in Great Britain 2023
by Mills & Boon, an imprint of HarperCollins*Publishers* Ltd,
1 London Bridge Street, London, SE1 9GF

www.harpercollins.co.uk

HarperCollins*Publishers*, Macken House, 39/40 Mayor Street Upper,
Dublin 1, D01 C9W8, Ireland

Undoing His Innocent Enemy © 2023 Heidi Rice

In Bed with Her Billionaire Bodyguard © 2023 Pippa Roscoe

ISBN: 978-0-263-30707-8

12/23

This book is produced from independently certified FSC™ paper
to ensure responsible forest management.
For more information visit: www.harpercollins.co.uk/green.

Printed and Bound in the UK using 100% Renewable Electricity
at CPI Group (UK) Ltd, Croydon, CR0 4YY

UNDOING HIS INNOCENT ENEMY

HEIDI RICE

MILLS & BOON

To Rob and our beautiful boys, Joey and Luca,
who shared a marvellous adventure to Finnish Lapland
with me once upon a time. So glad I finally managed
to feature that wild winter landscape in a book!

CHAPTER ONE

CARA DOYLE EXHALED SLOWLY, allowing her breath to plume in the icy air. She lifted the camera she'd spent a small fortune on and watched the lynx in the viewfinder as it prowled across the powdery snow.

She had been trailing the female huntress for over a week—in between shifts as a barista at a resort hotel in Saariselkä—but today she'd got so many exceptional shots excitement made her heart rate soar. Which was good because, with the temperature plummeting to minus thirty degrees this morning, she couldn't spend much longer out here before she froze.

A shiver ran through her body as the camera's shutter purred through its twenty frames per second. Even with six layers of thermal clothing she could feel the cold embalming her. She ignored the discomfort. This moment was the culmination of six months' work doing crummy jobs in a succession of Lapland hotels and resorts, all through the summer and autumn, to pay for her trip studying the behaviour of the famously elusive wildcats for her breakout portfolio as a wildlife photographer.

The lynx's head lifted, her silvery gaze locking on Cara's.

Hello, there, girl, you're grand, aren't you? Just a few more shots, I promise. Then I'll be leaving you in peace.

Cara's heart rose into her throat. The picture in her

viewfinder was so stunning she could hardly breathe—the lynx's graceful feline form stood stock-still, almost as if posing for the shot. Her tawny white fur blended into the glittering landscape before she ducked beneath the snow-laden branches of the frozen spruce trees and disappeared into the monochromatic beauty of the boreal forest.

Cara waited a few more minutes. But the lynx was gone.

She rolled onto her back, stared up at the pearly sky through the trees. It was almost three o'clock—darkness would be falling soon, with only four hours of daylight at this time of year in Finnish Lapland. She had to get back to the skimobile she'd left on the edge of the forest so she didn't disturb the wildcat's habitat.

But she took a few precious moments, her lips lifting beneath the layers protecting her face from the freezing air.

It only took a few heartbeats though to realise her body temperature was dropping from lack of movement. It would be no good getting the shots she'd been working on for six months through summer, autumn and finally into the short crisp winter days, if she froze to death before she could sell them.

She levered herself onto her feet and began the trek back to the snowmobile, picking up her pace as twilight edged in around her.

Feck, exactly how long had she been out here?

It had only seemed like minutes but, when she was totally focussed on her work, time tended to dissolve as she hunted for that single perfect shot.

At last, she saw the small skimobile where she'd left it, parked near the hide she'd been using for weeks.

She packed the camera away in its insulated box in the saddlebag, aware that her hands were getting clumsy, the piercing cold turning to a numb pain.

Not good.

The delight and excitement at finally capturing the creature she'd been trailing for months began to turn to dismay though as she switched on the ignition, and nothing happened. Annoyed, she went for option two. Grabbing the start cord, she tugged hard. Again, nothing, not even the clunking sound of the engine turning over.

Don't panic...you're grand...you know the protocol.

But even as she tried to calm herself and continued yanking the cord, all the reasons why she shouldn't have followed the lynx so far into the national forest, why she shouldn't have stayed out so long, bombarded her tired mind.

Eventually, she was forced to give up on starting the snowmobile. Her arms hurt and she was losing what was left of her strength, plus sweating under the layers of clothing only made her colder. Maybe the engine had frozen—it had been inactive here too long. She should have left it running, but she hadn't expected to stay out so long and fuel cost a fortune. She fished the satellite phone out of her pack.

There was no phone signal this far north, and no communities nearby. She knew there were rumours of some reclusive US-Finnish billionaire, who lived in the uninhabited frozen wilderness on the far side of the national forest in a stunning glass house few people had ever seen or located... The resort workers whispered about him because apparently there was some tragic story involving the murder of his parents, and the fortune he had inherited as a kid before he disappeared from the public eye. But whatever the details were, they hadn't reached Ireland, and she couldn't rely on stumbling across some mythical Fortress of Solitude in the middle of nowhere—which could be hundreds of miles away. If it even existed at all.

She tuned into the last signal she'd used.

'Mayday, Mayday. I'm in the n-national forest about f-forty miles north-east of Saariselkä. My vehicle won't start. Please respond.'

Her eyelids drooped, the strange numbness wrapping around her ribs and slowing her breathing, as the last of the sunlight disappeared. She continued to broadcast as her energy drained.

If she could just sleep for a minute, she'd be fine.

No, don't sleep, Cara.

Just when it seemed the situation couldn't possibly get any worse, she felt the first swirl of wind, the prickle of ice on her face.

What the...?

There had been no suggestion of a snowstorm today in the weather forecast or on the radar. Because she'd checked.

But as the swirl lifted and twisted, and a whistling howl picked up through the canyon of trees, turning the winter silence into a wall of terrifying sound, she could barely hear her own voice, still shouting out the Mayday.

She burrowed into the gathering drift beside the broken snowmobile, to shelter from the wind. No one had responded. No one was coming. The battery light on the phone started to wink, the only thing she could see in the white-out.

Her mother's voice, practical, and tired, hissed through her consciousness. Bringing back their last frustrating conversation two days ago.

'You're a fine one...why would you want to go all the way there when we have more than enough creatures here to photograph on the farm?'

'Because a wildlife photographer photographs creatures in the wild, Mammy, not cows and sheep.'

'Shouldn't you be settling already? You're twenty-one and have barely had a boyfriend. All your brothers are having babies already.'

Because my brothers have no desire to get out of County Wexford, just like you, Mammy.

The answer she'd wanted to say swirled in her head, the icy cold making her eyes water.

Don't you dare cry, Cara Doyle, or your eyelids will stick to your eyeballs and then where will you be?

Everywhere was starting to hurt now. The six layers of expensive thermal clothing she'd maxed out one of her many credit cards to buy felt like a layer of tissue paper against the frigid wind.

The dying phone, forgotten in her hand, crackled and then barked.

'Yes… Yes?' she croaked out on a barely audible sob.

Please let that be someone coming to rescue me.

'The cat's lights. Turn them on.' The furious voice seemed to shoot through the wind and burrow into her brain.

Relief swept through her. She nodded, her throat too raw to reply. She pushed herself into the wind with the last of her strength. Her bones felt so brittle now she was sure they were frozen too. She flicked the switch, then collapsed over the seat.

The single yellow beam shone out into the storm—and made her think of all those stories she'd heard as a child, in Bible study as she prepped for her first holy communion, about the white light of Jesus beckoning you, which you saw before death.

Sister Mary Clodagh had always scared the hell out of them with that tale.

But Cara didn't feel scared now, she just felt exhausted. Her sore eyelids drooped.

'Keep talking.' The gruff voice on the phone reverberated in her skull.

She pressed the mouthpiece to her lips, mumbled what she could through the layers of her balaclavas.

'Louder,' the shout barked back.

'I'm trying…' she managed. Her fingers and face didn't hurt any more, because the embalming warmth pressed against her chest like a hot blanket.

Whoever Mr Angry is, he'd better be getting a move on.

A dark shape appeared in the pearly beam, the outline making her think of the majestic brown bears she'd spent the summer in Lapland observing and photographing… The hum of an engine cut through the howling wind as the bear got closer. It detached from its base, the dark shape looming over her.

Piercing silvery blue eyes locked on hers through the thin strip of skin visible under his helmet and above his face coverings and reminded her of the lynx—who she'd photographed what felt like several lifetimes ago.

Hard hands clasped her arms, lifting her. She tried to struggle free, scared her bones would snap.

'Don't fight me,' the bear shouted. 'Stay awake, don't sleep.'

Why was the bear shaking her? Was he attacking her? Shouldn't he be hibernating?

She tried to reply, but the words got stuck in her throat as his big body shielded her from the ice storm. The slaps were firm, but not painful, glancing off her cheek.

'Your name, tell me your name. Don't sleep.'

Why did a bear want to know her name? And how come it could talk?

She couldn't say anything, it hurt to speak. It hurt to even think.

She just wanted to sleep.

She heard cursing, angry, upset, reminding her of her father when he came home from the pub... So long ago now. Good riddance.

Don't sleep or he will come back and call you names again...

But as she found herself bundled onto a raft and being whisked through the storm, the icy wind shifting into a magical dance of blue and green light, the twinkle of stars like fairy lights in the canopy of darkness over her head, a comforting rumble seeped into her soul and chased away the old fear of her da.

Then the brutal, beautiful exhaustion claimed her at last.

Logan Arto Coltan III rode the utility snowmobile into the underground garage of his home and slammed the heavy machine into park.

He swore viciously as he jumped from the saddle and raced to the flatbed he'd hooked up to load supplies.

'Wake up,' he shouted at the body lying on top of the boxes of canned goods and frozen meat he'd been transporting when he'd picked up the Mayday. Accidentally.

He never monitored the emergency frequencies, but the dial must have slipped after he had called his supply pilot.

Why had he answered the call? He should have ignored it. Why hadn't he?

The person's eyelids—the long lashes white with frost—fluttered open. Revealing bright young eyes, coloured a deep emerald green.

He felt the odd jolt of something… And ignored it.

Not unconscious. Yet.

'Stay with me,' he said, then repeated it in Finnish—just in case English wasn't their first language—as he assessed the person's size under their bulky outdoor wear. Around five six. Probably a woman, he decided, as he stripped off the outer layers of his own clothing. The garage was kept at nineteen degrees, so he didn't overheat before removing his snowsuit to enter the house. But right now, he needed to be able to move, so he could get this fool inside.

Once he'd got down to his undershirt and track-pants, he headed to the garage's small utility room and grabbed the first-aid box. Dragging off his last pair of gloves, he found the thermometer, shoved it into his pants' pocket and returned to the trailer.

If this idiot had managed to give themselves hypothermia, he'd have to call an air ambulance.

He frowned, struggling to focus around the anger—and panic—that had been roiling in his gut ever since he'd answered the call.

Lifting the woman, he placed her as gently as he could over his shoulder. If she was hypothermic sudden movements could trigger a fatal heart arrhythmia. He toted her across the concrete space to climb the steps into the house. His home, ever since his grandfather had died ten years ago. A space no one else had ever entered while he was in residence.

'Avata,' he shouted to the house's integrated smart system, ignoring the roll and pitch in his gut as the locks clicked and he kicked the heavy metal door open with his boot.

'Tuli päälle,' he added to instruct the fire to come on,

as he walked into the vast living area. He set the girl on one of the sunken sofas that surrounded a stone fire pit.

The orange flames leapt up and reflected off the panoramic window that opened the luxury space into the winter landscape beyond, obscuring the night-time view of the forest gorge lit by the eerie glow of moonlight.

Safe.

He'd always been safe here, alone. But as he peeled off the woman's layers of headwear, a tumble of wavy reddish-blonde hair was revealed and the strange jolt returned, making him not feel safe any more.

Focus, Logan. You had no choice. It was bring her here or let her die.

She was still staring at him, her eyes glazed but somehow alert, in a way that immediately made him suspicious.

What the hell had she been doing on his land? So far from the nearest centre of civilisation, alone, as night fell?

'How do you feel?' he asked as he reached into his back pocket to grab the thermometer.

'C-c-cold,' she said, starting to shiver violently.

He nodded. Shivering was good.

He shook the thermometer, snapping off its protective covering. Then he pressed his thumb to her chapped bottom lip and placed it under her tongue.

He clicked the timer on his watch, to count down four minutes.

'Wh-wh…?'

'Don't talk.' He glared at the girl, who was staring at him now with a dazed, confused expression in those bright eyes as she continued to shudder.

Not so good.

The timer dinged.

He tugged out the thermometer. Ninety-four point nine degrees.

He cursed softly.

Anything below ninety-five was mild hypothermia.

Great.

'Come on.' He dumped the thermometer on the coffee table, stood, and scooped her carefully into his arms. 'We must get you warm,' he said as he strode towards the wooden staircase that led to the guest bedroom that had never been used on the ground level.

As he marched through the house, with her still shivering, he considered his options.

Perhaps he should call the EMT station in Saariselkä. But she was young, still lucid, looked healthy enough. And he'd located her fairly quickly. Plus she was conscious and her temperature was on the cusp. If he could get it back past ninety-five quickly, there would be no need for hospital treatment and hopefully no ill effects. It would take over an hour for the EMTs to get here even in a chopper and the storm still stood between them.

And he'd be damned if he'd give up the location of his home to help out a stranger before he absolutely had to… And before he knew who this person was, and what she had been doing on his land—getting herself lost in a snowstorm.

That said, he thought grimly as he began stripping off the wet outer layers of her clothing, while she stood shivering and docile… This promised to be a very long night.

CHAPTER TWO

WHERE AM I? Who is this guy? And why don't I care that he's taking off my clothing?

Another violent shudder racked Cara's body as her rescuer kneeled in front of her and lifted each foot to tug off her snow boots. She had to grasp his shoulder to stop herself from falling on top of him—but he seemed oblivious, his movements swift and deliberate as he peeled off her sodden snowsuit and the ski-pants beneath.

His shoulder flexed beneath her ungloved fingers making her aware of the thin thermal undershirt he'd stripped down to—which moulded to his impressive physique like a second skin. Another series of shudders turned her body into a human castanet.

Maybe I don't care because I'm exhausted. And I'd rather be here, wherever here is, than out in the storm.

Something about Mr Angry felt, if not safe, exactly, because he was big and grumpy, then at least not dangerous.

'Wh-who a-a-are y-you?' she managed through the shudders, so exhausted now she was astonished she was still upright.

'Save your energy,' he said, not answering her question. 'You will need it.'

He stood, and his piercing silvery blue gaze locked on her face, the icy glare trapping her like a tractor beam.

Suspicion flashed across his features. His jaw hardened under a rough stubble, which looked as if he'd forgotten to shave for a while, rather than grown it intentionally. His hair was a thick dark brown and long enough to touch his collar. He swept the unkempt waves off his forehead, but they dropped back again almost immediately. He didn't look as if he'd had a proper haircut in years, Cara thought vaguely. How odd, that he couldn't afford a haircut, when his place—if this place was his—looked so exclusive.

Much like the living area they had first entered, the sparsely furnished bedroom had a massive glass wall at the far end of the room, which took in the view of snow-laden forest and wide open sky, the darkness sprinkled with stars and brightened by the blue glow of a full moon...

His home was beyond stunning, a steel and glass minimalist palace that wouldn't look out of place in a glossy travel magazine. Or a Superman comic.

A Fortress of Solitude... She tried to focus her mind, grasp hold of that thought and the strange feeling of *déjà vu*. Why did she feel as if she knew this place? Or knew of it?

He was still staring at her as he pulled the zip down on her fleece and tugged her arms out. The fierce expression didn't just look suspicious now, it looked annoyed, and he was making no effort to hide it.

But as he knelt in front of her again, to take off her sweatpants, his hair flopped over his forehead again. She yearned to sweep the unruly waves away from his face, so she could see more of him, because however annoyed he was, he also fascinated her. Those pale, piercing eyes and the sharp angles of his face were not softened at all by his rugged, unkempt appearance. Although she'd only ever had the urge to photograph wildlife before now, she would love to photograph him, because there was something about him that seemed untamed despite the sophistication of his home.

She resisted the urge to touch him though, because her fingers were still cramping and she barely had the strength to stand—let alone lift her arm. Plus, she got the definite impression from his taciturn behaviour, he would not welcome her touch.

He remained silent as he continued to strip her out of the heavy clothing with brutal efficiency until all she wore were her panties, her bra, her thick woolly socks and the skintight thermal tights, which left very little to anyone's imagination.

She used all her strength to fold one arm across her breasts, feeling hideously exposed all of a sudden. And vulnerable. But her whole body was so shattered it was hard to muster a blush—even though, being Irish and a redhead, blushing was one of her superpowers.

What was worse than feeling naked in front of him, though, was feeling like a burden. She hated to be a burden—had always been self-sufficient, ever since her father had left and her mother had spent her evenings crying herself to sleep when she'd thought Cara and her brothers couldn't hear her...

Why are you thinking about your deadbeat da again?

The thought echoed through her foggy brain.

Luckily, she was too tired to muster the energy to be embarrassed about her dependence on Mr Grumpy as he leant past her to strip back the heavy duvet and then scooped her up and laid her in the middle of the enormous bed.

He tucked the quilt under her chin as she continued to shudder and shake. She still couldn't feel her feet, but her fingers and face were starting to burn as the blood flow returned.

The sheets smelled of laundry soap and a tantalising combination of bergamot and pine.

'I'm going to get a heated blanket and something hot to drink,' he said, his gruff accent a strange transatlantic mix of American and Scandinavian. 'We need to raise your temperature. Don't sleep or I'll have to wake you.'

She managed a nod, before watching him stride from the room.

As he disappeared through the doorway, she forced her gaze back towards the magnificent view through the room's glass wall.

The shaking had downgraded to a shiver when he finally returned. Somehow, she'd managed to keep her eyes open, even though the rest of her had melted into the mattress.

He perched on the edge of the bed, then tugged the duvet down to place the heated blanket next to her skin. He broke a heat pack over his knee and placed it under her neck. She flinched as he bundled her up in the blanket and quilt.

'I-it h-hurts,' she said, blinking furiously to hold back the tears scorching her eyes.

She'd rather die than cry in front of this guy.

'I know,' he said, but didn't offer any words of comfort or reassurance.

Your bedside manner really sucks, fella.

The antagonistic thought galvanised her despite her misery, at least a little bit, as he lifted her into a sitting position, banded his arm around her back and then reached for the hot mug he'd brought in with the blanket and heat pack.

As she inhaled, the scent of him got trapped in her

lungs, and she realised the tantalising aroma of bergamot and pine belonged to him.

Why did recognising his scent feel stupidly intimate? And make her feel even more compromised and vulnerable?

'Drink,' he ordered as he pressed the mug to her lips.

She gulped and spluttered, her tongue numb and her lips chapped. He ignored her grunts of protest, which somehow made her feel less compromised, keeping the mug pressed to her sore lips until she had consumed nearly half of the hot sweet mint tea.

At last, he let her lie down and took her temperature again.

As he checked it, the sharp frown on his face levelled out, a fraction.

'Ninety-five.' He stood, making her even more aware of his height.

He was so tall, his rangy body intimidatingly muscular. Whatever he did for a living, he was not idle.

All the better to rescue you with, Cara. Be grateful.

'Looks like you'll live,' he added, with a lack of enthusiasm that might have stung if she had been able to muster anything other than the deep desire to sleep for several millennia.

Trust me to get rescued by the most reluctant knight ever.

'I'll check on you during the night,' he added. 'Sleep now.'

Her eyelids shut on his command, but as she was whisked away by the foggy exhaustion—her body finally having stopped shivering long enough to sink into the mattress the rest of the way—all she could think was how odd it was that even though she was pretty sure she didn't like him, and he *really* didn't like her, she was glad he would be near tonight.

* * *

When she woke the next morning, Cara had a vague recollection of being awakened during the night by her rescuer. He'd taken her temperature and adjusted the heated blanket a few times… As she flexed tired, aching limbs in the huge bed, and inhaled that tantalising scent again, she realised the electric blanket was gone. So he must have retrieved it, to allow her to sleep comfortably during the night.

She blinked down tears as she turned towards the enormous picture window.

Now, don't you dare go getting emotional for no reason, Cara Doyle. He only did what any decent person would do in the circumstances. He could hardly be leaving you out there to freeze.

But even though she knew the emotion was simply relief after the painful, frankly terrifying ordeal of being stranded in the snowstorm, not sure if she would survive it, and that odd feeling of intimacy as he'd tended her through the night, it was hard not to feel indebted. And pathetically grateful.

For a guy who clearly did not want her in his home, he'd been remarkably diligent. And though brusque, also gentle with her.

Unlike the night before, when there had been a clear view of the forest through the glass wall, snow swirled now, and ice drifted across the landscape. The snow-laden forest on the edge of the tundra was obscured by what looked like another approaching storm.

She forced herself out of the bed, glad to discover her legs were still in working order, even if she did feel winded by the time she had crossed the room.

She pressed her nose to the frosted glass. Even though

she was in only her thermal tights and her underwear, the ambient temperature in the room felt warm and comfortable. Mr Grumpy's Fortress had much better insulation than her mammy's farm in Wexford, that was for sure, where she and her brothers had worn their outside coats indoors when the temperature had dipped to ten degrees. They'd have frozen solid in minus thirty.

There you go, thinking of home again.

She admonished herself. She had never been sentimental about Ireland, not since she'd left to pursue her dream of becoming a wildlife photographer, after spending years as a child watching and observing and finally learning to document the birds and small creatures in and around the farm.

The photos.

Panic pierced her heart.

She'd left her camera with the shots she'd taken of the lynx in the saddlebags of her broken snowmobile. The shots she'd nearly died to acquire... And which even now might be buried under a snowdrift.

She needed to thank Mr Grumpy for his help and get back to her snowmobile. But already she suspected the snowstorm was going to make that hard. And her weakened condition probably wasn't going to help either.

She wiped the mist off the glass as she spotted something... A large snowmobile driving across the frozen lake. The figure bundled in the necessary six or seven layers of winter clothing in the saddle handled the lumbering machine with casual grace, making him instantly recognisable.

Mr Grumpy. Aka the guy who had rescued her and tended her throughout the night, but whose name she didn't know.

A strange shudder shot through her, bringing with it a spurt of adrenaline to jolt her out of her maudlin thoughts of her family's farm—and her panic about the precious cargo she'd left in the forest. She tracked the snowmobile as it drove towards the house then disappeared beneath her, into what had to be the garage where she could remember them arriving the night before.

Before he'd carried her first into the vast living area then into this bedroom.

A weight formed in her throat, then swooped down into her belly as she recalled the feel of his hands, impersonal but also gentle, as he'd stripped her wet clothing off. The feel of his shoulder tensing under her hand, his arm braced against her back as he forced the hot drink on her, and those piercing silvery blue eyes locked on her face, studying her...

Sensation rippled over her skin, a lot more vivid now than it had been last night, when her brain had been foggy and her body too tired to experience much of anything but the intense cold, and those violent shudders.

Stop thinking about him. And figure out how to rescue your camera.

She pressed her forehead to the glass. And evened her breathing, trying to ignore the unfamiliar sensations rippling over her skin. She needed to formulate a plan as soon as she could, because the lynx photos were the crowning glory that would help her sell her Lapland portfolio to the stock photo site she'd been schmoozing for months.

She needed that income to pay off the credit cards she'd maxed out in the last six months to set up in Lapland. To take the next step in her career plan, she had to free up more time to observe and study the behaviour of the wildlife she wished to document and less time in the menial jobs—barista, waitress, hotel cleaner—that had just about kept her solvent...

Which would mean begging Mr Grumpy to take her to her machine, and—if it couldn't be fixed—then back to Saariselkä.

The good news was, he was clearly more than happy to travel in a storm. And, wherever he'd been just now, he was back. Not so good was the fact that—after she'd hunted the room—the rest of her clothes seemed to have disappeared, and she was now totally breathless.

Also not good... From her interaction with him so far, she did not think her host was going to be too pleased about being asked to do her another enormous favour.

Plus, charm had never been one of Cara's strengths. She knew that. She'd always been outspoken and fiercely independent, especially with men—thanks, Da—which was probably why she'd never had much luck in the boyfriend department. Something her mother had pointed out on numerous occasions.

But you're not trying to seduce him, Cara, you're just going to ask him for a favour. So it's all good.

After taking a hot shower in the adjoining bathroom—another striking, intimidatingly masculine and scrupulously clean architectural marvel made in quartz and glass and hand-carved stone—she found an oversized sweatshirt in the chest of drawers. On her it made a passable mini dress. At least it covered her backside, so she felt less naked once she'd put her tights back on. Finally, she felt human again.

But as she ventured out of the bedroom in search of her host, she could feel the hot brick dropping further into her stomach and jiggling about like a jumping bean. Which was just plain peculiar.

She didn't get nervous around men. It was surely just that she owed this guy more than she'd ever owed any man. And now she must ask for more.

But then, she'd never see him again after today. And she had a feeling he would be more than happy to see the back of her. So there was that.

Logan dumped the coffee jug back on the plate, sloshing the fresh brew over the kitchen counter. He gulped down a mouthful of hot black liquid and swallowed, focussing on the burn in his throat.

He was so damn mad his hands were shaking. He clasped the mug tight and willed them to stop, not caring that the hot china scalded his palms.

He'd found the camera in her gear on the disabled snow-mobile—and left it there. Just as he'd figured, the girl's appearance on the edge of his land hadn't been a coincidence. The hypothermia and the snowmobile's engine failure had been real. But she had risked her life to get a shot of him and his home—that had to be the explanation.

His grandfather had warned him long ago, the press was his enemy—that it was the media who had put a target on his parents' backs twenty years ago, reporting on their volatile marriage—the endless cycle of public arguments, private feuds, bitter silences, attention-seeking reconcili-ations—in minute and exploitative detail.

Logan thrust his fingers through his hair, the memory of the camera flashes like lightning bolts, the shouted de-mands for him to look up, to tell them how he felt about his parents' deaths hitting him like body blows all over again. He shuddered, remembering the sight of the muddy earth of their graves on that cold November morning. Panic assailed him, as another more visceral memory pressed at his consciousness.

He shoved it back.

He hadn't been able to cry at their funeral—had struggled to feel anything at all—cast into a media storm that had terrified him.

He'd been ten years old. An orphan. Trapped alone on the Coltan estate in Rhode Island with a staff of people paid to care for him. His life had been ruled and administered by a board of trustees until the Finnish grandfather he'd never met had brought him here.

And saved him. Protected him from all the people, so many people, who had wanted to exploit his loss.

He stared at the furious storm building outside the glass. And his hands stopped shaking at last.

His sanctuary. A place disconnected from the outside world. A place he'd built himself—in secret—at nineteen, because he couldn't bear to stay in his grandfather's A-frame house any more, without the old man there.

And now she had invaded it.

Hell, she hadn't just invaded it, she'd tricked him into bringing her here.

Into exposing himself all over again to the questions he couldn't answer as the memories tore at his chest.

'Hiya.'

He swung round to see the cause of his fury standing in his kitchen. She wore one of his sweatshirts, which didn't do much to cover the long, toned legs he'd noticed last night. The strange sensation in his gut flared, right alongside his anger.

He stared at her. Having someone—*anyone*—sharing his space felt wrong. An intrusion that he had never allowed, but there was something about having her standing on the other side of the kitchen counter, after the night he'd spent tending her, that felt wrong and yet also… Not.

'You don't need people, Arto. Nature is better. It does not scheme and exploit. It just is. Your mother was weak— she sought the limelight and was punished for it. You are not weak. You don't need those things.'

He ruthlessly ignored the flicker of exhilaration in his gut as his grandfather's voice echoed in his head.

Johannes Makinen had not been a talkative man. Never tactile or nurturing. But as austere as he had always been, he had also been as steady as the seasons, and fiercely protective of the broken boy Logan had been when he had first arrived in his mother's homeland, crippled by a fear of people that had taken years to become manageable.

The solitude, the silence here, had helped him survive those early years when he had been scared of every sound, every voice, except his grandfather's. He could not bear to be touched for so long, he had learned to survive without that too. And eventually the nightmares that tore him from sleep and dragged him back into the middle of that terrible night had died.

And that was when he'd understood, his grandfather was right. Even as his physical needs had changed as a teenager and eventually a man, he had learned to deny them—because he never wanted to be that broken again.

Something this woman would never understand.

But even as he tried to convince himself he did not want her here, he found himself studying her lithe physique and the flicker became a warm weight in his abdomen.

She cleared her throat, her pale skin bright with colour.

'I'd be after thanking you for last night,' she said. Her accent had a musical lilt that didn't match the sharp edges of Scandinavia, or the casual sway of the US. 'You... Well, you saved my life.'

The flush fired across her collarbone and made him notice the fascinating sprinkle of freckles there—and the rise and fall of her breasts under the baggy sweatshirt.

He gave a stiff nod. He didn't want her gratitude. He wanted her gone.

'You... You never told me your name,' she asked, as if she didn't know.

She was a good actress, he'd give her that, the curious light in her gaze almost credible. But he only became more annoyed when he noticed that the vivid green of her irises matched the deep striking emerald of the aurora borealis.

'Logan Colton,' he said, knowing he was not giving anything away that she didn't already know.

'Logan...? Colt...?'

Her eyebrows launched up her forehead, then her head whipped around, taking in the beamed ceiling, the huge open-plan space where he lived and which he had built on the footprint of his grandfather's old home.

'You're the billionaire recluse... This is it. The Fortress of Solitude... Of course,' she whispered, her voice low with either awe or astonishment, it was hard to tell. But then it hardly mattered, because this was no doubt an act for his benefit. 'You're the guy they talk about. You actually *exist*?' She gaped at him, and he realised she was worthy of an award—either that or she was not as smart as the fierce intelligence in her eyes suggested. 'I thought for sure that was a myth. Or a fairy tale.'

A fairy tale? Seriously?

He bristled. He didn't know any fairy tales. But what he did know was they were fanciful nonsense designed to scare young children. And he had never been a child.

Or scared of imaginary things. Because he knew exactly what terrors real life could hold.

Rain, endless rain, pounding down onto the dirty pavement. The scent of blood filling his nostrils, the cold dead weight pushing him into the filthy ground. His mother's broken screams. The pop of bullets like party balloons bursting. The fear clawing at his throat, making his heart rate accelerate to bursting...

He closed his eyes briefly to shove away the visions pushing into his consciousness again for the first time in years...

'Monsters exist, Arto. And they all take human form.'

His grandfather's voice eased the pain in his chest and pushed the worst of the memories back into the darkness, where they belonged.

'I'm sure I would have figured it out a lot sooner if I hadn't been so exhausted last night.' Her musical accent drew him sharply back to the present.

She wrapped her arms around her waist and gave a small shudder as if the memory of her ordeal disturbed her.

'Do you really live here all alone, then?' she asked, changing the subject. But then her eyes widened. 'I'm sorry, I'm sure that's not my business at all. I talk too much.'

Two things they could agree on.

'You're not a big talker, are you?' she added. 'Even for a Finnish person.'

Apparently, she was more observant than she appeared. But again, that was not a surprise—given that she was probably a journalist.

Her stomach made a loud growling sound, reminding him she hadn't eaten yet today.

He let his gaze drift down her frame, annoyed when it

lingered on the soft swell of her breasts beneath his old sweatshirt again.

He forced his gaze back to her flushed face, angry he had let himself get sucked into that response again. He didn't need human contact, and that must include women. He had convinced himself long ago his hand would do if he needed relief.

But having her in his home was distracting. And aggravating, for more than one reason. Already she was testing the boundaries he had made himself live by. And he hated that even more than the predatory reason for her intrusion into his home.

'There is food, help yourself,' he said, suddenly desperate to be somewhere she was not. His response to her would surely fade if he was not near her.

But as he walked past her, heading back towards his workshop, she reached out and touched his bare arm.

He was so shocked by the unsolicited contact, he flinched.

She dropped her hand instantly, but the ripple of sensation still buzzed across his senses in a way that only disturbed him more.

'I'm sorry...' she murmured.

He stiffened, hating the look in her gaze—confused, surprised but also somehow full of empathy.

'Where are you going?' she asked.

'Work,' he said.

'But... I wanted to ask you...' She swallowed, looking unsure of herself, again. 'Could you give me a lift back to my snowmobile today? So I can get out of your hair.'

'No.' He couldn't be around her, let her touch him again, until he was fully prepared for that contact, and his confusing response to it.

'Why not?' Her guileless expression only infuriated him more.

The truth—that her touch had had a profound effect on him—would make him look weak and foolish. So, he seized on all the other reasons why he could not take her anywhere today.

'The storm will become impassable,' he said, which was only the truth.

She did not know he had found her camera. If she lied about it, he would know the truth. So he added, 'And before you leave, you must tell me why you are really here.'

Her mouth went slack, those deep emerald eyes widening even further. 'But… You know why. My skimobile broke down in the snowstorm and you rescued me.'

'That is not the truth,' he said, or certainly not the whole truth. And until she told him that, he knew he could not trust her.

She simply blinked, as if struggling to process his statement. Another act.

He walked past her, the silence behind him layered with shock.

Despite his anger, and the disturbing unease—that visceral awareness that had made his skin prickle and the warm weight in his gut start to pulse—he felt a little of his power returning as he left the room.

At least he had finally found a way to shut her up.

CHAPTER THREE

CARA STARED AFTER Logan Colton's retreating back—
and his ridiculously broad shoulders—as her jaw dropped
so fast she was surprised it didn't bounce off the quartz
floor tiles.

She was completely and utterly speechless as he disappeared through the large doorway that led who knew
where in this enormous house.

What just happened?

She ran the conversation they'd had back through her
head.

Not that you could really call it a conversation—given
that the man had uttered all of about ten words on his end
of it.

She'd thanked him and asked him politely to return her
to her snowmobile. And okay, maybe her reaction hadn't
been the best when she'd figured out who he really was—
the billionaire recluse she had been convinced was a fig-
ment of everyone's imagination. But hey, she'd only just
recovered from a near-death experience. And surely she
could be forgiven for a little overfamiliarity—after all,
he'd seen her all but naked the night before. And saved
her from said near-death experience.

He'd looked at her with such intensity, she'd felt his gaze
roam over her skin like a caress, her unbidden reaction as

shocking as it was…well, shocking. For a moment she'd thought there was something there, something she probably shouldn't entertain—given her circumstances as a woman alone, in a stranger's home. But that searing gaze, dark with awareness, hadn't disgusted or unnerved her. It had made every one of her reliably dormant pheromones rejoice as if they were spending St Pat's Day getting plastered in Dublin's Temple Bar—instead of stranded in a stranger's ice palace in the middle of nowhere.

But then she'd felt him flinch at her touch, and seen the flash of fury in his eyes.

And her pheromones had stopped partying—because that look had transported her back to her family's kitchen, on the receiving end of one of her father's drunken tirades. And left her feeling miserable, and suffocated, and unfairly judged.

She was so shocked by his accusations, though, she was completely speechless for one whole minute.

But then the sense of injustice, of righteous indignation—which had got her through so much of her childhood, and finally dynamited her out of Ireland and away from the cruel memories of her father's abuse—kicked into gear.

Adrenaline charged through her veins, flushing away the last of the breathlessness that had dogged her ever since she'd woken up.

Maybe she owed Mr Grumpy her life and maybe she had invaded his privacy—something it was clear he was not happy about—and yeah, maybe she talked way too much. But what gave him the right to question her integrity? To suggest she had engineered a near-death experience… To do *what* exactly?

She shot through the doorway after him, finally finding her voice.

'Mr Colton, wait?' she shouted. The doorway led into another stunning architectural space. A wall of glass bricks revealed a panoramic view of the undulating forest rising across a gorge at the back of the property, which was blanketed in a thick layer of snow. The snow continued to cascade from the darkening sky in swirling gusts of white.

She slipped and slid in her socks on the stone floor, past the sunken fire pit and the couch she vaguely remembered being deposited on the night before. Two staircases led to other levels, one up, one down.

'Mr Colton, where are you?' she shouted, choosing the staircase down, because the staircase up might lead her to his bedroom, and she suspected heading there would not improve this situation at all.

She got no reply. Her indignation rose as she found herself lost in a complex series of passageways, lit by skylights. She walked past the door to a fully equipped gym—which had to explain those impressive pecs.

So not the point, Cara.

She didn't care if he'd saved her life. That didn't mean he got to be a judgemental jerk.

At last, she came to another staircase leading to a covered walkway insulated against the storm outside. It led to a large wooden structure constructed under the trees. She spotted him through the floor-to-ceiling glass panels on one side, standing in the light airy space, leaning over a worktable. He had his back to her as she burst through the door, her footsteps and heavy breathing covered by loud music—the tune one from a rock band from decades ago—blaring from an impressive sound system.

The workshop—for that was surely what it was—was the only messy place in the whole house, every available surface strewn with drawings, sketches, and an array of tools.

Organised chaos was what it seemed.

But then she saw the sculptures that stood in the far corner. Lifesize renderings of animal and plant life—the most striking of which was a black bear in full attack mode.

She drew a staggered breath…

The sculpture was exquisite. The bear looked so lifelike, but also stylised, its lumbering body rendered in the layered grain of the wood, the intent in its eyes, somehow both real and yet also mythic. The carving captured the power and strength as well as the natural grace of a species she had observed herself during the summer months.

Even her photographs could not have captured the magnificent creature so perfectly.

She stood spellbound for a moment.

But then her host turned, sensing her presence, and that searing blue gaze fixed on her face. He barked something in Finnish and the music died.

All she could hear was her own breathing.

The deep frown didn't alleviate the dark intensity in his expression one bit.

Breathe, Cara.

She forced herself to suck in a breath past the hot lump that had got jammed in her throat… And now sank between her thighs.

Oh, for the love of…

'Leave,' he said, in that charmingly erudite way he had—as if every word cost him a billion euros to utter.

But before he had a chance to turn his back on her again, she managed to locate her outrage, which had momentarily malfunctioned in the face of his staggering arrogance. And the striking beauty of his work.

'That's exactly what I want to be doing. But the storm is not my fault…'

'Leave my *workshop*,' he said as if she were an eejit, while completely missing the point. 'I want you where I am not.'

She would have congratulated herself on managing to get another whole sentence out of him—which, from the rusty sound of his voice, she suspected was an achievement. Except what he had said was just as rude and dictatorial as his two-syllable answers.

'Look, fella, it's clear you want me here even less than I want to be here.' She began again, holding on to her temper with an effort. From the rigid line of his jaw and the fierce suspicion in his gaze, she suspected losing her cool would only fuel his bad opinion of her. 'But that doesn't give you the right to insult me. Or imply that I tricked my way into your home when I was about to die of exposure last night.'

He leaned back against the worktable, crossed his arms over that wide chest—pumping up those magnificent biceps, annoyingly—and glared.

'You wish to play games?' he said, making even less sense now than he had before.

'What games?' she asked. Was that a trick question? Surely it had to be. As she had no fecking clue what games he was talking about.

'I know why you are really here.'

'You… What?' Her voice trailed off, anger and frustration replaced with confusion.

'I found the camera.' He spat the last word, as if it were an obscenity.

Okay, there was clearly some misunderstanding here. Because he was looking at her as if her camera were an unexploded nuclear warhead.

If only she'd listened more carefully to her fellow barista

Issi's stories about this guy, then she might have some clue what his problem was. But whatever his problem was, she needed to get to the bottom of it, before she exploded from frustration…and that damn throbbing in her gut got any more forceful—which had no business being there at all.

'You found my equipment in the snowmobile?' So that was where he had just been.

He gave a curt nod.

'Did you bring it back with you?' she asked, the flicker of hope in her chest almost painful. Maybe her work hadn't been lost.

'No,' he said.

The hope guttered out. And she had the stupid urge to cry. Six months' work. Lost. Not to mention the thousands of pounds' worth of priceless equipment that was now probably close to being frozen solid. That camera had been her future. A future she hadn't been able to afford to insure.

I hate my life.

She swallowed heavily, to contain the pain. The last thing she needed right now was to show him a weakness, because she had a feeling it would only increase his contempt. From his rigid unyielding stance, it was clear he didn't have a compassionate or empathetic bone in his body.

Her gaze glided over his impressive physique, the ridges of his six-pack moulded under the skintight thermal shirt.

His very *hot* body. The man was a ride and no mistake. She blinked.

Whoa, girl. Why are you getting fixated on his abs when it's his suspicious mind you need to concentrate on?

'Why not?' she managed, her voice breaking on the words. How hard would it have been for him to bring back her camera?

He didn't answer her perfectly reasonable question. He simply continued to glare at her—but she spotted the flicker of surprise cross his features before he could mask it.

It was only a small crack, but she'd take it.

'Why did you go out to find my snowmobile?' she asked. 'If you didn't intend to rescue my stuff?'

'To check if the machine was really broken.'

It was her turn to look surprised. Make that astonished. Exactly how cynical was he?

'You thought I faked being stranded?' she asked, even though she could see from the ice in his gaze he had thought exactly that.

He shrugged. 'Yes.'

'Why…? Why would I do that?' She knew she shouldn't be angry with him—she'd nearly died. But she was still too astonished by that brittle suspicion to be anything but dumbfounded. How could anyone be this cynical? This guarded?

'For the same reason you have the camera.'

That pale blue gaze glided over her figure. But despite the icy suspicion, all it did was make the throb in her abdomen heat.

Terrific.

'You've lost me again,' she said.

He crossed his ankles, drawing her attention to the muscles flexing in his thighs beneath the clinging brushed cotton of his sweatpants. She noticed for the first time, he wore thick woollen socks, which somehow softened the hard, unyielding stance.

But not much. Her gaze rose back to the rigid jawline, tensing under the thick stubble.

Why did he have to look so gorgeous, when he was clearly a paranoid eejit?

The quiet stretched out between them, only disturbed by the snowstorm outside the glass—its roar partially muffled by the triple glazing. She refused to say more, forced to bite her lip until he gave her an answer she could understand.

Obviously, he had decided she had some ulterior motive for being here... For nearly freezing to death yesterday. But he needed to tell her what it was, before she could defend herself.

'I know what your pictures are worth,' he said, being so cryptic it was starting to strain what was left of her patience. 'But you will never sell them.'

'You found my pictures of the lynx?' Was he some kind of wildlife photographer too? A rival? Although that made no sense either. Not only did he have a reputation for being extremely wealthy, but he also appeared to be an incredibly talented artist. Why would he be making a career for himself as a photographer when he could surely sell his artwork for a lot more?

It was his turn to frown. 'Stop the act,' he said.

The what-now...?

Frustration and fury blindsided her. She chewed on her lip, hard enough to taste blood, to hold the volatile reaction in check.

She would not let him goad her into losing her temper the rest of the way. Because she'd learnt at a young age, if someone insisted on judging you, on making you feel small and insignificant—the way her father had done so often, before he had disappeared from all their lives— the best thing to do was not let them see you cared about their opinion.

'Why don't you tell me what you think I'm guilty of? *Then* I can drop my act.' She ground out the words.

One dark brow rose up his forehead, the twist of his lips

flattening into a thin, intractable line. But he remained maddeningly silent.

Her motto had always been never defend, never explain. Because in her experience, that only led to more judgement… But he was leaving her with no choice.

'But just for the record, I'm a wildlife photographer.' She pushed the words out, determined to believe them, even though up until two days ago her main source of income had been menial jobs. 'The pictures on that camera were of a female Arctic lynx, which I have been tracking for weeks. You would also have found shots on the memory card of a wild reindeer herd from last week. I shouldn't have come so far out—should not have waited until it was almost dark to restart the snowmobile. And I'm still beyond grateful you rescued me. But I don't have an ulterior motive or a hidden agenda for being here…' She glanced around the structure. 'Wherever *here* actually is. I didn't even know you were a real person until this morning. But whatever your secret is, it is safe with me. All I want to do is rescue the equipment I've maxed out all my credit cards to buy. And, if possible, save the pictures I took of the lynx, which almost cost me my life. And then I want to return to Saariselkä so I can sell them to the stock photography company I've been trying to impress for months. If that's okay with you.'

She finally ran out of breath, the effort it had taken not just to speak, but to overcome her golden rule and explain herself, leaving her exhausted again. Her whole body slumped, the starch of her justifiable anger seeping away to leave her drained.

Unfortunately, his expression remained carved in granite. It hadn't softened one iota.

Well, isn't that just grand?

* * *

'Whatever your secret is, it is safe with me.'

Something leapt in Logan's chest, something unprecedented and fierce. And dangerous.

She looked so earnest, so honest, so forthright—which was precisely why he would be a fool to believe her.

The moment of doubt, though, that she might actually be who she said she was, made him almost as angry as the flood of hunger.

Her pale skin had flushed a deep red, her eyes were bright with purpose, her stance both belligerent but also brave. Making her look even more stunning than she had this morning when he'd first encountered her in his kitchen.

The desire, thick and insistent, which he had not even been able to name last night, settled in his groin. The throb of reaction was almost painful. Making it impossible for him to ignore it any longer. Or what it implied.

He was physically attracted to his uninvited house guest.

This wasn't just awareness, of her as a woman. It wasn't even the sexual appetite he had always been able to satisfy by masturbating whenever he felt the primal, basic and entirely natural urge to have sex. It was more specific than that. It was the desire to capture *her* plump lips and discover her taste. To feel *her* mouth moulding to his. To drive his tongue into the recesses and capture the sobs of *her* arousal. It was the intense longing to glide his palms beneath the hem of the shapeless sweatshirt of his she was wearing, to discover if her skin was as powder soft as it had seemed last night. The need to explore exactly what lay at the juncture of those long, toned thighs. The yearning to bare her body and caress every part of it.

He had never felt such desires before now—on the rare occasions he had encountered other women.

But somehow worse than his shocking reaction to this woman was the unprecedented urge to believe she was sincere. That if he asked her to, she really would keep his secrets safe.

He ground his teeth together, aware of the sweat sliding down his back. He unfolded his arms, the riot of sensations making him fidgety and tense. He shoved his fists into the pockets of his sweatpants.

The battle to draw himself back from the edge—not to let her see or even sense the yearning driving him—was harder than any battle he had fought in a while.

Surely this was precisely why he had kept himself away from other people for so long. So that he would never feel this driving need to touch, to hold? Because he knew he could not trust anyone to know his needs.

But he couldn't detach his gaze from hers as he noticed the way her eyes darkened.

She was no more immune to these sensations than he was—which only made this situation more untenable, more volatile.

He turned back to the sketches for his new piece, tried to concentrate on them and block out the yearning starting to claw at his gut.

'No camera,' he said, in answer to the question he had managed to grasp in her stream of consciousness. He picked up the pencil. 'Now leave.'

He heard her outraged gasp. But as he began to flesh out the wings of the eagle in the sketches for the new project, he waited to hear the sound of her retreating footsteps. They didn't come.

Her voice, when she spoke again, had a steely quality he had to admire.

'Congratulations, fella, you've just earned the title of the rudest eejit I've ever met. And I worked in a backpackers' pub in Temple Bar for two years.'

His breathing released as he finally heard the pad of her footsteps retreating. The door to the workshop slammed shut. He shouldn't turn around, shouldn't look, but he couldn't seem to stop himself. He tracked her through the glass walkway as she made her way back to the main house. His gaze devoured the sight of her through the swirling snow as she strode away—her head held high, her long legs eating up the ground—before she disappeared down the steps to the basement complex.

He threw down the pencil, the hunger surging through his veins.

He was unlikely to get much work done today. And from the look of the storm, which had been building all morning, they were going to be trapped together in the house for at least another twenty-four hours.

He frowned, annoyed all over again, as the unwanted desire continued to pump into his groin like wildfire. He thrust impatient fingers through his hair then glanced down at the prominent ridge in his sweatpants. He flattened his palm against the strident erection, to rub the rigid flesh through his clothing, furious that she had reduced him to this, and that any relief he found was likely to be temporary—until she was finally gone.

At least the storm would give him a chance to figure out the logistics of getting her back to Saariselkä without risking exposure. But concerns about how to do that took second place to getting her the hell out of his home, so he could control the desperate urge to touch her. Surely the fact that they did not like each other would help?

If last night had felt like the longest night of his life, the next twenty-four hours were going to feel like several hundred years.

CHAPTER FOUR

'WHAT ARE YOU DOING?'

Cara turned from the stove, to see her reluctant host staring at her.

Surprise, surprise, he did not look pleased to see her in his kitchen.

She sighed and placed the wooden spoon on the counter, then brushed her palms on the tea towel she had tucked into the waistband of her leggings.

'Making us supper,' she said, trying to push her lips into some semblance of a smile.

Not easy when he was glaring at her again. But this time, she was prepared for that hard, intense, judgmental look. And determined not to let it

get to her.

She'd managed to find breakfast then taken a long nap in what she now considered to be her bedroom in the huge house. After that, she'd gone to check on her reluctant host. Once she'd ensured he was still ensconced in his workshop, she'd gone exploring.

The house had three levels and was scrupulously clean and tidy throughout. Almost as if no one lived here. There was a library full of books, in a number of different languages, all of them dog-eared and well read. She hadn't managed to find anywhere to charge her dead phone, nor had she found any computer equipment. Which was just odd. Who lived so far from civilisation without benefit of the Internet? What did he do all day apart from read and work on his sculptures, and exercise? And how did he keep the house so clean, unless of course he had staff? But somehow she doubted that, because there was no evidence of anyone else ever having been here. And she'd noticed some kind of device busy remotely vacuuming the front parlour.

The storm had continued to rage outside for the entire day, until night had fallen about two hours ago in the middle of the afternoon.

Mr Grumpy had remained locked in his workshop the whole time. Maybe he had grabbed something to eat earlier while she'd been sleeping, but when she'd found a pantry just off the kitchen and a cold room full of frozen meat and fish, she'd had a brainwave.

She'd tried the stick. It hadn't even put a dent in his determination to think the worst of her. So now she was going to try the carrot. Or rather the carrots, onions, leeks, potatoes, cabbage and meat of her mammy's famous Irish stew, with a small twist, because the only unfrozen meat she'd found in the cold room were reindeer steaks.

For a moment, he was completely nonplussed by her statement. And she felt a strange pang in her chest. Not only did he appear to live here entirely alone, but she would hazard a guess no one had offered to cook him supper in a very long time.

Why that would make her feel momentarily sad for him she had no idea—given that the man practically had *Loner and Proud of It* tattooed across his forehead—but it did.

As much as she'd found her three older brothers a trial during her teenage years, because they'd always had their noses in her business, she had missed the energy and companionship of her big boisterous family once she had decided to set out alone to find her joy as a photographer. It was one thing about her chosen profession she could admit now she regretted—that she hadn't had the time to return to Wexford and visit for over a year.

He cocked his head to one side, staring at the pot she had bubbling on the stove. Then that silvery blue gaze connected with hers again.

'Why?' he asked, sounding not just suspicious now but also confused.

Her lips lifted, the forced smile becoming genuine. There was definitely something to be said for having this man at a disadvantage.

'Because I'm famished and I figured you would be, too. I made what I suspect is probably the first ever Irish Reindeer Stew with the supplies in the pantry.'

He didn't respond, so she felt compelled to fill the void. Conversation, after all, was another of her Celtic superpowers.

'Reindeer's a nice lean meat, it might even work better than the mutton my mammy uses from the farm for hers. But it's basically the same recipe. I couldn't figure out how to work your oven, so I had to slow cook it on the stove but it's—'

'Stop talking.' He held up a hand, cutting her off in midflow, his expression pained.

Disappointment rippled through her at his rudeness. But she tried not to take it personally. From the location of his home and his taciturn behaviour so far, she suspected Logan Colton was not a man well versed in conversation. Or any social graces at all really.

After years spent in the company of Irish men—who

tended to use great *craic* like a weapon, to charm unsuspecting women—this man's bluntness was almost refreshing.

'I did not ask you to cook for me,' he said, the brittle cynicism back, but it was more wary than accusatory now.

Progress, after a fashion.

'Consider it payback, for saving my life yesterday,' she said, because it was clear he was uncomfortable with being in her debt—and she wanted him to know how ridiculous that was, given what she owed him.

His brow furrowed, as if he was searching for the trap. She sighed.

Okay, they were really going to have to work on his suspicious nature. But when her stomach growled, she decided that would have to wait.

Switching off the burner under the pot, she set about ladling generous helpings of the stew into two big wooden bowls. He was still standing silently, observing her as if she were a science experiment he couldn't quite figure out. She walked out of the kitchen area with the food, then placed the bowls on the large table already set with cutlery and napkins and an array of pickles and condiments she'd found in the pantry. Like the rest of the house, the kitchen space had a huge picture window that looked out on the forest gorge that dropped below this side of the house. But in the darkness, the large space felt strangely intimate. Especially as she'd had to light a couple of candles on the table when she had been unable to figure out how to turn on the lights in the dining area.

Something she was now regretting, big-time. What on earth had made her think candles would be a good look?

Seriously, Cara? He probably thinks you're trying to seduce him now.

She'd also found a wine cellar. And had uncorked a bottle of merlot, which sat on the table now like another great big red flag to her bad intentions.

Heat flushed into her cheeks as her gaze connected with his.

'I'm sorry. I couldn't find a switch to turn on the lights over here when it got dark.' Luckily the lights in the kitchen had already been on.

'The house's systems are voice activated,' he supplied. 'In Finnish.'

'Grand,' she managed, feeling about as transparent as a new bride's negligee.

Yeah, maybe don't think about naked brides right now.

'That would explain why there wasn't a switch, then,' she said with a false cheeriness in her voice that made her feel like even more of a fraud.

To her surprise though, he didn't order the lights on. Instead, he came to the table and sat opposite her. If he thought she had been trying to seduce him with the candlelit supper, he didn't let on.

She pushed one full bowl across the table towards him, but drew her hand back sharply when his fingertips brushed hers. The frisson of energy that darted into her abdomen was not helpful at all. His gaze locked on hers momentarily. Had he felt it too? But then he bent his head and began to shovel the stew into his mouth without preamble.

She stared at the way the candlelight flickered over his features and made his tawny hair glow, highlighting a few golden strands in the burnished brown. The candlelight only made him look more rugged and handsome than he had that morning. His heavy stubble had grown into the beginnings of a beard, casting a dark shadow over that hard jaw.

She forced herself to stop staring and start eating.

The stew was rich and tasty—reindeer meat made a great substitute for mutton, who knew?—but she hadn't managed to swallow more than a few bites before she felt full. Eventually, the jumping beans having a rave in her belly made it impossible to eat another bite. Dawdling over her own meal, she took the opportunity to watch him eat unobserved—and the fascination with him, which had increased while she explored his luxurious but strangely impersonal home, grew.

He was methodical but also voracious as he chewed and swallowed, drawing her gaze to the tanned column of his throat. She noticed the paler skin below the neckline, the chest hair visible past the open collar of his thermal shirt. There was a small crescent-shaped scar high on his right cheekbone, just above his beard, another that slashed through his left eyebrow, and a slight bump on the bridge of his nose. Had he broken it at some point? There were nicks and cuts, some healed, some fresh, on his fingers as he handled the spoon with casual efficiency.

Despite his wealth, it seemed this man hadn't lived a charmed life.

His staggeringly beautiful home seemed to have all the mod cons and then some, but even so, it had to be dangerous, living so far out in the Arctic Circle all on your own.

Why had he hidden himself away in such a remote location? She'd racked her brains all day, trying to remember the details of Logan Coltan's story, which Issi had told her months ago during one of their breaks. She had a vague recollection of a tragedy—surrounding his parents' deaths when he'd been a boy... And the huge fortune in the US—built on his great-grandfather's wealth as some kind of railway baron—which he had become the sole heir to... But nothing more.

Why had he disappeared from the world, and built his very own Fortress? Rather than taking his place as the only surviving member of the Colton dynasty?

The compassion she'd felt earlier pressed against her chest. But surely, it would be foolish to feel sympathy for this hard man, as his solitary life appeared to be one he had not only chosen, but guarded zealously. Even so she couldn't help wondering what could possibly have happened to him to make him choose to starve himself of human companionship so completely.

Who did that?

He placed the spoon abruptly in the bowl, then his head rose. And she found herself trapped in that laser-sharp gaze again, caught staring at him.

The intensity in his expression unnerved her, making her hopelessly aware of the sensations pulsing under her skin.

But she refused to detach her gaze from his or feel guilty for watching him.

She lifted the bottle of wine and poured herself a generous glass. She wasn't a big drinker but right now she needed something to calm nerves that were fizzing and sparking and doing nothing to cool the hot weight in her belly.

She took a hasty gulp, then finally found her manners. 'Would you like a glass of your own wine?'

He seemed to consider the question then gave a slight dip of his head.

I'll take that as a yes.

She filled his glass. He took a sip of the fruity wine, continuing to watch her unabashed over the rim, but as usual he felt no need to fill the silence.

Unlike her.

'Was it all right?' She nodded towards his empty bowl. 'The stew?'

'Yes.' His husky voice seemed to scrape over her skin in the semi-darkness.

'That's grand. I'm glad you enjoyed it,' she said, then forced herself to shut up.

But so many questions burned on her tongue. Questions that had been swirling in her head all day like the storm outside as she'd discovered what she could about him from his home. The silence seemed to build in intensity, throbbing between them—not unlike the hot weight in her abdomen. Eventually she couldn't prevent herself from asking the most pressing one.

'Do you live here entirely alone?'

His eyes narrowed, the familiar cynicism making the pale blue of his irises look even more steely than usual. And she immediately wished she could grab the question back. She didn't want to ruin the truce she'd worked so hard to earn.

'Forget I asked,' she said.

At exactly the same time as he said, 'Yes.'

She blinked, surprised he had given her an answer. She already knew that he had never been seen in Saariselkä, which was Finland's northernmost town, and had to be well over fifty miles to the south if her calculations were correct. How did he even get his supplies?

She knew she really shouldn't push her luck, but the next question spilled out regardless. 'Don't you get lonely? Being so far from civilisation?'

His brows rose, as if the question made no sense to him. 'No.'

But then his gaze raked over her face, the penetrating look one that had her cheeks burning. And she had the weird sensation that even though he had told her the truth, he might not be entirely sure of his answer. Awareness— and that tangible spark of attraction she had felt when his fingers had brushed hers on the bowl—sizzled in the air between them.

She swallowed, her throat suddenly dry. But she couldn't seem to control the brutal pulse of awareness. His eyes darkened as his gaze dropped to her mouth. She licked her lips, feeling his perusal like a physical caress.

What was he thinking? Surely, he must be able to feel it, too? Whatever *it* was… Because she'd never felt like this before… Certainly never had to struggle to control her response to a man.

And if it was desire, what on earth were they supposed to do about it?

She jumped up, suddenly desperate to break the tension. But as she went to lift his empty bowl, intending to load it into the state-of-the-art dishwasher, he snagged her wrist.

Sensation pulsed and flared, the hot rock between her thighs becoming molten as their gazes locked again.

'Stay out of my way,' he murmured, the hard line of his jaw and the dark arousal in his eyes making it clear he was holding on to his control with an effort.

He dropped her hand, then stood and left the room.

She watched him go, mesmerised by the muscular grace of his movements as he stalked away. The flash of memory blindsided her. He reminded her of an Arctic wolf—the leader of a marauding pack—that she had photographed a month ago. That wolf had been predatory, deadly, dangerous, but also staggeringly beautiful in its ruthless pursuit of its prey. She rubbed her wrist where the skin still burned from his touch.

His warning had been blunt and unequivocal, just like

everything else about him. But it had also answered the question that had been hanging in the air between them during their meal.

He felt this devastating chemical reaction too.

The throb of arousal in her gut pounded harder, reckless and dangerous and like nothing she had ever felt before. The liquid heat settled, wedging itself between her thighs like a hot brick. Adrenaline surged, and an excitement she'd only ever felt for her work before now charged through her veins—reckless and intoxicating.

While she tidied away their bowls and cleaned up the kitchen, she tried to talk some sense into herself. And ignore the relentless pulse of desire.

She should do as he suggested. Avoid him. The house was big enough that they didn't need to cross paths at all—and surely the storm would clear by morning. But she couldn't shake the thought that the livewire sexual connection they shared was even more disturbing to him than it was to her.

She was playing with fire, she understood that. But there was something so raw and vibrant about this man, and she had always been drawn to the wild, the untamed... Which was precisely why she had made a career out of observing and capturing them on film.

Logan Colton was an enigma. A fascinating, compelling enigma. And imagining what it would be like to unleash the raw sexual energy she sensed pulsed just beneath the surface of that cast-iron control was as unbearably exciting as it was unsettling.

He'd told her to keep her distance. Made it clear he wanted nothing to do with her. Just as he seemed to want to have nothing to do with the outside world.

But she knew the truth was a great deal more complex.

Logan had needs, just like any man. Or woman for that matter. Needs she suspected he had been denying for a very long time—or he wouldn't be living out in the Arctic Circle entirely alone.

Needs that she could admit now she'd always denied too.

He had warned her off because he didn't want his control challenged. Didn't want to acknowledge this attraction.

But unfortunately, she'd never been very good at following orders. Especially orders imposed on her by other people. Just ask her mammy.

And she'd never been scared to pursue the things that fascinated and excited her.

And at the moment, the thing that fascinated and excited her the most was him.

CHAPTER FIVE

STANDING AT THE END of the jetty he had built two summers ago over the lake, Logan unfolded the long serrated blade. He began to saw through the ice to recreate the swimming hole that had frozen over during the storm.

He grunted in frustration as he shoved the blade into the ice.

He would not be able to take his unwanted guest to her vehicle now until tomorrow, as it would be dark again in only a few hours. He had worked out a plan to take her to the broken snowmobile, check the photos on her camera, and then let her call for rescue. If he left her in the forest clearing before rescue arrived he would not need to compromise his privacy. Without a working GPS she would never be able to find her way back through the forest to his home. But his plan had been thrown into turmoil today, because the storm had continued to rage all morning. It would take over an hour to get to her vehicle, and he could hardly leave her alone in the forest after dark.

Blast her.

He breathed through his annoyance. He had avoided her so far today and left her a note explaining the situation, so she would continue to stay away from him until they could leave at first light tomorrow. But getting out of the house had seemed the best solution today after he had found her cooking them supper last night.

He should not have accepted the peace offering—even though the stew had been delicious. He was still furious with the foolish decision and the weakness that had caused it, that visceral spurt of yearning to stay... With her.

He would not make the same mistake twice, which meant heeding his own warning, and staying away from her too.

The late morning sunlight made the freshly fallen snow sparkle and warmed his exposed skin. He preferred to use the traditional hand tools for this job. It was hard, sweaty work, but it reminded him of his grandfather—and provided a useful and much-needed distraction from the confusing thoughts and feelings that had been consuming him for twenty-four hours now.

He had already spent half an hour drilling the four corners of the hole into the ice, using a hand-powered drill, but it was the saw work that was the most tiring.

His muscles warmed as he segmented the square hole into two triangular blocks then stepped on each one in turn to dislodge them. Eventually, after much careful pressure he was able to employ the pick to lever the ice blocks under the edge of the hole. Then he dropped the ladder and fixed it to the ice.

Ice swimming was a three-hundred-year-old Finnish tradition, which he'd happily embraced as a teenager at his grandfather's instigation to help quell the night terrors. It was dangerous to swim on your own, but he had no qualms about having the brief dip whenever the weather allowed. It alleviated any stress in his life and unblocked his creativity when it stalled if he was feeling low. Or extremely frustrated.

Like now.

Because he would be forced to endure another night with *her* in his home.

Luckily the woman—whose name he had been careful not to ask—had stayed out of his way this morning. *Good*, he was glad she had listened for once.

That he had woken up after last night's meal with a strident erection had only frustrated him more.

It wasn't the first time he'd had erotic dreams. He was a grown man after all. But it was the first time those dreams had had a face, and a sultry spicy scent, and striking emerald eyes—the gold shards in the irises spellbound with arousal—that had bored into his soul. And made every one of his pulse points pound.

Stop thinking about her. Damn it.

At last, the *avanto* was ready. He stalked back to the cabin on the edge of the lake to prepare for his swim. After feeding more logs onto the fire that heated the cabin's sauna, he stripped down to his shorts and stepped inside. The dry heat relaxed tired muscles, while the sweat cleansed his pores and helped to clear his head of the many inconvenient thoughts... Of her. After ten minutes, he crossed the jetty and took the steps into the icy lake.

The water—its temperature hovering just above freezing—felt like sharp needles digging into his skin, but as he swam across the hole, adrenaline surged, bursting into his brain and dislodging the frustration.

The endorphins built to a wave as he climbed out and headed across the snowy dock in his shorts and a pair of sliders to protect his bare feet from the ice. But as he reached the sauna cabin, the cold rushing over his skin and making every nerve ending tingle with life and vitality, he heard a staggered breath. His head jerked up, and he spotted the woman who had been haunting his thoughts standing under the trees, wrapped up against the cold, her gaze roaming over his virtually naked body.

He swore abruptly, then clasped his arms around his torso. The frigid cold numbed his skin, but did nothing for the heat that blasted back into his gut.

Had she been watching him, swimming? And why did that only make the hunger worse?

Dislodging his gaze with an effort, before he froze to death, he stalked towards the sauna and ducked inside. Even though the last damn thing he needed was more heat.

She hadn't listened. Why was he even surprised?

As he doused the hot coals with lake water, the blast of steam hit his skin and the adrenaline rush from the cold-water immersion morphed into something a great deal more dangerous.

The arousal he'd been intending to dampen flared back to life. As he settled onto the sauna's pine bench, thoughts of her invaded his senses. Those full lips pressed to his chest, skating over his belly, surrounding his... The yearning to be touched by another human being, to be caressed by *her*, became so intense, the ache built until it became unbearable.

He swore viciously—unable to focus now with her so close, and unable to find another temporary release because it would only make him more ashamed of his weakness where she was concerned.

He stepped out of the steam-filled hut and got dressed in the cooler air of the outer cabin. When he stepped outside, she was no longer there. No longer watching.

The ripple of disappointment disturbed him, but not as much as the feel of her gaze rioting over his skin that still lingered, making the ache flare anew.

As he trudged through the forest, he found her footprints in the snow. And followed them back to the house.

But when he saw her through the kitchen's picture window, he detoured towards his workshop.

She had invaded his privacy, but worse, she had turned the solitude that he had enjoyed for so long—and relied on to make him whole—into something problematic, something not enough.

'Don't you get lonely?'

The question she'd asked last night pushed against his consciousness, opening a hollow space in his gut. He'd never been lonely. He embraced the quiet, had always loved being self-sufficient and self-contained, had never had any need for companionship or conversation—not since his grandfather had died.

But he couldn't shake the thought that there was something fundamental missing from his life now.

And that was her fault.

He tried to control the frustration and anger as he headed to his workshop. But as he selected the wood for his next project, it refused to fade. He picked up the different pieces that he had foraged for in the forest during the long summer days. But as he assessed the grain, tested for faults and knots that might ruin the design he had sketched, he imagined touching her skin. And wondered what it would feel like under his fingers. Those toned muscles, the soft contours of her body, her high full breasts, the taut nipples visible through the clinging fabric of her thermal undershirt...

The urge to make her gasp as she had in the forest, or shudder as she had when their fingers had brushed the night before, became desperate and demanding.

He dumped the chunk of silver pine he had been assessing back into the basket.

Swearing viciously, he stalked out of his workshop.

Avoiding her wasn't going to work, because she had refused to avoid him. Which meant they would both have to face the consequences now. Once and for all.

'Why did you spy on me?'

Cara glanced up from her breakfast to find her irate host standing over her. She'd seen him marching past the kitchen earlier to head to his workshop.

Guilt wrapped around her throat, making it hard for her to swallow down the spoonful of berries and yoghurt he'd caught her eating.

Accusation and anger shone in his eyes, turning the pale blue to a fierce steel.

'I—I didn't…'

She hadn't followed him intentionally. She'd read his curt note that morning, informing her they would leave at first light tomorrow—and also understood what he hadn't said, that he expected her to remain invisible until then.

She'd bristled at the commanding tone, but had been determined to control the reckless thoughts from last night—when she'd seriously contemplated acting on the passion that flared between them.

Because that was madness.

But when the storm had died, the shimmering white had beckoned her out into the quiet wilderness. She hadn't been able to resist the urge to get dressed in the clothing she'd found washed and folded in the laundry room off the garage.

She had ventured out to explore the land, on the pretext of figuring out if any of it was familiar. Maybe they weren't that far from the national forest where she'd left the snowmobile? After all, she'd been delirious the evening he'd brought her here, maybe the ride hadn't been as long as she'd assumed. But nothing had looked remotely familiar—the mountain gorge behind the house and the thick forest beyond a far cry from the frozen boreal forest of the tundra where she'd been tracking the lynx.

Changing tack, and mindful of not straying too far from the house, she'd been doubling back through the spruce and birch trees when she had spotted his tracks on the north side of the building. Without questioning the impulse, she'd followed his large footprints in the newly fallen snow until she had seen him through the trees busy sawing a hole in the icy lake beside a small wooden cabin.

She'd watched him work, becoming aware of what he was doing—because she had heard of the Finnish tradition of ice swimming in the resort in Saariselkä. She'd never tried it herself. But still she'd been fascinated by the methodical way he used the old-fashioned hand tools. The strength in his arms and shoulders—even visible beneath the heavy clothing—had drawn her to him as he'd finished creating the swimming hole. She'd been spellbound. And then he'd disappeared into the cabin. And come out a few minutes later virtually naked.

It was only then, as her pulse rate rocketed and the awareness in her gut flared like a firework, that she had acknowledged what she'd really been waiting to see—like the worst kind of voyeur.

His pale skin had been pink from the heat, the steam rising off those broad shoulders and long legs. Her gaze had devoured the defined ridges of his six-pack, the line of hair that tapered down from the light fleece that covered his pecs through washboard abs. As he'd stood at the ladder for several seconds, stretching and flexing before climbing in, she'd became fascinated by the way the damp shorts moulded to his backside framing a truly magnificent set of glutes.

He seemed immune to the cold, which was beginning to make her fingers numb and her eyelashes freeze in six layers of clothing, after standing still for too long spying on him.

The fervent wish that she'd had her camera equipment had consumed her. She would have loved to capture him on film as he lowered his body into the lake, his tall, broad frame somehow at one with the frozen beauty of his surroundings.

But once he'd been immersed to his neck in the freezing water, a rush of panic and fear had all but crippled her as she had waited what felt like several eternities for him to climb out again.

Wasn't it dangerous to swim alone, out here in the wilderness, miles from anywhere? Did he do this often? How could he be so reckless with his personal safety?

The fear and indignation returned in a rush as he stood over her now, thankfully masking her guilt and quelling the blush that threatened to incinerate her.

'I wasn't spying on you…'

Or not much, she told herself staunchly.

'I was making sure you didn't die.'

The dark frown became catastrophic. 'What?'

'You were ice swimming alone. That's dangerous. Even I know that and I'm not even Finnish, I'm Irish,' she added, warming to her theme as she began to babble. 'I've been living in Lapland for over six months. And I happen to know it's not safe to ice swim without back-up. If you'd had a pulmonary oedema while you were in there you could have become disorientated and there would have been no one to pull you out. I was just being your back-up.'

Getting an eyeful of his impressive physique and the way his bare body pulsed with vitality in the bright Arctic daylight had been a coincidental fringe benefit.

'My safety is not your concern,' he said, his firm lips pursing into a thin line, that steel-blue gaze going a little squinty with frustration.

Join the club, fella.

'Of course it is. You saved my life,' she said, becoming exasperated now with his rampant individualism. 'I owe you.'

'You owe me nothing.' He planted his palms on the table, and leaned over her, no doubt to intimidate her with that arctic glare, but she could see the awareness in his gaze as it swept over her face and dipped towards her breasts, which were moulded against the thin thermal undershirt she'd stripped down to after rushing back to the house. Something cracked open inside her, something raw and passionate. And the fierce feeling of connection—which she had been trying to deny ever since he had first appeared out of the storm like an avenging angel—careered through her body.

'There is nothing I need from you,' he added, his tone brittle with determination. 'Nothing I need from anyone.'

But she knew it wasn't entirely true, when his gaze swept over her again—and she saw the fierce hunger he couldn't hide.

She jumped to her feet, knocking her chair onto the floor. And stalked around the table, until they were toe to toe—possessed by a desire she had tried to deny all through the night.

He straightened, shifting away from her as she invaded his personal space. But the desire in her veins intensified, becoming hot and fluid and unstoppable.

'You're lying,' she whispered. Then she did what she had dreamed of doing all night. She placed her palm on his cheek, to soothe the rigid line of his jaw.

He grunted, the muscles tensing beneath her hand, as if he had been burned—not unlike his reaction the first time she had touched him—but this time, he didn't pull away. Instead, he closed his eyes, his breathing ragged as if he needed a moment to absorb the shock. When he opened his eyes again, what she saw had her breath seizing in her lungs.

Raw visceral need.

She ran her thumb across his lips, felt the firm line tremble, and became mesmerised as her own breathing accelerated to match the harsh murmur of his.

His pupils dilated, the vibrant steel in his gaze darkening to black, and she sensed the effort it was taking him to remain still.

So she went with her gut to break the deadlock.

'Can I kiss you, Logan?' she asked.

She saw the moment his control snapped, like a high-tension wire wound too tight.

He grasped her hips and dragged her against the un-yielding line of his body. The ridge of his erection pressed into her belly as he slanted his mouth across hers—and gave her his answer.

His kiss was firm, deliberate, possessing her mouth as his tongue thrust deep, and duelled with hers in furi-ous strokes, but it was the edge of desperation—so raw, so basic, so elemental and unskilled—that had the need pulsing at her core.

She grasped his head, threaded her fingers through his long hair, and opened her mouth to take more of those eager, untutored thrusts.

Consumed by passion, she sobbed, when he ripped his mouth free and pressed his forehead to hers. She could feel the shiver of reaction coursing through his body, or was it hers?

'I want you.' The words seemed to be torn from his throat—like a curse.

She released the fingers she had fisted in his hair, to press her palms to his hard cheeks and lift his head to stare into his eyes.

So many emotions swirled in the pale blue depths—desire, longing, but most of all baffled desperation.

This was madness. He didn't even know her name, because he hadn't bothered to ask. And she knew a part of him still did not want her in his home. A *large* part of him. But something about the desperation she could see in his face echoed in her heart—and called to her own loneliness. Her own denial.

She'd never truly wanted a man before. Always scared to take the risk. Scared she might end up like her mammy, tied to a brute like her father.

But this wasn't about affection, this was all about desire and chemistry. She'd never felt this rush of endorphins, of excitement and exhilaration. And she might never feel it again, because she already knew how rare it was, after too many botched and aborted make-out sessions as a teenager.

She'd been determined to be smart, sensible, in charge of her own destiny, always. But had she secretly also been holding out, hoping to feel the sensations she'd heard other women talk about? Sensations she had convinced herself might not exist for her.

And now she knew they did.

Why shouldn't they enjoy each other? If they were both willing? And they both needed it?

She had nearly died two days ago. What if he hadn't answered her Mayday, and she had perished out there in the frozen forest, a virgin? Having never known what it was to experience physical pleasure? Life wasn't guaranteed, she'd found that out while she huddled in that snowdrift praying for rescue.

And, to be fair, he *had* saved her life. And nursed her through the night. For all that he didn't like her.

However surly and uncommunicative he was, he had a core of honesty, of integrity, that made her sure she could trust him, with this much at least.

Ah, to hell with it. Stop overthinking this. Just do it already, Cara. This might be your only chance.

She kept her gaze fixed on his, threaded her fingers back into his hair, yanked his mouth back to hers. And told him the truth.

'I want you too,' she whispered against his lips, before licking across the seam, demanding entry.

His guttural moan made her feel powerful in a way she never had before.

This time, she took control of the kiss, thrusting her tongue deep into his mouth. Licking and sucking as he let her lead.

They devoured each other, but as they came up for air a second time, she knew it wasn't enough. Not to satisfy the ache building at her core.

His hands had remained on her hips, the tremble of reaction suggesting he was using the last threads of his control to keep them there.

She took one of his large hands and placed it firmly on her backside.

He shuddered, his fingers tensing and releasing as he stroked the firm flesh. Then he slanted his lips across hers and lifted her into another all-consuming kiss.

It seemed to take an eternity, but eventually he took the hint and slid one large palm beneath the waistband of her sweatpants and panties. His callused fingers rasped across her aching flesh, his moans matching her sobs as he pressed his palm to her vulva.

Her need soared, flooding her panties with moisture.

He found the sodden folds, then stepped back abruptly, yanking his hand out of her underwear. His gaze was fierce on hers and full of—what was that, exactly? Because it looked like a combination of awe and astonishment.

'You like my touch?' he rasped, his breathing ragged.

Why did he look so surprised? And why did that only make the hot weight between her legs rise to squeeze around her ribs?

She nodded, because he seemed to need an answer. 'Yes. I love having your hands on me.'

As he continued to stare at her, the heat from her core rose to burn her collarbone.

But before she could become embarrassed by her own enthusiasm, his gaze sank to her breasts. He cradled her neck, his touch firm again, and possessive, his gaze fierce as it roamed over the tight nipples clearly visible through the thin undershirt. But again, he hesitated.

The moment might have been awkward. She'd never met a man who hadn't wanted to take the initiative, especially as she had made it so clear she wanted him. But something about his reticence felt empowering.

Why not take the initiative yourself, Cara?

She grabbed the hem of her thermal undershirt and stripped it off over her head. His gaze narrowed, scalding her skin, the approval in his eyes almost as breathtaking as the desire.

She fumbled around for the back hook on her bra. How did you do this sort of thing gracefully? But it was clear she didn't need to worry about looking seductive. Because his gaze was riveted to her as she finally managed to discard the scrap of lace.

His face lifted to hers, awareness lighting his cheeks, the fire in his eyes turning them to a bright silver. It was all the validation she needed.

He appeared to be holding his breath. Then his lungs released, and he ran his tongue over his bottom lip.

'You are beautiful,' he said, his tone thick with reverence, his gaze rich with fascination.

And she felt truly beautiful for the first time in her life.

Her nipples hardened, elongating under that intense gaze. He lifted his hand, his expression reverent as he ran his thumb under the rigid peak.

Her own breath guttered out in an audible sob.

He paused, but didn't drop his hand, then he began to explore in earnest. His touch was careful and patient but full of purpose as he grazed the nipple with his thumb, lifted the weight in his palm, circled the areola in a methodical but profoundly sensual caress.

He watched her intently as the vice tightened at her core, the ache becoming painful.

She shuddered, the desire pouring between her thighs as he bent to lick the peak at last. He worked one nipple, then the other, sucking and tugging, making the arrows of pleasure dart to her core.

She felt trapped by her own desire, the insistent caresses, his determined touch reminding her of his long strong fingers on the pencil as he sketched in his workshop... Or his competent hands on the traditional tools at the lake. She grasped his head, her own dropping back, her body so alive with sensation she was struggling to breathe.

She'd never realised her breasts were so sensitive, but

she could feel the pressure building at her core. Insistent. Incendiary. Shockingly intense.

It wasn't enough to take her over though, not quite, and being suspended on the knife edge of release soon felt like torture.

'Please... Touch me more.'

His head lifted. 'How? Where?'

Again, she was momentarily nonplussed. How could he seem so competent, so hot and yet also not know how to touch her?

But then the desperation gripped her, and, grasping his hand, she shoved it back into her panties. He didn't need any more instruction, his blunt fingers finding the hot nub throbbing between her thighs.

She shuddered, and tensed as he circled, teased, then glided one callused forefinger right over the heart of her.

She bucked as he worked the spot ruthlessly—rubbing, touching, claiming, branding. She gripped his shoulders, riding his hand now, the orgasm so close...

She felt wild, wanton, and she didn't care, because it felt so, *so* good. He thrust one long finger inside her, then two, stretching her tight flesh unbearably, while still working her clitoris ruthlessly with his thumb.

'Oh... Yes.' She directed him, even though he seemed to know instinctively just how to touch her to drive her insane. 'Right...there...'

The powerful rush of pleasure burst over her at last, sending her senses reeling as she tumbled into a hot vat of pure bliss. He continued to stroke her through the vicious climax until she was limp and shaking.

She grasped his wrist, too sensitive to stand more.

'Please... I can't... It's too much.'

His fingers stilled, and he drew his hand from her panties.

She heard his rough chuckle and opened her eyes to see him sucking his fingers.

'Delicious,' he murmured.

She blushed, stunned by the renewed pulse of desire. The fierce approval in his gaze made her feel like a goddess.

'You are more beautiful when you come,' he said.

The words—thick with passion—seemed somehow incongruously poetic coming from this unsentimental and uncommunicative man.

Her body felt limp, sated, and strangely enervated. Her heart hammered her ribs.

The smile on his lips stunned her a little. She'd never seen him smile, hadn't imagined it was possible for him to be more handsome, more compelling. But the slight twist of his lips and the triumphant gleam in his eyes were as stunningly beautiful as the frozen landscape he lived in.

That would be the afterglow talking, Cara, you dolt.

She tried to talk some sense into herself, but with the endorphins still charging through her system, it wasn't easy.

'We should find a bed,' she managed.

'You wish to come again?' His eyebrows lifted, the surprise on his face making her laugh.

Good Lord. How could he be both scarily intense and stupidly adorable at one and the same time?

The man was an enigma and no mistake. An enigma she couldn't wait to figure out.

She cradled the heavy erection stretching the front of his sweatpants, feeling bold now with her new-found experience. She assessed the heft and weight of him—which were…*impressive*.

'Yes, but with you inside me this time,' she managed.

He tensed, but she could feel the erection strain against her palm.

He'd given her more pleasure than she had imagined possible and she wanted desperately to return the favour.

He grunted, but then nodded. 'Okay.'

Before she could protest, he dislodged her hand and scooped her into his arms.

She let out a shriek of shock and delight as she found herself being carried up the wide stairs leading to the house's top level. She knew she wasn't particularly heavy, but it was as if she weighed nothing at all.

Her laughter died as they entered an enormous room at the far end of the house.

Three walls were made of glass with a wide bed in the centre of it.

The breathtaking vista of forest and mountains beyond the glass stretched to the horizon, as the dying sunlight poured into the expertly appointed room giving it an eerily beautiful glow.

She'd made a point of not exploring the upstairs when she'd been checking out the house yesterday. But as he set her on her feet, she wished she had seen this room before. Because it might have helped to control the lump of emotion burning in her throat as he stripped off in front of her.

Moments later he stood before her naked—his strong body so much harder and firmer than hers.

'Your house is stunning,' she whispered, to cover what she suspected was her awestruck expression.

'Not as stunning as you,' he murmured.

She clasped her arms over her naked breasts, suddenly self-conscious at how she'd fallen apart so spectacularly at his touch. How was she going to return the favour when she knew nothing at all about pleasuring a guy?

He was magnificent. In every way. Not just the rough-hewn features, the muscular torso and long legs dusted with hair, but also the thick erection thrusting proudly from the nest of dark hair at his groin.

For a moment she couldn't seem to take her eyes off it. She swallowed past the rawness in her throat.

Oh... My...

'That's... It's... You're very...large,' she stammered, finally managing to finish the sentence while feeling both turned on and ridiculously gauche.

Sheesh, Cara, awkward much?

She'd promised him a temptress but was actually an untried virgin. What little sexual experience she'd had as a teenager had not been the best. And had certainly never been worth risking her father's wrath. She could still remember the awful fallout from her Debs—the Irish prom—when she'd returned home with her date an hour after curfew. Her father had branded her a whore and her mother had given her a lecture on where babies came from—as if she didn't already know that. But after that grubby, rushed and unsatisfying make-out session in the back of Barry O'Connell's mother's Skoda, and the names her father had screamed at her afterwards, she'd never had any desire to go further. Until now.

Logan tucked a knuckle under her chin and lifted her face to his.

'Is it too large?'

For a moment, she thought the blunt enquiry might be a boast, but then she registered the concern on his face.

'I don't know,' she replied honestly, feeling more awkward by the second, but no less turned on, weirdly. 'I don't think so.'

Surely in the grand scheme of things he wasn't so big she couldn't accommodate him. After all, his size was as big a turn-on as the rest of him. She pursed her lips, then spewed out the truth.

'It's just, I've never actually gone all the way before—which probably seems mad for a woman past twenty, but it's just…' She trailed off. Was this too much information again? Probably. He hadn't said a word, hadn't even flickered an eyelash at her confession. Was he put off by her lack of experience? Irritated? Annoyed? It was impossible to tell. 'So you'll be needing to take it slowly. Sorry,' she finished.

His brows lowered, but then his gorgeous mouth tilted in a breathtaking—and endearingly self-deprecating—grin. 'I am nearly thirty,' he said. 'And this is my first time, too, with a woman instead of my hand.'

For a moment she wasn't sure she'd heard him correctly. 'You're not serious?' she blurted out. 'You're a virgin?'

How could he have given her the best sexual experience of her life already—be so hot and gorgeous—and be as inexperienced as she was?

The information just wouldn't compute.

The smile on his lips died, his gaze becoming flat and direct. 'This is a problem?'

'No… No. Not at all.'

Wow, way to shove your foot down your own throat, Cara.

The concern had left his eyes, to be replaced by… Well, nothing. The shutters that had been lifted while he'd stroked her to orgasm—and she'd gone completely to bits under his instinctive and assured caresses—had slammed right back down again.

He turned away, lifting his sweatpants off the bed where he'd thrown them.

Panic assailed her. Had he changed his mind? Had she ruined it?

She grasped his arm, felt the ripple of muscle, making her frantic.

'Please, it's not… It's not a problem at all. It's just really surprising. And flattering,' she said, desperate to stop him from getting dressed again.

He'd never done it before with anyone. And he wanted to do it with her. Why did that suddenly feel like a massively big deal? She suspected his decision had more to do with opportunity than anything else. Just as hers had. Had he ever had a woman here before? Exactly how long had he lived here alone?

But even so, she felt the lump of emotion swell in her throat when he continued to stare at her, and assess her statement, with that blank look on his face—as if his emotions were not for public consumption. Ever.

Maybe he had only picked her because she had literally landed in his lap. And thrown herself at him. But it still made her feel special and important—in a way Barry O'Connell and the other guys she'd kissed as an inquisitive teen never had.

She gulped down the lump still expanding in her throat.

Now, don't go getting ahead of yourself. This is still just endorphins and chemistry and opportunity and sex…

But she was betting sex with Logan Colton—the most accomplished virgin in the northern hemisphere—would be really, really spectacular sex.

As long as she hadn't messed up her chance.

He slung his sweatpants back on the bed—and relief rushed through her. The intense look on his face was unnerving, but she could still see the fierce arousal in his gaze.

And that prodigious erection—which he seemed remarkably relaxed about—hadn't deflated one bit. That had to be a good sign.

'You are sure?' he said at last.

Her breath released in an audible sigh.

'Yes, I'm totally positive. It's grand.' Her gaze dipped to that gorgeous column of erect flesh—which she suspected no other woman had even seen before her.

'Could I...?' she began, then had to swallow past the newest constriction in her throat.

Oh, for pity's sake, Cara. This is your first time too, and weren't you just after telling him it's not a big deal?

'Can I touch you?' she asked.

He seemed to consider the question. Then nodded. 'Yes.'

She let out a nervous half-laugh, stupidly touched by his total lack of guile.

He didn't seem to be remotely embarrassed by his lack of experience. So why the heck was she?

'That's grand, then,' she said, feeling both strangely euphoric and also oddly moved.

Maybe this wasn't that big a deal to him. But in a lot of ways, it was to her.

Why had she waited so long to have sex? Why had she denied herself this experience?

Maybe because the few intimate encounters she'd had had been fraught with nerves and embarrassment—and marred by the spectre of her father's judgment. But this felt somehow new and different and impossibly exhilarating. Because for the first time ever, it felt as if there was no judgment here. And nothing to prove.

This was all about the elemental attraction between them and nothing more.

And after too many painfully self-conscious encounters in her teens, she found that impossibly liberating.

She sank to her knees in front of him. Then glanced up at his face when he grunted.

His gaze was bold as he threaded his fingers into her hair, caressing her scalp, his expression so full of that fierce yearning she was captivated. And humbled.

She curled her fingers around his hard shaft. A shot of adrenaline reverberated in her core when he shuddered.

He clasped her skull in both hands now, his fingers tensing, kneading. She leant forward, desperate for the taste of him, driven to do something she had never even considered doing before.

She licked the thick length from root to tip, gathering the salty droplet on her eager tongue. The erection jerked forward, as if seeking her touch.

He swore viciously as she kissed the swollen head, adoring the musty taste of him—excitement charged through her veins as he bucked against her lips. And groaned.

As he began to shake, his hips thrusting of their own accord, she opened her mouth as wide as she could manage and worshipped him with it. Determined to give him the glorious release he had given her.

Logan let out a guttural moan, the feel of her lips on his swollen shaft so exquisite it was almost painful. Watching her beneath him, on her knees, was the most erotic thing he had ever seen in his life, the thought of possessing all of her more than he could stand. The pleasure built at the base of his spine, his palms beginning to sweat as he resisted the powerful urge to thrust harder into her mouth.

He grunted. Tensed.

It was too good. Too much.

He clasped her head and dragged himself free. She stared at him, her eyes dazed with the same lust that burned in his gut.

'I wish to be inside you,' he murmured, his voice so

husky it sounded as if it had been wrenched from the depths of his soul.

He hooked clumsy hands under her arms to lift her off her knees. If she stayed down there any longer, he would not be responsible for his actions.

Falling to his own knees, he stripped off her sweat-pants, and the thin thermal tights she wore beneath. She clasped his shoulder, her nails digging into his flesh as she struggled to steady herself while he discarded the last of her clothing.

With his head level with her belly he could smell her desire. He licked his lips and sighed. Another time he intended to enjoy feasting on that scent. But right now, he couldn't wait.

He lifted her into his arms, then dropped her—without a lot of finesse—onto the bed.

He took a moment to absorb the sight and imprint it on his memory. Her soft flushed body—her skin glowing in the redolent twilight—lay on the white sheets, her reddish-blonde hair cast in a halo around her head.

'I do not have protection,' he managed around the hunger beginning to claw at his throat as well as his gut.

She seemed dazed for a moment—he knew how she felt—that sparkling green still riveted to his fierce erection. But then her gaze rose to his. 'I… I have a contraceptive implant.' She touched her upper arm and he noticed a small bump under the skin. 'It's to help with my heavy periods, because they used to be so excruciating. It would take me days to recover every month, plus periods are a pain when you're camping in the wild and…' Her soft musical voice babbled to a stop. But what had once annoyed him, captivated him now.

He stared at her, to process the barrage of information.

'I'm sorry, that's probably TMI...' She babbled some more.

He frowned. He had no idea what she meant by this TMI, but it did not matter. Adrenaline surged as his lust-fogged brain finally registered what she had said: he could climax inside her and it would not risk a pregnancy.

He climbed on the bed, his hands clasping her hips to angle her body. He would have preferred to turn her over, to sink himself deep inside her from behind, the desire to hide the effect she had on him instinctive. But he was aware he would need to gauge her reaction. She had seemed concerned about his size and he was her first lover, he did not want to risk hurting her.

But as she clasped his shoulders, and lifted her knees, her body cradling his, giving him better access, her gaze met his and he saw the same deep yearning in her eyes that pulsed so ferociously inside him.

He found her entrance, slid the thick shaft through the swollen folds, to nudge the spot he had found earlier.

She reared back and let out a guttural sob. 'Please, just do it, Logan, before I die of wanting.'

He grunted out a rough chuckle, astonished she could make him laugh when he was about to fall apart.

But he took the hint, and, gripping her hips, lifted her body to his, to find her entrance.

He pressed into the hot flesh. Then stopped abruptly when she flinched, but she shook her head.

'It's okay, keep going, it feels good,' she said, her fingers digging into his shoulder blades.

The feel of her, so tight, so tender, massaging him in spasms, had the last of his breath guttering out of his lungs as he thrust through the slight barrier.

He held himself deep, feeling her stretch to accept him, her pants matching his own harsh breaths.

Had he ever felt anything more exquisite in his life?

The question echoed in his consciousness but was swept away before he could engage with it by the tidal wave of yearning, of desperation as he felt her muscles twitch and pulse along his length, drawing him deeper still. The urge to move became so strong, he had to grit his teeth, to pull out slowly and thrust back as carefully as he could, amazed when he sank even further.

'Is it okay? You are not hurt?' he managed.

She shook her head. 'No, I'm good. You have to move, Logan.'

He didn't need a second invitation, the primal urge already clawing at his spine.

His rhythm was clumsy, uncoordinated at first, but her sighs, her shudders spurred him on. He rotated his hips, pulled out, thrust back, establishing the undulating thrusts, aware of what made her sigh, what made her tense.

The need built like a tsunami, claiming every part of his soul, in sweet, stunning increments, until he couldn't hold back any part of his need.

She clung to him, her nails carving deep grooves in his back, his body rejoicing as the sharp pain combined with the visceral pleasure.

She cried out, her body massaging him at last, and the pleasure exploded. He shouted out as his seed pumped into her—draining him, and shattering her.

He collapsed on top of her, throwing him over into a deep abyss of perfect gratification, pure pleasure, as one last coherent thought echoed inside his head.

I must let her go. Or I will want to do this again... And again... And again. Until I am lost for ever.

CHAPTER SIX

CARA LAY STARING at the vaulted wooden beams that made up the ceiling of Logan Colton's bedroom. His shoulder lay heavy on her chest, pressing her into the mattress.

She'd had two stunning orgasms in Logan's arms. *Two!* And while he still felt huge inside her, and she was a little sore, the glittering pleasure—and that heady feeling of fulfilment—was far greater.

But it wasn't just the endorphins barrelling through her system that were making her heart throb in her chest. She slid her hands over his shoulders, wanting to hold on to the moment a little while longer.

No one had ever made her feel so good. So right. And this man was a total novice. A smile curved her lips. Well, he wasn't a novice any more. If he had ever really been one.

And neither was she.

He groaned and lifted off her, rolling—or rather flopping—onto his back beside her.

They were both staring at the ceiling now.

She turned her head, to find him watching her intently.

'What is your name?' he asked, his tone gruff.

She chuckled. She couldn't help it.

That had to be the afterglow talking, surely?

Totally.

'Cara. Cara Moira Doyle. I'm named after my maternal

grandmother, who was by all accounts a fierce woman. I wish I had met her. Sorry, that's probably TMI again.'

Okay, Cara, stop talking before you exhaust the poor man.

She pursed her lips, but she couldn't prevent her smile spreading at the thought that he already seemed a little shattered, and she was the cause.

'Hello, Cara,' he said, and emotion tightened around her ribs.

'Hello, Logan, it's been a pleasure,' she said as another laugh bubbled out of her mouth.

For goodness' sake, stop giggling like a moonstruck girl.

But even as she tried to control the smile on her lips, it refused to leave her heart. She knew this was just sex— even if it was really spectacular sex—but the truth was, she felt impossibly grateful to him, for showing her that there had never been anything wrong with her. That the men— no, the boys—she'd kissed before, and Barry O'Connell in particular, who had treated her with so little care or affection or tenderness, then told her she was frigid when she had asked him to stop, had been as much to blame for her appalling experience of sex as she was.

She was twenty-one years old and she'd been avoiding sex ever since the night of her Debs—which would be appalling, if it weren't so pathetic.

Her first lover was staring at her now as if she were the most curiously puzzling thing he had ever seen. And strangely she liked it. Who said Cara Doyle couldn't be a femme fatale?

'What is this TMI?' he asked.

She choked out another laugh.

Ah, well, so much for being a femme fatale.

'It just stands for "too much information". I have a tendency to talk a lot when I'm nervous.'

'Why are you nervous?' he asked, a frown puckering his forehead.

'Because, well…' How to answer such a direct question without making it seem as if what they had just done had meant far too much to her? Far more than it should?

It was her turn to frown.

'Because I guess I don't know you… And we've just done something I thought I'd never do, and certainly never enjoy. And I enjoyed that a lot.'

She clamped her mouth shut, but the flush fired across her collarbone regardless.

'For me too,' he said easily as his gaze dropped to her breasts.

She folded her arms across the yearning flesh, before he could notice her nipples hardening again, the memory of how he had played with them so enthusiastically making the endorphins ramp right back up to eleven.

'I'm glad,' she managed, suddenly feeling exposed. 'Although that's not saying much, seeing as I'm the first woman you've ever had sex with.'

His gaze rose back to her face, that patient, probing stare as intimidating as it was exciting. 'And I am your first too.'

Ah, yes, you did let that slip in the heat of the moment. Strike one to Cara Doyle's big mouth.

'Well, yes,' she said as her blush incinerated her cheeks.

'We have a powerful sexual connection,' he murmured.

She stared at him, not sure what to say, having lost the power of speech. Had she ever met a man more forthright? She didn't think so. And why did it make her a little sad to think that was all he felt they shared?

'It would certainly seem so,' she said at last.

He lifted up on his elbow to lean over her, then ran his thumb down the side of her face, before hooking her unruly hair behind her ear. The casual, but surprisingly tender caress made her whole body shudder. A fierce emotion flashed into those pale blue eyes, as his gaze roamed over her face—gauging her reaction. But before she could read his expression, the emotion was banked again behind that intense stare. 'It is a shame we cannot explore it more,' he said, as much to himself as her.

'Why can't we?' she asked, then wanted to kick herself when his eyebrows rose.

Strike two to Cara Doyle's big mouth.

'Because you must leave,' he said.

But she could hear what he hadn't said.

Because I do not want you here.

She grabbed the sheet from the end of the bed and yanked it up to cover herself as she sat up. He was still lounging beside her, completely comfortable in his nakedness. Her gaze snagged on the evidence that he still wanted her, but clearly not enough.

'Yes, right,' she said, then cringed at the disappointment in her voice.

Seriously, Cara, could you sound any more needy? And desperate?

'No, it's grand,' she said hastily. 'You're right. I need to get back to Saariselkä and upload my photos. If my camera hasn't been destroyed by the cold.'

She shut her mouth, aware she was starting to babble again. Time to make a hasty retreat. And regroup. Her body was still flushed, and that semi-erection he was sporting was making her want to do foolish things again... With him.

But he no longer wanted to do them with her.

So what if he'd rocked her world—*twice*—and made

her feel special? It was all simply an illusion. Because he'd made it perfectly clear he wanted her gone now.

She tried to stifle the foolish feeling of rejection. What had she expected? She'd made it clear this wasn't a big deal—her virginity and his an inconvenience brought about by circumstance. That it had taken her this long to get over the stigma of her father's abuse, and the likes of Barry O'Connell's cruel taunts and teenage ineptitude, wasn't anything to do with him.

Plus, she *did* need to return to Saariselkä as soon as possible. She had her career to think about. Her new-found endorphins would just have to get over themselves.

She shifted off the bed, dragging the sheet with her, attempting to keep all the essential bits covered so she could make a swift and dignified exit. But as she stood, he leaned across the bed and grasped her wrist. The sheet slipped.

'You are upset,' he said as she grappled to cover herself and her dignity. 'Why?'

She stiffened, hating herself for the surge of emotion that felt stupidly like gratitude. Because he had noticed. And asked.

She tugged her arm free of his grasp, feeling exposed now and ashamed of how needy she was for any sign of affection from him. The afterglow had faded—and what had made her feel powerful, even cherished, during their epic sex session, now made her feel pathetic.

Cara, you eejit. Why did you throw yourself at him?

She swallowed past the shame threatening to close her throat, and reminding her far too forcefully of her teenage years, growing up with a man who had called her a slut more than once when she was still no more than a girl.

'I'm fine,' she lied.

But as she galvanised herself to walk away, he leapt off the bed and grasped her arm again.

'This is not the truth,' he said, although he dropped her arm as soon as she struggled.

'I'm *not* upset,' she said, as she rubbed her wrist where his touch still burned.

If her thigh muscles were still trembling, and her nipples as hard as torpedoes ready to launch, that was neither here nor there. Her body had a mind of its own where he was concerned, that much was obvious, but why was she letting her emotions become involved? He had offered her nothing. But nor did she want anything more from him.

He frowned. 'You cannot stay...' he said.

'And I didn't ask to, fella,' she huffed, furious now that he could see through her show of bravado so easily. Enough to know that she yearned for something more, some sign of intimacy, that went way beyond the physical.

What was that even about?

She bit into her lip and stared down at her hands, which had white-knuckled on the sheet, as she tried to control the brutal blush.

He raked his fingers through his hair, looking frustrated, then strode across the room to his dresser. Tugging out a fresh pair of boxer shorts, he put them on, but they didn't do much to hide the effect she still had on him.

She should walk out. Why was she still standing here like an eejit, waiting for something she shouldn't even need? Or want.

But she couldn't seem to detach her gaze from his.

He was watching her with that intense concentration that turned her thigh muscles to mush and made the lump swell in her throat.

What was he thinking? And why did he have to look so

gorgeous when he had treated her as if she were a...? She pushed the ugly word back down her throat.

That was her da talking.

Perhaps she was oversensitive about other people's opinions of her virtue, because of all the names that man had called her, when she'd barely understood what they meant. And why should she care anyway what Logan Colton thought of her? His opinion didn't matter—any more than her da's had.

But still, she couldn't seem to get her feet to move.

At last, his gaze detached from her face and glanced out of the huge windows.

Night had already fallen, and she could see snow swirling again in the frozen air outside the glass, depressing her even more. What if the storm kicked off again, and she had to stay another night?

How could she bear the humiliation? The knowing that somehow, somewhere, in some foolish corner of her heart, she had hoped for more from him? Had needed more?

'We will leave at first light tomorrow,' he said. 'Once you are returned to your vehicle, you can call for rescue.'

She nodded, but there was something in his voice— something wary and defensive—that didn't make any sense.

'Good,' she said, even as that foolish feeling of disappointment pushed at her chest.

She grabbed her discarded clothing and finally made her exit from his bedroom. But as she returned to her room, took a long hot shower, and found herself attempting to scrub off the scent of sex that clung to her skin, her father's angry words echoed in her head.

The brutal shame engulfed her again, because those words still had the power to hurt and humiliate her—after all this time.

But as she lay in bed afterwards, she thought of Logan, wild and untamed—and the intense silvery blue gaze that hid so many secrets. He had made love to her with such passion and purpose—she'd been the centre of his universe and she'd loved it. And then the memory of her father's words had turned the whole experience to crap.

But she could also recall the flash of regret in Logan's eyes as he had informed her he would take her to her snowmobile first thing in the morning. And suddenly, nothing seemed clear any more.

She had taken offence at his desire to be rid of her, because some of that abused girl still lurked inside her—needing validation and approval from a man.

Thanks, Da.

But what if his insistence that she had to leave had never been about her? Had always been about his fierce need for privacy, for solitude, his desperation to shun human contact?

She had breached his defences, but because of her own insecurities, she hadn't pushed her advantage.

She rolled over on the bed, curled into herself. And wanted to scream. Finally forced to admit the truth… She didn't want to leave first thing tomorrow.

He fascinated her and excited her in a way no other man ever had. Plus, she'd waited this long to finally know what all the fuss was about sex, and it had been glorious.

How did she let all that go, without any regrets?

But how did she ask him to let her stay, without seeming needy and pathetic? And how did she get him to admit he wanted to explore that connection too, without exposing herself and her emotions even more?

Damn the man!

CHAPTER SEVEN

LOGAN BRAKED HIS snowmobile as they entered the forest clearing where Cara's broken vehicle lay buried under a drift. Cara's arms loosened from around his waist. And let go.

His breath eased out through lungs tight with something he couldn't name… Something he did not want to name.

He'd spent the long winter night working furiously on his latest piece. Tempering the block of solid pine to carve it into the basic form of a golden eagle in flight. And trying not to think about the woman in his home. And the moment when he had come apart inside her.

But of course, it had been impossible.

He never should have touched her. He should have known it would make him lose focus. Force him into a situation he didn't understand.

He still hadn't figured out what they had argued about afterwards, but then his mind had been shattered, so no surprise there.

But as she climbed off his snowmobile and headed across the clearing towards her buried vehicle, his gaze remained fixed on her. She was dressed in six layers of thermal clothing, so it was hard to make out her shape, but the padded disguise did nothing to stop the memory of her skin—soft, malleable, responsive beneath his fingertips, his tongue—blasting into his brain.

He ripped off his goggles.

Aware that he was becoming aroused… Again.

This was an addiction, already. One single taste of her had turned him into a sex addict. Not good. When he had to let her go now.

They had barely spoken when she had appeared in the kitchen this morning. She had looked as if she hadn't slept well at all. He would have taken some comfort from that, except he had hardly slept himself.

He dismounted to follow her across the clearing.

He stood and watched as she dug through the snow with her gloved hands—frantic to get to the camera equipment he had left out here.

At last, she found the saddlebag. But the three pairs of gloves she had on made it impossible for her to open the bag and remove the camera equipment.

She pulled down her balaclava, to expose her mouth. Those full lips that had been wrapped around his…

He closed his eyes, trying to expel the memories, far too aware of the heat pooling in his groin.

'Can you help me get this undone?' she shouted.

Forcing himself to remember his plan—to check the camera and make sure she had not taken any pictures that might identify the location of his home—he took it from her. But after opening the bag and handing the camera back to her, he watched as she tried to get the equipment to start.

Five minutes later, they were forced to give up.

'It is too cold,' he said, aware that he would be forced to trust her, if he left her here without checking what was on it. 'Better to try and start it once it is warm.'

She nodded. 'How far is it to Saariselkä?'

'I cannot take you there,' he said, the old panic rising up his throat.

He could not step foot in the thriving tourist resort. It was too much to ask of him.

She seemed surprised, but then indicated the busted snowmobile. 'Can you help me to get this working?' she asked.

'I am not a mechanic,' he replied—which was not entirely true. He had learned how to service and maintain all the vehicles he kept on his property, including two motorised sledges and a snowmobile. He could usually fix most mechanical problems, so he would not have to seek outside help. It was one of the basic requirements of being self-sufficient in such a harsh environment. But, repairing the machine in this location, when the thermometer was scheduled to dip below minus twenty today, would be difficult, if not impossible.

Plus, he'd checked the machine two days ago, when he'd found her camera. It was a wreck. Who knew what she had paid for it? But she had taken her life into her hands riding it so far out into the wilderness.

His suspicions about her motives returned.

How could he let her go now, when he hadn't been able to check the pictures on the camera? Surely he had every right to insist she return with him now to his home? Just to be sure.

But even as he tried to persuade himself his desire to ask her to come back was all about preserving the privacy he had maintained for so long, he knew that wasn't the whole truth. Not even close. Because he could still recall the look of disappointment, even sadness, in her eyes last night, after they had made love.

A look that had triggered the yearning he had been trying to ignore all through the night.

The truth was, he wished to make love to her again... And again. To explore the longing, until it had run its course and he could return to the peace he had known before he had met her.

But what scared him more was the knowledge that his urge to keep her wasn't just about the livewire physical connection that was even now pulsing in his groin.

He had lain awake last night until the early hours of the morning, long before dawn, after working himself into a virtual coma in his workshop and then in the gym, thinking about that look, and the words she had said.

'Why can't we...?'

And the words she hadn't.

Explore it more.

Even though the request had made no sense, she had put the thought into his head. And now he could not dispel it. He had re-examined the tone and texture of her voice, recalled in exquisite detail the different tendrils of her scent as she stood so proud and belligerent in his bedroom, with that sheet barely covering her...

Until he'd finally fallen into a fitful sleep only a few hours before the sunrise.

When she had appeared in the kitchen, he had been struck all over again by the rush of adrenaline—the desperate yearning—that hadn't gone away during the night.

The woman was a sorceress. Letting her stay would threaten everything that had made him whole for so long. But still the thought could do nothing to dispel the insistent desire not to let her go. Not yet.

'So what do we do now?' she asked.

We? Why had she said we? When they were not friends.

And they never could be. He had never relied on anyone, not since his grandfather's death when he was a boy of nineteen.

He shook his head, trying to dislodge the confusing thoughts. And make himself concentrate on what had to happen now.

The plan had always been to leave her here, after checking her camera, while she waited for rescue. But after last night, he couldn't seem to commit to all the reasons why he had to stick to his plan.

'Don't trust anyone, Arto, they are all just vultures who want to hurt you the way they hurt your mother...'

His grandfather's oft-repeated warnings echoed in his head—but could do nothing to quell the insistent desire that continued to spike in his gut and make him want things he shouldn't need.

And an answer he didn't recognise spilled out of his mouth.

'I could arrange to have the vehicle towed and repaired. You can stay with me until it is ready?'

The reckless offer shocked him—but not as much as the strange yearning that assailed him as he waited for her reply. Or the brutal rush of relief when her face softened.

'I'd... I'd like that. If you're sure it's not too much trouble.'

It *was* too much trouble. She was a threat. Someone he would be a fool to trust.

But even so, he couldn't find the will to do anything but nod.

She remained silent as he called his contact in the local Saami community on his satellite phone and gave the older man the location of the broken snowmobile. He had always trusted the old friend of his grandfather's not to give away his whereabouts—but this was the first time he had asked for his assistance in ten years.

As he threw his leg over his machine, his breath blooming in the frozen air—he couldn't shake the thought that he had exposed himself.

But as he settled in the seat and switched on the ignition, he forced himself not to second-guess himself again. He couldn't withdraw the offer now. Nor did he want to. But surely this yearning, this need was about nothing more than the intense sexual connection they had discovered last night.

Of course, he would want to explore it. Why wouldn't he? Especially as she had made it clear she wished to explore it too. That did not mean he needed to trust her with anything else.

She climbed up behind him, then pressed herself against his back. Even through all the layers of clothing, he could imagine her subtle curves moulding to the hard line of his back. His heart stuttered as her arms wrapped around his midriff again and held him tight.

He manoeuvred the vehicle in a circle, to back it out of the clearing, then shot off along the tracks they'd made in the snow, to return to his sanctuary.

But this time, he was forced to acknowledge, he had invited her into his home… Willingly.

His heart hammered against his chest wall.

He did not know what that heavy beat was even about.

Until he convinced himself it was simply the bone-deep longing to have her again. In any way she would let him.

As they traversed the icy terrain, the adrenaline surged.

Why was he making this so complicated? And why was he second-guessing every decision? What possible threat could she really represent? The only reason he wanted, or needed, her company was to satisfy this vicious desire. This endless yearning. But once that was fed, once he had gorged on her, and she him, they would tire of each other. Solitude had always been his strength, and no woman could ever change that. Not even one as beautiful and confusing and fascinating as this one.

Cara felt the snowmobile's engine rumble through her over-eager body as she clung to Logan, her face buried into his back to escape from the wind.

She was tired, exhausted even, from a virtually sleepless night spent going over and over in her brain what she should do next.

But she could hardly deny the feeling of regret as they'd driven out into the wintry landscape this morning, or the shattered relief when he had suggested returning to his house. Together.

She didn't want to leave yet. Which was madness, she understood that. But at least she had her camera equipment now. So, she hadn't completely jettisoned her professional priorities in favour of her newly discovered libido.

Logan had been brusque and businesslike when she'd appeared this morning, waiting for her to have a quick breakfast then get dressed in the cumbersome thermal clothing before meeting him in the garage.

The forest thickened and then opened out onto the huge frozen lake system that surrounded Logan's home. The sun was high in the sky now, the eerie blue light making the snowy wilderness twinkle and glow. Her nose and eyelashes had begun to freeze even under her goggles, her extremities losing feeling even as he shielded her from the wind. She could feel his warmth through the snowsuit, his strength as he handled the cumbersome machine with consummate skill.

How could she have slept with him last night and still not know him at all? Had she made a mistake accepting his offer so eagerly? Especially as he still hadn't mentioned last night. Why hadn't she demanded to know exactly what his offer entailed?

She huffed, trying to slice off all the unhelpful thoughts before they could take root.

At last, the stunning glass and steel structure appeared on the horizon.

She frowned as her heart rate spiked.

As he arrived at the lakeside entrance to the house, and clicked the gizmo attached to the snowmobile, the garage door rose. He drove into the concrete bunker, the warm air like a welcome blanket as the door lowered behind them.

But inside Cara felt cold—and foolish. She'd jumped at the chance to return here—because he still fascinated and excited her. But why hadn't she made more of an effort to find out where they stood?

As soon as he braked, Cara clambered off the machine. She ripped off her head coverings, and tugged off her snowsuit, then took off her ski jacket and fleece while he parked the vehicle.

She reached for the camera box she had tucked into his saddlebag while he took off the first layers of his own clothing.

He slicked back his hair, damp from sweat, the day-old growth on his jaw making him look like a pirate as he walked towards her.

He reached for her camera. 'Let me see it,' he demanded.

She held the camera close to her chest and shook her

head. 'Why?' she asked, hoping against hope that her suspicions were wrong.

But the cold feeling spread as she waited for his reply. Because she suspected she already knew the answer to that question. Despite the offer to bring her back here, he still didn't trust her.

He tucked his hands into the pockets of his ski-pants and levelled that all-seeing glare at her, the one designed to intimidate her into not asking inconvenient or probing questions.

Well, to heck with that.

He'd been inside her. He'd been her first lover. And maybe that didn't make her any more trustworthy in his eyes. But it meant something to her.

Rather a lot in fact.

She didn't trust men easily, but on some elemental level she had trusted him. Enough to throw herself at him. Enough to want to come back here at his suggestion. But she would be damned if she'd do that entirely on his terms. He wanted her camera now, so he could check what was on it. She got that. And she didn't really have any objection to that. Because she knew her pictures would confirm her innocence.

But she would be damned if she would let him believe he had a right to make her prove her innocence, when she had done nothing wrong—except get lost in the snowy wilderness, and want him, the way he wanted her.

He continued to stare at her, and for once she could see the calculation in his eyes. He was trying to decide whether to admit the truth or not.

She was sure he was going to give her some lame excuse, but then he surprised her.

'Because I want to see if you took any pictures of my

home before you became lost,' he said. 'No one is allowed to know this exact location unless they have signed NDAs and I know I can trust them.'

'But what about the people who built this place?' she blurted out, a little stunned even now by the extent of his seclusion, and how fiercely he protected it.

'The construction crews, the architect and engineer were all blindfolded before they were driven here. And also required to sign NDAs.'

'But… How do you get your food delivered? What about if you need a doctor?'

'I have supplies air-dropped to a location twenty miles away twice a month. I can contact a doctor in an emergency. But I am fit and healthy.'

'But… *Why?*' She could see instantly the question had angered him, his eyes becoming flat and direct, the muscle twitching in his jaw visible despite the heavy beard scruff.

'Because I value my privacy,' he said.

He'd got away with the non-answer once before, but she refused to let him get away with it again.

'But why do you value it to that extent? What are you afraid of?'

The muscle hardened, his brows furrowing over those piercing silvery blue eyes.

'I am not afraid. I just do not need people.'

It seemed like a simple answer, but the stormy emotions on his face told a very different story.

Something had happened, something *must* have happened to make him so wary of social contact, so determined never to be found.

Sympathy pulsed in her chest.

'How long have you lived out here alone?' she asked.

'Since my grandfather died a decade ago. He brought

me here to save me from the vultures after my parents' death. And I have no desire to return to that circus.'

The vultures? Was he talking about the press? All she knew about him was the things she could vaguely recall her bar colleague mentioning—that he had disappeared from the public eye as a child.

Oh, for an Internet connection, or a phone signal, or a charger for her phone. There wasn't much she wouldn't do right now to be able to do an Internet search on him.

But somehow, she doubted she would find much. And why should she need to do an Internet search, when she had him right in front of her?

She decided to push her luck. 'How old were you when your parents died?'

His gaze narrowed, suspicion rife in his eyes. 'Ten.'

The sympathy contracted around her ribs like a vice.

He had come to Finland while still an impressionable child, after what had to have been a traumatic event, and then had been left in the care of a man who had clearly kept him isolated from the world. Was it any surprise he was a recluse?

'How did your parents die, Logan?'

He flinched, as if she had slapped him, and she saw the pain flash across his features.

'You don't know?' he asked, the sceptical tone only wounding her more.

She shook her head.

He glanced past her, his stance tense, his eyes closing briefly. She sensed the struggle he waged. This was not something he wished to remember, let alone talk about.

What right did she really have to ask him about any of this? They'd slept together once. But just as she said, 'It's okay, you don't have to answer—' He interrupted her.

'They were shot. A kidnap attempt gone wrong.'

'Someone was trying to kidnap them?' she asked, shocked to her core.

'Not them, *me*,' he murmured. But that rigid tone broke on the last word.

Had he been there? He must have been. Which meant he must have witnessed their deaths. The thought horrified her and made the sympathy tangle into a knot in her belly.

Before she could think better of the impulse, she stepped forward, and pressed her palm to his cheek. The muscle flexed and hardened, but she could see the brittle anguish in his gaze before he could mask it.

'I'm so sorry, Logan...'

He clasped her wrist, dragged her hand away from his face, the pain in his eyes turning to heat, and hunger. 'No more questions,' he said.

She nodded. 'No, no more questions.'

'I want you still,' he said, the brutal honesty, the need he couldn't hide, making the knot of sympathy turn into something fierce and visceral and undeniable. 'Show me what's on the camera,' he demanded.

A part of her wanted to refuse the request. But she understood now, he had answered her questions to earn her trust. How could she refuse to do the same? She pulled the strap off her shoulder and handed him the camera.

He took the Leica and switched it on. For several seconds that felt like years, the mechanism whirled as the camera's batteries warmed. Anticipation and hope clogged her throat. And fear. What if the camera still wouldn't start?

She swallowed heavily. Determined not to examine the fact that her desire to rescue her photos was all wrapped up in the desire to prove to him he could trust her too.

At last, the viewfinder lit. Relief guttered through her as he clicked methodically through the photos she'd taken.

He came to the end of the memory card. His gaze connected with hers as he turned the camera off.

'They are good,' he said.

Pride swelled in her chest. She banked it, ruthlessly. His opinion of her work shouldn't matter. She reached for the camera, but he held it away from her.

'You will not need it, while you are here,' he said.

She pushed her anger to the fore, to cover the well of disappointment. Apparently, she still hadn't earned his trust.

'I promise not to take pictures of you, or your home,' she offered, tightly. '*If* I decide to stay,' she clarified. Because he seemed to assume that was already a foregone conclusion.

Whatever happened now, whatever she agreed to, she refused to be treated like a stranger, or a threat—to be trusted even less than the people he had forced to sign NDAs.

'But it's my camera,' she continued. 'And if you can't trust me to have possession of it while I'm here, then I *can't* stay here… I won't.'

His brows flattened, his lips tightening. And the muscle she'd noticed several times before in his cheek began to twitch.

He did not like the idea of letting her have the camera. But she refused to back down. His gaze roamed over her face, gauging her determination.

The seconds ticked by as her ribs contracted, and the pounding in her ears became deafening.

But finally, he lowered the precious Leica and offered it to her. She took it hastily, determined not to examine the thundering rush of relief that flowed through her.

The concession felt huge though. Especially when he said, 'While you are here... I want you in my bed.'

It didn't really sound like a question, more of a demand. So what else was new? But he had at least finally acknowledged what he was really offering her.

And given her the opening she needed.

'Okay, but I have some ground rules,' she managed, not even sure what they were yet, but determined not to appear like some witless fool, completely captivated by his potent sex appeal... Even if she was.

Because, after all, the melting sensation in her core didn't lie as she sucked in a lungful of his delicious scent and sensation pulsed across her lips as his gaze centred on her mouth.

'Rules?' he said, the curve in those firm sensual lips even more captivating than the dark awareness she recognised in his gaze. She had no idea what was so amusing. 'What rules?'

She cleared her throat. 'I-important rules,' she managed. 'Uh-huh...'

The rumble of his reply streaked through her as he stepped closer. Close enough to touch. Close enough to have her body readying itself for him.

The storm of sensation threatened to derail her again. But she found the strength to plant her palms against his chest. The hard pectoral muscles flexed as she edged him back.

'A week, I can't stay more than a week,' she said. 'If the skimobile isn't fixed by then, you'll have to take me back to Saariselkä,' she managed.

'Two weeks,' he countered. 'A week will not be long enough.'

The fierce need in his eyes made her insides turn to

mush. Had any man ever looked at her like that before, as if he could not get enough of her?

No, never.

'T-ten days,' she said, even though she had the strange thought she was arguing against herself now, as well as him. 'And I get to keep working, during daylight hours.' She could build her portfolio here as well as anywhere—so her time wouldn't be wasted.

Plus, it was the principle of the thing… Wasn't it?

He hooked a finger into the waistband of her sweatpants and tugged her back towards him. She dragged in a lungful of his scent—that intoxicating mix of bergamot and pine that drove her wild.

'Two weeks,' he demanded again. 'In my bed. And you may take photos away from the house, as long as I am with you.'

Then he took the camera off her shoulder, placed it on the ground.

'Say yes, Cara,' he urged, his voice gruff with demand. 'Two weeks and then I will ensure you get back to Saariselkä.'

How could she resist him, when every cell in her body was begging her to give in?

And maybe this was what she needed, to finally become herself at last, a woman in every sense of the word, no longer bound by the shame of that little girl.

'Okay,' she managed, her throat dry, her panties already soaking wet.

He let out a triumphant huff, then scooped her into his arms and strode out of the garage.

Two weeks.

She'd agreed to two weeks, she thought vaguely as she

let him carry her back through his home to his bedroom. Like a trophy. A prize.

But as they stripped each other, and he sank back into her at last, his thick erection stretched her tender flesh as an orgasm barrelled towards her.

She'd taken a risk. And this was her reward. They had an understanding now. Maybe he still didn't trust her completely, but he trusted her enough.

She let herself shatter and held him as he crashed over into the abyss behind her.

Hadn't she earned this? she thought vaguely. After nearly killing herself to make her career a reality? Didn't she deserve the chance to be reckless and impulsive for once? And unafraid?

But as she sank into an exhausted sleep, her heart thundering as his big body wrapped around her, she made herself a solemn promise.

Take the risk. Just don't you dare risk your heart in the process, Cara.

CHAPTER EIGHT

'WAKE UP, CARA...you are getting lazy.'

'Huh?' Cara huffed and opened eyes heavy with sleep to find Logan leaning over her, with a disturbingly gorgeous smile on his face. This was new—he usually looked so focussed and intense. Her heart bounced in her chest.

'I'm not lazy. I'm shattered,' she murmured, her voice rough as she struggled to wake from the sex-induced coma he'd put her in last night. Sunlight sparkled through the floor-to-ceiling windows in his bedroom. How long had she been out? It had been pitch-dark when she'd finally plunged into a dreamless sleep.

The man was insatiable.

'*You* shattered me. Now get lost,' she grumbled, presenting her back to him as she rolled over and pulled the duvet over her head.

How on earth did he have the energy to get out of bed? Let alone look at her with that hot awareness in his eyes.

They'd made love too many times to count in the past week, in the seven energetic days and long sultry nights since they'd made their Devil's Bargain. They'd christened pretty much every room in the house, even the gym and his workshop, and then there had been that memorable moment yesterday afternoon in the kitchen—when he'd bent her over the work surface while she was slicing carrots, worked her into a frenzy with his tongue and then plunged into her from behind. She was lucky she hadn't lost a finger in the process.

Heat flushed through her tired—and frankly sore—body as she burrowed into the bedding.

The man was a sex machine. Inventive, inquisitive, generous and curious. And it seemed he had stored up a ton of fantasies over his long years of celibacy to practise on her. And while she had enjoyed every second of his attention—each orgasm more overpowering and overwhelming than the last as he discovered every possible way he could arouse and entice her—she was not in the market for any more orgasms until she had slept for at least twenty-four hours straight. Especially as in the last few days that disturbing sense of anxiety was never far behind.

She yelped as he flipped the duvet off her bare body.

'Up,' he said in that take-no-prisoners tone she had come to adore—and hate—in equal measure. 'We are wasting daylight.'

'Go. Away!' she shouted as she grappled with the duvet.

'No,' he said, before he won the duvet war and whisked it off the bed.

The arousal in his eyes darkened with intent as his gaze roamed over her yearning flesh. The answering heat in her belly flared. Because of course it did!

She knew what that look meant. And she had discovered she was powerless to resist it. But if she had any more orgasms, she might actually die.

'We are not having sex!' she announced, determined to persuade her traitorous body as much as him, because seriously, how could she be wet for him again? When she was still a little sore from their last epic session.

Clearly Logan Colton was not the only sex addict in

this room. Because the hot brick that had been jammed between her legs for seven days had already begun to pulse again.

'Understood,' he said, surprising her—because the man had to be able to smell her arousal. And she knew by now he usually pressed that advantage every chance he got.

But before she could evade him, or congratulate herself on sticking to her guns, he scooped her off the bed and hefted her onto his shoulder.

The air expelled from her lungs, and it took her a moment to find her outrage, through the shock.

'Logan, what the hell?' she yelped, holding on to the chuckle that threatened to burst out of her mouth.

If she laughed at his outrageous behaviour she'd be lost, because surely he would take that as an invitation… Because he took *everything* as an invitation.

She struggled, desperately trying to ignore the flutter of excitement and affection making her lungs hurt and the hot brick in her belly weightless. He was usually so serious about sex, his concentration whenever he caressed her his own special superpower—because it made him impossible to resist. Playfulness was a new look for him. The problem was, it only made him more irresistible.

She pressed her palms into the solid muscles of his back, trying to lift herself, twisting and turning and ignoring the swooping sensation in her belly that threatened to beckon emotions she'd kept so carefully in check for over a week.

Before she could get too sentimental though, his large hand landed firmly on her backside.

'Stop squirming or I will drop you,' he said.

'Then put me down, you *dolt*,' she yelped and struggled harder.

But as he headed through the house, apparently oblivious to her protests, and the fact that they were both stark nekkid, the laughter escaped.

When he finally deposited her in the garage—beside a pile of neatly folded clothing he must have washed for her while she slept—her heart bobbed into her throat, the wicked glint in those pale blue eyes turning them into a magnetic silver.

'Dress before you freeze,' he ordered as that stark possessive gaze raked over her burning flesh again. 'Or I decide to make you beg me for another orgasm.'

'I don't beg, fella,' she scoffed.

But she darted away from him before he decided to test that theory. After all, they both knew she was putty in his hands—whatever her best intentions.

As she scrambled into the layers of clothing, she watched him dress himself in a more leisurely fashion, immune to the lower ambient temperature in the garage, and tried not to regret not taking him up on his offer of yet more orgasms.

Because sex was safer than seeing this new, almost boyish side to the harsh, demanding man she had spent the last week with. A side he'd never let her see before now. A side she hadn't even known existed.

Not a big deal, Cara. In two weeks you'd have to find something else to do eventually.

'So where exactly are we going?' she asked as she stamped on her boots and zipped up the cumbersome snowsuit, feeling surprisingly enthusiastic about this new adventure. Perhaps she wasn't that tired after all. And getting out of the house had to be a good thing.

They hadn't left his Fortress of Solitude—now renamed the Fortress of Sex-capades—since last weekend, when they'd originally agreed to indulge their 'sexual connection'. The only times they'd been apart was while he worked in his workshop and she worked up a sweat in the gym. She hadn't even been able to venture out to check out the local wildlife because the weather had been terrible.

With the sun shining today for the first time in a week, it was way past time they found some new ways to amuse themselves. Because she was starting to get beard burn in places where it had no right to be. And that damn anxious feeling was starting to concern her.

Logan finished shrugging on his own layers, then walked to her. He zipped up her suit the rest of the way, then helped her to put on her outer gloves and the different face coverings that would protect her cheeks from the frosty air. Her heart pummelled her chest wall, her ribs feeling suspiciously tight at the methodical way he checked her clothing, to ensure she was appropriately attired. He lifted her chin, that mocking smile making her heart rate slow dangerously.

How could he look even more gorgeous when he was annoying the heck out of her?

'I am going to introduce you to the benefits of ice swimming,' he announced.

'Wait? *What?*' she asked, sure she hadn't heard that correctly. 'You're not serious?'

'It will revive you,' he said, that playful smile taking a wicked turn.

'No, it won't. It'll kill me,' she managed. Before she could object further, though, he had hefted her back onto his shoulder and ordered the garage door open in Finnish.

As the icy air hit her cheeks, her renewed protests—as he trudged out into the snow and headed towards the frozen lake—turned out to be completely futile. Because her cries of outrage were muffled by the three balaclavas covering her mouth. And her flailing arms and feet were bundled up in seven layers of Arctic clothing, insulating his broad back from the fallout.

The rat.

'I will go in first. You must descend quickly or your fingers will freeze to the ladder,' Logan commanded, unable to take his eyes off Cara as they stood on the edge of the swimming hole. She wore nothing but a pair of his boxer shorts, sliders to protect her feet and the thick robe he'd given her, which reached her ankles. With her arms folded tightly across her chest he could see the delicious hint of cleavage flushed pink from the sauna.

It had been an act of sheer willpower not to take advantage of all that lush skin as they had heated themselves to prepare for their swim. She hadn't commented on the erection stretching his shorts. But he could tell from the potent scent of her arousal she had noticed it.

But then, he was almost permanently ready for her, in a constant state of wanting to touch, to taste, to devour.

In the past week he had lost the last of his inhibitions, the fear that he might hurt her. And taken her whenever and wherever he could.

She had embraced the sex with the same enthusiasm, the same fierce, unquenchable desire—meeting all of his demands and making many of her own. And he had discovered a level of pleasure, of passion, he had never believed possible.

As he had watched her sleep this morning, her slender body laid out on his bed like a banquet, the heat had pooled in his crotch all over again, but he had forced himself not to wake her—and demand more. Because as he had studied her, he had finally noticed the ravages of the past week's endless sex-capades, as Cara had dubbed them, on her soft skin.

The small thumb-sized bruises on her hips where he had held her too tightly, the slight rash around both nipples where he had sucked her into a frenzy too many times to count—because she was so deliciously sensitive there. He had listened to the deep murmur of her breathing, a sign of her exhaustion, and been more than a little ashamed.

How could he have gorged on her again and again, and still not have satisfied this endless hunger? Was this normal? This desperate clawing need to touch and caress and excite? And to be touched and caressed and excited in return? After so many years spent avoiding any touch at all?

And when was it going to stop? Would this thirst ever be fully quenched? Because they only had seven days left and already he was terrified she had changed him in some fundamental way.

As much as he had tried to make their connection only about the physical, there were so many other aspects of her presence in his home that had begun to enchant him.

The inane chatter about nothing in particular, which had become a comforting background noise when they cooked and ate together. The flush that highlighted the freckles on her cleavage when he frustrated or aroused her. The way she whistled off-key, songs by an Irish band called U2, when she stirred the big pots of stew they had been devouring each evening before devouring each other.

Instead of enjoying his solitude, he now sought her company.

Instead of wanting to know nothing more about her than how to make her beg for release, he wanted to know everything. Who she was? Where did she come from? Who were the brothers she had mentioned in passing with such affection? Why had she waited so long to have sex when she was so responsive to a man's touch? What did that band's songs really sound like when she wasn't mangling them? What had driven her to come to Finnish Lapland and take the stunning shots he had seen on her camera?

He had even had to catch himself from offering to take her outside in a blizzard when he had found her studying a snowy owl as it swooped past the bedroom windows.

The woman was an artist, just as he was. He had seen her fierce desire to capture the bird in flight and understood it. So much so, that he was even beginning to feel uncomfortable about making her keep her promise not to use the camera around his home.

How had he come to be desperate to know everything about her? How could he want to please her, and not just her body? Because both were urges he did not understand.

He had never been curious about another human being. Never wanted to please anyone but himself. Not since he was a boy and he had first arrived in the care of his grandfather—and this frozen wilderness had become his sanctuary. A place of peace and solitude.

But his sanctuary didn't feel as safe and sure as it once had—when he imagined it now without her in it.

'I can't believe I'm actually doing this. It's madness!' she huffed, stamping her feet, her breath pluming out in a cloud.

He grinned at her disgruntled expression and shoved the wayward thoughts to the back of his mind.

Time to stop thinking and start doing.

They both needed time out from the unquenchable desire, and he couldn't think of a better way to control it than dousing himself in icy water. That he had wanted to share this with her too was problematic, but he had been unable to deny the urge.

He dropped his own robe, slung it over the ladder and climbed into the water.

The prickling pain fired over his skin as he immersed himself, his panting breaths helping to regulate his temperature.

'Come quickly, before you cool too much.' He beckoned her in.

A delightful frown puckered her brow, and she muttered something that sounded like, 'Oh, feck it.' Then, with the fierceness he had come to adore, she slipped the robe off, revealing those pert breasts, and flipped off her sliders.

Turning, she presented him with a perfect view of her beautiful butt, exquisitely displayed in his shorts. He kicked away from the ladder, giving her space as her toe touched the water.

She swore profusely, the profane words echoing off the quiet snow and making birds fly up from the nearby trees. He began to laugh, as he watched her scrambling down into the frigid lake. She ducked in all the way to her neckline, panting furiously and still cursing like a sailor.

'Good?' he asked, as he swam closer—the endorphin rush starting to shoot into his brain, making his whole body sing.

'F-f-freezing!' she shouted over her shoulder, then clambered back up the ladder again so fast her bright pink skin was a blur of motion. Her breasts jiggled adorably as she danced around trying to grab her robe, her nipples ruched into hard peaks.

His mouth watered as he considered how best to warm her breasts up again.

He levered himself out behind her as she bundled herself into the robe, covering up all that delicious flesh, then stamped her feet back into the sliders and rushed down the deck towards the sauna cabin.

He was still laughing, the adrenaline making him even more euphoric than usual as the door of the cabin slammed shut behind her.

He tugged on his own robe, his skin brilliantly alive from the cold, but his groin pulsing hot with a very different kind of vitality. He entered the large wooden cabin he had built several summers ago, stoked the fire, added a few more logs so they could stay inside for a while, then ducked into the sauna.

She sat on the top bench, shivering, despite the dry heat—the robe still wrapped tightly around her naked body.

Well, now, that wouldn't do.

He dropped his own robe, kicked off his sliders aware of the thick ridge in his wet shorts as the raw heat poured through his system now on the tails of the adrenaline overload.

'How the...?' Her brows rose in astonishment as her gaze snagged on the proof of his need. 'How can you possibly be hard again? After that?'

'Because I am always hard for you,' he said, his chuckle roughened by the familiar desire, although his heart stuttered at the realisation it was only the truth.

He placed his foot on the bench below her to ease the robe off her shoulders. 'Can you not feel it too? The rush?'

Her fingers released their death grip on the flannel and she let him cast the robe aside—to reveal the flushed flesh he adored. Her gaze met his, the depth of emotion making his heart stumble, when she nodded.

'Yes, it's...' She breathed in, the motion making her

breasts lift, drawing his gaze to the puckered nipples, so taut and ready it was as if they were begging for his mouth. 'I'd forgotten how good it feels, to swim outside in cold water. The rush afterwards is incredible,' she said, the wistful look in her eyes enchanting him.

'You have been ice swimming before?'

'Not exactly.' She chuckled, the sound light with pleasure. Her full lips curled, making her whole face brighten. 'There's a beach near my family's farm in Wexford called Curracloe. Miles of sand and dunes. I used to swim there as a girl with my brothers.' She closed her eyes, let her head fall back, the memories lighting her face like sunshine.

'We'd go all year round,' she continued as he listened intently—riveted by this glimpse into her past, her childhood. 'Sneak down after school before we had to do our chores. It was the perfect escape. The winter was the best time, even though the surf was brutal. The water was warm into November, and there'd be no tourists, you see. We'd have the whole beach to ourselves. But then...' She paused, and something stark flashed across her features— taking the sunshine away. Her gaze had lost the golden glow of memory, her expression becoming bleak when she opened her eyes.

'But then what?' he probed, even though he knew it was dangerous to ask. Dangerous to care about what had put the sadness in her eyes. Dangerous to want to know where that bleak look had come from.

'It doesn't matter.' She shrugged and smiled. But the innocent joy was gone.

She pressed her palm to the thick ridge in his shorts. 'Perhaps we should take care of this now you've revived me,' she added provocatively.

His aching flesh leapt to her touch. But he knew a distraction technique when he saw one.

He clasped her wrist, dragged those tempting fingers away.

'Tell me,' he said as he sat beside her on the bench. He pushed the wet locks of her hair back so he could see her face. 'Why did you stop swimming as a girl?'

She sighed. 'The story is a passion killer.'

Nothing could kill his passion for her, he thought wryly. But he only said again, 'Tell me.'

Her shoulders hitched, but for once he did not become fixated on the bounce of her bare breasts.

'Da caught us one afternoon,' she said. 'And took a belt to my brothers and me. After that, there was no escape in it any more. Just the fear he would catch us again.'

'Your father hit you with a belt?' he asked, unable to hide his shock, not just at the revelation, but the lack of emotion in her tone when she revealed this ugly detail.

He knew enough about Cara Doyle to know she was not an unemotional woman.

She folded her arms across her breasts, the flush of shame in her cheeks making him want to punch a wall.

'The man was a brute,' she said, without any inflection at all. 'And I hated him. But to be fair, it was the only time he ever hit me. My brothers all felt the end of his belt on a regular basis. But he preferred to spend his time calling me a dirty whore.' She let out a half-laugh, but it had no humour. 'If he could have seen me this past week, jumping you every chance I get and enjoying every second of it, I've no doubt he would have considered himself right about that.'

The revelation disturbed him, but not as much as the flicker of shame in her voice, or the rush of anger that flared like wildfire. His fingers curled into fists. He wanted to kill the bastard. For putting that thought into her head.

Was this why she had not discovered sex before now?

Why she had reacted so strangely when they had made love the first time?

Had the ravings of a bastard made her believe it was wrong to enjoy the connection they shared?

He cupped her cheek, stroked his thumb over the pounding pulse in her neck.

'We have been jumping each other, Cara,' he murmured, suddenly desperate to show her what they had together was good, pure. Meant to be indulged. And never dirty.

'True.' Her lips lifted, but he could still see the conflicting emotions in her eyes. Pain, sadness, confusion.

He took her hand, pressed her palm to the thick ridge still making him ache. 'Let me show you why this is not dirty,' he said. 'Why he was always wrong.'

Her gaze filled with something he could not name... Wasn't sure he wanted to name. Something bold and sweet and unafraid.

But when she nodded, he was glad, because the shame was gone.

'Okay,' she said.

He eased her folded arms away from her breasts. Until she sat before him, her skin glowing, flushed from the heat, her nipples rigid with desire.

Lifting the swollen weight to his lips, he captured the taut peak and sucked it deep into his mouth. She groaned, and braced her arms on the bench behind her, offering herself to him as he kissed and tugged at the ruched flesh, knowing how to make her ache.

Desire flared through him as she dislodged his mouth

from her nipple to ease down his shorts. She bent to capture the rigid erection in her lips with an enthusiasm he had always adored, but admired even more now.

She had conquered those demons, this week, with him. And he was glad.

He sat, shuddering, shaking, watching intently as she worked him with her mouth.

The passion built. Hard, fast. Until he was forced to grasp her cheeks, lift her from him.

He wanted this to be for her. Wanted to give her an orgasm that would obliterate the last of her father's lies. Until all that was left was the joy.

He dragged her off the bench, positioned her pliant body until she was bent over, her hands braced on the shelf. He held her hips, tugged down the shorts and eased into the tight wet clasp of her body from behind, knowing the penetration would be deepest from this angle. He let her take the full measure of him. The feel of her body contracting around his aching length was pure torture.

She groaned. 'Please, Logan, move.' Her whole body shuddered. 'It's too hot in here.'

He laughed at her double meaning. The sweat dripped from his brow onto her back as he stared at the place where they were joined. He wiped the moisture away. But shifted only slightly, to nudge the spot deep inside her he knew would drive her wild.

'Logan... For pity's sake...' she begged, tried to move, but he held her firmly for the deep stroking, rolling his hips, making her take only what he wanted to give.

He nudged, pressed, stroked... Torturing them both. Never taking her over, building the passion to impossible proportions.

The battle for control raged between them in fire and

ice as the titanic climax hovered a whisper away. Too close and yet not close enough.

Until at last, her swollen flesh pulsed and shattered, massaging his length. Her throaty cry of release triggered his own vicious climax.

He pulled out, slammed back into her. Once, twice, until his own orgasm crested.

They lay sprawled together on the floor of the sauna moments later, the dry heat all but unbearable now as steam rose from their sweat-slicked bodies. He dragged her into his arms, pressed a kiss to her forehead.

'He was wrong, Cara,' he murmured. 'There is no shame here. Ever.'

She glanced up at him. The cheeky smile she sent him—tinged with the innocent joy that had always captivated him—made his heart leap painfully in his chest.

'I know. But when we get back to the house, you may have to give me another demonstration, just so I can be sure.'

He was still laughing while he washed off in the sauna bucket, dressed hastily and then raced her back to the house in the fading daylight—more than ready to prove his point all over again.

CHAPTER NINE

FOUR DAYS AFTER she and Logan had started ice swimming each morning, Cara sat at the kitchen table—spooning down some yoghurt and fruit—and stared at the note she'd found on the counter when she'd woken up alone.

Had to go out. Back later.
L

She swallowed down the bubble of disappointment and irritation. And the dumb ache in her throat.

Why hadn't he mentioned he was heading out when he'd woken her up just before dawn to make slow luxurious love to her while she was barely awake? She might have liked to go with him. And where exactly had he gone when the nearest town was Saariselkä—which had to be at least fifty miles away by her reckoning—and she knew he never went there?

Curiosity, and boredom, were the only reasons she would miss him today, she told herself. That and the fact she could not ice swim alone, something she had become addicted to in the last four days.

She folded the note and stuffed it into the pocket of her robe... Or rather *his* robe. Her body was still humming from their session before dawn, her nerve-endings tingling with awareness and that reckless passion—that unquenchable fire—that he could ignite so easily. Her frown deepened. Had he woken her deliberately, to exhaust her, so that she would be fast asleep again when he sneaked off for the day?

She swore. A curse word her mammy would have washed her mouth out with soap for using echoed off the granite surfaces.

Of course, he had. Which could only mean one thing. He still didn't trust her—not completely. Not enough to let her accompany him wherever he had gone today.

The hollow feeling of disappointment—that he'd abandoned her for the day so easily—expanded in her chest and pushed against her ribs. She pressed her fingers to her eyelids, annoyed even more by the sting of tears.

What was wrong with her? She didn't need him to trust her. She'd entered into this liaison with her eyes wide open.

Just sex. Not intimacy. Not companionship. Not by any means a relationship. It wasn't what he'd offered and it was what she had happily agreed to.

But...

The pressure in her chest, the sting of sensation making her eyeballs hurt, refused to subside. They'd spent the last ten days together, barely apart. And it hadn't been just about sex, not any more. Not for her.

'There is no shame here. Ever.'

The words he'd said to her in the sauna four days ago echoed in her head. As they had a hundred times since that moment, when everything had changed. She'd shared something with him she hadn't shared with anyone. The shame she'd carried with her for so long, without even really acknowledging it. And he'd somehow made it better.

The ice swimming each morning now helping to reinforce her escape from that shame. That fear. That judgment.

He'd understood something she wasn't even sure she'd understood herself.

She'd always been sure she had got over her father's insults, had never internalised them. She had even been stupidity grateful that he'd only once used his belt on her the way he had so often used it on her brothers. Sticks and stones and belts were worse than names, she'd told herself.

But after feeling that rush on her skin again, after so long, from swimming in cold water, it had brought it all back. How she'd loved to go down to the beach with her brothers. How those stolen swims had been an escape, an act of rebellion, a secret pleasure they had all shared. The teasing and games, the larking about, even the shared misery as they'd scrambled back into their clothes in the howling wind, pressing sandy feet into damp shoes. Those swims had been a chance to get away from the miserable tension, the barely leashed violence, the cruel words and endless threats that had marred so much of their childhood. Those swims had allowed them to be children again.

And she'd missed it, unbearably, once it had been stolen from her. By their da.

So much so, she'd forced herself to believe she didn't need it. She didn't even want it anymore. The camaraderie with her brothers, the sweet rush of feeling, the stolen moments when they were just kids together—not hostages to her father's moods and binges, his violent, volatile temper.

And Logan had somehow understood that. And given it back to her.

He'd listened intently to her story. The good memories and the bad. And offered comfort, and validation. And even joy. With his words and then his body. And he'd reinforced that new-found freedom every day since, coaxing her to the *avanto* until she'd become as addicted to the rush as he was...

They hadn't spoken again about her past. But she'd begun to look forward to their mornings now as much as their nights.

But that was off the agenda today, because he wasn't here.

It wasn't just the swim. What was worse was the knowledge that the sense of connection, which had felt like so much more than sex—the new-found intimacy, the friendship she thought they'd built with the easy smiles, the playful gestures, the moments out of bed—couldn't have meant to him what they had to her.

Or he wouldn't have thrown away the chance to swim with her today. When they only had a few more days left together.

She picked up her mug and bowl, carried them over to the dishwasher and loaded them in, breathing heavily so the pressure in her chest—that feeling of loss—wouldn't crush her.

Cara, lighten up. He promised you nothing. If you thought this could be more, perhaps it's good now you know for sure it can't be.

She braced her hands on the counter and watched the precious Arctic daylight bounce off the surfaces.

It was already close to noon. And she had no idea when he would be back. And when he deigned to return, would he be expecting her to be waiting for him, naked and willing, like a dutiful little sex object?

The anger and frustration at his high-handed decision not to give her a choice this morning to accompany him, not to stay and spend time with her, pushed the regret and yearning back. Mostly.

A shadow floated across the room and she spotted the snowy owl—which she'd seen several times before—soaring majestically over the frozen lake. Its large tawny wings spanned the air currents as it dipped and dived, then rose again, its predatory grace making her breath clog as a small creature struggled in its talons, before it disappeared into the towering birch trees that edged the lake.

She pushed away the stupid sense of loss. Why was she moping about? When she could be doing something she loved instead, but had neglected for over ten days now.

She'd thought about photographing the owl every time she'd seen it fly past in the last week, but she hadn't been able to act upon it. The weather had been an excuse until yesterday, but the truth was she'd got sidetracked—because her time with Logan had been so precious. And finite.

What an eejit she'd been.

She marched towards the bedroom. After donning her first two layers, she headed for the garage where she kept her outer clothes—and the camera she'd had packed away for too long, her fingers already itching to use it.

After she had zipped herself into the cumbersome snowsuit, and double-checked the camera, she shouted out the Finnish command Logan used to open the garage door and headed out into the newly fallen snow. Her boots made crisp indents in the drifts, as she walked past his snowmobile tracks and headed towards the forest, her strides purposeful. Determined.

He had asked her not to leave the house without him, but he wasn't here to stop her. Because he had chosen not to be. And she'd be damned if she would pass up the opportunity to study the owl and maybe capture it on film—and start reaffirming her priorities.

* * *

Logan turned off the snowmobile's ignition and ordered the garage doors closed. He stripped off his outer layers, then began unpacking the food supplies he had picked up from the regular air-drop location on the edge of his land—even though every instinct was telling him to race through the house and find Cara.

He'd spent a whole day away from her, to prove that he could—so he forced himself now to complete the mundane task.

In three days, she would be gone. And his life would have to continue as normal. That he would miss her—the feel and taste and scent of her in his bed—was something he needed to get a handle on.

Except it wasn't just the sex he would miss any more, he thought grimly as he unloaded and stacked the dry goods. Because the more he tried to focus on the physical, the more he found himself thinking about all the other things he would miss.

He'd avoided any more revealing conversations about her childhood since their first ice-swimming session, had stifled all the questions that remained lodged in his head. Because that would simply encourage more intimacy. And she might expect him to return the favour. To revisit parts of his own past he had no wish to discuss.

But the questions still haunted him.

How had she survived such a brutal upbringing? And become such a strong, independent woman? Forthright, bold, brave, and so open.

He had become addicted to swimming with her each morning since, seeing her duck into the water, seeing her grin when the rush hit, warming her up afterwards in the sauna…

It had become a ritual that he had woken up this morning wanting so badly to keep that he'd known he had to leave her alone for the day.

But it had been torture to be without her during the long ride to the drop zone. How was he going to survive once she was gone for good? The chatter of her conversation in the evening as they cooked their supper? The sight of her first thing each morning, her hair a mess as she took that first gulp of coffee with an indulgent sigh? Her rouged skin as she shot out of the *avanto* with an ear-splitting shriek…

He breathed past the growing obstruction in his throat. *Damn it…*

All the moments he had greedily stored in his memory would haunt him when she was no longer here.

He slammed the cargo trunk shut. Then unhooked the sleigh. But as he tugged the towing vehicle past the shelving unit where they kept their snowsuits, he paused and frowned.

Where were Cara's outer garments? He checked his watch. It was edging towards three o'clock, close to nightfall.

Had she gone out without him? He left the sleigh and shot up into the house to check.

'Cara?' he shouted. No answer.

He searched the living area, the downstairs guest bedroom, jogged up to his own bedroom. The bed had been remade. But there was no sign of her.

Eventually he headed to the basement complex. The gym, the workshop. He even checked the freezer room as panic began to wrap around his chest, making his heart pound harder.

He should not have left her here alone. What if she had gone swimming without him? Surely, she wouldn't be so foolish? But even as he thought it, he imagined her face, that sweet grin splitting her features the day before as she'd managed to spend longer in the freezing water.

He charged back to the garage—the panic choking him—and checked that all the snowmobiles were still there. All four were accounted for.

Even so, his breathing continued to accelerate. Where was she? It would be dark soon. What if she had got lost? She had no idea where she was. The lake could be treacherous, the forests even more so. The bears hibernated at this time of year, but sometimes there could be one—sick or injured that could not hibernate and would be starving, desperate for food. And then there were the wolves that hunted in packs on the other side of the gorge. They never ventured near the house, but what if they had spotted her and come to investigate...?

He dashed outside as the sun dipped beneath the treeline. The brittle daylight had turned to the glow of twilight. He found her tracks, veering away from the trail he had taken to the drop zone that morning. But the boot prints had already frozen. She must have left hours ago.

Visions of her broken bloodied body, lying in the snow, or floating frozen in the water, made his lungs contract, his breath seize in painful gasps.

'Cara?' he rasped, but barely any sound came out, the shout trapped in his larynx.

The silent screams drew him back to that night, so long ago, as he stumbled through the snow, his legs so heavy he felt as if he were being sucked back into the terrible nightmares that had all but destroyed him once.

Instead of the quiet crunch of his boots, all he could hear was torrential rain, hitting the broken sidewalk in waves. The dirty water washed over his mother's pale face, and red blood spread across the starched white cotton of his father's dress shirt, like the fingers of a corpse. The heavy weight on his back a burden he couldn't shake. Stifling. Suffocating.

The screech of an owl jerked him back to the present, forcing him to focus. To lock the nightmares back into the recesses of his mind where they belonged. A shape appeared in the distance, through the trees, and stood up.

'Cara,' he murmured, his voice a rasp of sound.

Not broken...whole.

The fear released its stranglehold on his throat, the trapped air expelling from his lungs, but as he charged towards her, needing to hold her, to make sure she was real, she was his, she was safe, he spotted the camera in her hands. And the frantic fear became a rush of fury.

CHAPTER TEN

'LOGAN, OVER HERE!' Cara shouted, and waved.

She'd seen him return ten minutes ago, the snowmobile crossing the lake, and had struggled not to stop what she was doing instantly and rush to the house to greet him. Like a lovestruck fool.

He'd been gone the whole day. And she'd be damned if she'd give him the satisfaction of knowing how much she'd missed him.

Observing the owl and its nesting area, taking shots to document its habitat and flight paths, had managed to keep her mind off the feeling of rejection, of loss. Mostly... But she couldn't ignore the leap of exhilaration in her chest—or how much it scared her—as he trudged towards her.

But as he got closer, the exhilaration downgraded considerably.

He looked like he had when they'd first met. Maybe because his head was bare, the waves of dark hair dancing in the breeze, and without the balaclavas she could see the hard line of his jaw, the brittle expression.

'Hi,' she said, tugging down her face covering as a shiver racked her tired body.

She'd been out in the forest for a couple of hours and had noticed the discomfort a while ago. But each time she'd contemplated returning to the empty house, she'd decided to stay a little longer. The pictures she'd taken weren't great, but they had felt important somehow. A declaration of intent. A chance to regain her purpose after ten days of indulgence.

'You're back,' she added inanely, because he hadn't responded, the fierce expression on his face starting to bother her.

'You are freezing.' He grasped her arm and turned, dragging her back towards the house. 'How long have you been out here, putting yourself in danger?'

What the hell?

'Logan, let go.' She jerked her arm out of his grasp, almost dropping the camera. The sense of loss she'd been ruthlessly controlling all day was joined by a spurt of resentment, and fury. 'I wasn't in any danger. I'm less than a kilometre from the house. Not that you'd care anyhow— you've been gone all day who knows where.'

The minute she'd said the words, she wanted to snatch them back.

Really? Could she sound any more clingy?

Before she had a chance to contemplate the depths of her humiliation, though, or how he had managed to turn her into this pathetic creature she didn't even recognise, he bent and scooped her onto his shoulder.

'Logan, damn it, put me down,' she cried, thumping his broad back as he stamped back through the snow. Her fury quickly outpaced her humiliation as she kicked and twisted, but to no avail. The man was as strong as a damn ox—and twice as arrogant.

He had carried her like this before, the first time they'd been ice swimming, and she'd secretly loved it then, his strength, his determination and the playfulness beneath.

She wasn't loving it any more though, as she struggled

to get free of his hold—but only exhausted herself more—while he carted her back to the house like an unruly child.

They were both panting when he finally dropped her on her feet in the garage.

His cheeks were flushed from the cold, and the exertion, his heavy breaths matching her own. But she could see the harsh expression and it sparked the feeling deep in her chest she remembered from her childhood… When her da had arrived home from work, or the pub, in the kind of mood they all knew would cause trouble. For everyone.

She'd cowered then. But she refused to cower now.

She wasn't a little girl any more. And Logan, for all his high-handed ways, was not her father. But even so, she felt the pressure in her chest, that hole in her stomach, caused by the feeling of inadequacy, of judgement, which had made her feel small in the face of a man's temper.

'How long were you out there?' he demanded again, as if he had the right to question her decisions. Her autonomy.

The fury burst free, incinerating the anguish.

She dragged off her head gear, the balaclavas and the goggles around her neck, and threw them at his chest. He ignored them.

But he couldn't dodge her outrage.

'You bastard!' she shouted as she shoved the camera in its box with clumsy hands and placed it on the ground. The camera he'd all but forbidden her to use. The camera he could have broken with his stupid stunt.

Once the camera was safe—no thanks to him—she ripped off her gloves, all five pairs of them, and threw them at him too.

He barely blinked.

'I was working.' She ground the words out to stop from screaming. She tore down the zip on her snowsuit, began to struggle out of the layers as he continued to glare at her as if he were her keeper. 'And I wasn't finished.'

She didn't care about his anger. It would be a cold day in hell before she cowered before a man ever again. Especially a man who had been gone all day, without a word of when he'd be back.

'It was getting dark,' he shouted back, his own voice rising—the stony expression belied by the fire in his eyes as he threw off his own layers. His pectoral muscles heaved beneath the clinging nylon of his thermal undershirt as he kicked off his boots, and his ski-pants.

The spike of awareness as his big body was revealed only infuriated her more.

'There are bears, wolves and also the threat of storms, like the one which brought you here,' he growled as if he were speaking to an imbecile, his anger making a muscle tic in his jaw. 'They come from nowhere without warning. Even a hundred yards from the house you would be in danger.'

'So what? How is that any of your concern?' she replied, the rage making her body heat spike, even though she stood before him now in nothing but her thermal tights and undershirt.

She saw the awareness shadow his gaze as it roamed over her. And felt the answering hum in her abdomen, that hot, melting sensation between her thighs that meant her body was readying itself for him. Even though she hated him in that moment. Or wanted to hate him. For making her feel like that girl again—scared of being chastised.

He glared at her. 'You know it is my concern. When you are here, you are mine.'

'Well, that's where you're wrong, fella,' she yelled back, hating the dark possessive look in his eyes, the way his gaze raked over her with a sense of ownership. And the way her heart hammered her ribs in heavy thuds because a part of her wanted it to be true. The weak, needy part of her she thought she'd destroyed long ago. 'I belong to no one but myself,' she said, determined to convince herself as much as him. 'And I'll not be taking safety advice from a man who lives in the middle of nowhere alone. And can't even deign to tell me where he's been.'

She turned on her heel, to march away, so furious now—with herself and the stupid wayward emotions battering her—she was about to explode.

'Don't!' The low demand broke over her and reverberated in her chest, stopping her in her tracks.

Then his fingers grasped her arm and pulled her round. He pressed her back against the garage wall. His forehead touched hers, his staggered breathing hot on her neck, as he dragged her clumsily into his embrace. But then the hard ridge of his arousal pushed into her belly, making the heat flare at her core. She slammed her palms against his chest, determined to push him away, to deny that bone-deep yearning that had troubled her all day, and made her a woman she didn't recognise. A woman who needed his touch, his presence, his validation.

She struggled to get free of him—and the emotions that had sneaked up on her in the last ten days without warning, and which she had no clue how to navigate.

But then he murmured, 'Please, don't…'

She stilled, shocked by the raw plea in his voice.

'You had icicles on your lashes,' he said, his tone rough as he cupped her cheek, his hand warm against her chilled skin. 'I was scared you were dead.'

What?

She gripped his undershirt, registering the fear and anguish on his face.

'They died and I did nothing to save them,' he added, wild grief shadowing his eyes. 'I cannot lose you too.'

'Logan…?' she murmured, the last of her anger deserting her, the distress in his voice crucifying her. 'What are you talking about?'

The pain flared in his eyes and she thought she understood. Was this about his parents? About what had happened all those years ago? A fear she had somehow triggered, because he cared for her, too. Enough to want to keep her safe.

Anguish for him tore at her chest—terrifying, but also somehow liberating. Because she felt so much less alone.

'Logan, is this about your parents? Can you tell me what happened to them?'

He shook his head. But as he pressed his forehead to hers again, and held her tight, emotion rippled through him and she understood he was scared to let her go.

She cradled his cheeks, looked into his eyes. 'It's okay, Logan. I'm okay. I'm safe. I was never in any real danger, do you understand?'

He nodded, then pressed his mouth to hers, silencing the questions. The surge of need that had been building all day rushed in. He kissed her with a frantic passion—as if reassuring himself that she was whole. That she was his.

Suddenly they were tearing at each other's clothes, desperate to reach flesh—as desire bridged the last of the gap between them.

This was simple, basic, she realised. A way to cope with the devastating emotions churning in her chest and making her heart hurt. The yearning she had worked so hard to suppress fed the frantic need. Until he lifted her naked in his arms and impaled her on his thick shaft.

She sank onto the strident erection, taking him to the hilt

in one long, slow, unbearable glide. Her swollen sex stretched to receive him as she had done so many times before. But this time, as he began to move in frantic bursts, her back thumping against the wall, her heart soared into her throat.

The pleasure slammed into her, and her sobs were matched by his harsh shout of release.

Afterwards, she clung to his shoulders, and buried her face in his neck.

'I am sorry, Cara,' he mumbled against her hair. 'I should not have left you alone.'

Her ragged breathing cut through the quiet air, but even the wave of afterglow couldn't hide the gaping hole in her chest that swallowed her whole at his gruff apology.

He carried her into the house, and up to the bedroom, as if she were precious, cherished. But as he tucked her into his bed, then joined her, pulling her into his arms, the plunging pain in her stomach returned.

Had she made a terrible mistake?

How could she have fallen so hopelessly in love with this difficult, taciturn, untouchable man—enough to want to ease his pain and find out where it had come from?

Enough to want to save him? Even though he hadn't asked to be saved.

He hadn't even asked her to stay, and if he did, how could she accept? When it would surely mean giving up everything she'd worked for, everything she'd dreamed of, for a man… The way her mother had.

You couldn't save someone, couldn't change someone, who didn't want to be saved.

But as she lay warm in his arms, feeling the thumps of his heartbeat reverberating against her back, she recognised the well of hope that bubbled up under her breastbone.

She mattered to Logan, in a way no other person had

for a very long time. And that had to be as scary for him as it was for her. Maybe even more so. But surely that also had to mean something?

Now all she had to do was figure out exactly what it meant. And whether she could nurture and protect the well of hope… And turn it into something more tangible.

In the three days they had left together.

No pressure, then.

'Who were you talking about yesterday, Logan? When you said they died and you could do nothing to save them?'

Logan's hand stilled on Cara's belly where he had been lazily stroking her. The warm heat from the sauna and the drugging feeling of sexual satisfaction had relaxed him and made him feel in control of his emotions for the first time since yesterday's argument.

But as he glanced up from the lower bench, to find her watching him, her face flushed from their latest swim and the traditional warm-up afterwards, he tensed.

Why had he thought she would not recall the things he had let slip last night while he had been blindsided by the old fear?

When he had woken this morning, to find her already up and keen to go swimming, he had assumed she had forgotten their argument. And when she had said nothing as they conducted their wake-up swim, he had convinced himself all would be well.

But as she stared at him now, her gaze probing, the questions in her eyes unleashed the intense emotion from yesterday all over again.

'Were you talking about your parents?' she said softly as she stroked his cheek. Coaxing, curious, compassionate.

He sat up, deliberately dislodging her hand, because

he wanted so badly to lean into that consoling touch. And that would be bad.

He didn't want to revisit that night. Not again. Didn't want her to know about the fear that had broken him as a boy—and could break him again, if he let her in the rest of the way.

But as his mind raced, trying to figure out how to avoid her questions, how to deflect or ignore that look in her eyes, she added, 'Were you with them when they died, Logan?'

He flinched and shook his head, but he could see she had caught him in the lie. Because her expression was suffused with sympathy.

He stood, suddenly too exposed, too raw. He headed for the door to the sauna. They were naked, sweaty, his groin still pulsing with the aftermath of his recent climax and he had few enough defences already when she looked at him that way.

'It's getting cold,' he said, by way of explanation, even though his face was burning as he entered the changing room and began pulling on his clothes.

He concentrated on adding the layers necessary to return to the house, aware of her following him into the room, and silently getting dressed too.

As he tugged on his gloves, he could feel the guilty flags lighting his cheeks.

After getting rid of their snowsuits and outdoor layers in the garage, they headed up to the living area, and made their breakfasts—him a traditional Finnish porridge and her a bowl of fruit and yoghurt—as the tension and guilt knotted in his gut.

He stole glances at her as he stirred the thick multi-grain oatmeal on the stovetop, transferred it to a bowl and added slices of apple and a sprinkle of cinnamon, while she laid the table, and scooped yoghurt and frozen berries into a bowl then grabbed the coffee pot and poured them both a cup.

The domesticity struck him. And didn't help with the panic. When had he become so settled, so comfortable with her in his space? Enough to know he would miss her desperately when she was gone.

She didn't press him, didn't probe as they sat to eat, didn't say anything at all in fact. It annoyed him to realise he even missed the chatter she always used to fill the silence.

But something about her stoic acceptance of his refusal to engage in this conversation only tightened the knot in his gut, making each mouthful of the hearty porridge a chore instead of a pleasure.

She hadn't looked at him directly, not once, since he had walked out of the sauna.

Did she believe he owed her this information, because when he had asked about her past, she had confided in him? Was this some kind of pay-off? Some unspoken rule in relationships he knew nothing about?

But they didn't have a relationship, he told himself.

Except...

What about yesterday's argument? Wasn't that exactly what a relationship was?

Angry words? Charged silences? Broken promises? And then the inevitable make-up sex. Wasn't what had happened yesterday very much like the little he could remember of his parents' relationship?

Although, he thought miserably, when he had made fast frantic love after their argument, and held her in his arms, he hadn't felt used, or bitter, he had felt calm, and settled... And safe.

He blinked, the porridge like cement paste now in his stomach.

But he didn't feel settled any more, or calm, he felt agitated, on edge. As if more than just his control was slipping through his fingers—and he had no clue how to hold on to it.

Finally, he couldn't swallow another mouthful past the thickness in his throat. He pushed the bowl away.

'Yes, I was there,' he blurted out. 'I asked them to take me to the movie premiere that night,' he added, remembering for the first time details he had forced himself to forget.

He had begged to attend the new dinosaur movie, so he could boast about it to all his friends at the boarding school he attended in Boston. He rarely saw his parents—their social lives a whirl of high-profile events linked to his father's business interests and his mother's position as a former supermodel turned socialite. As soon as they had climbed into the limo together though, he had regretted the impulse, because his parents had started arguing.

The porridge turned over in his stomach as he remembered the cutting words, the furious whispers as the car had driven through lower Manhattan to the event. And he had sat staring out of the window, watching the rain pour down on the stormy October night, seen the people scurrying to get home along the sidewalks as he'd wished he could be anywhere but inside that car. With them.

He had so few clear memories of them. How strange he could now recall in such vivid details his unhappiness with them that night...

Cara's gaze connected with his at last. But the moment of relief, because she had looked at him again, was quickly destroyed when the shadow of sympathy darkened her eyes to a rich emerald.

She placed her spoon in her bowl and reached across to cover the fist he had clenched on the table with her hand.

'I'm so sorry, Logan,' she said softly. 'That must have been very traumatic. You don't have to talk about it, if you don't want to.'

He dragged his hand free. And stared out of the window—but instead of seeing the brilliant white landscape all he could see was that grey alley behind the theatre, and the man with the gun shouting. And the weight on his back, as he lay broken and scared, too terrified to move.

He didn't want to talk about this, about any of it. He had never even confided in his grandfather, when the old man had asked about the nightmares, which had finally faded over time. Nightmares he had deserved. But after the way he had overreacted yesterday, freaking out when she had chosen to leave the house, he realised he owed her this much.

He forced himself to look at her again, to absorb the compassion in her gaze.

While a part of him wanted to bask in the tenderness he could see in her eyes, another part of him was terrified of needing it. Of taking another treacherous step out of the isolation that had protected him for so long... But somehow the truth spilled out regardless.

'The man with the gun was shouting, telling me to come with him.' He stumbled through the memories, thrown back to the night he had avoided for so long. 'But I couldn't move. I was hiding behind my father. My mother was screaming and then...' He sucked in a breath, hearing the pops, feeling the impact as his father's body slammed into him, the dead weight crushing him as he lay on the pavement. 'I couldn't breathe.' He drew in a harsh breath, his lungs tightening up again. How could the suffocating fear still be so vivid? 'Not for a long time.' He stared at her, willing her to understand. 'Not until my grandfather brought me here.'

But as she looked back at him, her eyes deep pools of emotion, it occurred to him that he'd never felt so much. Not through all the years of isolation. Not until he'd met her.

The panic was swift and unequivocal, forcing him to acknowledge a truth he had never faced until this moment.

'Maybe if I had done what that man asked, they might still be alive.'

Instead of the contempt he expected to see in her face though, the contempt he felt for himself, all he saw was compassion.

'Oh, Logan, that's madness,' she said so simply he wanted to believe her. 'Surely you must know you had no part in their deaths.'

He shook his head, scared to believe her now, because it only made him feel more defenceless, more exposed.

'Is that why you've been alone here for so long?' she asked, gently. 'Because you're punishing yourself for something that happened to you as a boy that you had no control over? Can't you see how wrong that is?'

The words struck his chest, piercing the armour-plating he had built with a lifetime of solitude. Of abstinence. Armour-plating that had numbed his pain for so many years but had never been able to protect him from the yearning, the wanting, when it came to her. He clenched his fists, rose abruptly from his chair, his legs weak, his body shaky. He hated that boy who had been treated like a victim by the media swarms, and she saw as a victim too. Because that boy had lain on the broken pavement, suffocated by fear and the sharp metallic scent of his father's blood and been too scared to move, too scared to get help. But what he hated more was the thought of becoming that boy again.

Confused, terrified, defenceless.

She stood too, and came to stand in front of him, her eyes brimming with tears. Tears he was sure now he did not deserve.

'Logan, please don't be scared,' she said, her voice breaking as she touched his cheek. 'But I think I've fallen in love with you.'

He jerked his head back, the leap in his heart at her words swiftly followed by that crippling fear. Visions swirled into his mind, so close to the surface now he couldn't control them at all any more… The sweet, sickening aroma of death and day-old garbage, the violent shouts, the pounding rain, the cold weight of his father's body.

'I have to work,' he said, his voice barely audible, the present and the past combining as the suffocating feeling pressed in on him, like cold water closing over his head.

He walked out, aware of her standing alone in the kitchen.

He stayed all day in the workshop, working on the eagle, determined to close himself off, to rebuild the wall he had relied on for so long, so he would never have to remember that night again, and his part in his parents' deaths.

But when he found her in his bed, after a day spent trying to contain the fear, control the yearning, she responded to his touch with fierce passion, gave herself up to the driving need with unquestioning generosity. And he knew there would be no going back to that time when he had been able to protect himself from the broken parts of himself with denial.

So he took what she offered, and tried to convince himself he could keep her, as long as he never let her see the broken boy again, who he was terrified now would always lurk inside the man.

CHAPTER ELEVEN

CARA CLUNG TO Logan as the snowmobile trundled over the packed snow. She had to keep her head tucked into his spine, the icy wind biting the few spots of exposed skin. And keep her eyes firmly closed, so as not to encourage the tears that had been locked inside her heart for the past two days.

She'd told him she was falling in love with him. And he'd walked away from her.

She'd spooked him. In fact, he'd barely spoken to her since that morning.

She shouldn't have blurted it out like that. Shouldn't have burdened him with her feelings. Especially as it was obvious now he did not share them.

She'd wanted to help him, the way he'd helped her. She'd seen his pain, his trauma, understood a little more about why he had lived alone for so long when he'd spoken of his parents' deaths in that flat, raw voice. And her heart had broken for him.

Logan Colton, for all his wealth and self-sufficiency, his strength of character and carefully controlled emotions, was terrified of life. Of love. Of feeling too much. Of becoming that terrified child again. She got that now.

But that didn't mean he loved her. Nor did it mean she could change the course he'd set for his life, especially if he didn't want to change it.

And by locking himself in his workshop for the last two days, he'd made that very clear.

She'd debated whether to stay in his bed, had considered returning to the guest room she'd slept in when she'd first arrived. But ultimately, she'd been unable to take that final step. Because it had seemed pointless and self-defeating.

If all they could have was the sex—she'd take it. But each time he made love to her without a word, thrusting heavily inside her, bringing her to one shimmering orgasm after another—teasing and tormenting and provoking her, using all the skills they'd learned together over the last two weeks as if he wanted to bind her to him—she'd felt him pulling further away emotionally.

And she'd let him. Because what right did she have to ask more of him than he was willing to give?

She had no idea where he was taking her now—because he hadn't told her and she hadn't asked. But when he'd told her to be ready to leave at noon this morning, she hadn't argued with him.

The journey seemed to go on for ever, giving her far too much time to think of how she could have done things differently.

But as she held him, far too aware of the tensing and flexing of his muscular body through the layers of winter clothing, she couldn't find an alternative narrative that would give her the result she wanted.

Maybe she'd been a fool to lose her heart so quickly to a man who guarded his own emotions so fiercely. But she couldn't regret it. The last two weeks had been life-affirming in so many ways. She had never realised until this past week how scared she'd been to risk a relationship, because of the way her father had behaved. She'd taken so many risks to make her career a reality, while all the time denying or burying her emotional needs. She wouldn't do that any more. She had so much to give, so much to discover. And Logan had been responsible for luring her out of hiding. Her heightened emotions were just something she would have to learn how to manage when this was over.

At last, the snowmobile climbed out of the forest and headed across another frozen lake system. As the sun dipped towards the treeline on the other side of the ice, it highlighted a structure built on the opposite bank. As they got closer, she realised it was an A-frame cabin, constructed in wood, with a deck that would sit over the water in the summer months. Woodsmoke trailed up into the turquoise sky from a chimney in the peaked roof, and the glass frontage sparkled in the dying light.

As the snowmobile headed towards the ridge, her heart sank. Was this where he intended to leave her? With strangers? But as they drew closer, no one appeared from inside the house.

Logan parked the snowmobile in front of a garage, then pushed up his goggles as he looked over his shoulder.

'We stay here tonight,' he said.

She hated the way her heart rose into her throat, the stupid bubble of hope that had never completely died expanding in her chest.

Maybe this wasn't the end after all? If they had one more night together?

He swung his leg over the machine and dismounted, then helped her down from the saddle. Her legs were stiff and cold after the long ride and she stumbled.

'Easy,' he said and scooped her into his arms.

She marvelled, not for the first time, at his strength as he carried her effortlessly into the house.

As soon as they entered the well-insulated room, he put

her down. Warmth hit her tired body. A woodburning stove blazed in the centre of the open-plan space—which was equipped with a small kitchen and rustic but finely made furniture. She recognised the work as Logan's.

She could see a mezzanine level with a beautiful hand-carved bed covered in an embroidered quilt. Solar-powered fairy lights glowed through the glass spotlighting a hot tub on a platform outside and making it look like an enchanted bower.

The whole place was impossibly romantic. Why had he brought her here?

As they shrugged off their layers, she tried to figure out what to say, where to begin.

'Who lives here?' she asked finally.

He sent her a quizzical look. 'It is mine. I built it. I paid a contact to prepare it for us. There is stew for to-night and wine.'

'But why?' she asked.

Today was supposed to be their last day together. Was this a farewell, or more than that?

The bubble of hope died though, when he stripped off the last of his outer layers, and she noticed the prominent ridge in his ski-pants—which was always there when they were together, it seemed.

Of course, he'd brought her here for one more night of 'exploring their sexual connection'—which had been his purpose all along. She was the one who had lost sight of that, not him. She was the one who had wanted to build more than just a sexual relationship.

'There is something I wish for you to see,' he said, cryptically. But then he picked up the camera case she had brought in with her and pulled out her Leica. 'Do you have space on the memory card?'

She frowned, surprised to see him handle the camera without sneering. She nodded. She'd spent the last few days checking through all the shots and deleting any she didn't wish to download when she returned to Saariselkä.

'Good,' he said. And passed her the camera. 'You will need it.'

He strolled to the kitchen area and produced a casserole dish from the fridge. He set it on the woodburning stove. After stoking the fire, he peered out across the lake at the gathering darkness. 'We have an hour before it's dark enough.'

For what?

Before she could ask, he added, 'Do you want to use the hot tub while we wait?'

The intensity in his gaze, the dark arousal in those pure blue eyes, warm now with a need he couldn't hide, told her all she needed to know about what he planned to do to her there. Perhaps she should say no, tell him she wanted a clarification of where they stood. Was this their last night or wasn't it?

But somehow, she didn't want to ruin this new truce. Didn't want to think about the future. She was tired of pondering what might have been. Wouldn't it be better to stay in the now? To enjoy the moment, to enjoy what they *did* have, and live the pipe dreams she'd weaved about them one last time before they could be dashed tomorrow? They'd built something precious over the past two weeks. Even if it was only a sexual connection for him it was so much more for her. And here was her chance to own it and enjoy it for a few more hours at least.

She loved him. And she didn't want to hurt him. Didn't want to press and probe at wounds that clearly hadn't healed. And might never heal.

She forced a smile to her lips, grasped his shoulder and bounced into his arms. He grunted and caught her, the fire in his eyes dancing as she wrapped her legs around his waist.

'Absolutely, but only if you join me there.' She swept her gaze over the dramatic sweep of his brows, the high cheekbones and day-old stubble that made him look so breathtakingly wild and untamed.

You tamed him for two whole weeks, Cara Doyle. And he's still yours tonight.

'Try to keep me away,' he said and let out a gruff laugh as he captured her lips with a hunger she adored, as if no other woman existed.

Was it any wonder she'd fallen for this bold, unknowable, insatiable man—who made her feel so alive and unashamed?

As he tugged off the last of her clothing and his own, then carted her outside and dropped her into the gloriously hot water, she forced herself to revel in the moment, to let the snow-laden beauty of the forest night add to the adrenaline rush of making love to him in the crisp winter light, and not to think of the empty space in her chest.

Or what tomorrow might bring.

'There, can you see them?' Logan whispered, pointing over Cara's shoulder, feeling her body still beneath his as they lay in the hide he'd built especially to view the wildlife a few years before. A hide he had never imagined wanting to share with anyone.

Her awed gasp had emotion tightening his ribs as she spotted the wolves silhouetted against the leap of coloured lights on the forest ridge. Turquoise blue and a flicker of iridescent pink edged the pulsing emerald as the aurora borealis swirled and shimmered, cutting across the inky, star-studded night and providing the perfect backdrop to the hunting pack.

'Oh, Logan, that's… Absolutely stunning,' she murmured. 'They're all white.' He could feel her excitement as she lifted the camera to her face and began clicking off shots from their vantage point. 'I've never seen a pack like it before. Are they all albinos?'

'No, they are a rare subspecies, all but extinct now,' he murmured.

His grandfather had told him as much when he'd spotted a pack like this as a teenager.

Wolf populations were growing in the south and east of Finland, with around two hundred of them now living in the wild—the tourist board even arranged photography trips so visitors could view them. But no one would ever see these wolves—and he'd wanted her to have this.

The alpha female paused and turned as if sensing their presence, then stretched her head towards the sky and howled, galvanising her pack for the hunt as a moose crashed through the trees in front of them, obviously scenting the wolves' presence. For several seconds, the lead wolf's snowy fur—usually camouflaged by the winter landscape—was aglow with the green and blue lightshow above her.

The natural wonder of the wolf though was nothing compared to the sight of Cara, eagerly photographing her and her pack. Not to Logan. He lay still and watched her face, the slight frown of concentration, the ice that had formed on her lashes as they waited, the glow of excitement in her eyes lit by the Northern Lights as she worked tirelessly to capture the pack before they dashed past the ridge chasing their prey.

He thought of the sight of Cara earlier in the hot tub, as she rode him, her body bowing back, her skin alive with sensation, her face a picture of ecstasy as she came. And later as he washed her in the cabin's shower and she gave herself to him again, without holding back. And without demanding more from him.

And he knew he couldn't lose her, couldn't let her go. Not yet.

The pack and their prey disappeared into the trees, and she flopped over onto her back, her face lit by the ethereal lights of the Lapland night.

She lifted her gloved hand to his face, her eyes glowing with achievement. 'Wow, Logan. Just wow,' she whispered, her voice muffled by her scarf. 'Thank you for giving me this.'

He could see the love and trust that had scared him so fundamentally two days ago. And suddenly he knew how to make her stay. What he could give her without exposing himself any more than he already had.

There was a way to make this work. All he'd had to do was find it.

He nodded and pressed a kiss to her nose. Then crawled out of the hide and dragged her out with him. 'Come, it is time to eat. And get warm again,' he said, eager to get back to the cabin and tell her his plan.

His heart skipped a beat when she laughed and murmured, 'Oh, goody. Getting warm with you happens to be one of my favourite pastimes.'

'If you stay with me, there is much you can photograph. The wildlife on my land has been untouched for generations.'

'Stay? With you?' Cara murmured as she placed the

wine glass on the small table at the side of the bed, shocked not just by Logan's offer, but the casual way he made it.

She turned in his arms, so she could see his face, the harsh planes and angles lit by the firelight below them.

They'd made love again after supper, long, slow, lazy love, her excitement at the shots she'd taken only tempered by the thought of what the morning would bring. But as they'd sat on the bed, her wearing his boxer shorts and an undershirt, him in just his shorts in the warm room, sipping the last of the bottle he'd produced to go with the stew, she'd been unable to keep the empty space at bay.

Until this moment.

Anticipation dried her throat.

But then he nodded, placing his own glass beside hers, cupping the back of her neck, and brushing his thumb over the thundering pulse point.

'Yes. Stay,' he said.

The wave of emotion gathered in her chest then barrelled through her tired body. She'd hoped for such an offer, but she hadn't really expected it.

'I cannot lose you,' he said, the emotion in his voice matching her own as his eyes searched her face. This wasn't just hunger, it was affection, caring, much more than a physical connection just as she'd hoped. 'Not yet.'

Not...*yet*?

The single word echoed through her, bringing a discordant note to the symphony of joy and excitement.

The bubble in her chest deflated as what he was really offering her became clear. A relationship on his terms. An arrangement such as the one they already had, which involved her living a life of exile—and never probing too much, so he never had to face his demons.

'What do you say, Cara? Will you come home with me?'

he asked, taking her hand in his and lifting her trembling fingers to his lips.

The yes lodged in her heart sat on the tip of her tongue as he kissed her palm. But somehow, she couldn't seem to utter it.

She tugged her hand free and fisted it in her lap, shifting away from him on the bed, suddenly knowing she couldn't give him what he wanted, or she would lose herself in the process.

'I... I don't know if I can,' she said, hating the words and the need to say them.

'Why not?' he asked, tilting his head to one side as he studied her, the way she'd seen him study one of his sculptures. As if she were a puzzle to be solved. 'You would be able to build your career as a photographer. Is this not what you want?'

'But how? How would I be able to show my work or sell it, even?' she asked.

It wasn't just that his home was isolated, that he had no Internet as far as she knew. He hadn't left his land in years. But more specifically, he hadn't let her in, not really.

She didn't expect him to give up his isolation. Nor did she expect a declaration of undying love.

They'd only known each other for two weeks. And she knew the last fortnight had been tumultuous for him too, as well as her. Maybe *too* tumultuous.

But she needed something, a sign that there could be more eventually. That he was committed to making this a real relationship, at some point in the future. That he was prepared to bend for her, too? That he wouldn't close her out of his heart for ever.

'There are ways, we could figure it out,' he said. 'I sell my work to a gallery in New York through a subsidiary.'

'But I would have to leave occasionally, Logan. The wildlife here is incredible and I would love to spend time observing it and photographing it, but if I'm really going to make a career, a living, out of my work I can't limit myself to one location.' She sighed. 'Especially not while I'm trying to establish myself. And I'd want to go to Ireland to see my family, too.' Maybe she hadn't been to see them in over a year, but did he realise what he was asking of her? 'Is that what you want?'

He frowned and she could see he hadn't considered the ramifications of what he was offering her. And what he wasn't.

'I have a lot of money, Cara...' He huffed out a breath. 'You would not need to support yourself, while you were with me,' he said. 'There would be no need to leave. And if you must see your family, I would figure out how to do that.'

Her heart broke at the rough emotion in his voice. And the dark intensity in his eyes.

'It's not about money, Logan.'

His frown deepened. 'Then what is it about?'

She got off the bed, wrapped her arms around her waist as she stared out into the night. The Northern Lights still flickered on the horizon, the magical play of colours over the forest so beautiful it hurt.

But the life he lived here wasn't a real life. Not for her. She would tumble the rest of the way in love with him, sink so deep she could never get out again. He would bind her to him, with sex and affection—something she had yearned for without even realising it—and she would want to save him. Just as her mother had once wanted to save her father, from the demons that had turned him into a cruel and bitter man.

Logan wasn't cruel or bitter. He was a good man, even a tender man in his own way. Forceful and possessive in another. But he was a damaged man.

A damaged man who had no desire to face his demons either. She wasn't even sure he understood that he had demons too. How much good would she really be doing him by helping him avoid them?

She heard him come off the bed behind her. He stroked her hair, then banded his arms around her waist and pressed his face into the back of her neck.

She leaned back against him, because she couldn't seem to stop herself.

It felt so good to be in his arms, so right. But how could it be, when he was still hiding from the world, and he wanted her to hide too?

'Don't complicate this, Cara, when it can be simple,' he said. 'You said you loved me, why is this not what you want?'

She spun round, her heart cracking open in her chest at the forthright expression on his face. 'Logan, you have refused to talk to me for two days... And you still can't bear to be around people. Can't you see why that's a problem?'

'No.' He shrugged. 'Because all that matters is that I can bear to be around you.'

She pushed her hair out of her eyes, agitated now, and heartsore. And desperately frustrated with the intractable expression on his face. He wasn't listening to her, because he chose not to.

'But can't you see, if I went back with you, if I lived with you, I'd want to talk about everything,' she said, trying one last time to make him understand. 'Because I'd want to know you, *really* know you.' She cupped his cheek, felt the muscle bunch under her palm as he stared back at her. 'Not just who you are now, but also that little boy, who you're still punishing.' He flinched, but she forced herself to continue. 'And I'd want you to know me. All my flaws and weaknesses. As well as my strengths. Because love is curious and demanding, emotionally as well as physically. Can't you see that?'

He placed his hand over hers, pulled it away from his face then said softly, 'Why does it need to be, when what we have is already so good?'

Good for you, she thought, and the ripple of bitterness was surprising, but there, nonetheless. Couldn't he give her anything? Not even an indication that with time things might change?

'You're asking me to give up too much, Logan. I'd lose myself, and my independence. One day, I might want to have children, a family of my own...' It wasn't something she was thinking of right this minute, but when she felt him stiffen, she suddenly understood. He wasn't going to budge about any of it.

'*Might* is not important,' he said, grasping her elbow, pulling her against his body. 'Nothing in life is guaranteed. We have only the now. What we feel, what we want. And I want you and you want me. That is enough.'

It was hopeless. Logan was a fatalist, a man bound to his past. Who couldn't break those chains. Wasn't even prepared to attempt to break them.

'I can't live like that, Logan, I won't.'

'Really?' he asked. 'You would deny us both this?' he said, then covered her mouth with his, kissing her with the furious hunger she recognised. And responded to always.

Her body quickened as he grasped her bottom, thrust the thick erection in his shorts against the melting spot between her thighs, rubbing her clitoris with expert intensity through the thin layers of cotton. His fingers sank beneath the waistband of her shorts, finding the slick nub and working it with ruthless efficiency.

She gasped, sobbed, the brutal climax already too close.

'You are wet for me, always, Cara,' he said, his lips devouring her throat as she rode his fingers, unable to deny his mastery over her body. Or the tearing pain in her heart.

Somehow she managed to scramble back, to push him away. 'Don't, Logan.'

He stopped instantly, his face flushed, his eyes dark, the muscle in his jaw clenching.

'It won't work, not again,' she said, even as her body yearned for him. 'Sex isn't the answer—not this time. I need more than that. If you can't give it to me, that's okay. I understand. But I can't stay with you on your terms.'

He grunted as pain slashed across his face. He turned away from her, to stare out at the night sky, his arms crossed over his broad chest, his breath heaving. Everything inside her gathered. The stupid, foolish hope building again. Maybe, just maybe, she had broken through to him, to the man she suspected lay beneath that wall... The man she'd had tantalising glimpses of over the past two weeks. The man who enjoyed her company, who wanted to please her, and protect her, who she knew would be lonely without her... The man who had denied himself so much because he blamed himself for his parents' deaths.

But as the seconds ticked past, she saw the veil come down again. His breathing evened out, and his arms relaxed, to fall back by his side. And when he finally turned back towards her, the need, the desperation, the confusion were gone, until all that was left was the same implacable mask—tinged with impatience and frustration—she remembered from when she had first met him. He had retreated back into the shell where she couldn't reach him.

He nodded. 'I will sleep downstairs. We can talk again in the morning.'

It was a dismissal. Maybe even an ultimatum. But as he walked away, picking up his clothing to take the stairs to the living area below, she didn't stop him.

Talking more tonight was pointless. She was over-emotional. And they were both on edge, both tired, and when you factored in that endless hunger that never seemed to die between them, and his determination to use it against her... She wrapped her own arms around her body as she heard him making up a bed for himself on the sofa downstairs.

She crawled under the embroidered quilt, curled up in a ball, taking in a lungful of his clean fresh scent, bergamot and pine, rubbing her thighs together to ignore the sensation still humming at her core, where he had touched her with such purpose, such skill.

The low howl of a wolf in the distance cut through the crackle of the fire from downstairs and the thunder of her own heartbeat as she closed her eyes. And squeezed them tightly shut around the stinging tears.

Maybe tomorrow, once they'd both slept, she could reason with him again. She wasn't giving up, not yet. Not entirely.

But her heart felt unbearably heavy, as she finally drifted into a fitful sleep.

CHAPTER TWELVE

*Your snowmobile is in the garage. It is fuelled and
has a GPS to guide you to Saariselkä. Leave early
and do not travel at night. If you change your mind,
I will be waiting.*

*Contact Grant.Andrews@ColtonCorp.com and he
will arrange everything. But until then tell no one
of our time together.*
    Logan

A TEAR BURNED Cara's cheek as she stared at the note left
on the coffee table. She brushed the moisture away with
her fist. The empty living area, which had seemed so romantic last night, now felt vacant and oppressive.

She walked onto the deck and spotted the empty space
where Logan had parked his snowmobile the day before.

Logan was gone. He must have left early, before she
had woken up. And all she had of him now was this curt
message.

Hopelessness opened like a black hole in the pit of her
stomach.

If you change your mind, I will be waiting...

A part of her wanted desperately to cling to that phrase. He had given her a chance to rewrite last night's argument—and get to the outcome they both wanted. To be together.

But as she sucked in an unsteady breath, trying desperately not to dissolve into tears, the pain in her chest refused to ease.

Because he hadn't given them a chance. Not really. What that phrase really meant was either you do this on my terms, or not at all.

But it was worse than that, because she knew the next few days and weeks, even months, were going to be torture—as she forced herself to resist his invitation.

She was going to miss him, so much. Miss him and the intense time they had spent together. Alone. In his stunning home on the edge of the world.

Not just the moments when he had given her more pleasure than she had realised she was capable of, hell, had even known existed before he had touched her, and tasted her. But also, those moments out of bed, as they prepared meals together or enjoyed the silence. The rush of ice swimming with him. Even the passion and anger of the arguments they'd had felt more real, more intense, than anything she'd ever experienced. She'd miss his home, too, that open, airy space, which should have felt like a prison, but never had. She'd loved the moments when she simply took the time to absorb the stillness, watching him work with those capable, skilled hands, carving something beautiful and compelling from the wood. The husky rumble of his voice as he teased or cajoled her, discovering a boyish side to his nature she was sure he'd never realised was there before her.

They had been good for each other. In so many ways.

Because Logan hadn't been the only one living in isolation. The only one who had been lonely and alone before they'd met.

She left the note on the table, swallowing past the huge constriction in her throat. And let out a shout of frustration—that no one could hear but her.

Damn it, how could she hate him and love him at the same time?

She forced herself to put on her outdoor layers, to douse the fire in the wood burner, and leave the cabin, closing the door behind her firmly—even if she knew she would never be able to close out all the memories.

She found her snowmobile in the garage—repaired, just as he had promised her two weeks before. It occurred to her he must have arranged to have the machine brought here so he could avoid having anyone visit his home...

But when?

Had he always intended to use his invitation as an ultimatum? To discard her if she didn't agree to his terms? Or had last night's invitation been an impulse that he had regretted?

She opened the garage door, climbed onto the machine. As soon as she turned the key in the ignition, the well-oiled hum of the engine—so different from the ominous rattle it used to have whenever she started it—suggested no expense had been spared making it roadworthy again.

She gulped down a sob. Why did the thought of the effort he had made to prepare for her departure only make this that much harder?

She shoved the goggles down, twisted the accelerator and drove the machine out of the garage. She turned on the GPS tracker attached to the machine's handlebars.

Three hours, the route said.

But somehow she knew it would take her a great deal longer to leave this cabin, this forest, and her time with Logan Colton behind. Maybe even for ever.

As she headed south, following the route round the lake, past the place where they had huddled together waiting for the wolfpack the night before, she felt a part of her heart being torn away, and left behind her bleeding in the snow...

She arrived at the outskirts of Saariselkä nearly four hours later. Night was already closing in. The lights that lit the resort town made the snow-covered streets sparkle. She was exhausted, in mind and body and spirit, as she pulled up to the hotel where she had been working before she'd left two weeks ago to photograph the lynx. But as she turned off the ignition and dragged her camera box out of the saddlebag, she noticed the flashing lights of several police cars and one of the forest ranger's trucks parked by the entrance.

Odd.

The region only had a small police presence, and the nearest station was over two hours' drive away. She didn't think she'd ever seen a local cop in the town the whole six months she'd lived here.

She trudged to the hotel's entrance, but as she ripped off her head coverings on entering the building, the warmth enveloping her, she spotted a tall man with dark wavy hair standing by the reception desk flanked by a couple of policemen and the local ranger. His voice hit her first as he remonstrated with the cops.

Recognition streaked through her. 'Kieran?' she gasped. What on earth was her oldest brother doing in Lapland?

He swung round.

'Cara!' He rushed towards her, then grasped her arms, the wild panic in his eyes making her touch his cheek. To soothe. Kieran was a rock, he never got over-emotional, but right now he looked a wreck.

'You're here, you're okay,' he murmured as the police followed him across the lobby. As well as a middle-aged woman, who began to snap photos with her phone.

'What's wrong, Kieran?' she asked, frantic herself now. 'Is it Mam?'

'No. Are you mad?' He swore, the panic turning to fury in a heartbeat. 'It's you. We've been searching for you for days now. You didn't call Mam for two weeks. We were frantic.'

'But I told her, I was taking time out to work on my portfolio,' she said, her mind reeling.

She usually called her mammy once a week, but she'd missed the scheduled phone call before. It had never occurred to her that her family would take on so.

'But where have you *been*?' he shouted, his fingers digging into her biceps, as if he was scared to let her go in case she disappeared. 'They found no trace of your vehicle and you haven't been back here in over two weeks.'

'Miss Doyle…' The older of the two policemen—who had a bold silver strip on his dark blue snowsuit—intervened. 'We began the search two days ago, at your brother's request. We were about to bring in the army,' he added in perfect English, despite the Finnish accent. 'Can you tell us where you have been residing over the past sixteen days? Have you been kept against your will?'

'No, I… No, I haven't been kept against my will,' she said, evasively, remembering Logan's request. She didn't want to reveal his whereabouts. To anyone.

But then the policeman frowned and her brother said,

'Then where the hell have you been, Cara? Because we know you haven't been here.'

'I… I can't tell you,' she managed. Her brother swore, while concern darkened the policeman's penetrating stare.

'Why can you not tell us, Miss Doyle?' he asked again, in that patient tone.

'I just… I can't say, but I was fine. Really. It was my choice.'

'Cara, this is nonsense,' her brother announced, his temper igniting. Although she didn't blame him. He must think there was something up.

'Mr Doyle, you must remain calm,' the policeman added. 'Your sister is well and found. These are just follow-up questions that—'

'Were you with Logan Colton, the sole heir to the Colton empire?' The probing question shot out of left field, but the guilty blush had suffused Cara's face before she could even register it had come from the woman who had been hovering nearby and was still taking photos.

'I… I'm not answering that,' Cara blurted out, then realised how incriminating that sounded. Her answer only seemed to encourage the woman—who Cara suddenly realised had to be a reporter.

'What's he like, Cara?' The journalist clicked an app on her phone then shoved it in Cara's face, her eyes glowing with excitement. 'Is his home as stunning as they say? Is *he*? You know he hasn't been seen in public since he was a boy of ten? And he witnessed his parents' brutal murder.'

'Get away with you,' Kieran announced, trying to shield Cara from the woman's aggressive questioning, just as the policeman took her other arm.

'Miss Doyle, let us take you to a more private place,' he said, but as he led her away she knew it was already too late. The reporter was dictating the exclusive story into her phone—throwing out words like 'billionaire recluse' and 'kidnap victim' and making Cara want to fold in on herself and disappear.

The exhaustion and sadness clamped down on her heart, making her feel even more alone, and far away from Logan. As if she'd travelled a million miles today, instead of under a hundred.

She would never be able to go back to him now.

Why hadn't she tried harder to win his trust? Before she had betrayed it so comprehensively?

The story broke in the Finnish press the next morning, and had been splashed all over the Internet by lunchtime. By nightfall, the hotel in Saariselkä had been besieged by photographers and reporters and celebrity journalists from all over the globe, trying to get an interview or even a glimpse of the woman who had been 'trapped in Colton's love nest' or 'kidnapped by a reclusive billionaire' or 'the first clue in decades to a billionaire enigma' depending on your news source of choice.

The whole thing felt unreal to Cara. Only twenty-four hours ago she'd been in Logan's arms. And now it felt as if her life had become disconnected from reality, because she was sleepwalking through a nightmare she couldn't escape.

Knowing that she was the focus of a media storm—that she couldn't even leave the hotel—was only one aspect of the nightmare though. Because her appearance from no-where, after two weeks in the wilderness, had triggered a hunt for the location of Logan's home.

He'd managed to stay safe from scrutiny by keeping under the radar. There had been whispers that he was liv-ing in Finland, but nothing concrete, and she knew what lengths he'd gone to, to keep it that way. Now she had effectively outed him by default, she knew he would not be able to stay hidden for much longer—without hiring an army to protect himself, and that would defeat the purpose because he would no longer have his solitude.

She felt sick to her stomach, had been unable to eat or sleep for twenty-four hours. But even so, she had refused to talk to the police. Logan had done nothing wrong, and neither had she, so she owed them no more of an explanation than she owed the press.

Eventually the police had left.

Her brother Kieran, however, had been far more persistent.

'Why won't you talk to me, Car?' he said, stalking across the suite she had been given by the hotel for her own protection.

'*If* he didn't hurt you,' Kieran added, raking his hair with impatient fingers, '*if* he didn't kidnap you, why won't you tell me what happened while you were with him?'

She'd told him nothing, she hadn't even mentioned Logan's name, but that hadn't stopped Kieran from jumping to all sorts of ludicrous notions.

'I'm not talking about it, Kieran, because it's none of your business. Nor is it anyone else's. It's private.'

'He's one of the richest men in the US. ColtonCorp has been a *Fortune 500* company for two generations. If he exploited you, we should demand compensation. Damages.'

She jumped up from her seat by the window, where she had been watching the press horde amassing all day. 'We'll demand nothing from him. He owes me nothing. He saved my life, so I'll not be paying him back by suing him,' she cried out.

'So you *were* with him. The reporter had the right of it.' Kieran's eyes narrowed.

Her bastard brother had tricked her into admitting the truth.

She slumped back in the armchair. Defeated. 'If you say his name to anyone, Kieran, I'll murder you,' she hissed, but she could hear the weary resignation in her own voice.

Enough to know it was an empty threat. She was too tired, too devastated to do anything.

He knelt down beside her armchair, rested his hands on the arms of the chair. 'Just tell me, Cara, did he hurt you?'

She shook her head, wiped away a tear. A pointless, self-pitying tear. 'No. He saved me, I told you.'

'Then why are you crying?' he asked, his voice gentle now, coaxing and full of the concern that made her feel like a little girl again, after being called names by their da.

Kieran had always been the one to come and tell her it meant nothing. To hold her and keep her safe. But as she turned to him, wanting to be held, to be reassured, she knew the only person who could do that now was Logan.

And he would never want to see her again. Not when the swarms of reporters and photographers found his home—which was surely only a matter of time.

'Because I love him, and I've destroyed his life,' she said simply.

She would have to leave Finland. The longer she stayed here, the more the story would grow. She'd had a lot of lucrative offers to buy her photographs, but she knew every one of them had nothing to do with the quality of her work and everything to do with her new-found celebrity—which meant she couldn't and wouldn't accept any of them.

By leaving Logan, she had destroyed the career she

had been so determined to save. It would be ironic, if it weren't so pathetic.

'Hey, sis,' Kieran murmured, pulling her into his arms and holding her as the sobs began to rack her body. The sobs she'd held in ever since the long drive back to Saariselkä. 'Don't take on so. None of this is your fault.'

Except it was her fault. She'd been a coward, scared to trust her love. Scared to give them a chance, scared to believe Logan could change, if she gave him time. And now he never would.

CHAPTER THIRTEEN

Three weeks later

'CARA, HEY. HAVE you seen today's headlines? Yer man is back in New York. It's all over the news.'

Cara lifted herself off the rocky ledge to see her middle brother, Connor, running up the bank towards her waving his mobile phone.

Her heart jolted in her chest. Her eyes burned.

Logan. He had to be talking about Logan.

She'd been avoiding the news ever since the press had finally left her alone, convinced at last that she had no intention of giving any exclusive interviews. And once 'Colton's Secret Lair' had been uncovered in Lapland, the press had switched their attention back to Finland.

So, Logan had finally been forced to return to the US, the place where he had only bad memories. Probably for his own safety.

Anger roiled in her gut, right alongside a wave of guilt. What gave those vultures the right to change his life? To force him out of his home? His sanctuary?

'I'm not interested, Connor,' she said, trying to convince herself it was true. 'He's not my man.' And he never really had been.

Connor let his phone drop, his breath heaving after the run up the hill from the farm.

'Well, you should be,' he said breathlessly. 'Because that's not all. Darragh has just phoned Mam,' he said, mentioning her youngest older brother, who worked at a bank in Wexford. 'The manager wanted him to inform you, there's been a huge deposit in your account. He says you should come in to speak to their investment advisors—as it makes no sense to leave it there.'

'What?' She stared at him blankly, not sure she'd heard that right.

'Darragh says it's millions of euros. It has to be coming from him, for sure,' he added as his lips tilted in a mischievous smile. 'Unless you've been trapped in some other billionaire's love nest we don't know about.'

'Oh, shut up, Connor.' She stalked past him, the nausea building under her breastbone.

Why would Logan give her money? It made no sense.

She dragged her phone out of her back pocket, switched it on. News notifications popped up, the headlines hitting her like bullets.

Billionaire Recluse Goes Home to the US

The Colton Orphan Returns from Lapland Exile

ColtonCorp Heir Outed as Celebrated Wood Sculpture Artist LAC

But the pictures were so much worse. Logan at JFK airport, his head covered, as he was rushed into a waiting limo with bodyguards either side of him surrounded by the press. All those people, so many people, how could he survive it after so long alone?

She sucked in a breath, covered her trembling lips with her hand as she clicked on a photo taken through the car window and enlarged it.

Her breath clogged in her lungs. The pain in her heart clawed at her throat.

His eyes were all wrong, the fierce silvery blue now cold and empty and devoid of expression. Like a wounded wolf, defending what little territory it had left.

The vultures had besieged him. Forced him to face the trauma he had spent years protecting himself against.

Just as you tried to do, Cara, because of some foolish notion you could make him whole. When he was already whole.

What Logan did now, what he was forced to do, was none of her business any more. She wiped away the errant tear that leaked down her cheek, like too many others in the past three weeks, and clicked on the home screen to her banking app.

She gasped as the balance displayed.

She'd been close to a thousand euros overdrawn yesterday. Now her account was in credit by… Her brain short-circuited as she tried to register the amount. How many zeros was that now?

Connor whistled beside her. 'Cara, that's ten million euros.' He grasped the phone, began clicking. 'Comes from a numbered Swiss account,' he said. 'No name. But it has to be him, right? Where else could it have come from?'

She took the phone back, feeling numb, the smell of the elderflowers starting to grow in the nearby hedgerow doing nothing to stem the nausea in her gut.

What was the money for? Her silence? The sex?

Why would he think he owed her anything at all?

And why hadn't he contacted her to tell her about the money? Did he hate her that much now? He couldn't even speak to her?

She'd received no messages from him, even though she'd been stupid enough to check the post and her emails every day, just in case. Stupid enough to hope, against all the odds, that he might reach out to her, might need her.

If you change your mind, I will be waiting.

The phrase echoed in her head, only making her heart hurt more. But it fuelled her anger too. Why did she have to be the one to make the move? Why did it have to be her decision to make, and not his?

'It doesn't matter where it comes from,' she said, slowly, carefully. Her heart pulsed so hard in her chest she was surprised it didn't burst through her ribs. 'Because I'll be sending it back.'

She headed back across the fields she'd spent three solid weeks wandering in like a ghost, feeling guilty and compromised and heartbroken and alone, anesthetising herself against the vivid emotions Logan had awakened.

But they weren't anesthetised any more.

Connor jogged alongside her. 'Are you an eejit? That's a fortune. You can pay off all your debts and work on your pictures again. Why would you be giving that back now?'

She gathered pace, the purpose she'd lacked for the past three weeks, ever since he'd left her with that damn note, finally returning. He'd given her over ten million euros, a ridiculous amount, but hadn't even bothered to contact her, to tell her what it was for. Was it a bribe? A payment for services rendered? Because whatever way she looked at it, it was insulting. To her and to what they'd had, what they'd built together over those two glorious weeks in Lapland.

'Because I don't want his money,' she said, feeling scared and raw still, but also fierce and increasingly furious. 'I want him.'

Logan stared out at the rocky outcropping and the bay beyond from the roof terrace of the Colton Mansion in Rhode Island.

Built in the Colonial style in the nineteen hundreds, as a summer residence for his robber baron great-grandfather, the house had sixteen bedrooms, ten bathrooms, indoor and outdoor pools, tennis courts, a golf course—now covered in a sprinkling of snow—and a stone guest house on the edge of the ten-acre property where he had been living since his return to the US three days ago.

But he couldn't sleep in the stone guest house, any more than he had been able to sleep in his home in Finland...

Everything here was different from the steel and glass structure he had built in Lapland. The ornate furniture that had been covered in dust sheets for over twenty years, until a week ago. The dull, expensive pieces of art his father's mother had packed the house with long before he was born. The carefully manicured lawns and gardens that had been cared for by a ground staff of forty people for twenty years while no one lived here.

Even the light was different from the light in the Arctic Circle, not clean and bright but dull and grey. There were no Northern Lights here, no flashes of brilliant colour amid the startling starry night...

He had run here, believing he could somehow escape the pain...

But here as in Finland one crucial thing was exactly the same.

There was no Cara.

He turned away from the view as he heard Colton-Corp's managing director, Grant Andrews, step out of the terrace doors.

'Logan, how are you doing?' the older man asked, his breath frosting in the winter air.

'Good,' he lied smoothly. He did not want any more sympathy. Or suggestions on therapists that could help him 'adjust to his new role'.

The truth was, he hadn't made the decision to return to the US because the press had finally discovered his home. He had already made up his mind—less than a day after leaving Cara at the cabin—that he couldn't live in Lapland any longer, because everything had changed.

And she was the cause.

What had once been his sanctuary, his fortress, had become a prison. Because he couldn't hear her voice, couldn't see or touch her, and yet her presence suffused every space, every room, every single scent and sound.

At first, he'd resented her. And blamed her for his misery, the loneliness that had never been a problem before she had appeared in his life.

Why hadn't she taken what he had offered? If she loved him, why wasn't she prepared to do anything to be with him?

Memories of her and their time together had tortured him—so he'd taken the decision to leave Finland. To come back, to prove that it had always been a choice to live in isolation, that she had been wrong to suggest there was something about the way he lived that needed to be fixed.

The only problem was, returning here hadn't made the misery stop. Hadn't filled the huge hole she'd left in his life. If anything, it had made it worse.

He still wanted her. Too much. But it wasn't just a physical yearning. It was far worse than that. She had somehow hijacked his mind, and his soul too.

He thought about her constantly. So much so that he'd had ten million euros deposited in her account in Ireland... And he wasn't even entirely sure why. Was it supposed to be a pay-off—because he'd had some vague notion of forcing her to sign an NDA, even though she hadn't spoken a word to the press about their time together?

Or was it even more pathetic than that. An attempt to force her hand, to get her to contact him, because he wanted her back, so much, but he had no idea how to reach out and ask her...beg her, even, to come back to him.

How could he have become so dependent on one person, in such a short space of time, after being alone—and happy—for so long?

Because you were never happy...you were hiding.

The damning truth whispered through his brain, making him tense as he followed Andrews back into the study and closed the terrace door. The study where he was supposed to be pretending to take an interest in a seminar on ColtonCorp's investment strategy for the next fiscal year— but which had begun to bore him in seconds.

The Colton Corporation had been managed well for twenty years by a board of trustees, and, whatever the press said, he had no intention of taking the helm. But, unfortunately, his work as a sculptor held no pleasure for him any more either.

His life was in flux. He had no purpose, and no interest in finding one any more.

All of which was Cara's fault too.

'I'm glad you're adapting,' Andrews said, although Logan could see wary concern in the man's eyes.

Grant Andrews had clearly been chosen by the board

several years ago to oversee ColtonCorp's vast investment portfolio because he was not an imbecile, and he knew how much Logan hated the press intrusion now he was back in the US…

What the man didn't know was that everything Logan had once feared so much—the loss of freedom, the press attention, the constraints on his movements, the constant social interactions that would push all the memories from the night his parents had died back to the forefront of his consciousness again—didn't scare him nearly as much now as the thought of spending the rest of his life alone. Without her.

'I left a couple of messages on your cell this morning,' Andrews said. 'But you didn't respond to them.'

'What messages?' Logan growled. 'I do not use the phone.'

Being constantly available and connected to other people by that thing was something he doubted he would ever get used to.

'Messages about Miss Doyle,' the man said.

The mention of Cara's name detonated in his chest like a nuclear bomb.

'Cara has contacted you?'

His MD nodded. 'Her bank returned the funds we transferred two days ago apparently. Although no one bothered to inform me until this morning. And I've just had an email from her, personally, demanding to see you.'

'What?' he said, his voice cracking on the painful burst of hope.

But the shock of hearing her name—and discovering she had not accepted his money—was nothing compared to the thought she might be nearby, close enough to touch.

'Cara is in the US?' he asked.

Grant nodded again but looked supremely uncomfortable. 'Actually, she's at the gatehouse. I spotted her as I drove up here. According to the guard, she's threatening to sue ColtonCorp if we don't let her in to see you. You need to make a decision, because if the press get wind of it, we'll be besieged again and we've only just got them off our back.'

Logan barely registered the last of the man's words though, because he was already charging towards the door of the study. His heart hammered his throat as adrenaline surged through his body, for the first time in over three weeks, ever since he had left her, lying in his bed. And he'd made the decision not to wake her. Not to try and persuade her to stay with him, one last time.

The wrong decision, he realised with a stunning burst of clarity.

He raced down the stairs, the sound of his footsteps echoing around the empty house, and threw instructions over his shoulder. 'Tell them to drive her to the house, then you must leave,' he managed as the combination of anger and hurt, guilt and desperation, threatened to strangle him.

She had come to him. And he would not give her a choice to leave him a second time.

He could not. He needed her. Now more than ever.

Because he couldn't function alone. Not any more.

He was only half a man—had *always* been half a man— without her. He knew that now. And he wanted to be whole again.

Cara climbed out of the car, not waiting for the security guard to open the door.

Nerves assailed her as a tall man in a business suit appeared from the imposing entrance to the huge mansion at the end of the spit of land.

The house, with its ornate gables and elegant, austere façade, was intimidating.

But not as intimidating as the man as he headed towards her across the frozen lawn.

Logan.

But not Logan. Not as she remembered him. This man was clean-shaven, his once long wavy hair shorn close to his head. And he wore a suit, the jacket lifting in the chilly wind, and flattening against his big body.

Her heart pulsed hard, battering her ribs, as he came close enough for her to register his expression. Not blank. Not the way it had been in the press photos she'd scoured a dozen times while on the budget flight to Boston she'd caught early this morning in Dublin.

It had taken her two bus rides to get here from Boston airport. Her stomach rolled over as she debated the wisdom of coming all this way. Of being so determined to see him again. She tried to find the fury that had gripped her two days ago, when she'd made the decision to come. But it had died during the long journey. Until all that was left was sadness, and confusion and guilt… And the endless regret.

He stopped in front of her. His jaw clenched tight as his gaze roamed over her.

Was that heat, longing, she saw in the steely blue? Or accusation?

A shiver ran through her, although she had on her winter coat. And was dressed a lot more warmly than he was. How could he look so invulnerable, dressed only in his indoor clothes?

He nodded to the security guard behind her, dismissing him. As the man left, and she heard the vehicle drive away, she wrapped her arms around her body, the chills running through her now not from the cold, but his fierce perusal.

He took her arm. 'Come inside, before you freeze,' he said. Her breath shuddered out as the familiar yearning pressed at her chest from his touch, but she didn't stop him as he led her into the house.

The place was enormous, the vaulted ceilings, the antique furniture, the sombre lighting, the smell of old wood and lemon polish, so different from the clean, unfussy lines and open airy spaces of his home in Finland.

She couldn't picture him here, not at all. Couldn't imagine he could be happy here.

But she forced herself not to say anything. His happiness was no longer her concern.

He led her into a library off the main hallway. The view across the sound through mullioned windows took in a pool, covered for the winter, and the rocky coastline, a private beach. She'd always know he was rich, but this was next level. And only intimidated her more.

'Cara?' he said, turning and propping his backside against the desk. He folded his arms over that broad chest, making her too aware of his body in the tailored suit. 'Why are you here?'

The direct question finally unlocked the blockage in her throat.

'The money. Ten million euros, Logan? What was it for?'

He sighed, then stared down at his shoes. Bright flags of colour hit his cheeks as he shrugged. 'I think,' he said at last, his gaze finally meeting hers again, 'it was an apology.'

She was taken aback, but only for a moment. 'An apology for *what*, Logan?' she cried, the anguish that she'd kept locked in her heart during the long journey making her voice crack. 'For letting me fall in love with you? For letting me ruin your life?' she asked, the tears stinging her eyes. The last of her anger crumbled, breaking open inside her... Because she'd never been angry with him. She'd only ever been angry with herself. Why hadn't she taken the risk? Gone back with him to his home? Taken a chance on love? Why had she needed guarantees? Why had she wanted him to change? They could have had a good life there, she could have pursued her photography, her passion and...

'If it hadn't been for me,' she said, 'you would still be in Lapland. Still be safe.'

'Stop.' He grasped her hand, yanked her into his body, then wrapped his arms around her. 'Stop, Cara. I was never safe there, I was simply hiding, because I was a coward. You were right.'

'That's not true, Logan.' She stared up at him, the fierce intensity in his eyes turning them to a pale, silvery blue. She could hear his heart beating as he dragged her against his chest. 'I was the coward,' she said as she burrowed into his warmth. 'I was the one who was too insecure to trust her own feelings. I'm the one who should apologise.'

She banded her arms around him, pressed her face into the clean linen of his shirt. Wanting to hold him for ever and never let him go.

'Why should you apologise,' he said, his voice husky with emotion, 'when all you did was make me face the truth?' He grasped her cheeks, dragged her face up. His gaze was so expressive, so full of feeling now, she felt her heartbeat gallop into her throat. 'I was terrified of living,' he added. 'Terrified of confronting the past. Terrified even of being touched. I shunned people because it was so much easier to be alone. So much simpler to avoid the emotion of others, when I could barely deal with my own.'

'Because you suffered a terrible trauma as a young child, Logan,' she interrupted him, unable to bear the self-disgust in his voice. 'You learned to cope the only way you could. There's nothing wrong with that,' she said, wanting him to see who she saw when she looked at him, not that broken child, but a strong, resilient man. 'It was wrong of me to make you think that wasn't enough.'

'Yes, I learned to cope... But at what cost?' He let out a harsh laugh, the sound painful, the shudder of emotion making her hold him tighter, trying to absorb the pain of that traumatised boy that swirled in his eyes. 'My solitude became my sanctuary for so long that, when my grandfather died, I did not want to return here...'

He looked around, the emotion in his gaze raw enough to make her shudder, but when his gaze met hers again, the turmoil had passed to leave only the bone-deep yearning that yanked at her own heart. 'But this is just a place, like any other.' He cupped her jaw. 'My grandfather helped me to cope, the solitude taught me how to heal. But *you*, Cara, you taught me how to live. I know this because, without you there, the silence became oppressive. The tasks I had once found so fulfilling no longer mattered to me. My bed was empty. But my life was emptier still. I even missed your inane chatter.'

'Inane chatter?' she asked, trying to sound offended, but unable to contain the joy spreading through her like wildfire—at the longing in his eyes he was making no effort to hide.

'Mostly...' His wry chuckle folded around her chest like a hug. 'I didn't come back here because the press found me. I came back to escape from the loneliness I found there without you.'

Her heart bounced in her throat, the bubble of hope becoming a boulder. 'Did you?' she murmured.

'The money was an apology,' he said again. 'An apology for leaving you that morning without a word. An apology for demanding you live in isolation with me. For pretending that all I ever wanted from you was sex. When there is so much more I need. An apology for leaving you to face those bastards alone. But the money was also a pathetic attempt to force your hand, to get you to acknowledge me...' He huffed. 'Because I was too much of a coward to contact you myself and beg you to come back to me.'

She reached up, and clasped his cheeks, pulling his lips to hers, then whispered against his mouth. 'Ask me again, Logan.'

'Stay with me, Cara?' he said, the questioning tone crucifying her.

'Yes.' She threw her arms around his neck, and as he grunted and grabbed hold of her instinctively she whispered in his ear. 'Now just see if you can get shot of me a second time.'

The snow fell in fat, heavy flakes outside, with night falling over the Colton Estate. But several hours later, as Logan lay on the library rug, drawing circles over Cara's naked hip as the firelight flickered over her pale skin, and she slept like the dead, he realised he had found a real sanctuary at last.

Because his sanctuary, his home, his safe place, wasn't in Rhode Island or Lapland, or anywhere in between, it would always be where this strong, smart, fierce, beautiful woman was—so close to his heart.

EPILOGUE

Eighteen months later

CARA STARED AT the two clear blue lines on the pregnancy testing stick. Then pressed shaking fingers to her lips. She bit into her knuckles, hard enough to leave a mark—the tumultuous combination of shock and joy and panic impossible to contain.

She was pregnant, with Logan's baby. And she had absolutely no idea how he would respond to the news.

The last year had been nothing short of...*idyllic*. That wasn't to say they hadn't argued at times.

They were both strong-willed, determined individuals, who had never had to compromise their desires before now. So they'd clashed more than once in the last eighteen months as they adapted their lives—so that they could live together.

First there had been the argument about whether Logan needed some therapy. She'd won that one outright when he had struggled with the nightmares that had come back with a vengeance, after the press ordeal that had continued to rage on and off while they were living in Rhode Island.

Then they'd clashed about whether they should return to Finland. With him insisting he had no need to return to Lapland, even though she knew the opposite was true.

He had wanted to prove he could live with people, for her. But she could see the toll it took on him, not just the nightmares, but also the stress of living in a world where he was constantly 'available'. She'd eventually won that one too—by simply telling him the truth, that she wanted to return to the house in Finland as well. That her career required it, and so did his, because she knew he struggled to focus outside his workshop. And she loved the quietness, the solitude—and he was more than enough for her.

But even their disagreements had felt constructive—because they were the sort of wild, passionate arguments that always led to lots of great make-up sex.

But this news was different.

She glanced out at the landscape beyond the glass, the huge lake that surrounded their home on the edge of the forest. The cabin where they had used the sauna to warm up for their ice swimming now doubled as a storeroom for the kayak Logan had purchased recently for the campout they'd been planning ever since the snow had finally melted a few weeks ago.

In May, this far north, they now had over eighteen hours of daylight.

She pressed her shaky palm to her still flat stomach, realising that this baby would be born in February—while they were back in the grips of winter.

Their baby.

She let out a careful breath.

How did she broach the subject of a child with him, when they hadn't planned this? Hadn't even spoken of it… And he'd endured so much change already. For her.

She must have slipped up with the timing when she'd chosen to change her contraception. And all the spectacular make-up sex had done the rest.

The spurt of joy began to diminish. Considerably. As the panic and anxiety charged to the fore.

She didn't want to put any more pressure on him. He had worked so hard to exorcise the demons from his childhood, they both had. But how would he adapt to this new responsibility? What if he disappeared back into the shell he'd once used to protect himself from feeling too much…? And how did she deal with the fact that she didn't think she could give him a choice?

When her period hadn't arrived, the possibility of a pregnancy had slowly begun to dawn on her. And it hadn't taken her long to realise she wanted this baby.

She jumped when there was a knock on the door.

'Cara, what are you doing in there? If you wish to arrive at the campsite before nightfall, we must go soon. It is not safe to travel through the gorge at night,' he said in that typically protective tone.

'Okay, Logan. I'm coming.'

She dumped the stick in the waste bin. And washed her hands, still stalling.

When she finally got up the guts to leave the bathroom, he was gone. Probably finishing loading up their supplies for the camp-out they had arranged to observe the bears as they emerged from hibernation and began mating.

She finished packing her own backpack, then left the house. She trudged round the edge of the lake, but her steps slowed as she spotted him coming towards her. In a plaid shirt, worn jeans and work boots, the long hair she adored touching his shoulders, he looked more like a rugged mountain man than the heir to a billion-dollar fortune.

Her rugged mountain man.

You have to tell him you're pregnant now it's official.

He grinned, the spontaneous smile whenever he saw her

just one of the many changes from the guarded, wounded man she had first met. Changes she had come to adore.

Logan was so much more open now. He still hated to talk about his feelings... But at least he was no longer afraid to admit he had them.

She couldn't bear to risk losing that man, even a little bit.

He pressed his callused palm to her cheek, the unguarded affection in his eyes making her heart stutter.

'At last you are here,' he said, the amused frown making her own heart ache. 'The bears will not wait for ever, you know.'

She swallowed. She had to tell him now, before she lost her nerve. Whatever the consequences they would work through them, together, because that was their superpower now.

So as he leaned in to kiss her, she pressed her palms to his chest—the arousal something she didn't want to encourage... For once.

'Cara, what is it?' Logan asked as Cara pushed him away. And avoided his kiss. 'Is something wrong?' he asked, aware of the panic in his own voice. The panic he had kept ruthlessly at bay for close to a week.

Something wasn't right. Cara had been quieter than usual for days now. The inane chatter he loved drifting into silence too many times to count. Plus she'd made a trip to Saariselkä yesterday, and had insisted on travelling there without him.

She'd told him it was a routine meeting with the rep from the stock photography site she now supplied. But he suspected it had been more than that, because she had clung to him this morning, after they made love, so tightly, then disappeared into the bathroom.

She had been so excited about the camp-out they had planned to observe the bears. Until a week ago. But what had changed?

She blinked, and he could see guilt shadow her eyes.

'Whatever it is, you need to tell me,' he demanded now. She was scaring him.

The last year and a half, with her, had been the best eighteen months of his life. Bar none. Everything about her still fascinated and excited him. And there was nothing he would not do for her... Even agreeing to see that nosy shrink, who had forced him to talk about his feelings for hours on end.

He wasn't hiding any more, he was living. He had no fear of people now. Although he had no specific need to spend too much time with any of them. Except her.

Was that it? Had she begun to feel smothered? Her life curtailed by his need for solitude? This was precisely why he had not wanted to return to Finland full time, even though he had missed the quiet and serenity here. He hadn't wanted to risk the chance that she would feel suffocated.

But she had seemed to enjoy it here too. They had both become immersed in their work and building their life together. He hadn't seen the signs.

He cursed silently as she continued to look at him. Of course, he hadn't seen the damn signs. Because he was still learning. How to negotiate rather than demand. How to temper his desires, and adjust his own needs so he didn't risk overwhelming her.

But she had seemed as enthusiastic about their life here. How could he have been so wrong?

He watched her swallow, unable to stop himself from cupping both her cheeks now, from touching her.

She grasped his hands and pulled them away from her face. 'It's okay, Logan… It's… I don't want to scare you. But I have news that you might not… Well, you might not like.'

'Tell me,' he said, unable to keep the edge from his voice.

If she was going to tell him she was leaving him, he might have to kidnap her, he decided—completely irrationally—as the panic began to consume him.

'I'm pregnant,' she said.

'You're…*what*?' he rasped, not sure he had heard her correctly, even as the pressure in his chest released in a rush, to be replaced by the instinctive spurt of joy and excitement.

Had she just told him she was having his child?

His gaze dropped to her belly. Her very flat belly. As his hands lowered to bracket her hips the thought of seeing her become heavy with his baby, of watching it grow inside her, made the spurt of joy turn into something so strong and fluid and powerful he couldn't speak. He could only feel.

'I… I'm going to have your baby, Logan. I know it's not something we've talked about. If it's too much… If you don't want to become a father you have to tell me, and I hope we can figure it out together… But I want this baby, because this baby is part of us. And I love us so much…'

She was talking, babbling really. The chatter he loved was back. But it wasn't inane any more. It was filled with love and possibilities… So many glorious possibilities.

'Please, Logan, say something.'

He raised his head at last. And looked into her eyes, the smile spreading across his face like the sun that had risen early that morning and bathed the landscape in glorious light.

He couldn't talk though, because his heart was jammed in his throat. So he gave her an answer the only way he knew how.

He cradled her face, drew her into his embrace and captured her mouth. The kiss was hungry, famished, but as he fed on her sobs and sighs, felt the tension and guilt melt from her body, it also became full to bursting with hope and excitement and joy.

When they were finally forced to come up for air, he rested his forehead against hers. And wrapped his arms around her hips, until she could feel exactly how much he wanted her. Always. And for ever.

She had given him so much already…he had never believed there could be more. Who knew?

'I'll take that as a yes,' she said, and the laughter in her voice echoed in his heart.

* * * * *

IN BED WITH
HER BILLIONAIRE
BODYGUARD

PIPPA ROSCOE

MILLS & BOON

This book is for Julie Chivers,
for reasons including, but not limited to:

- Answering random and overly complicated contract
  and copyright queries

- Knitting in meetings

- Sharing your fantastical reading journey

- Supplying me with a carefully curated and constant
  stream of high-quality TikTok videos

- Unwittingly inspiring THIS WHOLE BOOK!

So thank you, Julie!
It's a pleasure being your friend.

PROLOGUE

LUCA CALVINO SAT trying not to stare at the man in the hospital bed attached to more monitors than Luca had seen in his entire life. That the man was Nate Harcourt, billionaire businessman and barely a few years from Luca's own age of thirty-three, was mildly disconcerting.

'It's not as bad as it looks.'

'It looks pretty bad,' Luca replied truthfully.

'It's not.'

'Okay.'

The private hospital in Switzerland was as luxurious as some of the finest hotels Luca had ever had the pleasure of staying in and the security was top-notch, as it should be. Large windows looked out onto a wintry forest fit for a fairy tale. Warm leather and wood accents decorated the room that might look like the lounge of some metropolitan apartment but hid almost half a million euros' worth of medical equipment to suit any emergency.

'Pegaso has a pretty impressive portfolio for such a young company,' Nathanial Harcourt said, bringing his attention back to the matter at hand.

'Is ten years that young?' Luca enquired with a hint of sarcasm, disliking that he was only slightly rising to the Englishman's bait.

'It is when you have a family business that spans four hundred.'

'Fair point,' Luca conceded. Until a year ago, Nathanial Harcourt had been the rising star of the business world. He might have come from so much family money it reeked of established nepotism, had what he'd done with it not become legendary. But then he'd disappeared off the face of the planet—reportedly to go and find himself in Goa.

This was a far cry from Goa.

'Cancer?' he asked, curious as to what Nate would choose to tell him.

There was a moment; an appraisal between two dominant men.

'Aneurism. Cerebral.'

Luca nodded, unable to stop his eyebrows rising in surprise and reassessing the man in front of him. The upper part of the hospital bed was raised, across which hung a half table on a metal arm that was doing an excellent job of supporting what looked like an office's worth of paperwork and a laptop within Nate's reach.

'Pegaso's revenue was significant last year, not such an easy thing to do in today's economic climate. You have contracts through the majority of mainland Europe with several businesses, including this,' Nate stated, his hand opened to gesture to the hospital they were in—a discreet medical facility that employed the best of the best to those who needed the utmost privacy. Luca knew this because, as Nathanial had noted, Pegaso oversaw the security of the entire facility.

'I'm familiar with my CV.'

'But you haven't managed to break into any English-speaking markets.'

'It's funny,' Luca said with a gentle shoulder shrug,

'I would have thought that as a businessman who sits on three boards, is the CEO of two more, and is *very* high up in your own family business, you'd have a little more common sense than to alienate someone you are about to ask a favour from.'

'It's not a favour, it's an offer.'

The discreet monitor trilled sharply and Luca didn't miss the wince of pain and the jerk of Nate's hand as if he'd wanted to press it against his head, but wouldn't concede to such an open display of pain. Stubborn. Luca could respect that.

'Spill, before it's time for more meds,' Luca said.

'It's not as bad as it looks.'

'Keep telling yourself that.'

Nate managed a smirk and the beeping on the monitor settled again.

'I need you to protect my sister.'

Nate pointed at a folder on the half table and Luca stood to retrieve it. He had no problem verbally sparring with the English billionaire, but he had no intention of degrading the man by making him reach for it himself. A cerebral aneurism was no joke.

Luca opened the folder: Hope Harcourt, twin sister of Nathanial Harcourt, twenty-nine years old, single, Director of Marketing for Harcourts, the world's leading luxury department store. He sat back, looking at pictures of a blonde with delicate features. Although Hope and Nathanial Harcourt were twins, there was no more than a normal sibling similarity between them. His eyes grazed over high cheekbones and fine hair, working hard not to be distracted by the bolt of attraction that struck him hard. He purposely ignored the dark, espresso rich eyes that seemed to pick at his focus and pushed aside the pictures and bio, to pick up the press articles in the back.

More Than Just a Pretty Face? Hope Announced as Harcourts' Marketing Director.

Luca scanned the next few headlines for lesser or increasing degrees of offensive misogyny, unsurprised that the by-line bore the same name.

Harcourt Fiancé Reveals Socialite's Deep Insecurities.
Harcourts' Flawed Diamond! The Truth Behind the Breakup.

Luca rode out the familiar burn of resentment towards the tabloids who would take advantage of anything and anyone for a scoop. But he also understood that for every journalist there was someone ready and waiting to reap the rewards.

'My sister gets hit pieces like this all the time.'

'So why now?'

'Because I'm…here. I can't protect her.'

For the first time since meeting Nate Harcourt, the frustration was genuine, the anger palpable.

'You want Pegaso to protect her from the press?' She wouldn't be the first woman to court the press to advance her career, sales or reputation, Luca mused. 'What makes you think that she would even want it?'

'Because she's not like that and because something's coming. I don't know what. But the shareholders at Harcourts are being tight-lipped and they've cut me out of the loop since they believe that I'm swanning around South West India trying to find my third eye.'

'Could you have told them the truth?'

Nate stared at him long and hard.

Luca nodded, understanding without the Englishman having to explain. He knew this world too. 'They would forgive ludicrous frivolity, but not a medical complication that could see you drop dead at any minute, putting stocks and shares at risk.'

Nate nodded as if satisfied that Luca had answered his own question correctly.

'My sister and I grew up in a nest of vipers, Calvino. It may not seem like it, but she's all alone out there and I can't be there to protect her from this.'

Luca could feel himself swayed by the sibling loyalty and reached into his pocket to start recording the conversation on his phone. 'Are there any specific threats we need to know about?'

'Simon Harcourt, for sure. He's our cousin. I've never been able to pin anything on him, but he's clever enough not to get his own hands dirty. And then there's the usual hangers-on, people after her money.'

'That happen a lot?' Luca asked, taking another look at the, quite frankly, beautiful woman in the pictures.

'There was an ex. I dealt with it.'

'Name?'

'In the file. But I dealt with it.'

'Sure you did,' Luca said, knowing it would get a rise out of the man who had a no-nonsense manner and a quick, dry wit he was beginning to like.

'I'd have thought you'd have more sense than to alienate someone who's about to do you a favour.'

'You're not doing me a favour, you're making me an offer,' Luca pushed back, a smile curving the edge of his mouth. 'I'll put a team together. We can be in play in—'

'You will handle this personally.'

'That's not going to happen.'

While his company was renowned for their careful handling of high profile, very public contracts, he personally didn't. Ever.

'It is. Because if you do this—if you, just you, handle this personally, as a *favour* to me—you will have the sole security contract for Harcourts. That's not just store presence, that's internal, industrial, cyber—and all of it international. You'll have the biggest first step into the English markets by any company ever. You'll be set for life.'

Nate Harcourt was offering him everything he needed to take Pegaso to the highest heights he could imagine. Luca looked at the black and white photo of a woman exiting the world-famous front doors of Harcourts, bag perched in the crook of a bent arm and large oversized sunglasses covering half of her face. How hard could it be?

'When do I start?'

'Christmas is only a few days away. Am I taking you away from your family?'

'No,' Luca replied without even a thought of the day he'd planned to spend in the office after visiting Alma and Pietro on Christmas Eve, as he did each year.

'A girlfriend?'

'You asking me out, Harcourt?'

'And if I was?'

Luca let out a laugh. The English billionaire was a renowned womaniser. 'Very kind of you to ask, but you're not my type.'

'No. I didn't think so. And as long as my sister isn't either, then we're good.'

CHAPTER ONE

SWEAT DRIPPED DOWN her back and breath poured from her lungs and still Hope Harcourt pushed on. She flicked a gaze to the monitor, four point five kilometres, twenty-three minutes... So close. Her feet pounded against the treadmill in a rhythm that felt primal. She needed this. Needed the moment that effort became effortless, where her body felt fluid with the movements, and her mind felt calm. It didn't last for long and she didn't always get there, but when she did it was...perfect.

The monitor ticked five kilometres at twenty-five minutes and Hope hit the cooldown button. As her pace slowed to match the treadmill, she grabbed the towel she'd hung from the bar and wiped her face, her breathing coming back to normal just in time for the morning call from her assistant. She caught the time on the screen before answering. Six thirty a.m. on the dot.

Elise's chirpy voice came through the wireless headphones as the treadmill slowed even more.

'And how are we this morning?' Elise asked.

'We are wonderful,' Hope replied, hitting the stop button on the treadmill and grabbing her bag. She'd been in the apartment for three years and not once seen anyone else using the building's private gym. She left the blessed air-conditioning and made her way to the lift that would take her up to her sixteenth-floor apartment.

'Was there anything in my inbox from Kinara this morning?' Hope asked. It had taken several years to develop a work strategy that suited her, but now that she had, everything ran much more smoothly for it. She didn't check emails until she got into work, but her assistant would give her a brief rundown before she got ready that day. She got top line info on what to expect, without the drama—*that* could wait until after she'd had coffee. But it helped to know what to dress for.

She'd learned that the hard way. Over the years, the press had made it a sport to catch her at her worst. Whether it was the sixteenth birthday party where she'd been photographed wearing an unflattering and inappropriately short dress, or the frumpy suit she'd worn to her graduation, she'd been shamed one way or another. By the time she'd come to Harcourts, she'd developed an iron-clad sense of fashion that had helped her in her role as Marketing Director just as much as her degree and master's.

As Hope got into the lift she wondered why, of all the articles and hit pieces over the years, it was her sixteenth birthday that always stung that little bit more. Perhaps it was because the photos could only have come from the people around her—her friends.

'Kinara wants to meet. They're doing a shoot on Friday morning but it's the only time they can make it.'

Hope mentally scanned her diary. 'We can do that, right?'

'Yes.'

'Brilliant. Put it in the diary.'

'Doing it now.'

Hope and Harcourts' buyer, Steven, had been trying to

court Kinara ever since the deal Nate had tried to make with Casas Fashion had fallen through. And, just like that, her stomach roiled beneath the memory of the day that Nate had collapsed. She had been the one to call the private ambulance, had waited with him as he lay on the floor, his eyes unfocused, the quick, sharp mind that Hope knew almost as well as her own hazed and confused.

He was being treated by the best and, thankfully, on the road to recovery. But, outside of the medical facility, only two people knew about what had happened to her twin brother: her and their grandfather. A secret necessitated by the desperation of businessmen who would willingly step over her brother's sick body to get one rung higher on the Harcourts' ladder. Nate had people in place in his other businesses, but Harcourts was different. And in his absence she'd been fighting off those who would love nothing more than to usurp his position at Harcourts in order to further their own agenda and bank balance.

It was a strange thing to love where you worked but loathe a lot of the people who worked there. She shook her head at the way so many of the shareholders were out of touch with the customers and their needs, uncaring of anything but what ended up in their bank balance. It infuriated her that they couldn't see that by taking the time now, by making smart decisions now they would secure the future of Harcourts for so much longer. But what would they care for that when they wouldn't be around to see it?

'Is there anything else?' Hope asked as the lift let her off at her floor. She took a left and placed her thumb on the keypad beside her door.

The momentary pause from Elise was enough to stir a sense of unease.

'Don't check the socials.'

For a moment Hope's head dropped against the wooden door, safe in the knowledge that she was alone, unseen. A momentary weakness she indulged in before clenching her jaw and pulling herself up. 'What is it this time?'

'Nothing that can't wait.'

'Elise.'

'It's Martin.'

Hope yanked open her door and slammed it behind her, letting loose a string of curses that would make a sailor proud. It didn't matter that Elise had heard. There was very little she kept from the assistant who had been with her for nearly ten years now. Elise had been there when Martin de Savoir had burst into her life with charm and seduction and Elise had also been there when he'd left it, bitterly and loudly, crying 'poor me' to any journalist that would listen.

What Elise didn't know, what no one knew, was the conversation she'd overheard between Martin and her brother. Her stomach turned, already sore from the crunches she'd done before the treadmill. The ache that reminded her that the number of people she could trust could be counted on one hand.

'I—'

'You don't want to know.'

Hope stared out of the window of her apartment. On any day, come rain or shine, the view was spectacular. But she didn't see the impressive outline of The Shard across the Thames, she didn't see the historic Tower of London, or the iconic Tower Bridge stretching from north to south across the river. In her mind she heard Martin's laugh, bitter and nasty, in a way that—at the time—she could barely recognise.

'I have all the proof I need, Martin. I know you're only after her inheritance.'

'God, it's about all she's good for, Harcourt. Every-one knows that.'

'Is there anything else?' Hope asked, breathing through the pain of that devastating moment from the past.

'No.'

'Okay, I'll see you in forty minutes.'

'Don't check the socials.'

Hope hung up the phone and tossed it on the bed. She peeled off her sweaty exercise clothes and stood beneath the powerful jets of water, scalding her skin pink for longer than she usually allowed herself.

Unable and unwilling to spend the day hiding in her shower, as tempting as it might be, she got out, dried herself off and chose her clothes carefully. It was tempting to check Twitter and Instagram, but she genuinely wanted to dress today as if she neither cared nor knew what her ex-fiancé had done this time. She wanted to dress for herself. So she chose a cashmere skirt in camel that hit her mid-calf and nipped her in at the waist, a white silk shirt with a neck bow, and would pair it with buttery soft tan leather calf-high boots and a long cashmere duster coat.

She spent a little more time on her make-up today, knowing that, of all her armour, this was the most important. It took twice as much time to make it look as if she wasn't wearing any, but she'd been doing this for so long it was second nature. She checked herself in the mirror before leaving the apartment—to make sure that she looked as she'd intended, she told herself. Not because she was worried about whatever new wave of press interest would be stirred up by Martin's latest escapade.

But as Hope rode the lift down to the reception of her apartment block, the thing picking at her pulse wasn't anger about what Martin might have got up to this time, but anticipation. Anticipation about a certain tall, broad-shouldered individual who had stepped in to cover when her usual driver, James, had left to attend a family emergency. The naïve kind of anticipation that reminded her of silly schoolgirl crushes which, Hope decided as the lift doors opened, she was far too old for.

But when she saw him waiting for her, through the glass entrance doors of her apartment building, her pulse still reared and bucked like a skittish horse. Hope ducked her head, sliding on her sunglasses to protect her eyes from the early morning's wintry sun and *not* to covertly check him out. But she couldn't help it. She could only hope that he wouldn't notice the blush she felt across her cheeks as she took him in.

Dressed in a black suit, the breadth of his chest caused the lapels to pull open enough to hint at the power beneath but not make it look as if the suit was too small. A white shirt and black tie that disappeared beneath a suit jacket buttoned at lean hips. It should have screamed uniform not boardroom, but there was something about the man that made him look *more*. Her gaze ran upwards, and she decided that it was his face.

His jawline was as sharp as his collar and, clean-shaven, the morning sun glanced off angles that would make a supermodel weep. Dark waves were swept back neatly, shorter at the sides and longer on top, and not a single hair was out of place. Neat. Compact. Efficient. The large dark glasses hid his eyes, making him look inscrutable. Dispassionate even.

And *that* was what frustrated her. Luc's utterly professional behaviour only made her wildly inappropriate reaction to him more obvious, she thought, as she emerged from the apartment complex.

* * *

Luca took a moment to brace himself against his body's unwanted and most definitely wayward reaction to Hope Harcourt. It infuriated him that she seemed to have more control over his body than he did. And it was untenable to have such a reaction to his client. Or, technically, the sister of his client. Either way, she was under his protection, whether she knew it or not, and that put her beyond his reach. Luca had argued against keeping Hope in the dark about his identity, but Nate had been resolute and the carrot he was dangling was big enough to sway him.

Following their meeting, Luca had spent Christmas and New Year planning how the detail would work for Hope Harcourt. Her usual driver had been easily paid off, especially with Nate Harcourt's backing, and Luca's assistant had found him an apartment with easy and immediate access to Hope, but not so close as to risk an accidental run-in. Nate had been able to ease the wheels with IT, allowing him access to Hope's professional emails, and Luca knew, if he deemed it necessary, he could gain access to her private ones, but he was unwilling to breach her privacy at this point.

He had arrived in a snow-covered England six days ago and had immediately thrown himself into the work that would finally see him break into the English-speaking territories. That one thought had driven him like the devil ever since Nate had made the offer back in Switzerland.

For years he'd been trying to break into the market that would finally make him a global success. From the very beginning he'd had that goal and he'd stuck to it. But, no matter how many satisfied customers or glowing references, or how many multinational clients Pegaso had, it wasn't enough for the UK and US markets. They wanted *old* money and familiar faces, if not accents. And the rejection had stung. But with Nate's offer he would finally crack open the lock that had been on the last territories Luca needed.

Hope emerged from the revolving glass door, cutting into his thoughts, and slipped into the back car seat without sparing him so much as a glance. Luca understood how many could think her cold—especially if they indulged in the rags that called themselves newspapers—but if you looked closely enough, she looked... He rolled his tongue across the roof of his mouth.

Rich. Warm. Luxurious.

The camel colours she wore suited her complexion. Expensive in a way that was so rich it was priceless. There was a subtle golden sheen to her skin that only reinforced the fanciful notion, making him want to run his thumb over her cheek to see the flush of colour bloom beneath it. Her nose was small and slightly upturned, but it suited her. Although hidden, he knew her eyes were a deep brown that should have looked slightly out of place with the blonde of her hair, but didn't. Her jawline led to an angular chin, just perfect for holding between a thumb and forefinger. Perfect to angle to...

Basta! Enough!

He was here to protect her, not lust after her. And that was most definitely what was coursing powerfully through his veins. Hope settled into the back seat as he closed the door, cutting off the gentle enticement of her perfume. Today's scent was different from yesterday's, he noticed. Today's had something with bite.

He got into the driver's seat and turned the key in the ignition, ruthlessly regaining control of his senses. Before starting work as the replacement driver, he'd checked over the car with a fine-tooth comb and was satisfied that not only was it in excellent condition, it contained no tracking or covert listening devices. It seemed unlikely, but Luca was nothing if not thorough. And although the car remained in his apartment's parking space overnight, he still checked it every single morning.

Pulling out into the traffic on Upper Thames Street, he decided on his route to Harcourts' flagship department store in Mayfair. In the rear-view mirror he watched Hope gazing out of the window at the morning London scene. He found it strange that Hope never reached for her phone on her morning commute. There was something almost serene about the image.

A motorbike zipped past him and Luca refocused on the road until his personal mobile vibrated against his chest. The single burst of vibration meant the message from his team wasn't urgent, and he could only conclude that they hadn't yet found proof linking the Harcourt twins' cousin, Simon, to the journalist responsible for a shocking seventy-eight percent of the negative press against Hope. Lucas was sure it was there though.

Even the tech analyst he'd put on the search had been angered and shocked by the sheer volume of hate and vitriol directed at a woman just going about her business. The same analyst had been tasked with looking deeper into Hope's history to check areas of vulnerability in case there was something they needed to know.

As an oncoming car took a right turn across the lane, the headlights swept across his eyeline and he saw flashbulbs, thousands of them, the calls and yells of the crowd between him and his mother...

'Give us a smile, Anna! Come on!'

'Over here, Anna!'

'Is it true that you're involved with your co-star, Anna?'
'When are you going to settle down, Anna?'

Without pause, Luca moved the car forward, inching towards their turn-off, despite the direction of his thoughts. Despite the memory of how his eternally glamorous mother had thrown her head back and laughed the sexy, throaty laugh she was known for and replied to the baying crowd, 'Never, darlings. I'll *never* settle down!'

And she hadn't. Italy's most famous actress had never married, never had a relationship lasting more than the promotion of her latest film, and had never—not once—acknowledged the fact that at sixteen she'd had a child out of wedlock, who had been raised by two members of her family in secret.

Disconcerted to find himself surprised as they pulled up to the majestic front doors of Harcourts in Mayfair, Luca mentally slapped himself. It was unacceptable to have been so distracted with a client. Frustration made his actions sharp as he exited the town car and held Hope's door open for her. Getting out of the car, her skirt rose barely enough to show an inch of creamy skin between the hemline and her boots, and he looked steadfastly ahead. He saw the briefest frown above her sunglasses, as if she'd noticed the staccato edge to his actions.

She paused. 'Elise will let you know when I'm done for the day. All meetings are internal so I won't be needing you until then.'

'I'll wait,' he said simply.

'It won't be necessary,' she replied, that little frown still in place above her sunglasses.

'I'll be here.'

She looked at him for a moment more, before disappearing beneath the world-famous gold and purple awning into the building. He had frustrated her and, while that hadn't been his intention, he hadn't missed the moment where fire had ignited in the air between them. Two competitors wrestling for control, tension and force of will coming up against each other.

And he'd wanted it, he realised, cursing himself. Wanted to test the strength of it.

His phone vibrated against his chest again and he turned back to the car to drive it round to the underground car park, where he could check out what his people had found. It was time to stop messing around and get his head on straight.

Hope shook off the strange tension that still zinged in her blood from her interaction with Luc and entered her office, walking straight to the large window that looked out onto a snow-covered Hyde Park.

There was something magical about this time of year, especially for a department store like Harcourts, where people would come from all over the world to look at their festive display windows and the beautiful, bright Christmas decorations. There was an almost constant hum of excitement and holiday happiness from the staff and customers alike, but even that wasn't as glorious as London in the snow.

Her office was in what the staff called 'the old wing', directly above the Mayfair store. The traditional character of the original building's features remained strong, unlike the 'new wing' to the back of the large sprawling building, where the offices were all sleek chrome, glass and granite and full of the ego contests that spun back and forth between her brother and cousin.

Hers was larger than the smaller modern offices, but

that wasn't its appeal. This office had once belonged to her father. It was where she had visited him as a child and it was where she remembered him best. It was her connection to her parents, especially when the past grew a little less clear each and every day she grew older. *That* was why she loved it.

It was later that day when she turned back to her computer, casting one last look at the email that would greenlight a brand-new marketing campaign in the US. She'd travel out there later in the year, once it was underway, but she was excited by it. It was sexy and contemporary—things she wanted for Harcourts, rather than the dusty and predominantly old campaigns run in the past.

She'd had a good day so far. She'd nudged Daniel, the acting Financial Director covering for her brother, back on track after a showdown with Simon had knocked his confidence. She'd try to keep that from Nate if she could. The last thing her brother needed was to be worrying about Harcourts.

Elise stuck her head in the doorway, a light frown across her brow. 'Just a heads-up. I've heard that the Chairman is attending the shareholders' meeting this afternoon.'

'Really?' Hope asked. Her grandfather usually spent the period between Christmas and the staff party at home in Tunbridge Wells. Home being a sprawling family estate about as old as the Harcourts building. Frowning herself, she scanned the agenda for the meeting taking place in fifteen minutes' time. 'There's nothing here that would warrant his attention,' she noted, looking back at Elise.

Elise shrugged, seemingly just as confused.

'Anything else?'

'No,' Hope replied absently.

'Are you sure?' Elise asked.

'Yes,' Hope hedged, half curious about the wicked gleam in Elise's eye.

'Really? You don't want to know what I've heard about TD and H?'

'Elise!'

'What? He *is* tall, dark and handsome.'

'*He* has a name.'

'And it's *Luc*,' Elise said, drawing out the sound of his name and swooning dramatically against the door frame.

Hope couldn't help but laugh.

'And I've heard that—'

'Nope! Don't want to know,' Hope insisted.

'Yes, you do,' Elise teased.

'I really don't.'

'It's just that I've heard he has a really big—'

Elise's sentence was cut off by the sheaf of paper that had been an agenda and was now a missile striking its target. Elise's scream startled a passing member of staff and dissolved in to giggles.

'Bike,' Elise muttered quietly picking up the agenda from the floor. 'His motorbike. I've heard it's really big.'

'Out!' Hope demanded, trying to smother her own laughter as she gathered her things for the meeting because the only frustrating thing about this office was that it was a ten-minute walk from where most of the meetings were held. But it gave her a chance to enjoy the feeling of a day well spent. Too many things had been up in the air recently, but today…it was shaping up to be a *good* one.

Thirty minutes later, the sound around Hope was deafening. Shareholders rose from their seats, some were shouting and jeering while others were clapping. She caught her grandfather's purposely blank gaze before she turned to glare at her cousin. Simon was smiling and clapping the

CEO, who had just thrown the room into chaos by announcing that he was stepping down, without warning or thought to the impact on Harcourts.

No! Hope's head spun. It wasn't supposed to be like this. For years, Nate had been primed to take over from Johnson. He'd done the required schmoozing and courting of the shareholders; he'd put in the time and effort. From the looks being shared between Simon and Johnson, the now outgoing CEO, Hope clenched her jaw and decided it was nothing short of a coup. And they had waited until Nate was out of the picture to make their move.

Her grandfather slammed his hand down on the table three times, silencing the baying crowd. 'Clearly this news is unexpected, but we thank the outgoing CEO for his work and dedication over the years as he has safeguarded Harcourts' clear dominance in the luxury goods market.'

Hope wondered how much that had hurt to say. Johnson had been nothing but a stick-in-the-mud, holding Harcourts back by penny-pinching and the least progressive business direction she had ever seen.

'Leonard Johnson has steered our ship with singular focus and the utmost dedication and as Chairman it is my duty to ensure that the handover to the incoming CEO is smooth, efficient and quick. Nominations for the incoming CEO will take place in two days' time. The vote for CEO will happen in two weeks' time. That concludes the meeting.'

Hope bit back a curse. There was no way that Nate would be able to get here in that time. She looked to Simon again, who finally deigned to turn a smug, satisfied gaze in her direction. Her pulse raced from outrage and indignation, even as she became aware of the weight of several pairs of eyes turning on her.

Her grandfather stood, and so did everyone else in the room, a courtesy and a tradition upheld from an earlier time until the Chairman of Harcourts left the room, and instead of screaming and shouting her anger she smiled and nodded to the few people who had encouraging words on their lips but pity in their eyes.

CHAPTER TWO

Luca resisted getting out of the car. If it wasn't for the thirty or so members of the esteemed British press, he'd have gone in there and given Hope Harcourt both barrels. He messaged her again.

The garage is safer. I can bring the car there in two minutes.

Her reply was instantaneous.

No.

He wanted to growl. This was part of the trouble with having a client who didn't know they were a client. They didn't listen to him when he made genuine decisions about their safety. He cursed Nathanial to hell and back, before remembering that he'd probably already been there.

The press had started to gather before he'd arrived and in the last five minutes even more had appeared. Luca had been about to call the analyst assessing the Harcourts case, when Nate had called to warn him that the current CEO was stepping down in order to ensure that Simon was the only viable option to take his place. The background info was welcome, but the warning about the resulting press attention came too late. Clearly someone—most likely Simon Harcourt—had tipped them off. Luca was beginning to seriously dislike the man and he'd never even met him.

Luca's mobile was in his hand, his finger hovering over another message to Hope, when he saw her emerge into the famous foyer of Harcourts department store. She was walking at quite a pace and he readied himself to exit the car to have her door open for her, when a tall man sidled up beside her and stopped her.

Simon Harcourt.

Luca narrowed his gaze. Through the strobe lighting of camera flashes, he could just make out the way Simon leaned into her space. Instinct warred against staying in the car and simply observing the interaction. He cursed Nate again, whether he'd been to hell or not, for the limits that he'd put on Luca's ability to do his job. If he'd been beside Hope instead of stuck out here, the cousin wouldn't have got within two feet of her.

Luca assessed the situation quickly. From outward appearances, it was two colleagues—cousins—simply having a quick chat on the way out. But he could read the lines her body was making. Sharp and tense, she was trying very hard to suppress her anger. He'd done it on purpose, Luca realised, cornering her in front of the press. He fired off a message to the case analyst, demanding all info on Simon Harcourt to be sent to him immediately.

The moment Hope moved, he moved.

He was out of the car and, even though he'd expected it, he was still slammed by the wall of sound that had been muffled in the car's interior. Journalists jostled and shouted, trying to get a soundbite on the internal fighting that was about to take over one of the world's most recognisable companies.

'Hope, what would your brother be saying if he was here?'

'Will Nate come back from his travels for this?'

'Hope, who do you think the next CEO will be?'

She ignored them all, Simon having hung back to watch her walk into the braying madness from inside the department store. Sunglasses hid her gaze, as they did his, but despite that, he knew she was looking right at him, locked onto him as if he were her lifeline.

He closed the door behind her after she'd slid smoothly into the back of the car and resisted the urge to violently remove the paparazzo who tried to get a photo as Luca opened the door to get into the driver's seat. He gently manoeuvred the car through the crowd and onto the road, leaving the chaos behind them. He counted down from ten and was surprised to get as far as three before she spoke.

'Don't question my decisions again,' she said, her voice clipped.

Understanding that she was referring to his request to pick her up in the garage, he replied with a careful, 'No, ma'am.'

'Do you know the address in Tunbridge Wells?'

'Yes, ma'am,' he confirmed, having made a point of knowing all the likely locations she might need.

'We're going there now.'

'Yes, ma'am,' he said, making a left-hand turn towards the river.

A few minutes of silence passed between them before she spoke again.

'It would have looked as if I was hiding.'

'Yes, ma'am,' he agreed. But it would have been safer.

* * *

Darkness fell as they travelled further and further away
from the mess of the shareholders' meeting, which was a
metaphor for something, Hope was pretty sure. But out
here, as they turned off the M25 and onto the A2, on the
way to her grandfather's estate, it felt almost as if it were
just her and Luc alone in the world.

Luc.

She'd felt his frustration that afternoon. As if he'd
wanted to protect her somehow. The thought was laughable if she were being unkind to herself, and fanciful if she
were being charitable. Ridiculous was what it was, which-
ever way she looked at it. Her thoughts changing tack, she
reached for her phone and hit the dial button.

Nate answered on the second ring, as if he'd been waiting for her call.

'I didn't know,' he said immediately. 'I thought something was going on, but I didn't know what.'

'And you didn't think to warn me?' she demanded, some
of her feelings bleeding out into her tone.

'I didn't want to worry you,' he replied.

She bit back a harsh response and swallowed around
the hurt reminding her that her brother didn't think she
was strong enough to handle things like this. Just like he
hadn't thought she was strong enough to handle the truth
about Martin.

'What are we going to do?' she asked. 'The nomination
for CEO is on Friday, the vote is in two weeks.'

Nate's response was a curse. She understood his frustration. They both wanted great things for Harcourts, things
they'd imagined that he would be able to do as CEO.

'I'm on my way to see Grandfather.'

Silence met her statement. She knew his relationship

with their grandfather was strained in a way that hers wasn't, but she'd never understood why.

'There's…nothing I can do from here,' Nate admitted, sounding defeated.

'You can get better, Nate. That's all I want,' she insisted truthfully.

He ended the call without a reply and the silence rang loudly in her head. She knew her twin brother as well as she knew herself. And she knew how hard he was finding his body's slow recovery from the life-threatening aneurism that had nearly stolen his life. And renewed anger that Simon and Johnson had taken advantage of that weakness fired her blood.

As the car arrived at the family estate, she didn't see the grand sweeping drive, the ancient stone fountain in the centre, three majestic horses lit from beneath. She didn't even give Luc directions as to where to wait or park. Her focus was solely on getting to her grandfather, hoping he could tell her what was going on.

Her heels crunched on gravel, then on stone steps, then on parquet flooring and then on the wooden floor, clipping at a pace that kept time with her racing pulse. She ignored the greeting of Mrs Conwary, the housekeeper she had known for as long as she'd been alive, and her husband, the butler, who waited outside her grandfather's office as if he'd expected her.

She caught his gaze from the other side of the hallway and he nodded, saying, 'You can go in, ma'am.'

She didn't pause on the threshold, didn't knock, didn't do any of the things she would usually have done when visiting the grandfather who stood on ceremony above all else.

He was standing behind his desk, looking out of the

window into the darkness. The fire in the fireplace flickered and the lighting was subtle and soft.

'Grandfather.'

'You made good time from London,' he observed without turning around.

'Why didn't you tell me?' Hope asked, finally giving voice to the question that had run in her head on a loop since the announcement.

'Because I don't do favours for family.'

No. Hope knew that first-hand. Her grandfather believed that the hard way was the only way.

'Simon knew,' she replied.

'If he did, it didn't come from me,' was her grandfather's clipped response.

Hope bit back the breath aching in her chest. 'It wasn't supposed to be this way.'

'Of course it wasn't. It was supposed to be your father.'

The slap of his words was a shock and she inhaled through the pain. But it was a pain she saw reflected in his eyes as he turned to face her.

'I don't play favourites, Hope. I can't. Because *they* won't.'

She clenched her teeth against the harsh love he'd always shown her, Nate and presumably even Simon. She knew he was talking about the shareholders. The board. She knew he was talking about more than a job or a role—their inheritance.

'What kind of guardian would I have been if I'd mollycoddled you and given you special treatment?'

'Special?' she huffed out scornfully. 'Any kind of treatment would have been preferable to—'

'Do you want it?' her grandfather demanded, cutting off her unexpected emotional response.

'What?'

'The CEO position.'

'It was *supposed* to be Nate.'

'Well, that's not going to happen now, is it? You can't sit on the fence any more, Hope. If you want it, do something about it. If not? Make peace with the fact that Simon is going to get it.'

Luca rubbed his hands together and breathed out a cloudy stream of breath. He prowled back and forth beside the car in the way he'd not been able to do earlier, outside Harcourts. He was used to being much more active than this, and not being able to work off the excess energy wasn't helping his mood.

Yeah, right. You keep telling yourself that.

'You can come in, you know?'

Luca looked up at the older man, sticking his head out of the back door.

'That's okay, but thank you.'

'You'll freeze your testicles off in this weather. Get in here or my wife will have mine over coals.'

Luca bit back a laugh at the rough talk from the old man who reminded him somehow of Pietro. He recognised the man as the butler from Hope's file. Mr Conwary had been with the family for his entire working life. There were only two reasons a man did that. Loyalty or greed. There was nothing about a man who proudly admitted that his wife would roast his testicles over hot coals that suggested greed.

He looked back at the car, worried that he wouldn't be there for Hope when she'd finished with her grandfather.

'She'd be more unhappy that you'd waited outside in the

cold than having to look for you with us,' the man said, jerking his head back towards the house.

Relenting, Luca nodded his thanks and followed the old man through the back parts of the house and into a large, very recognisably English, country kitchen. A woman matching the butler's age turned to welcome him. Mrs Conwary. He'd have known it even without the background info. Cheeks pink from cooking something that smelled delicious, she smiled big and hugged hard. Luca was somewhat startled by the easy affection from these two and was hastily trying to fit it into what he knew about Hope and Nate's upbringing.

'Have a seat. Tea? Stew's not ready, but it'll do if you're hungry.'

Luca translated her words from English to Italian and got the gist. 'No, thank you, ma'am.'

She cooed in delight. 'Did you hear that? Me, ma'am? Charmer.'

Luca couldn't help but smile at the couple. This appeared as much their home as their employer's but their easy way around him was something he'd never experienced, not even with Pietro and Alma.

'You've started with Hope?' Mrs Conwary asked.

'Yes,' Luca said, readying himself for who knew what.

'How is she doing?'

'I can't believe that little toerag waited until Nate was... was...' her husband growled, cutting a glance at Luca '... away. What is Hope expected to do?'

Luca wasn't sure what a toerag was, but it didn't sound good. Mrs Conwary was staring at Luca intently, still clearly hoping for an answer.

'She is okay,' he hedged, not about to share his true

thoughts on the subject of Hope, no matter how friendly the couple appeared to be.

Mrs Conway hummed disapprovingly. 'She's not as tough as she looks.'

'I don't know about that, Mary,' the old man mused. 'She'll have to be if she's to throw her name in the hat.'

Luca kept his expression blank, but he was surprised that the family staff seemed to be as well-informed on the political wranglings at Harcourts as they were.

'I'd like to give that Simon a piece of my mind.'

Mary grabbed her husband's wagging finger and gently pushed it away from Luca's face. One part of him was amused, the other—the one focused on Hope Harcourt—was very much not.

'She used to be such a happy girl. Had a laugh that was like sunshine,' Mary said wistfully, staring at a series of old photo frames placed along a sideboard. 'Sorry, it's the time of year. Brings back the bad.'

The bad? Luca's confusion must have shown on his face.

'Memories. Bad memories. Hope's parents died in a car accident. Terrible thing. Patch of black ice took the car on the way back from a fancy party in London.'

Mr Conway rubbed circles on his wife's back to soothe her and an odd twist in his conscience caught Luca by surprise. He had known about her parents' death, noted it but not taken in the date. It was around this time of year, he vaguely remembered.

'Mr and Mrs Conway,' came Hope's voice from behind them all.

She was standing in the doorway, head resting against the frame, with a smile on her face that suggested she might *not* have heard what they had just been discussing.

Mrs Conwary looked aghast for a moment, but covered well and rushed to envelop Hope's thinner frame in her larger one. Mr Conwary shot Luca a glance that said he wasn't fooled either.

Luca got up, but Hope gestured for him to sit back down and he waited while she caught up with two people who just beamed in her presence. And while there was still something watchful about her, braced in a way he couldn't explain, she softened around them in a way that felt more naturally *her* than he'd seen so far.

Hope spent twenty minutes listening to the Conwarys talk about their children and grandchildren. She ate the small bowl of stew that was put there 'just in case' she changed her mind and decided she was hungry. She exchanged their hugs with promises to be back soon on the steps of the back entrance to the house as Luca got the car ready and warm. And all the while he couldn't shake the conviction that she was wearing another mask as she once again slid into the back seat as he held the door open for her without looking at him.

It was about half an hour into the journey. Hope was looking out of the window and said, 'You can ask, you know.'

'Pardon, ma'am?'

'Don't call me ma'am. It makes me feel old,' she admitted, her tone softer than the words sounded. 'Ask. You've been wanting to all evening.'

Luca inhaled, torn, knowing he should ask about her meeting with her grandfather, but needing to hear what her cousin had said to her. Either question could blur professional boundaries, but she had offered him the chance to ask of her own free will.

'What did Simon say to you in the foyer before you left Harcourts this afternoon?'

Hope continued to stare out of her window. It looked as if she might not have heard him. It looked as if she hadn't spoken. But then... 'He apologised that the timing of the vote coincided with the anniversary of my parents' death.'

Luca's hands white-knuckled around the steering wheel.

She could have lied. She probably should have, because the moment that the words came out of her mouth she felt it again. That thrum of awareness, almost a sense of connection. However it had happened, something had built between her and Luc.

'I'm sorry.' The words were gravel thick and forced.

'For Simon?' she scoffed bitterly.

'For your parents.'

Her heart turned, and she resented that. Resented that his words meant so much to her. Hated that just two little words worked to soothe the ache she hid so deep.

Luc knew more about her than James did—her driver of nearly five years. James was cordial, jovial even, but she couldn't imagine Luc being anything other than... She'd been thinking *cold*, or *distant*, but that wasn't quite right. He might be aloof, but beneath was a heat, a driving force that was absent in her normal driver. She'd seen it in the way he'd responded when she'd refused to let him pick her up from the garage earlier that day. She felt it now, shimmering in the air between them as Luc digested what Simon had callously taunted her with. It was anger. For her. An anger she didn't know what to do with, because it stirred her own already twisting emotions from her grandfather's words.

And suddenly she didn't want to go home to an empty apartment, for a few hours' sleep, before her alarm went off and she started the day all over again. Gym, Elise's call at six thirty, fighting whatever the press could throw her way again, the vote. Just the thought of it was stifling.

She cleared her throat. 'Can we take the scenic route back, please?'

'Scenic?' he asked, frowning at the nightscape beyond the car.

Her lips pulled into a small wry smile. So much for subtlety... 'I don't want to go home just yet. Is there a longer route we can take?' she clarified.

'*Sì,*' he replied. 'Yes,' he repeated unnecessarily.

She gazed out at the passing scenery. The roads were clear at this time of night, the sound of the tyres rolling over concrete soothing in its monotony. She'd never learned to drive—not after what had happened to her parents—and it usually took her a long time to become comfortable enough with a driver, but she'd not had that with Luc. From the very beginning she'd felt...*safe*.

She looked to the rear-view mirror which, from where she sat, showed Luc's brows and eyes and just a section of that patrician nose. With his focus on the roads, she gave herself free rein to look her fill. Now that it wasn't hidden behind the sunglasses he wore during the day, she could lose herself in the silvery gaze. The pools of gunmetal grey were arresting, strangely unique and out of place with his Mediterranean colouring and the heavy brow that hung above his eyes made him seem sterner than he was. She should look away, but she couldn't quite bring herself to. Until she became almost convinced that he knew she was watching him. Heat burned her skin, her breath caught in her chest and her pulse pounded in her throat before she finally wrenched her gaze away.

Personal. That's what her perusal of him made her feel.

As if she were taking something back from the man who already knew too much about her.

'How long have you been in England?' Hope asked, attempting to break whatever it was that had thickened the air in the car's interior.

'Not long,' he replied, his monosyllabic answer providing only frustration. Hope needed a distraction; she wanted the mindless conversation to take her thoughts away from the dark. She wanted not to have to think so hard about so much.

'Is it very different? Driving here than in Italy?' she tried again, knowing that the questions were asinine.

'Yes.'

'Whereabouts in Italy are you from?'

'The south,' he replied.

Hope huffed out a little breathy laugh. 'Luc, are you sure you're not a spy?'

Luca forced the curve of a smile to his lips in case she could see it, hoping that it would keep him on the right side of her joke. He flicked his gaze between the road and Hope's reflection in the rear-view mirror. In the past, women had complained that he always held himself back, that refusing to share personal information made him harder to know. But years spent keeping his entire existence a secret had taken its toll.

'I was born in Bari, but raised in Palizzi,' he replied, startled when he realised that he'd given her the truth.

'I've been to Italy many times, but not Palizzi.'

He smiled freely this time. Not many people knew of it. 'It's about as far south as you can get in Italy.'

'What's it like?' she asked.

He knew what she wanted to hear: the tourist spiel.

About its beach, the famous old medieval castle that loomed imperiously above the village from its rocky outcrop. But all he could think about was how, as a child, he'd longed to escape the quiet rurality of it all and join his mother in the fantastic adventures he was sure they'd have. He'd travel the world with her as her white knight, protecting her from anyone who would do her harm. That was what he'd told himself in the cold silence of Pietro and Alma's house.

Whenever he could, he'd escaped to run along the shoreline, exploring the azure blue bay that reached out into the Ionian Sea. He'd felt unwanted by them, but bound to the aunt and uncle into whose care he had been entrusted. And in those early years he'd believed it was them keeping him from his mother, rather than the other way round.

Luca felt Hope's retreat in the silence.

'I'm sorry, I shouldn't have—'

'It's beautiful,' he said, interrupting her apology. 'It's quiet, nothing like London,' he said, trying to cling to the role of chauffeur while answering her questions with as much truth as possible. He was good at it usually—after all, he'd learned from his mother, and his mother was the best of the best. But something about Hope Harcourt was throwing him off.

'Above the village is an old castle,' he said, noticing how that had caught Hope's interest in the glance he shared with her through the rear-view mirror. 'Not that kind of castle,' he said around a smile. 'It was reconstructed in the mid seventeen hundreds and looks more like a military garrison than anything else.'

'Sounds…charming,' Hope said wryly, and Luca's lips quirked into a half-smile.

'It had its moments,' he admitted.

'Why London?'

'I had a client who brought me with him when he came to London,' he hedged. 'And when he went back, I decided to stay.'

She flicked her gaze to his in the mirror as if she hadn't quite believed him, but the moment he met her eyes he felt it—the jolt, as if he'd been zapped in the chest. It was like being gripped by fire and soothed by ice at the same time. She held his gaze for a beat too long, and this time it was Hope who looked away, leaning back against her seat and turning her attention back out of the window.

His pulse thudded sluggishly, forcing blood away from his groin and back to the brain he needed to drive. It had been so long since a woman had had such power over him. Yes, he'd been with attractive women over the years—and his last mutually beneficial no-strings relationship had only been six months before. But when he thought about it, he knew that the desire they had shared was nothing compared to the incendiary heat that had absolutely no place being between him and Hope.

An hour later he pulled up outside her apartment block and she exited the car with a 'Goodnight,' and a quiet, 'See you in the morning.'

He waited until the lift doors closed on her, watching him watch her.

He shook his head and pulled the car back out into the night. His own apartment was barely three minutes and two streets away. He guided the car into the underground garage and pulled into the reserved parking space as he thought about what Hope had been through today.

He made his way up to his penthouse apartment and poured himself a drink, all the while unable to shake the feeling of her eyes on him, watching him as he drove, as he waited for her with the car. Having spent a lot of his professional life watching other people, he'd never once realised how intimate it was. Intrusive? Absolutely. But with Hope it was something else.

He took the tumbler of ice and whisky out onto the balcony, the slap of the cold, wintry night air enough to cut through the hazy hangover from her attention.

This. This was what it was about, Luca reminded himself as he looked out across the London skyline. This was what was at stake. Expanding his company, ensuring its global viability. He wanted a piece of it. And the key to making that was keeping his hands off Hope Harcourt.

CHAPTER THREE

HOPE WOKE BATTLING a headache. As the day of the nominations had drawn closer, she had felt sure that Simon had done this on purpose—engineered the nominations to happen on the anniversary of her parents' death. That he had waited for Nate to be away, that he had waited until no one was there to stop him. Tension and anger made her headache worse and no amount of running on the treadmill would help.

She missed Nate so acutely that morning and was torn between wanting to reach out to him and not wanting to bother him. He needed rest, he needed to get better, and he wouldn't do that if he thought for one minute she needed him. He'd always tried to protect her. Too much sometimes. But he at least understood her grief. She could usually share that with him, but not today.

Hope shook her head at herself. There was too much in her head, she needed to compartmentalise. She put thoughts of her parents gently aside until she returned home that evening. Right now, she needed to think of today—her meeting with Kinara and the nominations.

She pulled the oversized, soft as silk, black scarf from the hanger and looped it around her neck, over the cream cashmere rollneck long-sleeve top she wore tucked into black houndstooth wool wide-legged trousers. She grabbed her bag, slipped into her coat, left her apartment and waited for the lift to arrive, trying not to count the ways that Harcourts had already been damaged by Simon's penny-pinching and the CEO's laziness. Because Harcourts wasn't just a job to her. It was a legacy. Her parents' legacy. She wondered who would put themselves forward, but all she could see was her cousin. And if Simon became CEO...

The lift doors slid open and whisked her down to the ground floor.

You can't sit on the fence any more, Hope. If you want it, do something about it.

Her pulse tripped when she spied Luc waiting for her outside her apartment. If she'd thought that things might have changed between them after the drive back from Tunbridge Wells, she'd been wrong. Whatever intimacy she had imagined was absent the next time she'd seen him. It was as if it hadn't happened. Which would have been fine, had it not left a gaping hole in its place—as if something between them was missing and she couldn't quite say whether that was a good thing or a bad thing.

She found herself distracted by his aftershave, especially when he held the door open for her. It teased her senses, adding weight to the thump of her heart and a betraying flush to her cheeks. A part of her wanted to tell him to change it and the other part wanted to get closer, to stand chest to chest with him, to angle her head so that it fitted in the crook of his neck, so that she could get as close as possible to where it would be strongest, to where the scent was heated by his body, his skin, and where she could just *inhale*.

As Luc guided the car north, away from central London, towards Hackney, she ordered herself to get her head in the game. In less than twenty minutes she would meet with Kinara, the fashion designer she'd been hoping would help her bring Harcourts back into the twenty-first century.

They were a British designer, young but fresh and exciting and with no naiveté about the world they were working in. Born and working in Hackney, there was both a street element to their designs as well as a business casual style that spoke to Hope. It was the direction she desperately wished Harcourts would move towards. Intelligent, contemporary, broad appealing and sexy.

So Hope would get through the meeting with Kinara and go to the shareholders' meeting where the nominations would take place. Once she saw who was running against Simon, she'd be able to make a decision about what to do next. She would get through the entire day and she would get home and then she would let the walls come down around the pain of spending the anniversary of her parents' death alone.

Luca turned the car down a narrow street that looked barely fit for pedestrian use, disliking the menacingly industrial feel of the north London area. He hadn't been familiar with Hackney at all, and while the main road was urban but bright and clean, this…not so much.

He flicked a gaze to Hope, who was talking to Elise on the phone about the timing of the shareholders' meeting. She'd been doing her best to ignore him since he'd withdrawn behind a wall of professional civility following the visit to her grandfather's.

He glared at the display on his own phone as if it would make Nate Harcourt call him back. He'd hoped that he might have some information on what had passed between Hope and her grandfather, but Nate had remained unreachable and Luca had been forced to remind himself that it was hardly the man's fault that he was in a Swiss hospital.

The narrow lane finally opened out onto a large square surrounded on all sides by red brick buildings several storeys high, giving the strange impression of a modern-day amphitheatre. One that was, apparently, being put to good use.

Three models were posed around an old metal bin with real flames curling into the sky. A man leaned forward, hunched over his camera, clicking away while shouting directions at both the models and the staff. Another group of people were crowded around a laptop on a small table set up off to the left.

Luca shrugged off the thought that what he was seeing just made him feel old. He pulled up off to the far right, where a kid dressed in jeans hanging too low and an off-the-shoulder T-shirt was pointing.

He exited the car and went to Hope's door, holding it open for her as she got out and trying to ignore all the natural danger points of what was essentially the spatial equivalent of a shooting gallery.

Hope barely paused long enough to tell him to 'Wait here,' before walking away, and he told himself that her sharpness was the least he deserved, as his eyes tracked her to a table where three people stood staring at a monitor and speaking quietly.

One of the teens, a young woman with blue eyes and brown lazily curling hair that fell halfway down her back, was now the sole focus of the photographer.

'Look over your shoulder, Tina,' called the man with the camera, and Luca's pulse jumped.

The woman didn't even remotely look like his mother.

But between the posing, the photographer, the press, it was all hitting a little too close to home.

It had been nearly fourteen months since he'd last seen Anna. It had been another cloak-and-dagger meeting in a hotel in some city that happened to be a midpoint of nowhere for them both. And it had been the time he'd finally realised what he most disliked about these less than yearly meetings.

'Sit down and tell me all about how you're doing,' she'd said, patting a space on the chair opposite her.

As if he were still the same child she'd said exactly the same thing to when he was nine. As if twenty years hadn't passed. Always focused on him and never sharing about herself.

That last time it had hit him more forcefully than ever before, because it was exactly what his last lover had accused him of as she'd left.

'You don't share yourself, Luca. You give me everything I could possibly need, apart from yourself.'

He'd not even been consciously doing it. And it made him wonder whether his mother realised she did it too, that she kept their relationship on those terms, *her* terms, or whether it had just become habit. And as difficult as it had been growing up with only one foot in her life and the other in Palizzi with Alma and Pietro, he'd wondered what it must have been like for her. To see her child grow up over a handful of days across a handful of years, rather than day in, day out. To see how he had become an adult in less than a month's worth of time, while she had miraculously stayed the same.

'Now, look away?' the photographer called and Luca wondered about these people's families. Did they have them? Were they waiting at home? What would these people choose to sacrifice for fame and money?

He became aware of someone's eyes on him and searched through the crowd of people to see who it was. He managed not to react to the amusing and utterly obvious way a young male model was ogling him. If he'd been off-duty he would have smiled graciously at the guy while discreetly refusing any advance—just in the same way he would have done with the female model next to him, also devouring him with her gaze.

But he wasn't. He was working and he returned his focus returned to Hope, who was talking to a person he presumed was Kinara, and he forgot about the two models laughing and giggling over the looks that were one of only two things he could thank his mother for.

'That man is *fine*,' Kinara observed.

Hope raised an eyebrow as if unaware that they were speaking about Luc.

'Oh, girl, don't play coy with me. Every single person here with a pulse has checked him out. He could be in front of that damn camera. In fact, if he wants to go and put on some of my—'

'Hands off,' Hope interrupted.

Kinara laughed, a rich, joyous tease of a laugh. 'All that was missing from the end of your sentence was *my man*.'

Hope shook her head. 'He works for me.'

'And that stopped who, exactly?'

'Precisely. How am I supposed to be better than all the men that dipped their fountain pen in the company ink if I just do as they do?'

The tease left Kinara's assessing gaze. 'Fair. But seriously, though.'

Hope couldn't help but smile, just about resisting the urge to look over her shoulder to where a significant amount of attention was gathering on her Italian chauffeur. 'Seriously though' was ringing in her head as she tried to get them back on track.

She caught the eye of Anita, a Harcourts marketing assistant, and sent her a wave. Anita would be gathering behind-the-scenes photos and interviews to put across their socials just before the launch. Hope, Kinara and Anita had worked hard on the marketing campaign that would start four months before on-sale, and go hard two months in. There were levels to it, digital, in-person, celebrity endorsement, TV advertising, billboards and even client-generated content after sale, each part purposely curated to ensure that Kinara's collection sold as forecast. It all stretched out before them in lines that Hope could see and would pull together to make one hell of a campaign.

'I want to bring you in to meet with the senior staff.'

Kinara squinted. 'Am I ready for that?' they asked a little nervously.

'Absolutely,' Hope replied, knowing that it was right she had come here today. 'This is your first shoot for your first collection for us and I couldn't be happier or prouder with what you're doing.'

Kinara, who had always been tactile and utterly themselves, swept Hope up in a hug. The sudden contact surprised her, her already precarious emotions teetering on the brink. Hope hugged Kinara back with as much enthusiasm as she was given and eventually they started laughing at themselves.

Pulling back to level Kinara with a gaze, 'I love this collection,' Hope said sincerely. 'And I know with absolute certainty that I am the lucky one who got you before all the others come calling and want you in their stores.'

Kinara waved off Hope's words before pulling her over to the monitor, where they explained the styles and coordinated sets that had been put together for the collection. Hope stayed at the shoot for as long as her schedule would allow, letting herself enjoy Kinara's fierce concentration and determined view of what they wanted. It was a part of her job she really enjoyed, helping to choose new stockists. And, although as Marketing Director it wasn't common, she'd worked hard with the Harcourts buyer to make this happen. Because she believed in it.

She quietly started saying her goodbyes so as not to disrupt the notoriously pedantic photographer.

'Listen, you know that Gabriella Casas has been trying to reach your brother?' Kinara asked.

Hope frowned. The interim Financial Director had mentioned Ms Casas trying to reach Nate too, but Hope shook it off. It would wait until Nate was better, even if nothing else could.

She shrugged off Kinara's question and looked back to where Luc was still standing by the car. No one could deny that he was striking, the deep blue suit and crisp white shirt mere window-dressing for the main attraction that was *him*. She heard the giggles of the models, clearly checking him out, but instead of preening under the attention, Hope was half convinced that, beneath his dark glasses, his focus was—as it always seemed—on her. Embarrassed by the sudden thump of her heart, sluggish and heavy at the thought, she made her way slowly towards him, suddenly conscious of everything between them. The sound of her breath, the slight tightening across his shoulders, the clench low in her belly, the flickering muscle at his jaw.

The door was opened for her by the time she reached the car, and Hope kept her silence as Luc manoeuvred it around and back through the narrow lane. And while her thoughts should be on the nomination, she couldn't shake Luc from her thoughts as the brooding Italian navigated the London streets with a calm, serene ease.

'You didn't like it,' she observed.

'Like what?'

'Back at the shoot. The attention?'

'No.' The word was clipped and should have ended the conversation.

Hope frowned. 'Can I ask why?'

For a moment she thought he might not answer.

'It's not real,' he said with a shrug. 'It's not me that they are attracted to. It's what I look like.'

And the smile dropped from Hope's lips, startled by the fact that this particular sentiment linked them in a way that made her think he might have understood that about her too.

Before she could pursue the conversation, he pulled into the car lane in front of Harcourts and she couldn't believe her eyes. There was a crowd of paparazzi spilling from the pavement into the road.

'We should use the underground garage,' Luc insisted.

'They've already seen us,' she replied, angry that her cousin had managed to turn everything into a circus. She was the one who was supposed to control the media, but PR and Marketing were two different departments.

'There are too many people out there.'

'If you won't let me out here,' she said, reaching for the door, 'then I'll do it my—'

'Don't!'

The natural authority in his tone, the sense of irrefutable command, held her so still that she didn't move until he opened the door for her. Furious with him for his authoritarian streak and herself for obeying, she got out of the car, refusing to spare him a glance.

But she was unprepared for the sudden press of people around her. Hope was jostled to the side before Luc could reach her and, tipped off-balance, she landed awkwardly. Suddenly she felt an ice-cold slap across her chest and heard the collective gasp from hundreds of journalists who had caught the moment that someone had knocked iced coffee across her cream cashmere top.

She was still reeling, not just from the spill but the sheer volume of paparazzi, when Luc pulled her against him and tucked her under his arm. He escorted her singlehandedly through the throng and into the foyer of Harcourts.

It was all too much. The flashbulbs, the sticky ice-cold liquid soaking into the fine wool, the heat of Luc's body and the way he just…protected her. He didn't stop in the marble foyer, instead pressing them forward, through to the staff-only area and the staff lifts where, thankfully, one had just arrived.

Luca ushered Hope inside the lift and slammed a palm on the buttons to close the doors before she could even speak. She looked up at him, horror, anger, shock and fury all vying for dominance, and cursed. Loud and furiously. Luca watched as she turned to the mirror lining the back of the lift and took in her ruined top.

'Are you okay?' he demanded.

She was staring at herself, the obvious damp stain

spreading down her chest and across her stomach. Angrily, she pulled the ruined cashmere from her waistband.

'Hey!' Luca said, louder, grabbing her shoulders and pulling her around to face him. 'Are you okay?'

'No, of course I'm not okay,' she replied, gesturing to her top.

'That's what you're worried about right now?' he said, wrestling his anger under control. He reached behind him to pull the stop button on the lift. The lights shifted from bright to a standby glow, casting them both in shadow.

'No, Luc. What I'm worried about right now is Harcourts. This means something to me. If I'm to go in there and put my support behind someone other than Simon then I can't do it looking like I've just crawled out of a garbage bin!'

She spun round, turning her back to him, clearly trying, and failing, to get her emotions under control. She shook her head. 'This company, this business, my family—they all deserve better than Simon Harcourt.'

In the reflection, he saw how her chest rose and fell with the sheer power of her anger. And then, when she caught his gaze in the mirrored wall, anger morphed into a heat that frayed the edges of his resistance to her. He braced against the way that her hungry gaze flicked down to his jaw and back. He slammed his eyes closed, hoping to sever the intimate connection he felt stirring in him when she looked at him like that.

Get. Your. Head. On. Straight.

He forced himself to think practically about what she needed. Her ruined sweater. Appearance was important to her—not through vanity, he knew, but as a tool.

'Do you have time to get something from the store?'

'Not now,' she replied. 'The press outside held us up.'

Frustration at the entire situation made his movements harsh and stiff. He flicked the button of his suit jacket and shrugged out of it, dropping it on the floor beside him.

Hope watched him with large round eyes.

'What are you—'

Her words were cut off when his fingers reached to yank his tie loose, as he drew one silk strip from the other, pulling it from his neck and casting it aside onto his jacket. He angled his head slightly to flick the button at his neck and started on the next when she held up her hands between them.

'Stop! What are you doing?'

Despite her words, her hungry gaze was locked onto the progress his hands had made, and damn if that didn't send a thrill straight to his groin. He ignored her and the way his pulse pounded through his veins and his stomach tightened, tugging the shirt from his waistband.

He wished he couldn't see the naked desire in her gaze dancing through her confusion. It was wrong—inappropriate—and somehow that only turned the screw tightening his arousal. For someone who spent his life watching others, the feel of her gaze on him was like a weight, pressing against all the places she was looking. Pressing *hard*.

'You need something to wear,' he said, his voice like gravel, shrugging out of the sleeves and passing his shirt to her.

And, just like that, he felt her attention slam against his entire body. He felt it as she took in the breadth of his chest and shoulders, the musculature of his arms, the flare of surprise at the tattoo that wrapped around his bicep and disappeared beneath the white vest tucked into his suit trousers.

His skin was branded by the heat of her gaze, flames

licking across his body burning hotter than he'd experienced before. His blood was thick in his veins, making every part of his body hot and heavy. He wasn't into self-delusion. He knew what this was. He knew how dangerous it was. And that single thought sliced through the heat connecting him to her.

He pressed the shirt she still hadn't taken towards her again and Hope blinked.

Hope was glad he hadn't spoken again because she wasn't sure she'd have heard him through the blood rushing in her ears. She took the shirt, still warm from his body, and he turned so that his back was to her. His head was bowed and she realised that he was both giving her privacy and protecting her modesty.

Jesus. Where had her modesty been when she'd been utterly undone by just the way he'd taken off his shirt? If he'd taken even a minute more she might have done something stupid, like reach for him.

The tattoo decorating his bicep…a horse's flank disappeared beneath his vest and she saw feathers in black and white detail that made her think of winged horses and gods.

Pegasus.

Luc cleared his throat and she realised he was prompting her again. Embarrassment burned her cheeks and she turned her back on him. She pulled the soaked cashmere top from her body and threw it aside.

In the mirror she caught sight of their reflections and her breath caught. They stood back to back. Luc tall, tanned skin, white vest glowing in the half-light, breath expanding his chest, stretching that cotton across muscles that made her weak. And her, dark trousers almost a match for his, skin pale and her nude bra making them look like…like…

She bit her lip to stop herself from betraying the kaleidoscope of erotic images twisting into her mind. Luc's head jerked as if he'd sensed it somehow, but he didn't turn to look. But that he'd fought the need to look burned a desire she had never experienced before deep into her chest.

No. She had to stop this. He worked for her, she warned herself. He was her subordinate and she couldn't… Something about that thought snagged and stirred. Because the one thing that had become so clear in her mind was that there was nothing subordinate about Luc. She shrugged into his white shirt, and immediately the scent of him that enveloped her pulled at her thoughts. It was expensive, the cologne. Too expensive for a chauffeur.

She filtered through the possibilities and as she began to bring her conclusions together, quick, determined fingers threaded buttons through holes and sharp, efficient movements tucked the shirt beneath her waistband.

She turned to the mirror, pulled a little at the shirt to ensure that it sat right and refused to look Luc in the eye as she leaned to press the button to release the hold on the lift and braced as it jerked back into life.

Heat burned her cheeks as she thought how foolish, how stupid she had been not to see it sooner. She'd been taken in once again, and she cursed herself for not learning the lesson that had already cost her too much.

Luc frowned, as if sensing the change in her. He bent to pick up his jacket from the floor and shoved his tie in his pocket and Hope hated herself for the desperate hunger that somehow surpassed her anger.

The lift opened out onto her floor and they both ignored the stares following them as they made their way to her office in silence. And she realised in a heartbeat that *he* was leading *her*. It had happened that quickly. He had assumed control, *just like that*.

He walked straight over to the large window, probably drawn by the impressive view of Hyde Park. She didn't really care, as long as it put space between them. She waited until he turned towards her, a small power play she so desperately needed in that moment.

He stood there, hands in pockets, his black suit jacket over a vest, looking so damn gorgeous it made her knees tremble. Anger, she told herself, lied to herself. That was what she was feeling. Fury, even.

'You're not a chauffeur, are you?' It was less a question than a statement.

He inhaled and squared his shoulders, and stood tall, as if pulling himself to his full height. It only made him seem *larger*, more *him*. As if he'd shed a false persona before answering.

'No.'

She clenched her fists, bracing against the hurt and anger crashing through her.

'Security?' she asked, remembering the way he'd protected her.

'Yes.'

'My brother?'

Luc nodded.

'Hope? The meeting is about to start,' Elise said gently from the doorway, as if she knew she was interrupting.

Hope glared at Luc. 'Stay here,' she ordered, even though she wasn't sure she still had the right to do so.

She hurried down the corridors that took her from the old wing towards the meeting room where the shareholders had gathered to decide a future they barely had any interest in, so angry she wanted to cry. But she couldn't afford to think about Luc and Nate and how betrayed she felt that her brother thought so little of her. The nomination. That was all that mattered in this moment, and she shoved any other thoughts aside. She walked into the meeting room and a staff member closed the door behind her.

Simon was standing beside her grandfather and, *oh, God*, she was so sick of the power moves and game playing.

'We've been waiting—'

'Then let's get on with it,' she interrupted, drawing a few surprised glances her way.

She went to her assigned seat, to the left-hand side of the Chairman, and sat down, her teeth clenched together so hard her jaw ached.

'We have a nomination for Simon Harcourt,' her grandfather informed the room.

Hope waited for a counter-nomination, looking out across the faces of the thirty or so board members, none of whom met her eye. They might have voted for Nate but without him here, no one would stand against Simon. Her stomach clenched and her heart plummeted.

The silence was deafening and she was sure that everyone in the room could hear the dull thud of her heartbeat. *No, no, no.* This couldn't be happening. She wasn't enough. She couldn't do it, not by herself.

'Are there any other nominations?'

Her breath, locked in her chest, felt like a bomb that was about to explode.

You can't sit on the fence any more, Hope.

'If not, then we will forgo the vote and—'

'Me.' The word burst from her lips. 'I nominate myself.'

CHAPTER FOUR

LUCA PACED THE breadth of the room, furious with himself. On the one hand, now that Hope knew who he was, it would make it easier to protect her. On the other hand, he had never dropped the ball so hard before in his life. His company's future was on the line, for heaven's sake. A contract that would launch him light years ahead of any expectations he'd had for Pegaso. So he needed to get his head out of fantasies of Hope Harcourt and back on track. He was about to start another lap of the room when he heard the click of her heels on the parquet flooring outside the office.

He turned expectantly. 'That was quick.'

She threw a folder onto her desk and glared at him. 'You're fired.'

Luca accepted her response as his due, but still shook his head slowly. 'You didn't hire me.'

She held his gaze for a beat before producing her mobile from her pocket. His guess was that she was trying to reach Nate. And if she could get through? Brilliant. Luca had a few choice things he wanted to say to his client. But, unfortunately for both of them, Nate didn't answer.

'You need protection,' Luca warned her as she hung up the phone.

'*If* I need it, I can get it for myself.'

'But you haven't.'

She glared at him again, before turning her back to him to throw her phone on the desk. He gave her the time to gather herself. A lot had happened in a very short space of time.

'Luc?' she asked, without turning.

'Lu*ca*,' he corrected. 'Luca Calvino.'

He saw the line of tension across her shoulders, the grip of her hands on the table. He could only imagine the sense of betrayal she must be feeling, but that wasn't his job, nor his responsibility, he argued. Nate was his client, not her.

'The meeting?' he asked.

'Do you care?'

Her question nudged at his conscience. 'For professional purposes,' he lied.

'Well, I've pissed off three-quarters of the board, my grandfather and my cousin. Though, admittedly, I'm not too crushed by the last one. Apparently, they wanted to give Simon the easy win, celebrate over the weekend and resume work as normal on Monday.'

She turned back to him, her cheeks a little pink, her eyes glittering angrily. 'You're not just a bodyguard,' she accused.

'CEO. Pegaso Securities.'

Her gaze flew to his shoulder, as if she were seeing his tattoo beneath the layers of his clothing.

Focus. Hope's protection. His future contract.

'I'm not going anywhere,' he warned, 'so you might as well use me properly, rather than as just your driver.'

Hope let out a laugh that seemed far too cynical for her. 'You're not driving me anywhere ever again, Calvino.'

He levelled her with a gaze that pretty much said, *Think again.*

'I. Don't. Need. You,' she spelled out. 'I can handle it myself.'

'Of course you can,' he replied without missing a beat, his agreement clearly taking her by surprise. 'You can court shareholders; you can make your deals. I'm not interfering with that, but what you can't do is all of that *and* watch your back.'

She turned, her hands anchored on the desk behind her, and he fought the urge to look away as his shirt pulled tight across her chest. Now was not the time for errant thoughts.

'And what is it I have to watch my back for? Journalists with cups of coffee?' she replied, her tone full of scorn.

'Your cousin is mounting a coup. And it seems his weapon of choice is the press.'

Hope rolled her eyes and he ignored it, stepping closer to her to emphasise his point. Her eyes turned to him, flashing warning signs he also ignored. She needed to hear this.

'Every single time you challenge him, a story comes out. Every single time he feels slighted, a new series of articles comes into the press.'

'It's a coincidence. I'm in the public spotlight. I have to be, for my job.'

Luca shook his head. 'It's not. When you argued against him moving the Harcourt brand manufacturing factory to cut costs, the next day the headlines were about you snubbing an invitation from the royal family.'

'There *was* no invitation.'

'When you argued against the change in staff hours, the headlines the next day were about you firing a designer.'

'He went on paternity leave.'

'And when you stopped him from switching transportation contacts, this happened,' he said, showing her the screen of his phone.

'That was…' She trailed off, looking at the newspaper headline he'd pulled up. 'He couldn't have had anything to do with Martin. That was different… It was…'

'Personal? You think your cousin is above that? Your engagement had been broken for six months by that point. Why would the papers suddenly be interested in digging it up then?'

'Because I'd been out with friends?'

'Such a rare occasion that it demands a hit piece about how you broke the heart of your fiancé, when we all know that what really happened was—'

'I was there, I don't need reminding of what happened,' she yelled at him. She ran her hand across her forehead, as if thinking through his accusation.

'The journalist? Just happened to be at Oxford with Simon. Same year, same social circle, and a rather invested interest in any scandal related to you.'

She started to pace the room, just as he had done earlier. She shook her head. 'I didn't see it. I always thought it was just normal unhealthy interest, but not targeted in *that* way.' She shook her head again, as if trying to refute it, but Luca needed to press his point home now.

'Right now, you need to focus on the vote next week, so I'm going to focus on what you don't have the capacity to do.'

'I could hire my own security,' she said, repeating her earlier threat.

'You could, but you won't. Why?' he asked, before answering his own question. 'Because you need to figure out how you're going to win the vote. And that starts with what happens at the Harcourts Winter Party at the opera tomorrow night.'

Understanding and realisation dawned in her eyes. She knew he was right. Luca was now ninety-nine percent sure he had her. And *finally* he could actually do the job the way he wanted.

'And what do you get out of it?' she asked, catching him by surprise.

'What do you mean?'

'A CEO doesn't usually get this hands-on, even for a client like Nathanial Harcourt,' she said, a dangerous glint in her eye. 'I want to know what makes me—*this*—so special?' she demanded.

'Hope—'

'What are you getting out of this, Luca?' she demanded, and he hated how it looked. How whatever had passed between them—and something *had* passed between them—would be tainted by this.

She held his gaze steadily until he answered.

'The global security contract for Harcourts.'

Even braced for his response, she blanched. 'He had no right to do that,' she argued.

'Perhaps,' he agreed, trying to ignore the fact that he suddenly felt like a bastard. 'But really? Right now? That's not what's important. Look, forget your brother. Forget who's paying the bill. Forget what happens next. I'm here,' he said, taking another step towards her. 'And I'm good. I'm *very* good. Let me do my job.'

He held his breath. And he wondered if, for a minute, she was doing exactly the same.

'Fine,' she said, turning to walk around to her seat behind the desk.

He breathed and nodded. 'I'll be outside when you are ready to leave. Am I taking you home?' he asked.

'Where else would you take me?' she asked, the ice in her tone freezing him to the bone. But the words—he couldn't keep them back, even if he tried.

'To your grandfather's? A friend's? You shouldn't be alone tonight.'

'There are a lot of things I shouldn't be tonight. But that is neither any of your business nor anything to do with my protection.'

Chastised, with lines redrawn, Luca Calvino left her office.

The next evening, as Hope got ready for the Harcourts Christmas party, held each year at the Royal Opera House, she wrestled the feelings oscillating dangerously between anger and humiliation. Betrayal and a sense of her own stupidity. A part of her desperately wanted to cancel, but now that she had thrown her hat in the ring as the new CEO, she *had* to be there.

Luc had driven her home in stony silence last night.

No. Not Luc.

Luca, she corrected. Luc had been a handsome Italian chauffeur she'd had a silly feminine reaction to. *Luca* was a billionaire businessman whose only interest in her was an international contract with Harcourts and nothing more.

She'd praised herself for having enough self-control to at least wait until she'd got home before doing a search on him, although the fallout from putting herself forward for the CEO position meant she had more than enough to deal with. It was actually a testament to Simon's popularity that only a third of the board 'popped by' her office to show their support. Of that third, she was probably only guaranteed half of those votes, the others just doing it for show.

But, finally at home, she'd not been able to stop herself. With a large glass of Tempranillo, she'd typed his name into the search engine and found...very little. There was a single photograph from a few years ago on his bio, and she'd had to squint to make sure that it was, in fact, him. There was little to no personal information and therefore no way to see whether he'd been telling her the truth about growing up in Palizzi. She didn't know why, but it had become important that at least one piece of what he'd told her had been real. Even if it was just that. But not knowing only added to her feeling of insecurity.

Because she'd done it again, hadn't she? Seen and read too much into something, some*one*, who was only out for themselves. She looked at her reflection in the mirror-lined lift of her apartment building and found it hard to feel anything other than disdain for the woman staring back at her. After Martin, she'd promised herself she'd learnt that lesson, but clearly she hadn't.

When her phone had rung last night with Nate's name appearing on the screen, she hadn't been able to answer it. Even though she'd wanted to speak to him, even though she *should* have. But she hadn't. Because he'd not trusted her. He'd not thought she was strong enough to handle things, so he'd gone behind her back. Just like the way he'd done with her ex-fiancé.

And if Nate didn't think she could handle that, what would he think when he found out she'd put herself forward as CEO? He'd probably think it was nothing short of laughable. Even though she had two degrees in business and marketing and had just as much family knowledge as either of them.

She'd never be able to get away from the fact that her father had always wanted Nate to have Harcourts. For his son to take the lead of the family business and that thought, last night, of all nights, had hurt.

Hope bit her lip as she emerged from her apartment to find Luca waiting for her beside the open car door as if nothing had changed between them. And then she remembered that, for him, nothing had.

Forcing down her feelings, Hope got into the car and smoothed the black silk skirt of the haute couture dress one of the designers exclusive to Harcourts had made for her. Wide-strapped V-neck panels were flattering and tight over her top half, and the layered high/low skirt provided drama and a hint of sex appeal. Not enough to scare off the shareholders attending the Harcourts Winter Party, she had ensured. But enough to remind herself that she was still a desirable woman in her own right. A reminder she needed very much in that moment, with the weight of Luca's gaze on her.

As she studiously ignored him, she considered the night ahead. The party was a tradition started nearly one hundred years ago. On the second Saturday in January, Harcourts would hire the ROH for a night to delight the staff and their families. Its success had been replicated across their international locations and, although the Sydney Opera House was magnificent, this had always been her favourite. And she used that memory to ground her, used the strength of her feelings for Harcourts to give her the focus she needed. Tonight was about making the connections she needed to beat Simon and now, more than ever, that had become vital.

'We're here.'

'Thank you,' she replied automatically, ruthlessly relegating Luca to someone of no more importance than any other member of staff.

Hope checked her reflection in the mirror one last time, unable to afford any smudged make-up or any more photo disasters. That morning's headlines had been a montage of various images of her horrified face and some very unnecessary close-ups of her chest.

Luca opened her door and, ignoring the goosebumps that flashed over her skin from his proximity, she stepped out onto the red carpet, a touch of glamour that the staff appreciated. Photographers and journalists waiting for a glimpse of one of the most prestigious business events of the year were kept at bay by a rope and various security staff. She looked ahead through the glass-fronted entrance to see her grandfather surrounded by a group of tuxedoed men and their wives in impressive ballgowns.

Hope braced herself. She was used to arriving alone to these kinds of affairs—having learned a long time ago that it was better to spare both her date and the press the kind of speculation that followed—but somehow, after what had passed between her and Luca, she felt it more acutely. Leaving him in her wake, she smiled at the press, made a joke about no one having any iced coffee, at which most laughed, and made her way into the foyer of the Royal Opera House.

Smiles greeted her, as many fake as real, and she mingled with the shareholders and their partners for a drink or two before they heard the five-minute curtain call. Once again, that dip in her stomach returned. Tonight would be the first time that she'd be alone in the family box.

Her grandfather had his own, Simon's side of the family would be in another. Usually, she'd be here with Nate and they'd spend the evening gossiping about the board members and their snooty behaviour. But Nate was still recuperating and she would have to bear the attention alone.

As people started to peel off for their respective seats, she caught her grandfather's eye and thought for a second that she saw understanding and compassion in his gaze. But she knew better. Smile bright and eyes glittering, she made her way along the red-carpeted staircase to the door that opened onto the private box that she remembered from her childhood. She walked in and stopped just behind the seats, cast in shadow, watching the auditorium fill with Harcourts' staff and friends and family.

The noise rose up from below, gentle chatter, a laugh punctuating the hum. She wished the excitement was infectious enough to distract her, but it wasn't. Directly opposite her box, on the other side of the stalls, Simon gently slapped his father on the back, whilst scanning the auditorium. He looked up and found her watching him. She clearly wasn't as well hidden as she'd thought. He nodded in acknowledgement, the civility of it making Hope angry, until he purposely cut the connection to look at someone in the stalls below. Curious, she followed his gaze, and her fingers tightened to white as she fisted the evening's programme.

'What is Martin de Savoir doing here?'

The question made Hope jump and the sting of adrenaline pricked at her skin as she pressed a hand to her chest.

'Don't turn around,' Luca commanded. 'I'd rather people not know I'm here.'

Hope huffed out a bitter laugh. 'How novel. Someone who *doesn't* want to be seen with me. What are you doing here?' she demanded in a harsh whisper.

'My job,' Luca replied tightly.

He'd spent three hours that afternoon familiarising himself with the ROH layout and communicating with their security, before clearing a suspicious package sent to Hope's office that turned out to be flowers congratulating her on the nomination. It had been a miracle that he'd made it to Hope's apartment on time. And while he bore the lion's share of the responsibility for her animosity towards him, dealing with their acidic interactions was something he could do without.

From the shadows at the back of the box, he peered down into the auditorium to see Hope's ex-fiancé smack in the middle of the stalls, halfway between her and Simon Harcourt.

'Do you know who he's with?' Luca asked. *He* knew, he just wasn't sure how up-to-date Hope was on her ex's love life and what it would cost her to hear it.

He watched as Hope purposefully turned her attention away from the lower level to scan the rest of the auditorium. He imagined that she had a practically perfect smile on those incendiary red lips he'd caught sight of in the rear-view mirror of the car earlier. He was sure she'd been aiming for elegant rather than downright carnal, but anyone looking at the perfect bow of her lips painted in fire engine red would have to have been dead from the neck down not to think wicked thoughts.

'That is Imogen Frotheram.'

'That's quite a mouthful,' he observed, peering at the young blonde woman who looked remarkably like Hope.

'Twenty-four years old, with an inheritance of nearly one million pounds, and presently engaged to Martin de Savoir,' Hope informed him in a dispassionate tone.

Luca caught Imogen casting a look between her fiancé and up at Hope in the grand tier box, suggesting that perhaps she was only just becoming aware of what she had been drawn into.

'De Savoir doesn't work for Harcourts,' he said, his tone dark with suspicion.

'No,' Hope replied, still looking out as the remaining guests began to take their seats. She even waved at someone in the stalls.

'Then how did he get a ticket?'

There was barely a pause before she replied. 'That area is reserved for Simon's friends and family.'

Although her voice was carefully level, he could only imagine the fury that she must be feeling. To have her ex-fiancé here, with his new fiancée? The day *after* she'd gone head-to-head with her cousin? Simon was trying to get at her, undermining her on every level he could, publicly in front of the shareholders. And doing it all without even getting his hands dirty.

Hope moved forward to take her seat, the voluminous skirt swaying with her hips in a way that made him want to bracket her waist in his palms. *Graceful.* It caught his attention when he should have been thinking of so much more.

'Do you like opera, Luca?' she asked, holding the programme in front of her mouth to disguise their conversation.

'I do.'

She cocked her head to one side as if surprised, and he smiled.

'It's a national crime not to adore Puccini.'

'And Turandot?' she asked.

'One of my favourites,' he admitted begrudgingly of the opera famous, mostly, for the song Nessun Dorma.

'Really?' This time Hope had been unable to hide the surprise from her voice. 'I didn't picture you as a romantic.'

Luca clenched his jaw so hard he nearly broke a tooth

in order not to ask, to demand, how she had been pictur-
ing him. The silence screamed between them and he was
about to say something when the conductor tapped his
baton to ready the orchestra.

The entire way through the first act he tried to keep his
focus on his surroundings, but Hope was more distracting
than the dramatic death of the Prince of Persia.

Hope. One of the answers to the three questions Turandot asks of her suitors. Should they answer incorrectly,
they are put to death. Only the one who answers each of
the riddles can become her husband. He wondered what
Hope made of the heroine so angered by the assault on
her ancestor, she sets about taking revenge on all of her
would-be suitors.

From where he was standing, tucked into the rich red
velvet curtain enveloped by shadows, he could see the
delicate lines of her shoulders and neck. Hope's blonde
hair was looped into an elaborate twist, held in place by a
gold hairpin, leaving her long slender neck bare and begging to be caressed. The V on the front of her dress was
mirrored at the back and the dim lighting played in shadows across her shoulder blades and spine. Instinctively,
his hand flexed before he fisted it and shoved it behind
his back.

He usually had more control over himself than this, but
he had to admit he'd never encountered anyone like Hope
before. His mind returned to his earlier conversation with
Nathanial Harcourt. He'd expected a fight on his hands, to
keep the contract, to keep their agreement, but Nate had
seemed distracted.

'It's fine. As long as she's safe, that's all that matters.'
The Englishman's voice had sounded strained, but Luca
knew that he wouldn't appreciate any show of concern.

'Keep me informed,' was all he'd said before severing the call. He doubted her brother would have been so accepting if he'd had any idea of the erotic desires she evoked in Luca.

As the curtain dropped on the first intermission, Hope took a moment to gather herself. She hadn't seen a single second of the opera that was a favourite of hers too. Instead, the entire time, she'd been aware only of Luca. Of the weight of his presence, hidden in the corner, like a protection she both wanted and hated at the same time.

Shaking off the thought, she needed to get out to the main foyer. Intermissions were an important part of social networking and while she'd always begged off in the past, it was no longer a luxury she could afford. Standing from her seat, she turned, unable to stop her gaze flying straight to where Luca was standing—and instantly wished she hadn't. She'd been so focused on ignoring him earlier when he was with the car that she hadn't really taken him in. But now?

If he'd looked good in a suit and tie, Luca Calvino in a tuxedo was devastating. She wanted to press a hand to her stomach like some Victorian miss, for the first time truly understanding that flip in her core. *Deep* in her core. Her lips parted on nothing but air and she didn't miss the way that his gaze flickered between her mouth and her eyes. She was about to say something when there was a knock on the door.

Luca's brow dropped in question and Hope, understanding, shook her head to convey that she wasn't expecting anyone. She crossed to the door, gently batting aside Luca's raised hand warning her to stop, and opened it, regretting it instantly.

Her ex-fiancé lounged against the frame as if he had come to charm her rather than taunt her. Burying her anger deep, she waited. She had learned long ago that nothing frustrated Martin more than having to do things for himself.

'Not going to invite me in?'

'No,' she said, keeping her tone neutral and her expression purposely bland.

The wave of anger she felt coming from where Luca stood in the shadows heated her skin like a fierce caress. But all it did was make her aware that he was seeing this. Seeing that *this* was the man she'd nearly married. Shame and anger licked at her like flames.

Several guests passed in the hallway, casting them curious glances, clearly aware of the history between them and already beginning to gossip. Just as—she imagined—he'd planned.

'Don't you want to know why I'm here?' Martin taunted.

'No.'

'Even if I had something that you might want?' he leered.

'You have *nothing* I want, Martin. I promise you that,' she said, struggling to keep herself calm. He peeled himself angrily from the door frame and stood there glaring at her.

'Everyone wants something, Hope. Sadly, I was never going to give you what you are so desperate for,' he said, with so much false sincerity it curdled her stomach.

'And what was that?' she asked before she could stop herself.

'Love,' he whispered meanly, leaning into her ear.

She slammed the door on him, hating that she could hear his taunting laugh as he walked away.

* * *

Luca hadn't made out Martin's reply, but it took nearly everything in him not to wrench the door open and go after the bastard. What on earth was wrong with these people? No, his own wasn't exactly the perfect nuclear family. He didn't know and didn't care to know his father, he barely saw his mother—only when she deemed it safe and secret enough, but this?

Vipers.

It was a description Nate had used too and it barely touched the surface.

Hope stood facing the door she had just slammed shut, the rapid breaths pressing against the black satin crossed over her chest. She was looking down, that curved line of her neck bent. Until she rolled her shoulders and straightened her back and he watched as Hope rebuilt her armour, brick by brick, thought by thought.

'Can you get the car?'

'Sì,' he replied, unaware that his emotions were riding him hard enough for him to answer in his native Italian.

'Have it ready in five minutes.'

'Sì,' he said. Before he left, he marvelled as she resumed her seat in the private box. And just before the curtain rose on Turandot's second act, she even smiled and waved to some of the staff who caught her eye, looking for all the world as if nothing had happened.

What had Martin said to her?

The question become an urgent refrain as he made his way from the theatre to the garage where the car was. Luca barely breathed until he had the car at the entrance to the Royal Opera House and saw Hope making her way towards him.

Head high, back straight and as poised and regal as a

queen, sophistication and class dripped from every pore and no one would have guessed that she had just been emotionally eviscerated by her ex-fiancé. Luca exited the car without taking his eyes off her and, reaching for her door, he held it open and closed it behind her.

He wasn't sure what made him look back at that moment but, when he did, he saw Simon Harcourt standing at a second-floor window with an inscrutable expression on his face.

CHAPTER FIVE

HOPE WAS BARELY holding on. All she wanted to do was get back to her apartment, take this wretched dress off, wipe off the make-up and… No. She wouldn't cry. She wouldn't give in. Martin had been purposely baiting her. Distracting her. He'd done what he'd set out to achieve—what *Simon* had set out to achieve, that was. Instead of making the rounds at intermission and forging valuable connections, she'd remained in the opera box and had run away at the first chance.

When would she stop being such a fool? She *had* to be better than this. Cleverer. But all she could think—hear—was his parting words to her on a loop.

'I was never going to give you what you are so desperate for.'

She hated him. Hated that he was right.

As the car arrived at her apartment block she felt Luca's curiosity pressing against her, filling the car, suffocating her. The moment they pulled to a stop, she flung the door open and fled, desperate to escape. She didn't want him to know. Didn't want him to have any part of her. Not when she couldn't trust that he wasn't just the same as Martin.

As she pushed through the revolving doors, she felt him fall into step a little way behind her and though she wanted to tell him to leave, to stop following her, she didn't trust herself to speak.

The doors were open on the lift when she reached it and Hope tapped the button for her floor again and again to close them. She needed him to stop. She needed to be alone. To lick her wounds. To hurt. She turned back in time to see him pound a fist against the wall as the doors closed, cutting them off.

She sucked in a lungful of air, willing back the tears and trying to ease the pressure on her chest, thankful for the reprieve from Luca's constant attention. He saw and knew too much. She shook her head at herself, gathering the shreds of her dignity, and got out of the lift.

Her thumb was on the access pad to her apartment door when Luca came stalking down the corridor. He must have run up the flights of stairs. She turned in the doorway, refusing to let him over the threshold.

'Go away,' she commanded.

He pulled up opposite her, studying her with an intensity she felt tripping over her sensitised skin, pulling at her core, at what made her a woman and what she, as a woman, wanted. There were questions in his eyes, dark and angry. His gaze fastened on hers as if he was willing himself not to look anywhere else on her body and that annoyed her as much as it relieved. A muscle pulsed at his jaw and it seemed he was as on edge as she was.

'No.'

'No?'

He shook his head. 'I won't go away. Not until I know you're okay.'

Hope huffed out a bitter laugh. 'I am fine. Just another day in the life of Hope Harcourt.'

He looked over her shoulder at the sliver of apartment

he could see through the open door and looked back at her. It was all the warning she got.

'No, wait—'

He slipped past her before she could do anything.

'Luca!' she gasped, outraged that he was in her home. 'What do you think you're doing?' she demanded.

He stalked through her apartment like a jungle cat, peering into the rooms with a dispassion that was nearly offensive.

'My job,' he growled, and she wanted to growl right back. She was getting sick of hearing those two words. She didn't want him to be doing his job, she didn't want him here because he *had* to be. If he and her brother hadn't lied to her, she wouldn't be in this mess, feeling one thing and wanting another.

Luca turned, feeling Hope's frustration roll off her in waves. Good. He wanted her frustrated, he wanted her angry. Anything was better than the pain and hurt he'd seen hidden deep only moments before.

He caught sight of a wine fridge in the corner of the neat kitchen that opened onto the dining room. 'Drink?'

'Excuse me?' Hope demanded, a red flash across her cheeks.

'Would you like a drink?'

'You're offering me a drink in my own home?' She stared at him as if it were the greatest breach of etiquette she'd ever seen.

'I know I could do with one,' he bit out under his breath as he crossed to the kitchen. Hope's apartment was exactly as he had imagined—not that it was hard, having reviewed the floor plans and the original sales brochure. He probably knew more about her apartment than she did. He bent down to the wine fridge and scanned the labels. What he really wanted was to know what Martin had said to her. Instinctively, Luca knew it was important. Really important.

'I don't know what you think you saw tonight—'

'What I saw,' he interrupted as he pulled a very decent white from the fridge, 'was a vile, objectionable man using social pressure to keep you in your place while he tried to emotionally manipulate you.'

He reached for two wine glasses from the shelf above the countertop, liking the ergonomic feel of the apartment; everything was in reach where it should be, or was expected to be.

'Did he do that while you were together?' he asked, trying to keep the dangerous anger simmering beneath his skin at bay.

He felt the breath she held, the fury she tried to contain as if it were a living presence between them. He waited out her silence as he poured the pale wine into each glass. He looked to where Hope stood in the middle of her apartment, waiting until she gave up the fight.

She placed her bag and wrap on the arm of the sofa and came to stand with the breakfast bar between them. He slid the glass of wine across the gleaming marble and she took a sip before answering.

'No,' she said, putting the glass back down on the bar. 'No,' she said, shaking her head again. 'He was many things, but he doesn't have the intellect for that kind of emotional manipulation. But he was very good at hiding his true nature. I had absolutely no idea,' she admitted. 'And I should have,' she said, as if admonishing herself.

'We were twelve when our parents died and my grandfather became our guardian. He decided that boarding school was the best place for us and sent my brother to

Eton, and me to St Saviour's.' The words became thick
on her tongue. 'It was the first time I'd spent even a night
away from my brother. As twins, we'd been unusually
inseparable and suddenly my parents were gone, my life
was upside down and I was alone.'

She turned to the window, perhaps unseeing of the il-
luminated London nightscape beyond the glass.

'It was…an adjustment. Because of my parents' death,
the publicity, the tragedy, the family notoriety, everyone
in the school knew who I was. It counted among its number the daughters of dignitaries, ambassadors and even
princesses, but I was *famous*,' she said, smiling bitterly.

'I didn't quite realise what that meant until a picture of
me trying alcohol for the first time, in a desperate attempt
to fit in and find a place in the schoolgirl hierarchy, found
its way onto the front page of a daily rag. After that, it was
a photo of me getting changed after gym.'

She shrugged, trying to hide how much it had hurt, how
much it still hurt, but he could see it. Could tell how much
it cost her to remember, to open this up for him, because
he'd demanded it. Hope was describing exactly the kind
of invasive press attention that his mother had told him
she'd been trying to avoid. But with one difference—his
mother had only been trying to protect herself. It sounded
as if there had been no one to protect Hope. Until it was
too late. It struck him then that they each lived on opposite sides of public life—him in the shadows and her in
the glare of the spotlight.

'So you'd have thought I'd have learned my lesson by
the time I met Martin, but apparently not. At university,
things were easier. I was as anonymous as I'd ever been
and I let my guard down. I was *wooed* by him and fell for
his lies, hook, line and sinker.

'I thought myself in love,' she said, the cynicism dripping from her tone like acid that would only ever harm herself. 'And I would have married him, had my brother not realised he was only after my money.'

Luca didn't miss the way she had tripped over those words and his chest ached, not from anger but with understanding. He could easily imagine the kind of hurt she had felt.

'I overheard them talking. Nate confronted Martin about a month before our wedding, at a family event in Tunbridge Wells. And, to this day, they don't know I heard them.'

Luca's glass paused midway to his mouth.

'Nate wanted to pay Martin to leave me, but I broke it off before he could. Martin must have hated that. To not have got a penny out of us. I think that's why he threw his lot in with Simon. And that's how I became the "The Cold-Hearted Harcourt", dumping her fiancé weeks before the wedding.'

'Hope—'

'Better that than to be left by the bastard,' she bit out through clenched teeth.

How her brother had ever thought her weak was beyond Luca. He shook his head.

'So now you know,' she said, her eyes shining. 'And now you can leave,' she ordered regally.

He didn't want to leave her alone, but he couldn't be sure that his reasons were purely professional any more. And that alone was enough to tell him that he should. He left his half-drunk wine on the bar and Hope followed him to the door.

He turned. He wanted to say something but the look in

her eyes, powerful, angry and determined, warned him against it and only then did he feel it was okay to leave.

On Sunday evening Luca received a message from Elise, letting him know that Hope was working from home the next day. And the day after that. During that time, the press made Martin's approach to Hope at the opera into a secret assignation, a fight between jealous ex-lovers, and everything but a plot to dethrone the King. His mother's film also grossed millions at the Hollywood box office and there was something jarring about seeing both of their names in the same newspaper that put Luca in the foulest of moods.

And that was before he received the email about Austria. He picked up his phone and pressed the dial button before he'd even finished reading it.

'What's in Austria?' he demanded.

'Sun, ski and *après-ski*,' Elise replied dreamily, unconcerned by the growl in his voice.

'Clearly. What is she *doing* there?'

'You could ask me *really* nicely…' Hope's assistant drew out, 'but even then, I wouldn't tell you.'

'And this is where she intends to stay?' he asked, scanning and dismissing an image of the large central hotel, with so many access points it was nothing short of a security disaster waiting to happen.

'It's where she usually stays. Angelique has a chalet within the same village and they always go there and they always have so much fun and I'm always *so* jealous.'

The words poured from Hope's assistant so quickly, he barely managed to get the gist of it.

'And if we needed to change the location?'

'I wouldn't recommend it. Hope wouldn't like it one bit.'

Luca stared at the screen, thinking that it would be the least of what she didn't like about him at that point and reminded himself that it was probably not a bad thing either.

The next day Luca was already on the private jet when Hope entered the cabin of the small craft. Her glasses this time were almost completely opaque, leaving him clueless about her reaction to him.

Outwardly, she seemed not to spare him a glance as she took a seat at the furthest end of the cabin, on the opposite side, with her back to him. He smiled inwardly, having expected nothing less, before his conscience stirred. Yes, she was mad at him and she had good reason to be.

He had breached professional lines on the night of the opera. He might have told himself he had good reason, but it still had the same outcome. They were on rocky ground and he needed to get back to solid, professional. He couldn't lose the future contract with Harcourts. It was what he had been working towards for the last ten years.

The air steward came to settle Hope into her seat, asking if she wanted anything to drink before take-off. She kept her voice low, making him strain to hear her, making him work for it. He respected it as much as it frustrated him.

Her phone vibrated with a call and as she held up the screen, he realised he could see it from this angle. Not that he needed to. The sound of the video call cut through the quiet of the cabin.

'Darling! Tell me you're on your way,' came the cooing voice of a brunette with bright blue eyes.

'Just waiting for take-off.'

'Yes!' The word screamed into the phone and buzzed the speakers harshly.

The laugh Hope allowed herself hit him just as hard.

'So, are you ready to get up to no good?' the brunette demanded.

'Absolutely.'

'Good, because Simon arsehole Harcourt deserves to get sucker punched after all these years.'

Luca frowned, disliking how open the conversation was and very much disliking that he didn't know who the brunette was.

'That he does. I should be there in two hours.'

'The champers is on ice, darling, and I can't wait to see your gorgeous face!'

The switch in atmosphere in the plane the moment Hope disconnected the call was like whiplash, the soft humour severing into serious contemplation, and it reminded him of the time that his mother had been caught by a fan once when she'd been visiting.

At eleven, he was already painfully aware of the need to keep the identity of his mother a secret.

'It's to protect me, Luca. You're doing such a good job protecting me.'

A young woman had nervously approached her idol, asking if she would sign an autograph for her.

'Of course,' Anna had said, pushing Luca aside.

He knew the routine by then. He would walk on, just like any other fan who had been dismissed. Usually, he would find the nearest corner, or maybe even just head straight home. But this time he'd watched Anna, how she had lit up, the smile seeming so very genuine, happier even than when she'd been with him only moments before. And he'd felt resentment towards the woman who'd asked for the photograph, jealous that she was the recipient of all that focused joy Anna was capable of when she wanted to be.

Luca shook himself free of the thought. He wasn't usually so preoccupied with thoughts of Anna. In fact, as time had gone on and the visits between them had become more awkward and few and far between, he'd begun to wonder what the point was.

But it was this client. This case. He'd known when Nate had approached him that it would hit a little too close to home, to exactly what he'd spent his life trying to avoid— the press, public scrutiny. And he probably could have argued, after the night at the opera, that someone else would be better suited for her protection detail. But he'd given Nate his word, and that meant something to him.

Hope said her thanks as the air steward placed the espresso beside her and moved off. She'd never thought of the jet as small before, but when so much of her focus was taken up by her awareness of Luca it now seemed almost claustrophobic.

She had been purposely avoiding him since he had left her apartment that night after the opera. And if she'd thought she could have escaped London and come to Austria without him noticing, she would have. But it seemed that Luca was, indeed, very good at his job.

'Who was that?' he asked from behind her.

She'd have liked to pretend that he'd caught her by surprise, but he hadn't. She'd felt the distance between them getting smaller and smaller with every leap of her pulse. She could try to ignore him for the rest of the trip, but she doubted that she'd have much luck. There was simply no way to ignore Luca Calvino.

'Angelique,' she said on a sigh, wishing that his gravelly voice didn't make her tummy flip in that way.

'You trust her?' he asked, waiting beside the table for

her to invite him to sit. Like she'd thought, not that subtle, and not mincing his words today, it seemed.

Locking her gaze on his, direct and unquestionable, 'With my life,' she said honestly. 'I'm sure that you heard the call, and I'm sure that you drew all manner of conclusions about someone who says *champers* and *darling* and who has a chalet in an Austrian ski resort. And you're entitled to draw those conclusions, Luca. But, as I have quite clearly demonstrated to you, I know what it's like to be sold out by someone I deemed a friend. This isn't one of those times and Angelique isn't one of those people.'

'What are we doing in Austria, Hope?' he asked, the bite of exhausted frustration colouring his tone.

She considered whether to tell him the truth. She didn't like the way that he seemed to take over, without her permission or consultation. So many people did that to her, but with him it seemed all the more important to fight it.

'You have to let me know your plans if I'm going to do my job properly,' he insisted.

'If you need me to tell you my plans, then perhaps you're not up to the job,' she replied tartly.

'It doesn't have to be this difficult.'

'No, you're right. It doesn't. And had I wanted this, rather than you and my brother going behind my back, then it wouldn't be this difficult.'

'That is a very naïve view of the situation,' he said, dismissing her argument. 'It's this simple,' he went on, his index finger tracing an arc on the table. 'Either I'll follow one step behind you, wherever you go, during which time it's entirely possible that a lack of communication could lead to an accidental slip-up, and that the press, who are clearly also following you and looking for a story, will see,' he said with a careless shrug as her ire built and built. 'Or we can work together and make sure that the press see and discover nothing.'

'Are you threatening me?' she demanded.

'I will do whatever I have to do, to get the job done.'

'To get your global contract with Harcourts, you mean.'

Although her verbal jab was little more than a diversionary tactic, it was clear that it meant a lot to her. And he wished he hadn't had his hands tied by her brother, but they had been.

Luca hated the idea that he had to threaten Hope to get her to play ball, and if she'd had any idea that he had absolutely no intention of ever being noticed by the press, she'd have been able to call his bluff. But she didn't. In truth, if he could live in perfect anonymity, Luca would die a happy man. He'd have managed to live his life without ruining his mother's. No matter how large the distance between them, or how difficult the relationship, knowing that his very existence was a constant threat to his mother was a terrible burden to live with. So no, Luca had absolutely no intention of being discovered by the paparazzi, but neither did he have any intention of doing a bad job.

His question hung in the air between them. *What are we doing in Austria?*

'The shareholders don't like me,' she said with a shrug as if she didn't care, even though he doubted that to be true. 'Whether it's the fact I'm a woman, the fact that Nate and I want desperately to take Harcourts into the twenty-first century, or whether I'm not willing to schmooze them in the way they believe they are entitled to. It didn't really matter before now.

'Nate was supposed to be the one who took over the CEO position when Johnson finally stepped down, but clearly we underestimated the deals he'd made with

Simon.' She shook her head, as if annoyed with herself.
'Nate had been working on a business deal with Casas
Fashion.'

'The Spanish conglomerate?'

'Yes. But something happened and the deal fell through.
And before Nate could…he…' She looked out of the window again. 'Well, you know.'

Luca nodded, wondering when Nate had last spoken
to his sister. He thought of the Conwarys and how they'd
talked around the medical crisis that had struck him down,
and realised that there was more than one way to keep a
secret.

'Everyone wants something,' she said, repeating words
from the mouth of that snake de Savoir, making his hackles rise. 'So I need to give the board something that they
want, in order to vote for me and not Simon.'

'And what's that?' he asked.

'An obscene amount of money.'

Clever. Very clever, he thought, satisfaction a shimmering gold in the molten chocolate gaze staring back at him.

'I have to do a deal that will make them forget all their
prejudice. Because if avarice is their weakness, it will be
my success.'

Hope followed Luca down the stairs from the jet as the
luggage was loaded into a sleek, dark SUV with blacked-
out windows, her breath misting in the cold air. The private airstrip was in a basin protected by a mountain range
on one side and a lake in the distance on the other. The
air crisp and cool and promising a snowfall that would
be sure to delight the holidaymakers hoping to get in a
few last runs before returning their children to school or
work after the festive winter break. The runway had been

cleared to allow for landing, the snow banked up around the edges looking dirty and industrial, taking just a little of the shine from the alpine fantasy and showing the reality hidden beneath. Something that felt a little too close to home at that moment for Hope.

'Would you like to sit in the front?' Luca asked. She considered it. Thought of the way she'd watch his hands as he steered the wheel, changed gears, the power of it...

'If I sit beside you, the press will want to know who you are.'

It was true, but she still disliked how it forced them back to the roles of employer and employee, even if it wasn't strictly true. Luca's stiff nod in response served to acknowledge as much, as he held the passenger door open for her.

She immediately swiped across the screen of her phone to access her emails. Work. She needed to work, she was *here* to work, and as long as the elaborate scheme she had created with Angelique was a success, she'd meet with her potential business partner that evening and be on her way back home tomorrow, all being well.

Hope had spent two days pulling together the details of what she believed would be the making of Harcourts. Her brother had tried with Casas Industries and while a deal with the Spanish fashion house would have been a solid investment, exciting up to a point, it wouldn't have changed anything. Hope wanted more. Hope wanted bigger. With Sofia Obeid, Hope was almost sure she had it. And while that familiar part of her wanted to speak to her brother, to ask if she was doing the right thing, if the deal was actually as good as she'd hoped, another—stronger—part wanted to keep this to herself. In case she failed.

She tried to focus on the inbox on her screen, but soon

became distracted by the view beyond the window. She had always loved snow-covered mountains. There was a wildness inherent in them that she felt she was never allowed to be. A raw, unmatched, solid force to them that was not action or reaction, push or pull, it just *was*. Simply power, unquestionable and immovable.

Like Luca.

No, she argued with herself. *Like* me. *Like how* I *want to be.*

She watched as the familiar turn-off to the village just outside of Kitzbühel came up on her left…and then disappeared as they passed it.

'Luca, I think we've missed the turning.'

'No, we didn't.'

'Yes,' she said, craning her neck back to where they should have gone. 'We've passed it.'

Her statement was met with silence.

'Luca?' she asked, her tone a warning which was also ignored.

CHAPTER SIX

THE SLAM OF her car door cracked through the snow-heavy silence like a gunshot. A bird erupted from a nearby fir tree, sending a flutter of wings and snow off into the forest just behind the sprawling wooden chalet.

Not even on pain of death would Hope admit that this place looked as if it had been plucked out of her daydreams. Not that Luca seemed to be bothered in any way whether she liked the ski lodge or not. He had hauled open the boot of the car and was removing their meagre luggage and carrying it up the stairs towards the front door, his movements quick, efficient and laced with a controlled impatience.

'You went behind my back,' she accused, following him as he made the trip back to the car. She turned to stare up at the accommodation. It seemed almost wasteful to use it for just a night. She counted the windows along the second floor of the chalet, bracketed by wooden eaves and a balcony. The entire place—built to house at least fifteen, from what she could see—looked as if it belonged in a chocolate advert. The luxurious promise of sweetness, warmth and decadence just behind its doors.

Her mind threw up a marketing campaign just like that—a couple very much in love, sinking to a white fur rug before a roaring fire, mulled wine on one side and seventy percent dark chocolate on the other. The mountains, perhaps a few slopes visible in the distance through an open window.

The slam of the car boot made her jump and Luca stalked past her, refusing to spare her a glance, up the stairs and, after entering a code in the door's keypad, into the chalet. She stamped her boots on the snow-covered driveway, kicking out the cold from her feet, and followed him reluctantly into one of the most beautiful places she'd ever stayed.

The door opened onto a large utility-style hallway, perfect for hanging coats and taking off boots. Along one side was a rack for skis and poles, snowboards and holders for boots and every kind of winter sport that could be imagined. At the end of the utility room was a door that stood partly ajar.

Braced and ready to give Luca a piece of her mind, she swept through the door and…

Oh.

The ground floor was as serene and soothing as any spa. A sauna glowed gently from behind its glass front, the wooden seating and panels promising a bone-deep warmth that Hope suddenly craved more than she could have imagined. On the other side was a hammam, offering a slick, humid heat that reactivated fantasies that she'd desperately wanted to put away. A small pool lay just beyond the bounds of the building, beneath a canopy of fairy lights covering what must be the underside of the large balcony above. Hope was hardly unfamiliar with the luxury that money could buy, but even she felt as if the world had tilted on its axis the moment she had stepped through the door.

On the second floor, she found an impressive gym that

stretched the entire length and width of the chalet, filled with machines that would work any muscle group imaginable, and a matted floor space just in front of the same floor-to-ceiling windows that separated it from the swimming area below. The third floor comprised of enough bedrooms for several families to share but it was the fourth floor that really impressed.

The entire open-plan floor wrapped around a chimney that hung down from the ceiling. Beneath it, a firepit blazed seductively. The floor-to-ceiling windows that had below displayed the incredible snow-covered landscape of forests and far-off chalets, here, with the elevated height offered by the fourth floor, showcased the mountain range that had become a piece of art in its own right.

Large plush cream sofas faced the central fireplace on one side, and an exquisite wooden hand-carved table ready to seat sixteen stood on the other. She became aware of a boiling kettle by the sound of it franticly rocking on its base.

Luca emerged from a doorway to her left and absently asked her if she wanted a cup of tea.

'No, Luca. I don't want a cup of tea. I want to know why I'm here and not in the apartment I had arranged for in town,' she said, throwing her coat onto the side of the sofa.

'Because that apartment was not a secure location.'

Hope rolled her eyes, the lack of sleep as she'd worked her way through the last two days, the stress of the nomination before that—it had all worked to reduce the filter she usually kept between herself and the world.

'I'm not POTUS. Or Whitney, or any other kind of person who needs *actual* protection, Luca. Are there deeply awful and intrusive and eminently frustrating headlines about me? Yes. Do they hurt? A little bit.' A lot, actually, but she had no intention of letting him know that. 'But is my life at risk? No.'

He had patiently pulled out a cup, added a tea bag and poured the water over it throughout her little speech.

'Are you done?' he asked, without looking up.

'Excuse me?' she demanded, bristling at the inherent disrespect.

'Are you done?' he asked, turning around to face her, his hands braced behind him on the countertop and she'd have had to be blind not to see how devastatingly attractive he seemed at that moment. The black knit turtleneck jumper clung to his chest like a second skin, the matt black brushed metal of the buckle of his belt clasped tightly over his lean hips. Legs clad in dark denim, lovingly wrapping around thigh and calf muscles even the most dedicated gym fanatic would have been proud of. Lethal, deadly and downright sexy. But suddenly she became aware of the flare of his nostrils, the dragging inhalation of oxygen. He was mad. At her. Very mad.

'I don't care if you're not the President of the United States. I don't care that you're not a multi-million-dollar music industry icon. I don't care that the chunks taken out of you are done by words not weapons. That's not my business or my concern. I have been paid to do a job, and I will do that job, whether you like it or not,' Luca warned.

'I was supposed to be in town. I was supposed to be *seen* in town. *That* was the point of the distraction, Luca.'

And that just pushed him even closer to the edge. Wanting to be seen, playing with the press—she thought she was using them and couldn't see the price she was having to pay.

He stalked towards her, closing the distance between them with barely two steps.

'A job I cannot do,' he said, as if she'd not spoken, 'if *someone* in your office is leaking your every move to the press.' His words weren't shouted or yelled. They were quiet even, but hit their mark with surgical precision.

Luca saw confusion cloud that bitter chocolate gaze of hers.

'What do you mean?'

'How am I supposed to keep you safe if the press knows what you're doing before I do? The leak didn't come from my team, because *we didn't know*,' he stressed, as infuriated by the message he'd received from his analyst now as when he'd read the email. 'How do they know you're going to a club called Meister? What on earth are you playing at here, Hope?' he demanded, a red haze beginning to press at the edges of his vision.

'I am playing the hand I've been dealt, Luca,' she threw back, matching her heat to his. 'This is the life I have and I'm making it work.' Fire blazed in the molten depths now that he'd lit the fuse and he could either stand by and watch or help her burn it all down and, God help him, he wanted it all to burn.

'And what kind of life is that?' he demanded, through the flames turning his vision red. 'It's vapid. It's ridiculous,' he dismissed with a slash of his hand. 'It's all for show without any deeper meaning. You're being used for someone else's momentary fascination and you're allowing it. It's pathetic and beneath you and you should know better.'

'You don't know anything about me, Luca,' she hurled back.

And he wanted to tell her. Tell her what he knew about her. Not just what had been in her file, not just the facts that he'd gathered, but the smaller things he'd noticed. The kindnesses that cost nothing but meant everything. The concern for her staff, for the future of her employees, for her customers. But he'd also seen the loneliness. The hurt she hid from everyone—even her brother. The way that she stood beneath the gaze of those who underestimated her constantly, but still she bore it. One day he wanted to see her rise above it, because he knew she could.

'You cannot keep me on the outside looking in,' he insisted. 'If I am constantly having to play catch-up, someone will get hurt.'

It hadn't happened yet, not on his watch, and not for any of his clients, but he couldn't take that risk, couldn't let his guard down. Not once. Not ever.

'You're doing such a good job protecting me.'

He turned his back on Hope, feeling a little too exposed, too raw. Because he'd seen it. He'd seen the moment that she'd realised he wasn't just speaking about her, about Harcourts.

'You'll tell me what you're planning?' he said, uncaring that it was more of a command than a request.

'Yes,' she said, looking at him with questions he'd put in her eyes.

He nodded and left the room.

Luca felt the loud bassline pumping out of Meister's speaker system bone-deep. It hummed beneath his skin, strangely subtle rather than jarring. He shouldn't have been surprised. He'd spent the afternoon exploring the layout, and had even done a quick walk-through before they'd opened—not that Hope would know about that.

He'd thought he'd have calmed down by now, but no. She was there, like that bassline, simmering beneath in his veins. But she was a client. Ignoring that—technically, Nate was the client—Hope was still under his protection.

A client that the future success of his company rested on. A contract with Harcourts would be the first step to a global operation.

He looked around the bar area, easily spotting the press photographers who thought they were being discreet, with their camera phones pointed straight at the VIP area blocked off by two imposing security figures—one male and one female.

He wondered where his mother was right now. What she would do if she were here. She'd have been on the other side of that rope, naturally. And if she'd seen that he was here? She wouldn't have spared him a glance as she left, unwilling to risk being in the same space as the biological son she had made sign a non-disclosure agreement at the age of eighteen about their relationship. In exchange for a small inheritance, of course. She was, after all, his mother.

He willed the tension headache back from where it began to press against his temples. Hope, his mother, the press, his childhood. This was why he didn't take the lead on public image clients any more.

Hope's laughter cut through the sounds of the bar as if he'd tuned into her very essence, his awareness of her beyond professional. He clenched his teeth as he saw someone jostle her and, for the first time ever, was furious that he'd been relegated to the shadows. And while he knew that it protected them both, it grated that he was so far from his charge.

A man leaned in to whisper something in her ear. Hope smiled up at him, and he saw the gesture catch the interest of one of the paparazzi in the club. Hope cocked her head to one side, the man shifting slightly so that Luca caught a head-to-toe glimpse of her and clenched his jaw until his teeth ached.

The ruched midnight-blue satin dress which stopped at a heart-attack-inducing level on her toned thighs was enough to make a grown man weep. Although the silky material cowled around a high neck, the back was where things got dangerous. The high neck was a collar, the sleeves closing beneath the arm to keep the entirety of her back bare, announcing to the world she was braless.

From the mutinous look she'd thrown him as she'd reached for her jacket before leaving the chalet earlier that evening, he'd half believed she'd done it on purpose. Just to rile him. He hid the bitter direction of his thoughts by taking a sip of the soda that would have passed as vodka to anyone other than the barman he'd paid handsomely to ensure that Hope's drinks were un-doctored and his were non-alcoholic.

The man Hope was talking to ran a hand boldly up and down her bare arm and when she reached for him, leaning in perilously close, Luca wanted to turn away. But, grim-faced and focused, he was here to do a job, and he'd do it. So he watched from the shadows as the man pulled Hope to the dance area of the VIP section, the press in the club dropping all pretence now and simply snapping away on whatever format they could get their picture of Hope Harcourt.

As the man pulled Hope against her and Luca clenched his fists, as she let him nuzzle her neck while his hands anchored on her hips, he saw one photographer laugh, the glint of a gold tooth catching his eye and turning his stomach. Feral. Luca felt feral.

Hope spun in the man's arms, a smile across her face and, taking one of his hands, and after throwing a flirtatious wave goodbye to Angelique, she led him away from the dance floor. The man practically covered Hope with his body, blocking her from Luca's sight, and Luca stalked across the lower level, keeping them locked in his sights.

Another of the paps was already checking the pictures he'd got, a satisfied smirk pasted on his features as he probably imagined the amount of money he'd get for that shot.

Luca watched Hope open a discreet door to the back of the VIP section and disappear through it. He waited a minute, popping his jaw with a click, and left the bar.

The moment Hope got through the door to the private floors of Meister, renowned as a hook-up place for those who wanted quick, easy and discreet, she leant back against the wall, looked at Marco, the guy she'd danced with, and they both started laughing.

'Think they bought it?' Marco asked.

'Hook, line and sinker,' Hope said, returning his smile.

'Pleasure doing business with you,' replied the actor, presently trying to keep his sexuality a secret, long enough for his long-term boyfriend to prepare for the media storm that would hit the moment they went public. And they *would* go public, Hope realised, having seen the genuine love and connection the two men shared.

Envy. That was what she felt, she realised as Marco waved his goodbye and disappeared off into the car waiting for him in the underground parking garage beneath the club. But now wasn't the time for romantic hopes and dreams. Now was the time for business.

Hope made her way towards the upper floor, where a series of rooms were set out for whatever the club's clients had in mind. Meister was a sister club to the famous private members London-based club Victoriana and had been the absolutely perfect place to secretly meet with Sofia Obeid.

Hope knew the lighting was kept purposely low to ensure anyone crossing paths in the hallway would be hardly recognisable, but in the shadows she saw Luca downstairs, glaring at her. The dark promise in his gaze, desire wrapped in jealous wrapped in denial, ignited something in her. Something hot and needy. Something that had no place here, especially when she was on the brink of making a deal that would secure Harcourts' future for a *very* long time.

She reached the door of the room that she had booked for the night and knocked, aware that Sofia had arrived before Hope had left the VIP section.

'Come in,' called the voice from within.

Hope opened the door and walked in with a practised smile. She ignored the fact that she was dressed for a night of sin, in stark contrast with the sleek trouser suit worn by the other woman.

Sofia Obeid was tall and every bit as graceful as she was elegant. Hope had done her research in the two days between the opera and when she'd made her approach through a mutual friend.

'Ms Obeid, I'm sorry for the cloak-and-dagger. I know it may seem ridiculous.'

Sofia waved aside the suggestion. 'Actually, not at all. I understand what it is like to work against family. It's not pretty and we do what we must.'

Hope nodded, noting the genuine response from the astute businesswoman. It spoke of secrets and hurts and a shared understanding forming between the two.

'Please.' Hope gestured to the seats. 'Your time is valuable and I don't want to waste it.'

'I appreciate that, thank you. I'm glad that I was in London when you reached out.'

'Rossi Industries?' Hope asked, knowing of the work Sofia had done with the property development tycoons, Alessandro and Gianni Rossi.

'Yes, the Aurora project is going well,' Sofia said with pride and excitement. 'But I must admit I'm curious as to what you might have in mind. Harcourts department stores are a global brand with instant recognition. But what that has to do with my area, I'm not yet sure.'

And Hope could understand. It wasn't immediately clear why she would reach out to a woman who owned a global chain of high-end hotels as well as numerous building development holdings.

Hope poured them each a glass of water from the side table before sitting opposite Sofia.

'You're aware that Harcourts is currently in the position of appointing a new CEO?' When Sofia nodded, Hope continued. 'My cousin Simon has a very good chance of getting that position and it would be the downfall of my family's company.'

If Sofia felt any surprise at the candour with which Hope was speaking, she hid it well. Forcing aside the insecurities she felt about assuming the position herself, Hope forged ahead. 'I would not be the shareholders' first choice and I am not naïve to that. But I know that I would do a much better job than my cousin in leading Harcourts now and into the future. To do that, I need to bring the shareholders something they can't say no to. And that's money.'

Sofia nodded and gestured for her to continue.

'Harcourts is a brand built on the promise of luxury. Harcourts can provide whatever your heart desires, as long as you have the money to pay for it and it is legal, of course. The latest fashion, the most exquisite jewellery, the most expensive furniture, the most contemporary interior design…but I want to take it a step further. I want you to be able to *live* the Harcourts lifestyle—for just a while.'

Sofia's eyes lit as she began to connect the dots. 'You want to create Harcourts hotels.'

'Yes,' Hope said, nodding fervently. 'I want to create branded luxury hotels where you can access everything that the department store has to offer, but the main focus would be on Harcourts branded items. We would start in the countries where a Harcourts department store is already located and branch out from there.'

Sofia sat up straighter in her chair. 'Okay, I get it. Makes sense, you can commute items from the store to the hotel, you already have an existing customer base in the locale on which you could expand. But where would my brand sit?'

'Harcourts Obeid.'

'Not Obeid Harcourts?'

'You already have hotels. Harcourts doesn't. Putting Harcourts first announces that it's something new.'

Hope retrieved her phone and pulled up the documents she'd put together on the deal before passing her phone to Sofia. The other woman sat back to review the proposal as Hope tried to slow her racing pulse. So much was at stake here. Her brother might have been able to lure the shareholders with Casas Fashion, but Hope not only needed something bigger, she *wanted* something bigger. Something better for Harcourts.

'I won't lie,' Sofia admitted. 'I'm tempted. Really tempted. The potential is clear, the revenue projections not only seem viable but eminently tempting. But, Hope, I can't do a deal with a marketing director.'

The other woman's words struck harder than her tone. Hope knew she didn't mean them unkindly, but simply as a statement of fact.

'If we agree to this deal, I won't *be* a marketing director, I'll be a CEO.'

Sofia shrugged. 'I've got another offer on the table. Is it as sexy and exciting as this? No. Would I rather work with you? Absolutely. But you know that this will be a problem with anyone you take this offer to.'

Hope clenched her teeth, her worst fears confirmed. She knew Sofia was right, but she also knew how good her idea was.

'Tell me why you want this,' Sofia stated.

Hope's mind went blank for a heartbeat. 'For the good of Harcourts. It will secure my family company's position as a leading global brand and bring both our companies huge revenue.'

For the first time in their conversation, Sofia seemed a little disappointed. It was there and gone in the blink of an eye but, whatever it had been, Hope realised *that* was the moment she lost Sofia Obeid.

'Can you give me some time? Think on it? Please,' Hope asked, hating that she would beg, hating the desperation she felt clawing at her.

'I'm returning to London in an hour.'

Hope felt sick.

'I could be back here in two days,' Sofia offered.

Hope wasn't sure if it was a lifeline or pity, but she took it with both hands.

'Absolutely. You let me know when and I'll make it happen,' Hope said automatically as she tried to catalogue how badly the outcome of this meeting had affected her.

Luca leant against the wall in the seating area of the private floor above Meister, ignoring the plush leather sofas and chairs. The urge to pace like a caged animal was a need in his blood. He didn't like knowing that he couldn't see what was going on in the room.

It didn't matter that Hope was in there with a business associate—which was all she'd told him earlier as they'd made the plans for that evening. He wasn't sure which had annoyed him more, that she refused to trust him or the thought of her in there with another man.

But something had happened to him, watching Hope on that dance floor. Something that had turned him from cool, calm and in control to raging neanderthal. He'd been attracted to women before. He'd chased and been chased, but the sheer indifference that Hope hid behind—because he knew she was hiding her desire, just like he was—drove him to the brink in a way he hadn't known before.

A door in the hallway opened and a tall, elegant woman emerged. Head down and turning away from Luca, she disappeared towards the back exit of the club. He barely gave her a second glance before he was at the threshold of the room he knew Hope was in.

He waited in the open doorway, unwilling to enter the room, desperately needing to keep some space between them. It was the first time he didn't trust himself. The first time ever. But as he looked to where Hope sat, staring into the distance, he realised that the meeting hadn't gone well.

'We can't go back to London yet,' she said, staring at the wall.

'Okay.'

'We'll be here for another two days, maybe three.'

'What happened?' he asked, wanting to know so that he could fix it, so that he could take that look from her face.

She shook her head as if unable to put words to it.

'She said no?' he demanded.

She looked up at him as if seeing him for the first time. 'She won't sign unless I'm CEO.'

'But you won't be CEO if she doesn't sign,' he said, realising the predicament instantly. 'What did she actually say?'

'She wanted to know why I want to do the deal. And then that we should both think about it.'

He frowned, wondering how Hope had answered the question, wondering what would have swayed the woman who had just left the room by a discreet back exit.

'You'll make it happen,' he said confidently but absently, distracted by the hemline of her dress, which had ridden up on her thighs. She had turned him into an animal.

'Why?' she asked, genuine curiosity in her eyes. 'Why do you think that?'

'Because that's what you do,' he answered as if it were the most obvious thing in the world. 'People underestimate you and you prove them wrong.'

There was an imperceptible breath held between them. He'd been too observant. He'd betrayed himself in an instant. He knew it. She knew it.

Hope stood and closed the distance between them and he held his ground, refusing to back away from what had become nearly the greatest threat he'd ever experienced.

'Why are you angry?' she demanded.

'It doesn't matter,' he dismissed quickly. Too quickly.

'Yes, it does. Why are you angry with me?'

He felt it burning in his gaze. The frustration, the helpless fury, the indignation and the want. It was all too much.

'You let that man put his hands on you,' he growled.

CHAPTER SEVEN

HOPE BACKED UP as he stepped towards her, crossing over the threshold, closing the door behind him and coming into the room. Not because she was scared but because she didn't know what to do with all that testosterone.

'You let that man touch you,' he said, rephrasing his objection to what had happened in the VIP section of Meister, closing the distance between them so that his chest pressed up against hers.

And a purely feminine power unfurled deep within her, knowing that she'd made him jealous. That he wanted her enough to be jealous. Standing in the centre of the room, she knew there was plenty she could do to create space between them if she needed to. If she *wanted* to. But she didn't. She was tired of running from this, running from how she felt about this man, from how much she wanted this man. And instead she breathed deeply, the action pressing her chest against his with the force of her inhalation, causing fireworks to ignite in his silvery gaze.

Tonight, he was dressed in a dark grey shirt, a thin black tie hanging down the centre of his broad chest. His shirtsleeves were rolled back and he looked like he belonged in the shadows. What she wanted to do felt like it belonged in the shadows.

He peered down at her, his height requiring her to crane her neck just a bit, just enough.

'Yes, I let him touch me,' Hope said into the thick tension weaving between them. Taunting him was dangerous—instinctively, she knew that, but she also craved it.

A part of Hope registered that this was crazy. She didn't do things like this. Having been burned by too many people posing as her friends only for access to what they could sell to the nearest journalist, she was incredibly careful about who she spent time with.

But this was entirely different. *He* was different. She knew that as well as she knew her own name. It was in his clear distaste for the media, in his intense discomfort with anything to do with them, in the anger she'd seen barely restrained at the headlines he believed her cousin to be involved in. But whatever this was—her feelings for him—she didn't have control over it. It was as if she was being swept away by it and there was something inherently seductive about that. About letting go. About just letting go.

'Did he ask?'

'What?' she said, his question cutting through the fog of desire clouding her mind.

'Did he ask before he put his hands on you?'

Dark, swirling, thick and heavy, promises filled his gaze and she almost didn't answer.

'Yes. He did.'

'And if I asked?'

This time his chest heaved in a breath that she felt against her breasts, hardness pressing into nipples that were taut with need.

She could play dumb, she could pretend she didn't understand what he meant, but then she would have to walk away. She felt it. They stood there on the cusp, the brink of an edge she could still step back from. But she didn't want to.

'What would it mean if I said yes?' she asked, and for a second she thought he might tease her. Laugh at her, ask if she was demanding hearts and roses and promises she wasn't sure she wanted herself. Fear made her look straight ahead, staring at his chest and feeling the anticipated embarrassment beginning to burn her cheeks.

Her heart pounded in her chest as she waited for him to answer and, even though a second stretched into ten, she refused to raise her gaze. Finally, his thumb hooked beneath her chin and she lifted her head to look deep into his silvery gaze.

Dark tousled hair framed his face perfectly and she was instantly struck by how beautiful he truly was. Fine cheekbones balanced out the sharp angles of his face, but it was him—it was his power beneath the layers of skin and silver eyes, that made him so devastating.

'If you asked me to put my hands on you, it would mean that we would be adults about this. It would mean that when we get back to London, you'll have someone else who will look out for you. I'll oversee it, but I won't be involved in your close protection detail.'

'And what about my brother?'

'You want to talk about your brother right now?' he demanded, the gentle tease so much more welcome than what she'd feared only moments ago.

'What about the deal? He wanted you personally to—'

'He'll live with it,' Luca said, shifting his weight between his feet, somehow making her feel as if he wanted to walk her back a step, even though he hadn't moved.

'But—'

'He'll live with it,' Luca growled, and she got the distinct impression he was barely holding on.

'So if I *did* ask you to put your hands on me?' she asked, needing to know. Needing clarification before they both gave in to whatever madness was waiting to take over.

That she was even considering this was insanity. But perhaps it was because they both had so much to lose that she was willing to take the risk. He had the future of his company on the line as much as she had the future of hers.

'It would mean,' he said, his head dropping closer to hers, his breath puffs of air against her moistened lips, 'that I get to put my hands on you whenever I want, until we return.'

'Just until we return…' She didn't even know if she were asking or demanding and from the swirling in the grey of his eyes like molten silver, neither did he. She was almost dizzy with want, but her instincts kicked in just in time. 'In private,' she said.

'What?' he asked, as if struggling with the same heady sensuality.

'This is only in private.'

Something dark passed across his features, so quickly she wasn't sure that she'd seen it, but then she was half lost because he said, 'Of course.'

'I can't—' Something in her started to defend herself. The risks she couldn't take—the risks neither of them could.

'I get it. So, in private,' he said, pulling his hands from his pockets, where he'd fisted them, 'I get to put my hands on you whenever I want?' They were there, hanging seemingly loose, despite the tension she felt coursing through every inch of his body, inches from where she wanted them.

'Yes.' The word was sin on her lips.

'Say it,' he commanded.

'I want your hands on my body.'

The words were magic for Luca, making the iron-strong bonds of his restraint disappear in an instant. He'd wanted this woman from the first moment he'd laid eyes on her and he could have lied, told himself he didn't know where he wanted to start, but he didn't have time for that. He knew exactly where he wanted his hands.

He pressed the length of his body against hers, crowding her, thrilled when she didn't back up and give him space. He felt a wicked smile pull at the curve of his lips as his knuckles grazed the hemline of Hope's skirt, pulled tight across her thighs.

He flexed his thumb and brushed across the satin of her skin just beneath the skirt of her dress, sending a scattering of goosebumps across her thighs. He could tell that she was trying to hide her reaction to him, unsure whether it was a hangover from the days they'd spent fighting their attraction or whether she was making him work for it, and both turned him on just as much.

He slipped his hand between her thighs and gently pressed her legs apart just an inch or two. He watched her face like a hawk—the way her lips parted just enough to suck a shocked inhale through them, the way her brown eyes burned with even just the hint of heat between them. Her chest was still pressed against his, but he could see the pulse flickering at her neck and he wanted to cover it with his open mouth, to feel that beat on his tongue.

Wicked. What he wanted to do with her was wicked. The heat from her legs warmed his hand as he palmed both thighs, sweeping round to run his thumb across the curve of her arse. A gentle roll unfurled through her body as she grew slightly longer in her spine when the back of his hand met the damp material of her panties.

He held back from doing what he wanted, which was to walk her back to the bare wall behind her and devour her. While that would be delicious and something he would absolutely do before returning to London, tonight was about Hope—her needs and her wants.

He caressed her thighs gently, again and again, almost accidentally brushing against her core as it grew damper and hotter each time. He felt her urge to move, to take control, to seek the pleasure he was denying her, but she didn't—and he knew how much that must cost her. Because it was driving him out of his mind. Every inch of his body was sensitised and tuned to her frequency, to her.

She opened her mouth, the plea in her eyes before it made it to her lips.

'Don't,' he commanded. 'Don't beg—you don't ever beg with me. Just ask. Ask for what you want,' he said, not missing a moment of how she felt about what he'd just said. Relief, thanks, excitement, arousal. And it infuriated him that someone had taught her that she couldn't just ask. As if she didn't have the right to pleasure on her own terms. He forced down the anger and twisted it into something else, something deliciously sinful.

'Oh, Hope. I'm going to give you so much pleasure you're not going to be the same again,' he promised.

The taunt, the promise, the cocky arrogance he knew she would rise to meet, worked.

'Really? You talk a good game, Luca, but—'

Her words slipped into a gasp as he ran his thumb between the folds outlined by the damp silk of her panties.

She shivered beneath his touch as his caress became more purposeful and less playful.

Hope's head fell back, the long line of her neck exposed and, unable to resist, he bent forward to press his lips against her skin. Open-mouthed, he gorged on the salty sweetness of her. Her murmur became a purr of pleasure as his fingers slipped past the wet silk to tease her and finally, *finally*, he had what he wanted. Hope—hot, wet and wanting in his arms.

Impatience choked him, clogging his throat with a desire so thick he could barely breathe past it. His pulse pounded in his veins and his ears like a drum, an incessant refrain. Taste, taste, taste.

He hooked a thumb around the thin band of her panties. 'May I?' he asked, his voice gravel against the satin of her throat.

'Yes... Luca?' she asked, her head straightening, waiting until he pulled away from her neck and looked her in the eye.

'Give it to me. All of it. All the pleasure you promised. I don't want to ask again.'

Oh, she was incredible, this woman.

There, in her eyes, he saw the heat that matched his own, saw the need, the desire, the passion and the power. He didn't have to hold back with her and she didn't have to pretend to be less with him.

In response, he sank to his knees. Not quickly but slowly, so she could see, so she could imagine what he was going to do to her. Like this, he was level with the juncture of her thighs, and he didn't think he'd ever find anywhere else he'd want to be more.

One hand pushed up the ruched side of the dress as the other pulled her panties down, a delicious tension between the two opposing forces, revealing a delicate crosshatch of curls. Musk on the air and heat from her body so close he could practically taste it turned his own arousal from painful to near unbearable. His erection pressed hard against the zip of his trousers, but he ignored it over a much more pressing need.

He ran his thumb between her folds again, one hand behind her, supporting her as she shivered in response, the tremble of her legs a victory, the gasp of heady need his rallying cry and the taste of her as he spread her for him, as he pressed the most intimate of kisses to her core, the only reward he would ever need.

Hope was shivering between fire and ice. Her lungs sucking in oxygen like she was drowning, because that was what he was doing to her. Drowning her in pleasure, just like he'd promised.

Sex—and it had only been sex—with Martin, had been perfunctory. Bed based, missionary, near mathematical, calculated. As if it were something he was assessing himself on. But this? This was sensuality, this was exquisite, powerful, *arcane*. This was what femininity was. This was what adoration was, she thought, before Luca fastened his attention and his teeth gently on her clitoris.

She bit her lip to stop the groan of pleasure that begged for release.

'I want to hear you,' he said against her core, before laving her with his tongue in a way that nearly had her coming right then.

She wasn't sure she could do it. She wasn't sure that, after years of not, owning her pleasure vocally was something she could…and then she didn't have a choice. Luca didn't give her one. He teased his fingers into her slowly but surely, at the same time grinding his tongue against her clitoris, bringing her to the brink of mindlessness, where she had absolutely no control over the pants of need falling from her mouth.

Pushed by his relentless pursuit of her pleasure, closer and closer to stand before the impending orgasm that felt bigger than anything she'd experienced before, she tried to hide from it, but Luca wouldn't let her. He made her acknowledge the force of it, welcome it, bear it as it crashed down about her. Wave after wave collapsed over her as she sobbed for breath, for mercy, for more, she didn't know any more.

By the time she came back to herself, Luca stood from where he had knelt before her and was pressing open-mouthed kisses to her neck. His hands gently caressed her sensitised skin, warming her body to his all over again. Her pulse had barely settled into a satiated throb when his thumb found her taut nipple and he pressed his tongue over the material it strained against.

There were too many barriers between them. Too many layers. She wanted to feel him, to know the heat of his skin, the firm muscle beneath his shirt and the erection pressing against her abdomen—the weight of it, the velvety smoothness, the *taste* of it. Carnal and wicked images ran through her mind like a kaleidoscope and suddenly she was ravenous for whatever he could give her, whatever he would let her take.

Luca's hands bracketed her ribs, holding her to his mouth…to where he continued to fasten his mouth to her breast. The cowl neckline of her dress was too high for him to bare her to his tongue without damaging it or… Frustration and impatience had her reaching for the bottom of her dress and pulling it from her body, Luca reacting quickly enough to move out of the way to let her. And then she stood before him, her black heels with the red soles, and absolutely nothing else.

And that was when Hope truly understood what it was to be devoured. He consumed every inch of her. She followed his gaze as his eyes tracked over her breasts, lingering on them before following the curve of her hip, the length of her legs, the sweep of her calves, locking on the shoes, when she saw silver *burn*.

'Turn,' he commanded.

If it had been anyone else, she might have felt objectified, but with Luca? She felt *alive*. She felt desired. She felt as if she were the one with the power and he was simply asking for more. Slowly, inch by inch, she turned in a circle, feeling the heat of his attention like a touch, like a caress, warmed by it, wetted by it.

Restless, she rubbed her thighs together, knowing that the orgasm he'd brought her to was a taste of what was to come, rather than the culmination. He bit his lip as he tugged at his tie and shirt with staccato movements. Buttons were yanked, his belt released from loops in one smooth movement that defied rational thought, his feet were bare and she couldn't remember when he'd taken off his shoes.

He pulled his shirt from his body, the vest beneath hugging muscles she wanted easy access to. Refusing to be a spectator any longer, she closed the distance between them and tugged the vest from the waistband of his trousers, glorying in the hot, smooth muscles that rippled beneath her touch.

She traced the detail of his tattoo, the wing down to the body of the horse. Pegasus. Power, freedom, determination all communicated in black and white detail—it was a piece of art.

He let her explore his body with a patience that she marvelled at. It was only when she pulled the vest from his body, pressing her mouth against his, her head full of the scent of him, her tongue parsing salt from skin and the taste that was uniquely him, that she realised it wasn't patience, it was restraint. And it was fraying beneath her ministrations.

Satisfaction unfurled and her own impatience got the better of her. She pulled him to her by the waistband of his trousers, before reaching to undo the button and the zip. Matching his earlier sensual tease, she allowed the back of her hand to smooth down the long length of his powerful erection. The temptation of it, of what she would feel when he filled her, was too much. She turned her hand to grasp him, her hold firm but gentle, the thin cotton of his briefs doing nothing to disguise the promise of him, and even that barrier became too much. She wanted skin, she wanted... Her hand slipped beneath his briefs and held him, heat on heat, smooth on smooth, but, even then, less than they both wanted.

Her hand drew up and down the length of him, the slide erotic and bringing slashes of dark red to his cheekbones. His chest heaved with his breath, and she felt it, having him at her mercy, the power she wielded in that moment. The trust it had taken for her to give in to him shining back at her in his silvery gaze. His breaths became pants and groans as she flexed her grip at the base of his erection, as she reached to cup his balls, as he fought his own desire for more.

It wasn't enough. She wanted him inside her. As if he'd read her very thoughts, he pulled back slightly from her hold, breaking their connection, only to remove the trousers and briefs in one go. If she had even a moment to take in what they looked like, staring each other down, naked, aroused, panting, it was just that. A moment. Because Luca reached for her, picking her up in his arms, her legs instinctively wrapping around his waist, his erection pressing against her stomach, his hands beneath her, perilously close to her folds, teasing her and instantly making her throb. He held her as he walked back to the sofa and sat, laying her across his lap, looking up hungrily at where she rose above him.

Unable to stop herself, she ground against his erection, the pressure raking against her clitoris sending a thrill through her, and his hands on her backside only encouraging her to repeat the action.

He reached down beside them and returned with a condom and she sent a prayer of thanks that at least one of them was thinking sensibly. She rose onto her knees as he covered himself in the latex, before running his thumb between her folds again, teasing her clitoris from beneath her. Unrestrained moans of pleasure fell from her lips as she rocked against his thumb, as he guided the head of his penis to her entrance and then she slowly, inch by inch, sank downwards onto his erection.

Curses fell into the room, his or hers she couldn't tell as he filled her, stretching her aching muscles, pleasure feeding into her bloodstream like a drug she could become addicted to. From this position she had power, she had control, and that he knew her enough to know how important that was to her was both terrifying and thrilling. Back and forth she rocked against him, teasing them both, sweat slicking their bodies and heartbeats pounding through skin.

For what felt like hours, they simply gloried in the feel of each other, the sounds and feel and scent and taste of each other... It was languid, slow and utterly erotic, the slide and glide of his hard length in her. The pleasure merely banked from her previous orgasm nipped at her heels, building slowly and slowly, and all the while Luca's gaze locked on hers watched every single moment of it happen. He could feel it, she realised, the tightening of her muscles, the impending orgasm about to sweep her away.

But then he moved.

Luca reached around her back, his palms on the tops of her shoulders, and pulled her down at the same moment as he pushed upward and the earth tilted on its axis. He was so deep in her he felt lost and found at the same time. Again and again, he thrust, hard and deep and quick. His hold kept them joined, but each time he felt closer and closer to impossible. Sweat gathered at the base of his spine, Hope, slippery in his arms, her pleasure-filled cries burnt into his soul as he shoved them closer and closer to the brink he wasn't sure he wanted to cross.

More, he *needed* more.

He picked her up and held her to him as he changed their positions, laying Hope carefully on her back on the sofa, and nearly losing his breath as he parted her thighs, so that he could see the way his erection penetrated her body, that he impaled her, but it was Hope watching him that pushed him towards the cliff edge. Her pleasure in his pleasure, her arousal fed by his, and he reached between them, his thumb finding her clitoris, rubbing gently, furiously, wringing cries and pleas from a woman who had struggled to find her voice merely an hour before.

'Luca,' she cried, his name pulled from a voice stretched taut with desire. His chest felt thick, full with arousal, barely able to breathe as he shoved into her, deep and hard, pulling out only to shove into her again. Braced on a hand beside her head, he pounded again and again, pushing them to madness.

Her hands wrapped around his forearm, her mouth finding his wrist, biting, licking and hiding her desire, her skin flushed and sweat-slick as her moans reached a crescendo, the muscles wrapped around his erection tightening like a fist and the orgasm that struck them both at the same time pulled them into an abyss of two stars exploding together.

Hope couldn't stop staring at him. This man, who had given her the most sensual, erotic experience of her life. This man, who had promised to touch her whenever he wanted, in private. And, as clichéd as it sounded, she was changed by what they had just shared. She felt it, it had sunk into her bones. A secret knowing of what she was capable of not only giving but receiving. As if she'd accessed some previously unknown, untapped, potential for *more*.

Luca navigated the car effortlessly through the snow-covered darkness. A silence that should have been suffocating, stifling even, held nothing but satisfaction. But also curiosity, she realised as she watched him palm the wheel, turning into the near invisible road to their chalet.

Is it always like that? For you? she wondered.

It was only when he turned to look at her, the car slowly pulling to a stop, heat blazing in his steel-grey gaze that she realised she'd spoken out loud.

'No, Hope. It's never…' He trailed off, seemingly as incapable of describing what they'd shared as she was, soothing the thin thread of unease that had unwound within her. It was important to her that they were equally in this, whatever this was, until they returned to London. Two days. She had two days to work Luca out of her system—

if that was even possible. And two days to figure out how to convince Sofia Obeid to change her mind.

He leaned his head back against the rest and looked at her. 'Stop thinking so hard,' he said. 'It's late. And I still have things I want to do to you tonight.'

And on that sensual promise, Hope let herself be led from the car, into the bedroom, where Luca once again drowned her in a pleasure she could have barely imagined before that night.

CHAPTER EIGHT

HOPE WOKE WITH a stretch. The bed was obscenely comfortable, the snowscape through the windows a skier's fantasy. Her body ached pleasantly and her blood was still heavy with the drug that was Luca. She nestled into the pillow that still bore his scent and warmth. She squinted at the clock on the side table and rolled onto her back with a groan.

It was seven a.m. and, no matter where she was in the world, she never slept in this late. She should have been in the gym, showered, dressed and on her way to work by now. And even though she was in Austria, despite last night's diversions, she *was* here to work.

She slipped from beneath the covers and peered into the en suite bathroom. The shower stall took up half the wall and she approved. Hugely. With a smile, she worked out the buttons and within seconds was standing under a powerfully hot stream of water, bringing her mentally into the present.

Less than fifteen minutes later, she emerged onto the fourth-floor living area dressed in soft, easy yoga clothes and looking for Luca. She found him leaning back against the counter, looking out at the forest at the foot of the mountains and the smooth slopes that brought visitors here in their thousands.

She paused, her hand on her stomach, taking in the

sight. He stood there bare-chested, black silk pants hanging low on his hips, almost as if their sole purpose was to display the corded muscles that veed beneath the waistband. She knew what those corded muscles could do, she realised, the blush riding high on her cheeks. She should be hitting the brakes on whatever this was. It wouldn't, *couldn't*, last. But a selfish part of her wanted more. Wanted to luxuriate in it, *him*, just a little longer.

He looked at her then, catching her watching him. 'Morning,' he said, his voice gravelly, in the same tone he'd used last night to tell her all the things he wanted to do to her and more.

All she was capable of was nodding. He held out a mug of steaming coffee and the spell was lifted and she covered the distance between them, desperate to get at her *other* morning addiction. She was sure that things would make sense after even just half a cup. And if they didn't, then she would make them make sense.

She went to stand beside him and paused when she caught sight of his tablet, open on the website for the *London Daily*. There was a headline about a politician lying about his expenses next to a photograph of her and Marco dancing in the club.

Unable to stop herself, she reached for the tablet, clicking on the post.

Hope Harcourt Drowns Sorrows with Stranger!

'I don't think Marco would appreciate being called a stranger,' she commented, scanning the hastily written hack piece on her 'indiscreet night' following hot on the heels of her ex-fiancé's new engagement. At least there was no mention of Sofia. 'It worked,' she observed, intensely uncomfortable searching the headlines of other magazines and articles for news of her supposed scandalous affair, standing beside the man she *had* actually spent the night with.

She knew the cover story was needed—if Simon had even an inkling of what she was up to, he'd find a way either to ruin it or try to trump her. No, it was best if he and the board all thought she was sunning herself on a ski slope until she could execute her plan—*if* she could execute her plan. But it left a bitter taste in her mouth to use herself in such a way.

And that was exactly what she felt like. *Used*. Dirty in a way no man had ever made her feel before. And for once, just once, she wanted to have a day where she wasn't in the spotlight, where she wasn't fodder for another attack by either the newspapers or Harcourts.

'You're thinking too much again,' he growled as he watched her take her first sip, testing the heat, testing the strength. Of the coffee and the man, she thought, perhaps.

'I can't *not* think, Luca. Everything rests on this deal with Obeid,' she said, shaking her head, feeling that sense of helplessness again. 'If Simon gets his way, I won't be able to just sit there and watch him ruin the company my father...' She trailed off, unable to admit how much she needed this to work. For her father, her brother, her grandfather. She tried to ignore the way that Luca narrowed his eyes at her. 'I'm going to use the gym...'

She trailed off at the way Luca was slowly shaking his head and felt a flare of frustration. Being dominant in the bedroom was one thing, but if he thought for one minute that extended out of it, into her day-to-day life, then—

'We're going skiing,' he announced.

'I have work,' she said, her hackles rising.

'You know your work. You know that deal. You know what wiggle room you have, and so does Sofia Obeid.

What you need to do is work out what she wants. Because she does want this deal, or she would have given you a flat *no*.'

The reason in his tone was as infuriating as the fact that he was right. She *did* need to get out of her head. Hope looked past him to the golden rays of the early morning sun glistening on fresh snow. He was the devil, tempting her in more ways than one.

Luca was almost surprised that Hope had agreed. It hadn't actually been what he'd intended to say, or even how he'd intended they spent the day. But the shadows in her gaze hadn't been from a lack of sleep, even if there had been very few moments stolen in between the times they'd reached for each other through the night.

He'd meant what he'd said. It had never been like that for him and he wasn't sure what that meant, and he didn't want to try to find that out just yet either. He got the impression that Hope felt the same way.

Luca turned to find Hope making her way towards him, her ski boots crunching on the snow. Even wrapped up in insulated layers of ski gear, she was stunning. Most of her blonde hair was hidden by the helmet, aside from the few wisps that had escaped. Goggles hung around her neck and her cheeks had a healthy pink glow from a mixture of excitement and windchill.

Unlike him, dressed head to toe in uniform black, she'd found ski pants in a deep orange and a high-tech slender pale blue jacket. Obviously the latest fashion, but he knew the brand, knew its quality was of the highest degree. He wondered if she would ever not stand out in a crowd. It was just something about her. Something he wasn't sure she realised she had.

'There's a path through the forest that leads straight down to the bottom of the slopes. From there we can get the chairlift up and take one of the green runs over to the other side of the range, where the slopes are a little more challenging, if you like.'

She appraised him. 'You ski regularly?'

'When I can,' he replied. Alma and Pietro hadn't had any interest in the sport, but the school his mother had paid for had regularly arranged trips to slopes in Italy and across Europe. The innate grace he'd inherited from Anna meant that he was a natural, and he'd enjoyed the athleticism of it as much as the beauty of where skiing could take him. He'd loved every minute, until the coach journey home. Because he'd known then that it was only hours before he'd watch each and every one of his friends rush off the coach, eager to get to their parents, to tell them about their holiday, to get kisses and be enveloped in hugs. And he'd wait, making sure to be the last off the coach, so that there were fewer people who might see Pietro, standing beside his old car, grim-faced and unwelcoming.

Anna had never seen it or, if she had, she'd refused to acknowledge it, but Pietro and Alma had only ever wanted to please the famous actress. Anna had been such a bright, shining light to them that they would have done anything she'd asked of them. Even raise her child. But it had never meant anything more to them than a burden they bore for her.

Hope clipped her boots into the skis provided by the chalet, their boot and ski measurements provided in the booking so that the guests wouldn't need to go through the rigmarole of battling against the general population renting their equipment. Luca bent to check them for himself, ignoring the smirk pulling her full lips into a curve. Satisfied she was ready, he clipped back into his and pushed off along the private path that led through the forest.

The sound of the skis on snow, the *thunk* of the poles digging into the ground was soothing on nerves almost painfully and constantly aware of Hope. There was something almost magical about it: the seclusion of the trees, their rich, vivid emerald peeking beneath thick layers of white, the way that sound was dull and that the easy movement caused his pulse to raise gently. He felt Hope keeping pace with him and smiled, wondering how long that would last.

They emerged from the forest near to the chairlift that would take them up higher, where they could take a series of runs that would get them to where he wanted to take Hope. She pulled to a stop beside him, pulling her goggles down, her eyes bright with excitement and expectation, and he knew he'd done the right thing.

'Your chariot awaits,' he said, pointing to the bottom of the chairlift, surrounded by small groups of families, couples and what looked like a ski class of five-year-olds.

Anonymity. He'd given her anonymity, she realised, as she leaned into the gentle turn she took down the green run that both she and Luca could have made blindfold. But she enjoyed the ease of it, refamiliarising herself with the turns, the stops, the feel of it. She'd spent so long being the face of Harcourts, courting the press, for good or ill, because it was how she represented her family, that she'd forgotten about simple pleasures, of an enjoyment that wasn't on display—perhaps even of a romance that was secret, she thought, her stomach swooping in line with the wide arc she made with her skis as she turned to a stop at the bottom of another set of lifts. To one side was the button lift, dragging skiers up the side of the easy run full of children and newbies. To the other was the bubble lift and where Luca was leading her to.

They queued up with excited children and eager adults, all speaking a mix of German, French, English, Spanish and Italian. Hope felt happy. And excited. A family of four stepped into the bubble-shaped lift behind them, the heavy plastic affording a hazy glimpse of the slopes below them and the mountain range above. The little girl was jumping up and down, the thrill and excitement rolling off her in waves. But it was the little boy that caught Hope's eye. Solemn, perhaps a little scared, his mother quietly and gently soothed him with reassuring words Hope didn't need to understand.

She remembered her mother doing something very similar for her when she and Nate had been learning to ski. She caught Luca looking at them too and wondered what it reminded him of. And slowly the smile that had curved her lips dropped a little. The look in his gaze wasn't one of fond memories.

But the lift arrived at its destination and they only had a short time to grab their skis and disembark. She went to follow the family to the top of the blue run—a step up in difficulty from the green, but Luca gently guided her in the opposite direction.

'We're not taking the run down?' she asked.

'Not yet. There's something I want to show you,' he said. 'Trust me?' And even though she couldn't see his eyes, hidden by the wraparound sunglasses, there was a taunt, a challenge, without the edge and with all the tease that she enjoyed so much between them.

'Not as far as I can throw you,' she lied and Luca threw

his head back and laughed. It was a startling sound—one that drew more than just her glance his way.

'Come on,' he said, and he guided her towards a faint track. It was off-piste, so it wasn't under careful management, and there were no ski patrols keeping an eye out like there were on the runs. But Hope was confident of both her and Luca's ability and she knew he'd never put her at risk. Ever.

The thought was as startling as his sudden deep laugh had been and it rang in her ears, echoing in the silence created by the banks of snow that surrounded them as they crossed the ridge of the hill and swept down into the basin below.

Her stomach rose and fell as the momentum they'd created forced them back up the other side and, despite her absolute conviction that she would slide back down, she found herself cresting the other side and couldn't help but let out a whoop of pleasure.

She followed Luca as he cut a path across fresh, untouched snow, and she tried not to be distracted by the sight of clouds hovering close by. He called back to her to make sure she was keeping up and while the cold air pushed and pulled out of her lungs with a frequency that was as intense as any workout, it was so much more satisfying.

For a while she focused simply on that. Moving her body, following Luca's direction. Her mind emptied for the first time in what felt like for ever. Peaceful. It was peaceful. There was nothing here that wanted her to be, or do, something. There were no demands on her or for her to make. She settled into the rhythm and lost herself, until Luca slowed to a stop. There was a little wooden sign, but she missed what it said because the moment she gazed to where Luca was looking, she forgot her curiosity.

Breath left her chest in a whoosh, the sight before her so magnificent. The peak of a mountain rose up so close she was half convinced she could reach out to touch it. The clouds that had hovered near earlier ringed the peak below where they stood.

When Luca clicked out of his skis and took a seat in the small bank of snow behind them, Hope followed suit.

'It's beautiful,' she said, her tone reverent. It was as if they were close to heaven, she thought, the sun glinting off the snow, a pale denim blue sky bare from but a few spun-sugar clouds. It was spectacular.

Luca nodded, not needing to fill the silence between them. It was an unusual trait, she realised, suddenly aware of how much of her life was filled with distractions or information. She had wondered before if it were part of his role, his job. A chauffeur needed to be unassuming and invisible a lot of the time. In some ways, she supposed, bodyguards had to be the same. But she was beginning to realise that it was something innate in him. Something quiet that called to the near frantic energy of her life and drew it down a few notches, soothing her in a way she'd not experienced before.

Her grandfather tolerated her, challenged her to be better and more with his absent manner and his criticism. Nate sought to fix, to mend, to do, unaware that he was utterly overcrowding her, not even giving her the chance to prove herself. The board, the shareholders, they were simply blind to what she achieved daily. But Luca? He just let her be.

Luca felt the moment that she relaxed finally. For the first time since that morning, she took the breath he'd felt her struggling for. He knew the breakneck speed at which she worked; he knew enough about the life she led to understand why she felt the need to be that way. He just wasn't sure that she'd ever really sat down and thought about whether she wanted it or not.

It hadn't been Alma or Pietro, or even Anna, that had helped him to see what he wanted from life, but a teacher from his local school in Palizzi. Signor Arcuri had called him back after class, just before the end of his final term.

'It doesn't matter what you want to do, Luca. As long as you know why. That "why" will give you purpose. It will see you through hard times, self-doubt, poverty and riches alike. Find why you want to do what it is you want to do, and do it with absolute conviction and no looking back.'

It had changed his life, Luca knew. It had forced him to coalesce his thoughts, his wants, into a single goal: Pegaso.

Perhaps he'd never grown out of the idea of becoming the white knight he'd believed his mother had desperately needed, because even then he'd known that he wanted to protect people. To help those who couldn't help themselves. So he'd taken the money his mother had gifted him when he'd signed the NDA at eighteen and been clever. Sensible but clever. He'd invested half of that money while he'd done the training and groundwork needed to build Pegaso up from nothing. He was proud of that, and he'd never looked back. But he couldn't help but wonder if that perhaps all this action and forward momentum in Hope disguised the fact that she didn't know what it was that she truly wanted.

'Beats the gym,' Hope said, her breath a puff of air, her eyes squinting in the sun, having taken off her goggles to look at the view.

'Beats the gym,' he confirmed. He checked his watch. 'Come on.'

'Have we got somewhere to be?' she asked, laughing lightly. It was a sound he felt against his skin. One he wanted more of.

'A very important meeting,' he teased.

Another ninety minutes of skiing and one chairlift later and they came to a large chalet, similar to the one they were staying in, but here on the large wraparound deck were tables, half full of skiers and families. Hope's desire for anonymity was so different to his mother's near compulsive need for recognition that he didn't know how to make it fit with Hope and her life.

'Lunch?' she asked, turning that bright, full smile on him, and it had the force of a punch to the chest, sending all thoughts of his mother scattering.

'Best place in town,' he commented.

'It's the *only* place in town,' she observed, making a show of looking around at the miles of snow-covered landscape.

'Doesn't mean that it's not good,' he said, holding his hand out to her. When she took it, he led her up the busy wooden steps and towards the entrance.

Stop.

It was a feeling. The raising of hairs on his neck. He'd never not trusted it because it had always been right. He stopped and turned. Something had caught his eye; he just couldn't quite work out…

There.

The man had his back half-turned now, but Luca could just make out the high-quality camera. And yes, it could have been a skier using personal equipment, but there was something about him that was familiar.

The club. He'd seen the guy at the club. Luca remembered him because of his tooth, having tried to work out if it was a stain or a gold replacement that had caught his eye when the guy smiled.

Before he could think it through, Luca covered the distance between them and crowded in on the man, using their height difference to maximum effect. The photographer turned, ready to lash out, but shrank back instead when he realised it was Luca.

'Give me the camera,' Luca said, his voice low but determined.

'Hey, man, I'm just doing my—'

'Not today,' Luca said, reaching for the camera.

'You can't do that,' the photographer complained.

'I can delete the ones from just now, or I can take the SD card. Your choice.'

'How magnanimous of you,' the pap whined.

'Card it is,' Luca said, flipping the camera, pressing the button.

'No, wait—wait. That's my work.'

'And this is mine,' Luca said, a penetrating glare forcing the photographer's eyes away.

'Just the ones from now,' he said, his tone placating but his eyes furious. 'Please.'

Luca probably should have taken the SD card, but he knew he was skating on thin ice. With no justification for removing the pictures, other than the fact that he had wanted to give her, give them, this one day, he scanned through them. The clearest one showed Hope—and it clearly was Hope Harcourt—looking up at him and taking his hand. He paused for a heartbeat before hitting the delete button on the pictures.

Luca thrust the camera back at the photographer and stalked back to Hope, who stood waiting nervously, casting furtive glances over his shoulder at the man behind him.

'How did he find us?' she whispered.

'I don't know, but he has nothing now.'

'You deleted the images?'

He looked down at her, wanting so much more than he could do in public. It had been a timely reminder of the promise he'd made to her, and one that could have cost them greatly. And from the look in Hope's eyes, she felt the same.

'Yes,' he said, answering her question about the photos, and gestured with his head towards the chalet, careful to keep his hands to himself.

Luca led Hope to the greeting desk. On one side of the chalet's floor was a large canteen-style buffet where families, couples and even a ski class were busy piling plates high with delicious-smelling food, the other where tables and chairs were rapidly filling up.

Hope watched as he spoke to the waitress behind the desk, who smiled and nodded, gesturing for them to follow her up the large wooden staircase to the second floor, which opened up to a restaurant dining area. Tables covered in white cloth and silverware were half full with slightly more sedate customers than the raucous ski groups downstairs. Hope thought that they might stop there, but the waitress continued on to the balcony and, pulling back glass sliding doors, she led her and Luca out towards a private table for two. Luca thanked the waitress while Hope simply stared at the view.

Discreet outside heaters gently warmed them from above, and though only glass separated them from the dining room, there was the impression of privacy—they were alone with the view. Their chairs, covered in rich white faux fur, suited the silver, glass and green fir sprigs decorating the table. It looked like a winter wonderland but while her designer's eye appreciated the touches, it was the natural beauty of the mountains that called to her the most.

'You're spoiling me today, Luca. I'm going to have to come up with more words than stunning, beautiful, awe-inspiring.'

She turned to find him looking at her. Really looking.

'Now you know how I feel,' he said, and her heart fluttered in her chest, replacing the earlier discomfort from the encounter with the paparazzo.

For just a moment, she'd allowed herself to forget. Forget that they couldn't be seen in public together, that the easy affection she wanted to give was not possible. Forget that this, whatever it was, had limits before it had even started.

He pulled a chair out for her and she sat, before he took the seat opposite her.

'Thank you,' she said, not knowing how much she meant it until the words left her lips. He nodded, the look in his eyes understanding, rather than dismissing what the moment meant to her. And it was novel. To be so understood.

Being a twin was a connection that was hard to explain to most people. There was a bond there that went so deep, sometimes she'd wanted to break free from it. But then Nate had collapsed and the fear she'd felt that day, the genuine, honest-to-God moment of heart-stopping, mind-blanking fear had rocked her to her core.

And though that connection blazed strong between them, she sometimes felt that Nate didn't take the time to understand her. Sending Luca after her without speaking to her, believing that she needed protection—or that she couldn't have seen to that herself, believing that she wouldn't realise that there was more to Luca than being a chauffeur, were prime examples. Perhaps even doubting that she could be CEO of Harcourts was another.

But Luca? She felt he did actually understand her. He didn't underestimate her or what she wanted or could even achieve. And it frustrated her that she didn't know the same about him. It was possible that his reticence was just with her, but Hope felt that it went deeper than that, instinctively knowing that he would be just as much of a closed book with other women.

She thought back to the other day, when they'd argued about this lifestyle.

'What kind of life is that? It's bland. It's ridiculous. You're being used for someone else's momentary fascination and you're allowing it.'

She'd never forget those words as long as she lived. And now, she realised, truly realised, he hadn't been talking about her.

Hope waited until the waitress had poured both water and wine and left before asking the question burning in her chest.

'Who is she?'

'Who?' Luca asked with a frown marring his brow.

'The person you know who lives this life.'

Her gaze took in the pulsing muscle at his jaw, the living, breathing dragon that lived behind the blank gaze he'd erected between them. His body had betrayed nothing. But the energy that pounded beneath his skin, the change in temperature between them told her so much.

He stayed silent for so long, Hope looked away. What right did she have to pry into his life? She felt foolish and embarrassed for asking, for overstepping whatever line it was—as invisible as it might be—that lay between them.

She reached for her glass and her hand nearly knocked it over when he answered.

'My mother.'

CHAPTER NINE

THE WORDS ENDED years of silence and secrecy, landing between them like an unexploded bomb. Luca's heart pounded in his chest. He'd never told anyone. Thirty-four years of keeping a secret was a hard habit to shake and even now he felt nearly sick at the thought of it.

He could see Hope trying to make a mental connection between his name and someone she knew and, when that failed, she looked at him, searching for features she might recognise. His cut glass cheekbones, the rich dark hair, the unusual silvery grey gaze.

'Oh,' she said, blinking as she put two and two together. It was his eyes. They were his mother's. Anna Bertoli, the famous Italian actress who had managed to do the unthinkable: cross from Italy to Hollywood without disdain or derision. She was a screen siren with more global recognition than Harcourts could even dream of having.

'I didn't know she had children,' Hope said, without thinking.

'She doesn't.'

Hope flinched at the cutting edge of his tone and he instantly regretted it. But the internal battle raging between wanting to protect his mother and wanting to tell her was riding him hard. Because he thought she, of all people, might understand. Hope knew the weight of the attention of the press, of the importance of reputation. And because he thought she might be able to keep his secret. Hoped that she would, because a part of him wanted someone he didn't have to lie to, someone he didn't have to keep himself separate from.

Luca's sigh was a surrender. 'There are only two other people, besides Anna and myself, that know this.' He hadn't realised it, but his palms had turned upwards, a physical manifestation of the question he didn't have to ask.

'I will never tell,' Hope promised and he—who rarely trusted anyone—believed her with absolute certainty.

'I don't see her much. I *can't*,' he said, trying to explain his very complicated feelings about the press and public life. 'Anna forged her career as an ingenue, an enigma, an alluring woman who remained dedicated only to her career and her fans. That she's not had children is part of her brand,' he said with a shrug, as if he were running down the CV of a client rather than describing his mother's achievements. In part because all of those achievements had required him to be invisible.

'She must have been incredibly young when she had you,' Hope hedged. He knew it was a gentle probe. Something he didn't have to answer if he didn't want to.

'Sixteen.'

Hope cursed, the word almost funny in her crisp English accent. But there really was nothing funny about a pregnant single sixteen-year-old girl.

'He was a co-star, apparently.'

'Apparently?' Hope asked, her eyes getting darker and darker with an empathy that was new and unfamiliar to him.

'She never told me his name,' Luca said. Anna had, instead, told him that it had been a terrible mistake, that she wished it had never happened and that he had told her to just 'get rid of it'. If she had even realised the impact of what she was saying to her child, he'd never seen a sign of it. In Anna's world, she had simply been telling him how terrible it had been for *her*. He'd wondered once if it was a defence mechanism. If she'd *had* to see the world that way, to live with the decisions she'd made, but he didn't like to think that hard about it. Instead, what he'd clung to as a child was that she had stayed. His mother had stayed when she could so easily have not. How could a child not be thankful for that?

'At the time, her father was her agent, her mother had died a few years before. It wasn't too difficult to explain her absence by an eight-month stint on an independent film that didn't get off the ground. And after she had me, she returned to make *Il Cuore Vuole*, the film that made her an international star.

'But from that moment on, I was a threat to her,' he confessed. 'Neither Hollywood nor Italian cinema would have touched an unwed sixteen-year-old mother of one.'

Hope reached out her hand across the table and, as much as he wanted to take the comfort she offered—more than he'd ever wanted anything—he couldn't forget that they weren't in private. Just like with his mother, there were too many witnesses and something buried deep ached all over again.

She withdrew her hand, apologies in her eyes for the gesture of comfort she couldn't give.

It was strange speaking of it after all this time. For so long everything he'd thought about it, he'd felt about it, had been unspoken. Seeing the sadness for him in Hope's gaze legitimised his feelings in a way that was new for him.

He wished that didn't make him angry. He wished that he still wanted to protect his mother, the way he had been so desperate to as a child. But he wasn't a child any more. He had seen the way the world worked, and what Anna had told him then didn't make as much sense now.

'Who raised you?' she asked.

'Anna's older sister and her husband. Alma and Pietro. They'd never had children of their own and after their mother passed, they loved Anna like their own.'

But not you?

Her question might not have been spoken but he read it easily in her eyes.

He was saved from having to answer by the arrival of the food he'd ordered before he'd lost all appetite following their conversation.

Hope seemingly felt the same way as the food went untouched long after the waitress left.

'So, you have protected her secret?' Hope asked, reaching for the water rather than the wine.

'Yes,' he said with a conviction that went deeper than any vow. No matter what their relationship was like, Anna was his mother.

'Why?' she asked tentatively, as if afraid that the question would seem rude or thoughtless, even though he knew that Hope was neither of those things.

Why? It was a question he'd been asking himself a lot in the last few years. It had made sense when he'd been a child. He'd seen himself as her knight, as Anna's protector. But was he really that same little boy, still hoping that she'd love him? That she'd finally recognise him and claim him? Something he realised in that moment, with a start, that Anna Bertoli would never do.

'But she supported you?' Hope asked in the absence

of an answer, her concern that his mother had fulfilled at least some part of her maternal duties clear in her tone.

'She gave Alma and Pietro whatever they needed to raise me and, although it wasn't too much to raise suspicions, it was definitely enough. And then at eighteen there was an inheritance of sorts.'

'Of sorts?'

'Anna wanted me to have some money, but said that her lawyers were worried about it so they tied it into a non-disclosure agreement.'

'An NDA for what?' Hope demanded, already halfway to furious on his behalf.

'That I never revealed myself as her child.'

Shock punched the breath from her lungs. Her hand flew to her mouth. 'She…' Hope couldn't find the words. In all her years at an all-girls boarding school, throughout which she genuinely thought she'd experienced some of the cruellest behaviour, and even beyond that—seeing what Simon was willing to do for power and control—none of it compared to a mother not just disowning her son, but silencing him too.

'You can do a lot with half a million,' he said, as if he felt the need to justify his choice. She realised that he was worried what she thought of him.

She desperately wanted to reach for him then. She wanted to curl up in his lap and hold him and tell him words she had no place offering him. Because he couldn't even take her hand. And she hated that she couldn't offer it to him. It made her feel unworthy of him.

'It's okay,' he assured her, as if sensing her inner battle.

'It's not,' she replied, refusing to let him excuse it, the way he clearly tried to excuse his mother's behaviour. 'And she should never have done that to you,' she whispered harshly. 'You should never have had to sign such a thing, certainly not in exchange for your silence,' she insisted, and even though it made her want to question their own agreement, this was about him and about his mother, not them. No wonder he had made a career from living in the shadows, from keeping secrets. Yes, he had become a protector, a saviour to some—she was sure. But at what cost?

'Luca you did the *right* thing by taking the money. Because you made something of your own. Something you can be proud of. And that means something. The man you have become owes nothing to that woman,' Hope said, sure of her words, but unsure whether she had the right to say such a thing.

His eyes on her were fierce. She *felt* what it meant to him to hear that. And somewhere in that molten silver unwound passion and a heat so intense she felt a flush rise to her skin. But in spite of that passion, she still needed him to know one thing.

'You shouldn't have to live in the shadows. You deserve more, Luca.'

He nodded his acceptance of her statement, not once taking his eyes from her, but she still felt that he held a part of himself back.

'Hope, no one can know,' he warned, and she knew that this wasn't a request from the wrong side of a legal agreement. It was the request of a son determined to protect his mother. And she would do anything to honour it.

They spent the rest of the afternoon chasing each other across the runs and slopes of white powdery snow. After a few forced moments of happiness to change the mood over lunch to something lighter, the lie became the truth, as if they were both determined to put the past behind them and focus only on the present. As if they were both aware that time was running out before they returned to London and would have to stop whatever this thing was between them. Because even as every part of her being wanted Luca with a ferocity that scared her almost, she knew that their relationship wouldn't, couldn't, survive the scrutiny of the press.

So after a few slopes they embraced the freedom of their movements, allowing it to lift her heart that afternoon as they sped across dramatic vistas with barely a soul to see. The sweeping sound of her skis on snow, Luca's delicious—and sometimes wicked—laughter, all standing out against the backdrop of a clear blue sky without a hint of a cloud.

She convinced Luca to let them go to one of the ski bars on the way down the mountain, promising to keep her goggles on as they shared a mulled wine and were tempted to shots of Jägermeister, the syrupy sweet alcohol with a punch. It had almost been a game, how far they could push each other without the displays of affection they both so clearly wanted.

Stomachs growling from a full day of skiing and a barely touched lunch, they sneaked into a bistro and, after securing a table in the back of the restaurant, they wolfed down *schnitzel,* and buttery greens and mashed potato for Luca and *frites* for Hope, who rarely let herself indulge in so much naughtiness in a week, let alone a day. And as the crispy, salty crunch exploded on her tongue, she began to wonder just how much she had sacrificed in becoming the face of Harcourts. As if sensing the direction of her thoughts, Luca distracted her with a forkful of garlic mushrooms that she couldn't resist.

Reluctant to make the trip back on their skis through the wooded forest in the dark, Luca arranged for a car to take them back to the chalet, from a service he trusted, and the moment they were through the front door, Luca was peeling her clothes from her body and she was frantically tugging at his. He walked them down the hall to where the spa rooms were and guided her towards the hammam.

'Shower first,' she said against his lips and he simply shook his head, pushing her onto the glass-panelled room, his urgency, his need for her pressing against her stomach, and driving her beyond rational thought.

'I've wanted to do this all day,' he growled into her ear.

He picked her up, her legs instinctively wrapping around his waist, and backed against the door so that it opened for them, pressing a button on the panel on the side that filled the room with a delicate-scented steam that brought a slick sheen to her skin in seconds. He sat with her once again on his lap, only this time he brought her leg across so that she straddled him, the thick blunt head of his penis teasing her folds.

He took her mouth in a kiss that was carnal, invasive and possessive, burning her hotter than anything the steam room was capable of. She rolled against him, her hips, her thighs, her chest, unfurling inch by inch, her entire body craving the feel of him against her.

And she was in heaven until she heard Luca curse with frustration.

'Condom,' he growled, and he pressed his forehead against hers.

For a moment Hope's mind went blank and then rushed back in a heartbeat. 'I'm on the pill. Contraception. I'm on it. And I'm clean,' she said in a rush.

He looked up at her, she could see the warring in his

eyes. The desperation to be that intimate with her, but also the awareness of consequences, of mistakes. She wouldn't force this on him, it was his choice as much as it was hers. No one had the right to take that from anyone.

'I'm clean too,' he said, and she understood the incredible trust he had placed in her.

She nodded in answer to his unspoken question. She wanted this more than she wanted her next breath.

'But Hope, this is going to be hard and fast,' he warned, the wicked promise bringing a wetness to her core. In answer to his unspoken question, she rose onto her knees enough to reach between them and grip the length of his erection, hot and thick in her palm. Her thumb brushed the head of his penis, where a small bead of moisture already tipped against her finger.

'You'll be the death of me, Harcourt,' he growled against her lips, as she guided him to her entrance. His hands, one on each of her sit bones, palmed the backs of her thighs, spreading her for him, his fingers dipping into her folds.

'You're so wet, *cara*,' he said.

'That's what you do to me,' she whispered into his ear, before sinking down onto the steel of him as he rose up to meet her with a powerful thrust that drew a cry from her lips.

She spread her knees wider, sinking just that bit more onto him, and felt him pulse deep against her core. Her head fell against his shoulder, a sob exploding from her chest. With one arm around her waist and the other pinning her chest to his, he withdrew slowly, a delicious torture, before slamming back into her with a guttural cry. Bracing herself against his shoulders as he held her just slightly above him, again and again he pounded into her, forcing her towards an orgasm she wasn't sure she'd survive. Luca filled her so completely, she felt all of him as he moved within her, but when he found that little rough patch of nerves hidden deep within her, Luca hitting it again and again until he became so hard, so steely within her, it felt alchemical.

'I've got you,' he whispered as he thrust into her again. 'I've got you. You can let go,' he said.

As if that was what she'd been waiting to hear her entire life, she gave in, standing in the path of the orgasm building between them as it crashed down on them like a tidal wave and all she could do was surrender.

Luca had never come so hard in his entire life. Aftershocks still burst through his body, even as he picked up a thoroughly ravished Hope and walked them into the shower stall. Turning on the spray of warm water, he lathered his hands in the shower gel and gently began to wash her body. She felt delicate under his touch, but he knew the strength of this woman—even if perhaps she wasn't always sure of it herself. Lust-drunk dark eyes watched him as he ran soapy hands gently between her legs, caressing and cleansing as he went.

After seeing to himself, and before he could become even more of a neanderthal and take her again in the shower, he turned off the water, dried them off and wrapped her in a large fluffy white robe.

'Where are we going?' she asked as he led her out of the ground floor and towards the fourth.

It was a good question, and even though he replied, 'Upstairs,' his mind threw up many different answers to the same question. But what he wanted and what he could have were two different things. They always had been. Hope's life—so prominently in the public eye—was impossible for him. Within an hour of being seen together there would be deep dives into his background, his family. There would be photos and research, and while Anna Bertoli on paper had no connection to Luca Calvino, he knew it wouldn't take too much digging, too much work to uncover the truth. The only reason it hadn't been done before now was because of his anonymity. So the only answer his mind offered to her question was *Nowhere*, even as everything in him roared in denial. This, whatever it was, had an expiration date. But until then he would satiate every single craving or desire Hope Harcourt could conceive of.

He went to a cupboard and produced a very nice bottle of red while Hope retrieved the glasses. Hitting the buttons on the solar-powered heaters, having stored their energy through the day, he flooded the balcony with gentle warmth and a subtle glow. He flicked a button on the hot tub and Hope started to laugh.

'You're trying to turn me into a prune, Calvino,' she said, the lightness of her tone soothing his concern that he'd been too rough with her.

He turned, apparently, the question clear in his gaze.

She put down the glasses on the small table beside the bubbling tub. 'That was incredible,' she said, walking into his space, slipping her hands between the robe he wore and pressing herself against him like a cat. She reached up to cup his jaw. 'You gave me what I wanted before I knew to ask for it,' she said, easing any concern he'd had about what they had just shared. He kissed her, letting his relief, his thanks and his promises for more to come, bleed into the kiss.

'A prune, Calvino,' she teased, pulling back from the kiss, giving them both the chance to breathe.

She shrugged out of her robe, gloriously and utterly unselfconsciously naked as she stepped into the frothing bubbles of the hot tub. Lithe and graceful, and he'd have known that even if he hadn't spent the entire day watching her traversing the slopes and runs as if she'd been born to them.

Shucking his own robe, he joined her in the bubbling heat, steam rising around them and disappearing into the night sky.

Although the kiss had rekindled the arousal between them, the burning desire that had driven him almost the entire day had been sated enough for him to simply enjoy the feel of her next to him, to luxuriate in the easy touches that passed between them as they settled into their wine, talking of particular slopes or moments of the day they'd enjoyed. And although the conversation was easy, he knew that the revelation about his mother had left an imprint. It made him think of the anniversary of her parents' death. Of how she'd spent that night alone and he wished he'd had enough sense to fight her harder on that.

'What were your parents like?' he asked, wondering if she'd shut him down, hoping that she wouldn't.

She looked out at the view of the mountains and was quiet for so long he thought she wouldn't answer.

'Busy,' she said, surprising him with the choice of word. 'Harcourts is from Dad's side of the family, and he was groomed to take over from grandfather. Not something I think my uncle enjoyed very much. Perhaps that's why Simon is so determined to become CEO.' She smiled pensively. 'But they were busy. Mum was an interior designer.'

'Where you get your eye from?' Luca enquired.

She smiled up at him, as if thrilled he'd noticed.

'I'd like to think so. She filled the house with colour,

prints and paintings, everything that was bright and cool. She would take kitsch and make it classy, and would get lost in a fabric shop the same way others might get lost in a museum,' Hope said, smiling. 'We actually did that once. Got lost in a fabric shop. I would swear, even now, it took us nearly the entire day to find our way out.'

She grinned up at Luca, the memory pulled to the surface by his question, of that special, magical moment in time when it had just been the two of them. 'Nate was off with Dad, probably at Harcourts, but Mum and I spent the day pulling out reams of bright fabric and soft textures, sequins and silks.'

Her mother had promised to make her a dress for her twelfth birthday from the material they bought that day, but…then the accident had happened. Hope didn't remember seeing the material again. After the funeral their grandfather had closed down the house, put most of their parents' things in storage, sold the family townhouse in London and put the money into the trust fund that both Hope and Nate had access to when they turned twenty-one.

'And your father?'

The question pulled Hope to another memory. 'Tall,' she said instantly, remembering clinging to his leg and looking up at him as he reached down to pick her up. 'He had a bit of a temper, would shout, and of the two, we were definitely more scared of him than our mother. But she would soften him, soothe him. Coffee makes me think of him,' she said softly. 'And caramel makes me think of her.'

'How did they meet?' Luca asked, pulling her closer to him to rub soothing circles at her neck.

'She had been working as an assistant to a window dresser, but he was temperamental and had an artistic disagreement with Grandfather, who promptly ordered Mum to 'fix it'. That's the story they always told, anyway.'

'So Harcourts was the centre of everything?'

It was the heart.

'Mum worked there before having us and then, after we were old enough, took on some private interior design clients. But Nate and I grew up in the halls of Harcourts. Playing hide and seek before it opened and after it closed, waiting for Mum and Dad to finish up work. All the staff knew us. It used to be a family joke that the store was the biggest nursery in the world.

'Dad would sneak Nate into the board meetings sometimes,' she remembered.

'And you?'

'I would be outside with the secretaries,' Hope replied, losing a little of that smile. 'They were lovely, but busy. I sometimes wondered if less work was done in the meetings than outside of it.'

Luca nodded. 'Probably quite true.'

She turned to him to prise a kiss from his lips, trying to remove that anxious, uncomfortable feeling when she remembered things like that. Luca indulged her, but she realised it was precisely that. An indulgence that lacked the punch of heat she felt when he wanted her.

'He was grooming Nate even then?' Luca asked eventually when she came up for air.

Hope shrugged, not enjoying the questions now.

'I don't know,' she replied.

'Yes, you do,' Luca pushed, not unkindly. 'But he was a man with values imparted from an older man. And you were children with fully formed personalities and half-formed dreams.'

She wanted to push back at him, at his perceptiveness.

'You should forgive him,' he urged gently.

'For what?' she replied, despite knowing full well where Luca was leading her.

'He couldn't have known.'

'Known what?'

'How much you would love Harcourts. How much it's in your blood,' he said, taking her hand and pressing a kiss to the pulse at her wrist.

'Of course I do. It's—'

'Nate has three other companies,' Luca observed.

'And?'

'You don't,' he stated. 'Your brother loves *business*. You love Harcourts. And you have every right, if not more, to that CEO position. Even if you don't believe it yet.'

The unearthing of her vulnerability was painful and raw. She hated that she was jealous of her twin, hated that she had been angry with her father as a child, angry before she'd even really been able to put a word to the swirling emotion that had heated her cheeks and made her heart ache. And she hated that she wanted Harcourts so much that she'd do almost anything to get it.

Luca was right. She loved it with every ounce of her being.

He reached for her and Hope went to him willingly, to kneel in the space he made for her between his legs. Yes, there was arousal there, attraction that seemed almost constantly to simmer beneath the surface, but comfort was what she sought, and what Luca gave her when she most needed it.

CHAPTER TEN

THE CALL FROM Sofia Obeid had come in early the next morning and the air around Hope had been electrified ever since. Luca drove them to where Hope had arranged to meet Sofia, unnervingly happy that it wasn't another club and didn't involve another man to disguise the meeting. He peered through the wide window of the restaurant that was nearly half full of diners. This far from the slopes in Hallstatt, it was a classy establishment for those who wanted something away from the crowds of tourists.

The winding drive into the picturesque valley, down to the lake nestled in the basin of mountains, had failed to distract Hope from typing notes furiously into her phone. He'd asked her if she knew what she was going to say. She'd nodded, her fingers halting on the screen for just a moment, and then she'd nodded again and gone back to typing.

'Are you sure about meeting here? It's very public. I can't control photographers here,' he warned.

'I'm done with hiding, Luca. I'm done with pretending to be less than I am,' she said, her tone determined in a way that made him proud and pleased at the same time.

'Do you want me to come in with you?' he asked.

'No,' she said with a smile as she opened the door before he could even think of doing it for her.

He watched her cross the road and, even though he was parked in a no parking zone, he refused to move the car away from where he could see her. She entered the restaurant and a waiter took her to a table that was thankfully still in the view of the window.

He recognised the woman who stood up from the table, greeting Hope warmly, as the same woman who had left the club the night before last, tall, striking and slightly older than Hope. He wondered if the people in the restaurant had any idea of the power that these two women had at their fingertips.

He'd cast an eye over Hope's plan while she'd been preparing and while he didn't understand the specifics, he knew enough about numbers to know that the board and the shareholders would be absolutely out of their minds to ignore a deal that could net them nearly half a billion pounds in profit by the second year of the branded hotels' opening. It was clever. It was daring. It was global, and Luca had absolutely no doubt in his mind that it would work.

He just couldn't work out how she didn't know it. How she didn't know how brilliant she was. He wanted to throttle her brother and shake her grandfather. These were the people who were supposed to protect her and raise her with a confidence and self-assurance that she deserved.

Watching her sit down opposite Sofia Obeid, Luca realised that he didn't want this to end here, in Austria. Yes, there was a huge amount on the line if they even tried to continue a relationship moving forward—his business deal, avoiding the press, Anna...

These weren't inconsiderable things to him. He'd spent his entire life protecting his mother's reputation and he'd spent his entire adult life protecting and developing his own business. It was the one thing, the *one* thing, that grounded him in this world. The one thing that would prove he'd ever been here.

But a reckless, demanding part of him didn't want to give Hope up. He—who trusted almost no one—had trusted her with more of himself than he'd ever shown anyone. And he knew that he'd seen a side of Hope that no one else had ever seen, not even that bastard of an ex-fiancé.

His mind scrabbled to make the scenario work. Clandestine meetings, illicit encounters, ways around attracting the attention of the press… He'd do it, he realised. He'd do that for her. He could even see himself giving up the contract that Nate Harcourt had dangled in front of him like a carrot to protect Hope in the first place. He would stay in the shadows for her, like he had done for his mother.

And he didn't know whether that terrified him because it was a good thing, or because it was the worst thing.

'Thank you so much for making the time,' Hope said, surprised that she wasn't feeling nervous. The urgency and desperation that had driven her in their last meeting was strangely absent.

'I'm glad I was able to,' Sofia replied sincerely, her gaze assessing, as if noting the change in Hope too.

'I don't have any changes to the offer. I can't and, to be honest, even if I could, I *wouldn't* make any changes to what is already both a good idea and a good deal for us both.'

Sofia frowned slightly, her only outward sign of confusion about where this conversation might be going then. Hope didn't want to waste either of their time with unnecessary platitudes.

'But I did want to give you another answer to the question you asked before, about why I wanted this. If I'm honest,' Hope admitted, 'I wasn't aware of what was driving me then. And in some ways, if you hadn't forced me to question it, I might never have realised it, so I'd like to thank you.'

Sofia's eyes were impassive, but Hope didn't care. If the amazing businesswoman sitting opposite her didn't get it or understand—even as she prayed that wasn't the case—Hope realised that she'd find another way. Because she loved Harcourts and because she loved what she did. And she *would* find a way of making it hers.

'At the beginning I thought that I was trying to make this deal because it would wrestle the CEO position away from my cousin. I thought I was doing it for my brother, who had been groomed from childhood to become the CEO, first by my father and then my grandfather. I thought that I could maybe caretake it for him, until he returns, paying him back for all the times that he protected me after my parents died.'

Sympathy and a hint of understanding flared in Sofia's gaze.

'But… I don't want to give it away,' she said, finally admitting the truth out loud. 'I want the CEO position for myself. And I want this deal because it's an *excellent* idea, it's an *exciting* idea, and because it's *my* idea. I can see it so clearly in my mind, I can almost feel the gold handle of the hotel door, with our names across the top of it,' she said, conjuring the images in her mind as she said them. 'I want this because Harcourts is my legacy and my future. Because I want to thrust it into the twenty-first century, with new designers and a socially conscious ethos. I want Harcourts to speak to, not *down* to, the communities that it supplies,' she said, nearly out of breath with the passion pulsing through her body with every beat of her heart.

There was so much more she could have said, but Hope realised she didn't need to as she looked at Sofia smiling back at her with satisfaction and an excitement of her own.

'*Now* you are someone I would like to do business with,' Sofia stated confidently.

'I can't lie, I'm not the CEO yet.'

Sofia nodded, clearly debating what she was about to say. 'Hope, if they choose Simon over you, then you might have to think about leaving. Because as much as you love that business, it will never love you back.'

'But you're agreeing to the deal,' Hope said, refusing to let Sofia's warning dim the bright shining light building in her chest.

Sofia smiled. 'Did you bring the paperwork?'

Hope managed to contain her excitement until she got back into the SUV and turned to Luca.

'You did it,' he said, a smile splitting his handsome features, his steely grey eyes bright with silvery sparks.

She didn't answer. Instead, she grabbed him and kissed him hard and hot and deep, her hands pulling him to her meeting no resistance. She clung to the kiss, desperately almost, praying that Luca wouldn't notice—that she couldn't speak, couldn't think past the fear of how much him being there had meant to her. How much she'd wanted *him* to know that she'd got the deal. Not her brother, not her grandfather—the people she had spent her life wanting to impress, but Luca—who had come to mean so much to her in such a short space of time. Too much, she realised, as she responded to the pounding of his heart beneath the palm of her hand, where it rested on his chest.

He pulled back from the kiss, breath punching in and out of his chest. 'I'm taking you home,' he said, and she knew she should correct him, that the chalet wasn't their home, but the words stuck in her throat, the fiery passion blazing in his gaze setting her body alight with that very same need.

Luca didn't know how many speed limits he broke on the way home, and Hope hardly helped matters. She couldn't keep her hands off him, her palm smoothing over his thigh muscle, dangerously close to where he really wanted her.

She looked at him, and where he'd once seen disinterest and aloofness, he now saw so much more. He saw need, raw and unvarnished, in the swirls of espresso and heated caramel, making his whole body pulse with a thick arousal he feared he might never satiate.

All he knew was that by the time they pulled into the driveway to the chalet he was ready to claim her in a way that was primal and powerful, in a way he'd never experienced before. Which was why he kept his hands on the steering wheel, trying to claw back some sense of control.

He felt her gaze on him. 'Luca—'

'I need a minute,' he said, concerned by the intensity of his need for her, concerned about what that could lead to.

'I don't,' she replied.

'Hope…' Her name was a plea and a warning at the same time.

'I can see it,' she said. 'How much you want me.'

Clenching his jaw, he forced himself to meet her gaze.

'Don't you see that same want in me? That same ferocity? I want you like *this*,' she said, her words a silvery seduction enticing him to his deepest needs, as she leaned towards him, her lips already partway open when she pressed against his mouth, inviting his tongue, his hands, his heart…

This was Hope emboldened and she was magnificent. She shifted across the console, too impatient to wait, his hands reaching for the lever to pull the seat back in time for her to straddle his thighs, and too fast for him to explain that the chalet was just there.

Her kisses drugged him. Her hands reached between them, found his painfully hard erection and her palms teased more than soothed the heat between his legs. Unable to fight it any more, he reached for her, his hands wrapping around her, holding her in place above him, her blonde hair hanging around them like a halo.

He teased her breasts with his thumbs, the arch of her back pressing them closer to where he wanted, and he pressed open-mouthed kisses over the thin merino knit top she was wearing, the stiff peaks of her nipples punched against wool damp from his attention. He let her go, knowing she'd support herself, and reached between her legs, the same damp heat there just from her pleasure.

'Please,' Hope whimpered, rocking herself back and forth across his lap, his erection and his sanity. The wrap-over cashmere skirt she wore had slipped either side of his lap, showing slivers of perfectly smooth trembling thighs. Gasps shuddering through her, her hand reached between her thighs to ease her own need, but he pulled it away, pressing kisses into her palm, and growled the words, 'Not yet.' Her eyes flared, the pulsing in them matching the throbbing in his groin.

'Luca,' she cried from need and want.

Biting back a curse, he freed himself from his trousers, reached between the heaven of her legs, pulled aside the damp silk, sweat already beading at the base of his spine and the last coherent thought he had before he thrust into the hot, wet heat of her was that if this was madness, he never wanted to be sane again.

Hope's gasp of raw pleasure filled the car as she braced her palm against the roof, to push herself back down onto each thrust. He could feel the twitch of her muscles as they encased him, gripping him. She was already as close as he was.

Breath punched in and out of his chest as he fought to hold off the impending orgasm building deep within him. His hands palmed the underside of her trembling thighs, holding her in place as he pounded into her from beneath, his hips thrusting and pulse racing.

Instinct took over, and any concern that it was too fast, too hard, fled as Hope's desperate cries urged him on. He reached for the hand she had on his shoulder and moved it between them, his finger guiding hers against her clitoris.

Her eyes sought his, filled with so much dark desire and a desperate want.

'Now, *cara*,' he said, and watched with his heart in his mouth as she began to touch herself. Her head fell back as she gave herself over to the pleasure they were making together. She coated him as he withdrew from her agonisingly, only to thrust back into her with a dizzying force. She took everything but gave him more.

Luca raced against their impending orgasm, desperate to wring as much pleasure from this moment as possible, determined to hear one more pleasure-filled cry fall from her lips, to feel her grip him once more as he pulsed deep within her. To take one more breath through an arousal that made the air thick and fogged the windows. His thighs slapped against hers again and again as he pounded deep into her, as he felt her fingertips from where she brought herself closer and closer until they lost the fight and she came apart around him, drawing his own orgasm from deeper than he'd ever felt before.

It was the most intense orgasm Hope had ever had. She had let Luca carry her from the car and into the shower on the ground floor, and somehow he'd then taken her to their bed, where she'd fallen into a bliss-filled unconsciousness.

So when she heard the buzz from her mobile phone it took her a moment to try and orientate herself. She wasn't even sure what the time was. The room was dark and her screen so bright she squinted to see the name.

She blinked awake in an instant. Unplugging it from where it was charging, she slipped from the bed, hoping not to wake Luca. She tiptoed out of the room and upstairs to the fourth floor.

'What do you want?' she demanded when she finally hit the accept button on the call.

'Can't I just give my little cousin a call, now? Have we become such adversaries?'

'Simon, drop the crap. I don't have time for this.'

'No, I'm sure you don't,' he said insidiously.

Everything in her went still. He wouldn't call unless he had something. He wouldn't call unless he thought he'd already won. Her stomach turned in on itself.

'What do you want?' she repeated, not quite trusting herself to say anything else.

'Nothing. In fact, it's entirely the opposite. I have something for you,' he said, his tone overly civil. 'I managed to obtain something I thought you might be interested in. Check your inbox. I'll wait.'

She put the call on hold while she pulled up her inbox

on her phone. His email was waiting for her, but when she clicked on the attachment she nearly dropped her phone.

There were several pictures of her and Luca, taken when they had been in the hot tub only the day before. One of her in his lap, another of them kissing, and one of him looking at her as if he wanted to devour her. Her pulse rocketed and her skin stung, the violation of their privacy absolutely horrifying.

The photographer Luca had warned off, she guessed. If he'd been freelancing for the press, she wouldn't have seen these pictures until they were beneath a headline. The fact that Simon had them could only mean that he'd been the one to hire the photographer.

She bit back the wave of nausea turning her stomach, her mind racing, Although the pictures bordered on explicit, she didn't doubt there were worse ones she hadn't been sent. In an instant she saw it—realised what these photographs meant and her heart jerked in her chest. The press might be interested in who Luca was, but Simon would be a bloodhound. He wouldn't stop until he knew everything, in the hope that it would give him leverage to get what he wanted.

She closed down the email app and opened another on her phone and, after arranging what she wanted, she took the call off hold.

'What do you want, Simon?' she bit out, not even bothering to suppress the rage she felt in that moment. She was almost certain she knew, but she needed him to say it.

'Let's not be coy about this,' he snarled into the phone. 'I know you have some kind of deal on the table in an attempt to woo the shareholders into voting for you in two days' time. But I doubt any deal would trump another sex scandal from you.'

'There hasn't even been one sex scandal,' she growled into the phone.

'Oh, I'm sure your ex-fiancé has something up his sleeve, if this doesn't do the trick. I want you to back out of the CEO vote, or I'll start digging. Because though you may be egalitarian, you wouldn't be sleeping with the help, Hope. So, while I don't yet know who he is, it's only a matter of time.'

Luca paused at the top of the stairs. He'd woken just as Hope slipped from the room and he'd worried when she hadn't come back. He watched her pace the living room floor, whispering harshly into the phone. He couldn't quite hear her, but it was clear something was wrong. He frowned, and debated whether to go to her, but he could tell from her body language that it might not be a good idea. The call wrapped up and she turned to stare at the darkness through the window.

Quietly, he returned to the room and the bed and waited.

When Hope tiptoed in about half an hour later, he lifted the cover for her.

'Everything okay?' he asked.

'Absolutely,' she said, smiling back at him, not realising that her one word had eviscerated him. And neither of them slept again that night.

The next morning Hope packed her things while Luca was in the shower, stomach churning and heart aching.

She knew what she had to do, and that it hurt so much to do it only served to make Hope even more convinced that it was the right thing. Time and time again she'd seen that she could only trust herself; look what had happened with Martin, and wasn't she just making the same mistake in trying to rely on Luca? It wasn't as if they had a future beyond Austria anyway.

Just until we return.

Had she said that? Or had it been Luca? She threw a jumper into the suitcase angrily. That she didn't even remember, didn't know, just went to prove how much being with Luca confused things for her. And she couldn't afford to be confused right now. Her focus *had* to be on Harcourts, on beating Simon.

Yes, Simon had sent a photographer after her, but *she* was the one who had drawn Luca into the mess of her family struggles. The least she could do was ensure that Luca and his mother didn't get caught in the crossfire.

But if Luca knew what Simon had sent to her personal email, Hope knew that he'd try to find a way to protect her. He'd not stop until he'd protected her—whatever the cost to himself. And she *couldn't* allow that to happen. It was time that someone finally protected him for a change. Even if it broke both of them to do it.

She stopped pacing back and forth across the floor when she heard his footsteps on the staircase. She'd made them coffee and when he emerged she gestured to where it was on the counter. Luca closed the distance between them and reached for the coffee, his eyes flicking between her and her suitcase, his expression inscrutable.

'I've been thinking about when I get back to London. The vote is in two days' time and things will be crazy after that, if—*when*—I get the CEO position,' she said, the words ash on her tongue. 'It's going to be a while until I might be able to see you again.'

That unfathomable gaze was locked on her, as if he knew she was lying. But she wasn't, was she? That was the thing. She would be busy when she got back, no matter what happened with the vote. And nothing changed the fact that even if she could have a relationship with him, the press would still be there. They would still want to know about Luca, who he was, what he did, where he came from. Every single inch of his personal life would be scrutinised, and nothing could protect him and his mother from that.

'I'll wait.'

'You can't,' she said, retreating into herself, pulling the layers of polite civility over her once again. It had been a mask that Luca had stripped from her, but to protect him—to protect herself—she needed to put it on once again.

'Don't do this,' he commanded, and she struggled against the order, hating the anger in his eyes, barely masking the hurt that lay beneath it. 'Don't shut me out like she did.' His words eviscerated her. Knowing how much that had not only cost him to say, but also to feel. She was rejecting him, just like his mother, and that cut something deep in her. A wound in her conscience and her soul that wouldn't heal.

'Hope,' he said, her name on his lips so different to the way he'd said it last night. The night before that. No, this time it was pain. 'You don't have to do this,' he said.

'You're right. I don't have to. But it's what I'm choosing to do, Luca. This stays here in Austria. Just like we agreed. And when I'm made CEO, I'll honour the agreement my brother made with you too. But this,' she said, gesturing between them, 'this was never going to be anything more than a pleasant distraction.'

She saw it then, her words hit their target, striking dead centre, and it did something to her. No, they'd not shared words of love, and yes, she was pushing him away as hard as she could. But it was so desperately painful that he was able to believe her so easily.

* * *

Fury coursed through his veins, blotting out rational thought and reason. Blotting out the memory of her pacing back and forth on the phone the night before.

Fury, the lash end of the whip of pain that was racking his body in a way he'd not even begun to feel just yet. He was so angry he wanted to shake her. He knew that there was something wrong with her words, with the way she said them, but he could barely see past the fact that she was walking away from him, cutting the ties that had bound them so deeply he thought he'd lost his heart.

Fool. Bloody fool.

It was happening again. Another woman turning away from him. His mother couldn't be seen with him, Hope didn't want to. The walls came slamming down, cutting off everything but the ice that was forming around his heart.

'You didn't even give it a chance, did you?' he bit out, shaking his head. Hurt and self-recrimination descended in a red haze. 'Because that's too scary for you, isn't it, Hope?' He tutted and turned away, bracing his hands on his hips. 'Fine,' he said to himself, nodding once before looking back to her. 'This? It's done. As you wish.' His hand was a slash through the air, drawing an immovable line. 'But Hope? Know that you will never be loved the way you need and want, until you're ready to open yourself up to the possibility of being hurt.'

She flinched at his words and he couldn't even bring himself to feel like the bastard he knew he was.

'I'll take you to the airport and my team will pick you up in London.'

'I've called a car. It's better if we—'

'I'm taking you to the airport,' he growled, nothing but ice in his tone. 'My team will continue in my absence until the vote, and until you can arrange for your own security.' He went to the top of the stairs where her bags were. 'I'll be in the car,' he said, picking them up on his way out of the chalet.

They drove in complete silence, Hope returning to the back seat, which he was thankful for. He wanted to shake her, he wanted to push her, he wanted her with him and he wanted her as far away from him as possible. He couldn't trust himself to speak, anger and hurt were riding him so hard.

They arrived at the airport and he opened the car door for her, Hope hiding behind her large sunglasses once again. Each step she took felt like a punch to the gut. Each second she refused to look at him, acknowledge him, another cut of the knife. And he welcomed them, reminding himself that this was why he should have kept his distance. This was how he made sure he learned his lesson this time.

He stayed by the car as the steps were pulled up, refusing to move from his post as the small jet taxied to the runway. He thought he could see Hope in one of the round windows, but told himself it was probably just his imagination. He stayed by the car as the jet powered across the tarmac, lifting delicately into the air, and he stayed by the car long after the plane became less than a dot on a denim blue sky that he hated more than he'd hated anything in his life before.

Afterwards, Hope didn't remember the flight back to London. She knew that she'd stared blindly through the cabin window with one thing on her mind.

Don't cry. Don't cry. Don't cry.

When she climbed down the stairs from the jet, a uniformed driver had the car door open for her and Hope slid into the back seat.

She absolutely refused to break in front of one of Luca's employees, even though her mind played her a collage of all the moments she'd shared with him. The way he'd looked at her in the rear-view mirror as he drove, the way he'd stopped the lift and given her his shirt. The way he'd kissed her that first time in Meister, and the way that he'd held her in the hot tub when she'd needed it.

It was all and none of those things at the same time. Her heart felt bruised and raw and hurt in a way she had never experienced before. Not even when she'd discovered the truth about Martin. Because she'd never loved her ex-fiancé the way he'd expected her to. And at first he'd wanted her for that almost as much as he'd wanted her for her money. But the fact she gave him neither of those things had enraged him.

The only thing that had angered Luca was when she was in danger, from the press or from not being true to herself. He had seen beyond every mask she'd worn, every distraction she'd used, every wall she'd erected, and found her. The real her. The one who was still scared that she'd not live up to what her daddy had wanted. Until that very last moment, when he'd seen what she'd wanted him to see. And perhaps what he'd expected to see all along.

She shook her head, physically trying to break away from the direction of her thoughts, because if she looked too closely she'd hear it. The refrain in her soul, telling her that she loved Luca, that she adored him, and that only made it harder to push him away.

Tears pressed at the corners of her eyes and she willed them back. Just a little bit longer. She could hold on just a little bit longer. Her heart was aching and she felt more alone than she'd ever felt before. Through the car window, the streets of London looked grey and dirty. All she saw were the piles of rubbish waiting to be collected, and the drunks and the homeless who slept in doorways. It was the seedy underbelly of the glitz and glamour that Harcourts' customers paid exorbitant amounts to erase. And she felt it—the slick grime over her skin, choking her with the agreement she'd made with Simon.

'You will never be loved the way you need and want, until you're ready to open yourself up to the possibility of being hurt.'

Hope shook her head at Luca's parting words to her, believing that she didn't need the love he taunted her with. She didn't need anyone. She never had. She could do this on her own, she thought, sweeping away the tear that had escaped.

'Ma'am, the press are at the entrance to your building.'

Hope nodded her understanding.

The driver's wary gaze looked back at her in the rearview mirror.

'Would you like to use the garage?'

'No, thank you.'

I'm done hiding.

CHAPTER ELEVEN

LUCA TURNED THE glass in his hands, the ice sliding around the curve, lubricated by the last mouthful of whisky. He'd nursed one drink for half an hour and was considering ordering another and getting a cab back from the airport. Or maybe he could call one of his staff.

He found a bitter irony in the fact that, of all places, the meet had to happen here in Switzerland, where it had all started. He glared out at the passengers waiting for flights from behind dark glasses. The waiter had been casting nervous glances his way from the moment he'd sat down. His female colleague, however, looked like she wanted to devour him.

He rolled his shoulders and cracked his neck. The solid fist gripping his stomach since Hope had left Austria yesterday hadn't let up. He rubbed his hand across the beginnings of a beard that he might or might not keep.

He caught the commotion from the corner of his eye, the flash of bulbs and the raised voices, and for the first time in his life he didn't connect it with his mother—but Hope. He shoved back at the kneejerk jolt of concern. He clenched his jaw and ordered another whisky. He was receiving updates from his staff in London and that was all that he had now.

The glass door to the private lounge opened and in

glided Anna Bertoli, her entourage staying behind to block the frenzy. Luca knew the drill by now, they had it down to an art form—almost like two dancers performing practised moves. He got up from the bar and chose an empty table with several others, equally bare, around it.

Without a glance in his direction, Anna went to the bar, ordered her drink and took a seat at a nearby table with her back practically to him.

She was a beautiful woman, his mother. Her hair was a waterfall of ebony silk falling down her back in perfect waves. Her skin was perfect, as smooth as it had always been, and he nearly laughed at the bitter irony that it was probably the most natural thing about her.

'You look well,' he said, facing away from her.

That was how they did this. Two strangers talking out at the world, rather than to each other. In a paparazzo's photograph he would just be a hazy background figure; in a fan's memory he wouldn't even appear.

'So do you,' his mother observed, even though she had yet to actually look his way. 'Is everything okay? I was surprised to get your request to meet,' she said, and he wondered whether she was really worried about him or herself.

'Do you regret it?' It wasn't what he'd planned to ask, but the words came unbidden to his lips.

Anna froze, the moment so quick it was almost imperceptible, but he'd been watching, waiting to see it and, now that he had, he wasn't sure how it made him feel. She exhaled slowly, as if through pain, and he hated that he couldn't trust that she was being truthful.

'Every day,' she replied.

'Would you have made a different choice?'

'No.' The word was a bullet that hit its mark. 'We are who we are because of our choices, Luca.' That he be-

lieved. 'And you were a child. I was trying to protect you.'
The words were right, but Luca honestly thought in that
moment that his mother was talking about herself.

He bit down on a chunk of ice, watering down the
whisky in his empty stomach.

'The press intensity would have been truly awful for you.'

'Then.'

'Pardon?'

'Then. As a child, it would have been awful then. I'm
a man now and I can take whatever you think they might
throw at me.'

'Even your agreement to sign an NDA?'

Bile twisted his stomach.

'They'd eat us alive. The mother who hid her son and
the son who sold his silence?'

Rage tore through him at the thought that his mother
would even try to use that against him. He'd agonised over
that decision—between money he desperately needed, and
what…? Because there hadn't been an alternative offer that
was anything other than what he already had. There hadn't
been promises to recognise him in her life. There had been
no exchange. It had been a payment, pure and simple. Any
last hope of a familial bond frayed beneath the weight of
that recognition and a line appeared in the sand, between
him and her. Anna shifted in her chair as if sensing it.

'Is this because of the girl?'

This time, *he* froze.

'Hope Harcourt?'

'How do you—?'

'I saw you in the background on the front page. Even
when you try not to, you stand out, you know,' his mother
said with an edge to her tone that sounded a little too much
like jealousy. 'Even in the shadows.'

Luca shook his head at her choice of words as they struck a chord with similar ones Hope had said over lunch in Austria. Hope had lashed out, had been angry that his mother had wanted him to stay in the shadows. She'd said as much. And Hope would also have known that being with her would do exactly the same—force him to remain there, in the darkness, to keep his promise to his mother.

Like a fist to the gut, Luca realised that Hope had been lying to him that last day in Austria. That there had been something else instigating their separation. Something that must have been tied to the phone call she'd taken that last night.

And he'd allowed himself to believe her lies because he was scared. Scared by the power of his feelings for her, by his need—yes—but by the all-consuming love he felt for her too. Scared because he feared, even now, that Hope might not think him worth the risk.

I'm done with hiding.

He could have laughed at himself right then, and not with humour. Hope Harcourt had more strength and determination than anyone he knew. Now it was time for him to prove that he was worthy of such an incredible woman.

'Luca?'

'I didn't mind it, you know,' he said, even as his mind raced towards what he needed to do next. 'Being in the shadows for you. It was safe, for us both really. You got to keep your greatest acting role, that of the eternal ingenue, and I never had to ask you to prove your love.'

Anna Bertoli might have paled, or it could have been a trick of the airport lounge lighting.

'But Hope deserves more than that. She deserves someone who will stand by her side, and I deserve that too,' he said, standing up from the table. 'Get your staff ready, Anna. It won't take long for people to put two and two together.'

'I'm sorry,' she attempted.

'I'm sorry too. But I'm sure you'll find a way to spin it to your advantage. After all, you're about to begin promoting your new film.'

Luca left the airport and hailed a car. After giving the driver instructions, he contacted the analyst on Hope's case and asked them to look into the call that Hope had received that night. He had a suspicion he already knew, but he wanted confirmation before he did anything that might jeopardise the vote being held tomorrow in London.

His heart pounded so hard in his chest, powered by a forceful combination of self-recrimination and fear. Fear that it was too late. He never should have believed what she was saying. And the words he'd said to her that last time in the chalet had been terrible. He punched a fist against his thigh. *Bastardo.*

How could he have been so stupid? Hope had spent almost her entire life going it alone—unable to trust people, unable to count on people. And he'd gone and proved her right. He, who had fallen so hard and so fast in love with her he'd not even realised it.

Well, he wasn't going to make the same mistake again. If Hope thought she could shake him off that easily, she had another think coming. And this time he was going to bring reinforcements. Hope was about to face the biggest challenge of her life, and Luca was going to make damn sure she wasn't going to do it alone.

Hope had skipped her early morning workout for this. And as much as she disliked being off her routine, she also knew that she needed it. Her driver had dropped her off in the garage, and the cleaning crew had watched her as she'd stepped out onto the floor.

There was a smell to a department store. Clean, fresh—all carefully manufactured, but this was unique to Harcourts. Her heels clicked against the floor, echoing in the silence. The subdued pre-opening lighting made the shadows deeper and the sense of expectation greater. As if the store was holding its breath before opening time, when doors would be sprung open and streams of people would fill the aisles. Hope couldn't help but wonder if there was a sense that it was waiting for more today. Waiting to see who would stand at its helm and guide it forward into the future.

Was she doing the right thing? she asked herself.

She could only hope so.

She was putting all of her dreams and wants in one basket. Well, all but one, at least. She passed the perfume counters, the make-up stations, the cosmetics shelves and the skincare stalls. She reached out to adjust an expensive handmade Italian leather handbag on a tower of luxury purses and bags. She caught sight of the tie displays near the shirts—just a taster of what the men's section would offer on the third floor, and wondered what people would think of her plans for a non-gendered clothing section.

As she came towards the centre of the ground floor, in her mind she heard her eight-year-old self laughing as Nate chased her around the empty store. In the famous arch that had been used in at least three romantic comedy films, she saw her father kiss her mother under the mistletoe. She felt her grandfather's watchful gaze from the top floor, as he would stand there surveying his kingdom. A kingdom she wanted to inherit so badly it hurt.

But not enough to override the hurt caused by Luca's

absence. One day she might be able to go to him. To explain. One day when she wasn't a threat to him and what he guarded. But not today. No, today would decide her future. And it was one she would meet head-on.

She took one last sweep of the ground floor, the soft glow of the overhead lighting coating everything in gentle gold, and turned back towards the door to the staff stairwell that would take her up to the new wing, where the meeting was due to start.

Two uniformed staff stood either side of the boardroom doors and they greeted her with a small bow and shortly after she made her way to her seat the doors were closed. It always made her think of the phrase 'behind closed doors', of secrets and deals done in back rooms. And she hated that culture. Wanted it gone from the business that was as much a part of her as her family.

Finally, she forced herself to look at the man who wanted to blackmail her into stepping down from the vote. She wasn't surprised to find a smug grin and a knowing gleam in his eyes and for the first time she felt saddened by that, not angered. This man was also a member of her family—this man who had sold stories to the press about her, who had tried to push her and Nate aside so that he could reach for something that not only wasn't his by right, but by worth either. He just didn't deserve it. And if she hadn't already made up her mind, Hope thought that this realisation might have just swayed her.

Her grandfather stood from the head of the U-shaped wooden table and waited for silence to fall. Three rows of chairs behind each of the long wings of the table seated the entire number of board members and shareholders. The sense of heady expectation was thick in the air, most of the board darting frantic glances between her and Simon.

'Before we vote on the next CEO, is there any business to address?' her grandfather asked. Was she imagining the tone in his voice that made her think that Simon had warned him to expect her to step down? Or was it something else?

'I have something I need to bring to the table,' she said.

He gestured for her to proceed.

She stood, and almost instantly her legs nearly gave way. From the position of her chair, she'd not been able to see the rows at the back, and she hadn't even thought to look when she'd entered the room. She should have, though. Then she wouldn't have been so surprised to see not only her brother but Luca, standing right behind him, a mixture of thunderous frustration and admiration in his eyes, making her want to sob his name.

She hadn't wanted him here for so many reasons, but that he was, that he had somehow managed to get into this highly private and closely guarded business meeting meant the world to her. Apologies screamed from her silent lips and she could only hope that he might understand.

'Well?' Simon demanded, as if he had the right.

Refusing to give him even the courtesy of a glance, she faced her grandfather, the outgoing CEO and the CFO.

'Gentlemen,' she said, refusing to hide the emotion clogging her throat. 'Ladies,' she said, nodding to the hallowed few who had risen through the ranks. 'Before we get to the vote, I thought it would be good for you to know a little about me and Simon as people. You may think that because you've worked with us nearly all our adult lives,' she said, 'and knew us before that, even, you're aware of the kind of people we are. And it's possible that you do,' she admitted, shrugging. 'But, just in case you don't, I have something I'd like you to listen to.'

She removed her phone from her bag and tapped across the screen to pull up what she needed. To what she'd been able to record midway through the conversation which had taken place what felt almost like a lifetime ago.

Her voice broke into the silence from her phone. 'What do you want, Simon?'

'Let's not be coy about this. I know you have some kind of deal on the table in an attempt to woo the shareholders into voting for you in two days' time. But I doubt any deal would trump another sex scandal from you.'

'There hasn't even been one sex scandal.'

'Oh, I'm sure your ex-fiancé has something up his sleeve, if this doesn't do the trick. I want you to back out of the CEO vote, or I'll start digging.'

Simon stood up with such force it sent his chair falling back.

'This is outrageous,' he cried, increasing the volume of the disapproving muttering around her.

'No,' she said clearly, her voice loud enough to carry and quieten the voices of the shocked shareholders. 'What is outrageous is that you thought I would let you get away with attempting to blackmail me into giving up my desire to be Harcourts' next CEO. What is outrageous is that, once again, you—just like many others here—underestimated me terribly.

'And just in case anyone was wondering about the deal I have to woo you, let me explain. I have a signed deal with Sofia Obeid for the first of ten internationally located, exclusive luxury hotels to be branded Harcourts Obeid,' Hope said, pausing only long enough for that to sink in. 'They will be stocked with Harcourts' own brand and offer the ability to buy anything from the Harcourts' catalogue.' Excited whispers spread through the meeting.

'The revenue projections for the two-year mark,' she said, waiting to have everyone's attention, even Simon's, 'half a billion pounds.'

Now there was interest in the mix as well as excitement. She desperately wanted to look to her brother for confirmation, hating that she'd kept this from him, and hoping that he'd understand. Understand her need to have done this by herself, for herself. And then maybe, just maybe, Luca might too.

She turned to the head of the table, where she felt the weight of serious and heavy contemplation.

'I'm off the fence, Grandfather. I want the CEO position. So,' she said, turning back to the room, 'you can vote for someone who did absolutely nothing to forward Harcourts' interest and instead wanted to win by forcing out their opponent. Or you can vote for someone who refused to play games and instead made a business deal for your benefit. It's up to you,' she said, pushing back her chair and leaving the room without a backward glance.

Luca's heart was pounding so hard he was surprised it hadn't burst from his chest. He went to follow on her heels, and Nate held him back with surprising strength for someone who had needed a wheelchair to get to this room.

'Wait,' Nathanial Harcourt ordered.

'*Cazzo*, Nate—'

'Just wait. They need to see her leave. Alone. Powerful message.'

The truncated sentence concerned Luca and he looked back to the man beside him, who was beginning to sweat a little.

Luca cursed again. 'We should get you out of here,' he said, but Nate was staring off somewhere behind Luca.

Turning around, he saw that the target of his fierce gaze was his grandfather. There was a nod between the two men before the Chairman of Harcourts broke the gaze and turned to his colleague.

'*Now* we go,' said Nate as they worked their way to the side door, where some of Nate's assistants waited with the wheelchair to whisk him away from public sight before the meeting adjourned.

He waited long enough to see Nate settled, and after a glare and a, 'What are you waiting for?' from the other man, Luca rushed off in the direction he thought she'd gone.

Trusting his gut, he ran to the lifts and hit the call button, the doors parting instantly. He slammed his palm against the button for the ground floor, praying that Hope was doing the same just one or maybe two floors down. He held his breath and when the lift drew to a stop only moments after leaving the top floor, he knew he'd been right.

The doors parted and a startled Hope stared back at him. Before she could run away again, he reached for her wrist and pulled her into the lift with him and straight into an open-mouthed kiss.

It was punishment and pleasure; it was everything he couldn't say and everything he wanted to say. She gasped into his mouth and sagged against his body in willing submission, and everything in him roared in victory to have his hands on her again. He dragged himself back from the kiss only for enough time to hit the stop button, forcing a halt to the lift's progress.

A few seconds later, a voice came over the speaker. 'Is everything okay in there?'

'Yes,' Hope replied.

'Go away,' Luca commanded at the same time.

'Yes, ma'am, sir,' came the reply, as Luca let himself take the breath he'd not had since she'd flown away from him in Austria.

She pulled out of his hold, stepping back against the opposite side of the lift, her hands wrapping around the rail as if to stop herself reaching for him. Her eyes were full of hurt, shame and frustration.

'Nothing's changed, Luca.'

He shook his head slowly from side to side. Everything had changed, she just didn't know it yet. He wanted to prowl towards her, to press his body against hers until she melted against him again, but he knew they needed to speak first. There were things he needed to know and she needed to hear.

'Why didn't you tell me? About Simon?'

She bit her lip and clenched her jaw as if attempting to defy him and he wondered if she realised what hung in the balance here. But he was a patient man. He'd waited his entire life to meet her and he would wait for her to catch up, he would wait as long as it took her to realise that she loved him as much as he loved her.

She opened and closed her mouth and found her courage. 'My whole life people have been trying to protect me. My parents. Nate. You. Money made me a target, my gender made that easy. Simon's been undermining me as a way of getting to Nate for years. But all those things? They weren't about *me*,' she said, shrugging as if it hadn't hurt.

'People like Simon won't stop coming after me even if I do become CEO. So, are you and my brother going to find a way to protect me from every little threat I face? Or will you now finally trust that I can do this myself? That I have that power?' she demanded. 'I *needed* to do this by myself, to know that I could. Not for Simon, or the shareholders, or even you, but for *me*. I needed to know that I could do this.'

It nearly destroyed him that she hadn't known how strong she was. But he understood that need. The power of self-knowledge. Hadn't he felt it too when he'd confronted his mother?

'But now that I do know that, I realise that I don't have to,' she said softly, making him want to reach for her and pull her to him. It had been a terrible price for her to pay. Years of fighting to know herself. 'But that doesn't stop the threat of the news coming out about you and your mother. That hasn't changed, and I don't see how—'

He cut her words off with a kiss that he couldn't help any longer.

'Will you stop doing that?' she cried against his lips.

'No. Never. For the rest of our lives, if I think you are speaking utter nonsense, this is what will happen, just so you know,' he replied against her lips, though it was getting a little difficult to keep talking, kissing and smiling.

Hope pulled out of his hold, shock and hope pouring through her veins.

She stared up at him, cast in shadow by the emergency lighting, desperate to know what he'd meant by that. Questions he apparently read in her gaze.

'I went to see Anna,' he said, his use of her name telling.

Hope closed the distance between them, her hand reaching up to cup his jaw, to offer comfort and to be with him as he explained.

'She had been on my mind since we spoke and…she happened to be near to where I was already, so…' He shrugged but she saw the pain and the hurt that rippled across his features. 'I don't think she will ever be able to behave differently. Behave like a mother. Because she isn't one. Truly. I don't think she will ever be able to explain why she did what she did with the non-disclosure agreement. And for a moment there—I swear—I think she almost tried to blackmail me into silence again,' he admitted, the gravel in his voice dragging across her senses.

'Luca…' Hope said, his name conciliation on her tongue.

He shook his head. 'I protected her when I thought she needed it.'

'You protected her when she should have been protecting you,' Hope said gently, awareness flaring in her body when he locked his gaze on hers.

'Like you did,' he stated. 'You were never going to bow to Simon's threat, but you did it in such a way that he wouldn't have been able to reveal that threat without absolutely destroying himself in the eyes of his colleagues. You rendered his blackmail unusable. And I was that blackmail, wasn't I?' he demanded.

Hope looked away from the intensity in his eyes. She nodded, incapable of words at that point, her heart in her mouth. He was everything she'd wanted and more than she could have imagined and it was terrifying. A business wouldn't love her back, but he could. And she wanted it so much it made her sick.

'What did Martin say to you at the opera?' Luca asked. 'What did he say that you wanted?'

The question cut into her thoughts, spinning her back in time, and shame that he'd witnessed their encounter filled her again. She wanted to hide Martin's cruelty, but her loyalty and trust…they needed to be with Luca.

'Love. He said that I wanted love,' she admitted, tears pressing at the corners of her eyes.

Luca looked at her and she knew—she could feel his fury that her ex-fiancé had taunted her with such a thing—but she could also feel the need to give her that very same thing. She felt it shining from his eyes when he looked at her. She felt it in his touch when he held her.

And while she resented Martin for what he'd said, she knew, deep in her heart, that he'd been right. Beneath the mask and the facade she'd adopted to survive the loss of her parents, through boarding school, press attention and even working at Harcourts, had been a little girl just looking for someone to love her.

'You're ashamed of that?' Luca asked, his thumb under her chin, and a part of her was. A tear fell from her eye and he swept at it with his finger.

'Should I be ashamed of the same thing?' he asked gently. 'For surely that was the only reason I protected Anna's secret.'

'What? No, of course not,' she said, outraged at the thought until realising the point he was making.

When he saw that she understood, he nodded. 'I love you. I love you so much that it is beyond me. I can't contain it. Marry me,' Luca asked against her lips.

Hope's tears fell into their kiss and were swept away by passion and promises, and she felt as if something had finally slotted into place to make her complete. As if the world had been righted on its axis when she hadn't known it was off-kilter. And now she knew the power of what it was to love and be loved. This amazing, proud, powerful man would stand by her and support whatever she did, just as she would him, and she knew that as well as she knew the sky was blue and the earth was round.

'I don't have fancy words, but I have a declaration for you. You will never have to ask, or wonder, or doubt again.

I know your name,' Luca said, his voice a whisper and a quote she recognised from Turandot, the opera they had seen that night, her heart flaring at his words. 'I know your name,' he repeated. 'Your name is love.'

Overwhelmed by the love she felt from him, by the love she felt for him, she could only say, 'Yes. Yes, yes, yes…' over and over again until she believed it. Until she knew that she was going to spend the rest of her life loving and being loved by Luca Calvino.

'Erm, sorry to interrupt, ma'am.'

Hope waved an arm as if trying to get rid of the voice.

'We're going to have to start the lift up again, ma'am.'

The floor beneath Hope jerked into action just a moment later.

'And ma'am? The shareholders' vote just came in. May I be the first to congratulate our new CEO?'

Luca wrenched his lips from hers long enough to look at her in a way that told her so much. Love, pride, excitement, desire…and then went right back to kissing her socks off. And when the lift doors opened and the press caught sight of them, so wrapped up in each other they couldn't even stop kissing, they went wild and Hope and Luca didn't care one bit. They were done hiding their love.

EPILOGUE

LUCA LEANED BACK in his chair, making sure that the shade of the pergola covered both him and his daughter, fast asleep on his chest. He felt her cheek with the back of his hand, making sure that she wasn't too hot beneath the Italian sun, his concern easing when he found Felicity's skin warm but not hot. Even at four months old, his second daughter was far too much like her mother—refusing to complain or demand help when she needed it.

The papoose fit her snugly against him and he was sure he'd never tire of the feeling. He certainly hadn't with Bella, their first daughter, who—at the age of four—was ordering her twin cousins around the garden like a general.

'Gabbi, you should tell her to stop if she's too much,' he said to his sister-in-law, who was watching the three children from the seat beside him. They were playing out in the early summer sun in the sprawling garden that had become the cornerstone of Luca's heart and home.

Gabbi Casas waved him off with a sweep of her hand. 'It's wonderful to see. The twins need to be kept on their toes or they'll really start to believe that they rule over everything.'

Luca smiled. The twins were a rambunctious pair and the absolute love of their parents' lives—and they did rule over everything. He looked over to where his wife and her own twin brother were head-to-head over a small table between them, a fierce chess game taking all their concentration. What had started as a way to keep Nate's healing brain active and nimble had become deeply enmeshed in the siblings' relationship.

'I'm so glad she can play him. He just wins every time with me.'

'Don't try and pull that with me,' Luca said, laughing, 'I know that you let him win.'

Gabbi's face turned towards him, the blank expression making him laugh even more, and he struggled not to wake Felicity.

'You're secretly a chess master, aren't you?' he demanded.

'Only in my spare time, but don't tell Nate that.'

Luca's cheeks hurt from the happiness he felt here. This was his home. It was full of laughter and love and fun and ease. No, his marriage to Hope hadn't all been smiles. It had been a hard road to navigate as Hope struggled with the pressures of her job, and then with infertility issues— the fear and self-doubt that had come with that. Had she waited too long? Had she sacrificed too much for Harcourts? Luca shook his head, remembering the shock and the pain of those years. Thankfully, after only two rounds of IVF, Bella had come into their lives and Luca and Hope had thought their lives complete. And then, out of the blue, just a little over four years later, Felicity came along, determined to make everyone sit up and notice.

Looking back on his own childhood, Luca could never have imagined the sheer light that he lived in now. They had navigated—and survived—the fallout from the press linking him to Anna Bertoli, which they all suspected had been Simon's last jab after losing the vote for CEO before he'd retired to the world of private investment. Anna had pivoted the initial few days of very painful and public backlash against her into something positive as she became an ambassador for a single parents' charity and, despite fears, managed a number one box office hit in the wake of the attention. And while he and his mother had a strained relationship, the love that Hope and their children had brought into his life made it much easier to bear.

Hope had done incredible things with Harcourts. The deal with Sofia Obeid had been a roaring success, to the point where it was rolled out globally and had also led to another partnership of a different kind. Hope, Gabbi and Sofia had joined forces to create a small but hugely successful fashion brand, after launching three collections, male, female and non-binary. Gabbi ran the day-to-day business but it was a joint effort that each of the women loved. In the meantime, Harcourts had produced more accessible and specific lines for each department store's local community. It worked slightly differently to the rest of the store, but the small and often rotated stock and start-up brands regularly drew a lot of interest and support, selling out just as much as the more exclusive brands and designers.

'Hope, sunscreen!' he called out to his wife.

'The kids are fine,' Hope said, without raising her attention from the chessboard between her and her brother.

'I meant for you,' Luca shouted back.

Nate laughed.

'That goes for you too, husband,' chided Gabbi.

'It's okay for you two with your Mediterranean colouring,' Nate groused.

'Yeah, well, we can't all have been in a hospital for nearly two years,' Luca teased.

* * *

It was one of the things that Hope loved most about the relationship between her brother and her husband. They'd had it from the very start—a way of communicating that was as much a brotherly bond as Hope could imagine. She'd not realised how worried she'd been that they wouldn't get on until it came time to reintroduce Luca to Nate as her fiancé. She'd wanted more than civility, not only for herself but for Luca who deserved a huge, sprawling, loud, messy, chaotic family so different from the cold loneliness and rejection he'd had growing up. But she needn't have worried. The men were fast friends and firm in their loyalty and love. Which was pretty much the way she felt about Gabbi.

When she'd learned of the beginning of their relationship, she'd felt acutely aware that she had played an accidental part in keeping them apart, feeling as if she'd still needed to protect Nate's privacy back then. But at least and at last, they'd found their way back to each other and with a happiness that maybe matched—but not rivalled— her own. She looked back to the large wooden table beneath the pergola that looked out across the Italian hillside.

They spent every holiday possible at their villa in Tuscany and last year their grandfather had even come out. Interactions had been slightly stilted, but Hope had loved having all the generations in the house together. Usually, the big family occasions were Nate's family and hers, together all under the one roof, and Hope nearly had to pinch herself. Remembering the time when she had nearly lost her brother, and then when she had nearly let such an incredible man—Luca—slip through her fingers, it didn't bear thinking about. Goosebumps raised on her skin briefly as she applied the sunscreen as prompted by her husband.

For all her focus on the Harcourts CEO position back then, Sofia had been right. Harcourts the department store would never love her back. But the family? Her family? What she had made of it—even after being so scared to even hope what it could be—was everything. It hadn't always been easy—Luca was still commanding and demanding, and she was still stubborn and occasionally— *occasionally*—worked too hard. But it was hers, and the love she felt, it grew even more each and every day. She'd once thought that love had a capacity, a certain amount that could be given or received, but her husband and daughters showed her that, actually, the capacity for love was infinite, and it was a lesson she loved learning over and over again each day for the rest of her life.

* * * * *

COMING SOON!

We really hope you enjoyed reading this book.
If you're looking for more romance
be sure to head to the shops when
new books are available on

Thursday 18th January

To see which titles are coming soon, please visit
millsandboon.co.uk/nextmonth

Introducing our newest series, Afterglow.

From showing up to glowing up, Afterglow characters are on the path to leading their best lives and finding romance along the way – with a dash of sizzling spice!

Follow characters from all walks of life as they chase their dreams and find that true love is only the beginning...

Two stories published every month. Launching January 2024

millsandboon.co.uk

MILLS & BOON®

Coming next month

THE BUMP IN THEIR FORBIDDEN REUNION
Amanda Cinelli

'Sir, you can't just–' The nurse visibly fawned as she tried to remain stern, her voice high with excitement and nerves as she continued.

'She knows me.' The man stepped into the room, his dark gaze instantly landing on her. 'Don't you, Isabel?'

Izzy froze at the sound of her name on Elite One racing legend Grayson Koh's perfectly chiselled lips. For the briefest moment she felt the ridiculous urge to run to him, but then she remembered that while they may technically know one another, they had never been friends.

It had been two years since Grayson had told her she should never have married his best friend, right before he'd offered her money to stay away from the Liang family entirely.

She instantly felt her blood pressure rise.

True to form, Grayson ignored everyone and remained singularly focused upon where she sat frozen on the edge of the exam table.

When he spoke, his voice was a dry rasp. 'Am I too late…have you already done it?'

Continue reading
THE BUMP IN THEIR FORBIDDEN REUNION
Amanda Cinelli

Available next month
millsandboon.co.uk

LET'S TALK
Romance

For exclusive extracts, competitions
and special offers, find us online:

f MillsandBoon

X @MillsandBoon

o @MillsandBoonUK

d @MillsandBoonUK

Get in touch on 01413 063 232